Life has bigger plans for Jiggs Morgan as he adjusts to a world away from the battlefields of Viet Nam. *No More Forever* brings us a wonderfully human character in this epic novel. One of my favorite novels this year. Brilliant and heartfelt.

– Rabia Tanveer

NO MORE FOREVER

By
Christopher Britton

NO MORE FOREVER

Author: Christopher Britton

For permission, please contact:
    Christopher Britton
    cqbritton@hotmail.com

Cover design by Clark Valentine
Cover photo by Nancy Britton

Book layout/design by David Larson

Scott,
Best wishes
for many great seasons,
Chris Britton

In Memory
of
Georgia Quinn

ACKNOWLEDGEMENTS

Many thanks to my wife, Nancy, for the patience to be an author's widow and for her scrupulous proofreading and insightful suggestions.

Thanks, too, to my friend Jeannie Ferris, writer deluxe in her own right, for repeatedly telling me when I was wandering into realms of unreality.

I also received invaluable assistance from Dr. Joy Kennedy, Dr. Michael Stitt, Carol Steele, Steve Allen, Dave Larsen and the Tuesday Writers' Workshop, particularly Avery Kerr and Amy Christensen.

To one and all, my most sincere thanks.

"I will fight no more forever."

Chief Joseph
Chief of the Nez Perce

GLOSSARY

CLICK – One thousand meters.

COMPANY – An Marine infantry combat unit consisting of three infantry platoons and a weapons platoon.

OCS – Officer Candidate School, the training program located at Quantico, Virginia, that must be completed in order for an individual to become a Marine officer.

OD – Officer of the Day, the Commander's direct representative and first responder to routine problems, a duty that rotates among officers in the Command.

PLATOON – A small Marine infantry combat unit usually consisting of three squads of approximately twelve to fifteen troops, a guide, platoon sergeant and a platoon commander. Squads are divided into fire teams of four or five troops.

REMF – Rear Echelon Mother-F_ _ _ er, the infantry grunts' nickname for support personnel whose job does not involve actual combat.

SEABEES – Members of the Navy's Construction Forces.

SHORT or **SHORT-TIMER** – an expression signifying that the Marine to whom applied is within a very few days of being transferred, particularly of being transferred home from the war.

SQUID – Marine Corps' slang for a member of the Navy.

PROLOGUE

October 1968

Jiggs Morgan was so short he could rest comfortably in the shade of a dime. He was leaving Okinawa with nothing but an AM transistor radio and some scars, deep and indelible, seen and unseen. But he was leaving; he was finally going home.

In the three months since Camilla flew home, Jiggs had not allowed himself to wander south to Kadena Air Base, to the tiny Quonset, the seawall, their pizza place. Better not to dwell on a past that was no part of his future. So he stayed north, seldom leaving camp. He read a Bible he'd found in the desk he'd been assigned and thought about the future, his, Carol's, theirs, that ill-defined place from which they'd been sidetracked by the war.

But, now that his departure from the Island was imminent, the reality of what he would be leaving behind was gnawing a hole in Jiggs' heart. Probably he would never come back. The places he and Camilla had been together would remain behind, the healing that had happened there uncelebrated. Jiggs decided to make a final pilgrimage.

Wayne Handy looked up from his desk as Jiggs walked into his former battalion's office. "What are you doing here, Morgan? I thought you'd be down at the terminal with your nose pressed against the glass waiting for your flight."

"Flight's not until midnight. How about letting me borrow your bike? I need to make a farewell tour."

Handy dug into his pocket and tossed Jiggs a key. "It's in the lot outside my room. Needs gas."

The speed limit all over the Island was thirty-five miles per hour. Jiggs winked at it as the speedometer raced past. It had been almost two years since he had been on a bike. The wind in his face felt good, the engine vibration like an injection of electric energy. He gave the throttle a twist, and the big 450 leapt forward, rocketing him into his recent past.

Just outside the back gate of the Air Base, two taxis, *skoshi cabs*, were keeping their round the clock vigil for fares. The scene of uncounted after midnight partings, it was here at Kadena that Jiggs had decided to risk Camilla's friendship. Throttling down, Jiggs nodded, acknowledging the salute Handy's officer's sticker earned from the sentry as he rolled past the guard shack.

The Quonset was situated in a little cul-de-sac amid the Base's family housing area. Jiggs downshifted as he turned in and coasted to a stop. There was no one around. He straddled the idling bike, both feet on the ground. He didn't know what he expected to see. The rounded metal building looked smaller than when Camilla lived there. *Wonder who lives there now.*

Seconds passed. A bird on an overhead wire, evidently satisfied the creature on the big red machine could not fly, began to sing. Just the sight of the place, however diminished by Camilla's absence, filled Jiggs with guilty longing. Maybe it was healthy he would never see this place again.

There was no shade on the street where he was stopped, and, despite the breeze, it was a sultry day. Jiggs took a few deep breaths, inhalations that would have to last a lifetime. Then he turned and rode away.

Leaving Kadena, he headed further south along streets lined with the welter of ramshackle bars, massage parlors, used car lots and repair shops – Okinawa's emulation of America on the fringe of the great air base. Here the traffic was heavy until Jiggs found the cut-off he was looking for. Within a mile of the turn, he had cleared the smog and congestion and emerged onto a beach road bordered by sugarcane fields on its inland side. Here the breeze became a wind, and the spray from waves rolling in from the West refreshed him. *Rain coming.*

Steering around an old familiar turn, he came to the sea wall, a gigantic bulwark of three-legged concrete forms piled high to thwart the inland march of the China Sea. He pulled to a stop in the lee of this rampart and scrambled up to its rim. As soon as Jiggs' head crested the top, spray more stinging than refreshing assaulted him. He looked around and spotted the hollow among the forms where the two of them had spent so many hours exchanging lives, and folded himself into its shelter.

There he sat, listening to the wind search for him just above. Here the waves did not roar, they rumbled as they broke in among the spaces at the base of the fortress far below, as if a subway was perpetually passing beneath him. No one on Earth knew where he was at this moment ... unless Cam knew through some miracle of telepathy. The thought of that possibility gave Jiggs a measure of satisfaction he didn't fully understand. How many times had he sat in this very place in silence, brooding, wondering whether any of his friends were dying at that moment fifteen hundred miles away in the war? It was something Jiggs still wondered, would continue to wonder, until the war was over, if it ever was. He shook his head at the thought, folded his hands and began to pray aloud.

"Lord, it's me, Jiggs. You haven't heard much from me for a long time, so I have a lot of catching up to do. I have done some terrible things, and I need to ask your help. Please forgive me for fighting in that unholy, endless war. Forgive me for David Leslie and bring him peace. Protect those still fighting on both sides, and bring wisdom to their leaders in a way that enables them to disengage without regard to policy or pride.

"Thank you for Camilla's friendship and understanding. Help me to use what she has given me to make this world a better place and to forge a meaningful and fulfilling life."

It was the first prayer Jiggs had prayed in years.

After an hour his concrete aerie became too hard for further sitting and it had begun to rain. Jiggs climbed down, kicked the bike to life and rode north. He had paid his respects. He thought he knew what he had to do.

I

WALNUT GROVE

1

October 1957

The two teams aligned nose to nose along the line of scrimmage. Jim Hegman, the quarterback, stood behind the center and surveyed the defense. As he crouched to take the snap, the final gun sounded. Players on both sides of the line stood up. Everyone except the huge, bristle-haired Bjournquist, who lunged forward from his tackle position like a jet-propelled bulldozer and leveled two of his opponents across the line, both of whom had just begun to relax for the first time all evening.

"Nice block," said a teammate of the two flattened players.

After the moment or two required for others to assure themselves Bjournquist now intended to treat the game as concluded, helmets came off, some players shook hands with their opposite numbers, and both teams headed for the showers as the stands began to empty.

Jiggs Morgan, Central's long-snapper, was standing on the Central sideline at game's end. Between plays he contemplated the solitary grass stain on his otherwise unblemished tan uniform pants. *At least it's in front.*

The Central cheerleaders and members of the pep club were crowded around the field house door as the team tried to filter its way through. Mindy Lundberg, one of the cheerleaders and this year's homecoming queen, was standing directly in Jiggs' path with her back to him talking to Jim Hegman. Prevented by the crowd from going around them in either direction, Jiggs said, "Excuse me" in a voice loud enough to be heard above the din.

Hegman, who was facing Jiggs, looked up and attempted to move to the side. Mindy, who was the obstacle, paid no attention and went on talking, asking whether Hegman was going to give her a ride home. Bjournquist came up behind Jiggs and shoved him hard into Mindy's back. "Make a hole!"

Mindy whirled. "Why don't you watch where you're going, you little freshman toad?"

Bitch. Jiggs said nothing and walked past her into the locker room.

Central's dressing room was a jumble of benches pointing in all different directions. Some players wandered around, arms in the air, jerseys half off, looking for someone to help pull them the rest of the way over their shoulder pads. The floor, a sea of football pads, dirty uniforms, wet towels, used tape and dirt from cleats turning to mud from water tracked from the showers. Steam billowed, lockers banged, those in the showers yelled when toilets were flushed without warning.

Jiggs retreated to the corner of the room farthest from the door, sat down opposite his locker and began to undress. He did so slowly. Despite episodes like that with Mindy, he was happy to be part of the team, however small his role. As he bent down to pull off his socks, a shadow engulfed him. Looking up, he found Jim Hegman towering above him, filthy and obviously happy with the win, in which he'd played every down.

"That was a nice hit you put on that punt receiver, Junior," Hegman said, referring to a solo tackle Jiggs had made, his only one of the night.

"Thanks, Jim. The guy was probably another freshman."

"Hey, take it easy, Junior. Don't let all the hazing get under your skin. None of these assholes were even on the team as freshmen. That's why they ride you so hard. Don't feel so sorry for yourself."

"Yeah, that's what I keep telling myself, but about the time I'm half convinced, some deal like that with Mindy happens, and I feel about two feet high again."

"Ah, forget about Mindy. When she was a freshman, her zits were bigger than her tits. No wonder she behaves like she was never in ninth grade. Anyway, tonight's game gives you enough quarters for a letter, doesn't it?"

"Yeah, it does."

"Well, cheer up then. They can't take that away from you. Congratulations."

"Thanks. I appreciate it. I really do."

"Listen, Junior, some of us are going over to the Starlight in Lake City. Want to come along?"

Jiggs winced. To be invited to go with these guys was a sign of acceptance he never thought would come. However, the invitation was not without problems. *Will my folks let me go? What will the guys I usually hang out with think?* There was a bigger problem.

"Jim, I can't dance."

"Don't have to." Hegman laughed. "I've been to the Starlight nearly every Friday night the last three years and haven't danced but two or three times."

"What do you do?"

"Mostly lean against the booths and check everything out. C'mon with us. It's worth it just to see the girls' reaction when Bjournquist asks 'em to dance."

"Okay. I'll ask my folks. See you outside."

Hegman disappeared into the crowd of milling players. *What if they won't let me go? What if I make a fool of myself? What if ... What if ... The hell with it.* Jiggs threw a wad of tape at the barrel in the center of the room, missed, and headed for the showers. *Won't know unless I ask.*

Stepping outside into the late autumn air after the closeness of the locker room was like pulling a cool sheet over himself. His parents' car was parked on the far side of the lot back by the cornfield. As he drew near, he could see them waiting with his younger sisters, Marie and Darcy. They were talking with Mr. and Mrs. Johanssen, who farmed the place a mile north of the Morgan's.

There were still a few stragglers in the parking lot, mostly players or people waiting for players. The visiting team's bus was almost full. Across the lot someone was gunning his engine. Jiggs and his family were briefly outlined in the headlights of a car creeping out of the lot, glass packs crackling, gravel crunching under slow turning tires.

"What did you think of the game?" Doc Morgan had let a lot of hay get wet getting Jiggs to games on time, but this was all his dad ever said about games he watched Jiggs play. Jiggs sensed his father, a veterinarian, didn't share his love of sports, especially team sports. Whatever Doc's reservations, he kept them to himself, neither praising nor criticizing. Just the inevitable question, what did Jiggs think about the game.

"Seven plays is hardly enough to form an opinion," Jiggs replied, "but it's a step in the right direction." He drew a deep breath. "Dad, Mom, can I go to the dance in Lake City with Jim Hegman and some of the guys?" *Mention Hegman, they like him.*

Silence.

"Oh, Jiggs ... those boys are so much older than you. I don't think…"

"Just a second, Mary," Doc put his hand on Jiggs' shoulder. "Jiggs, are you sure you even want to go? Some of those guys have been awful hard on you all season."

Jiggs shrugged, looked down at the ground and then up at his dad. "I don't know. Hegman's never been a part of it. It almost seems like I have to go now that I've been asked if I really want to be part of the team."

"Is that the way the invitation was put?"

"No. Just a feeling I have."

"Is Ronald Bjournquist one of the boys you want to go with?" asked his mom.

"I think so."

"Oh, dear..."

"How late are you going to be out?" asked Doc. The way he said it told Jiggs he would be allowed to go.

"I don't know ... probably twelve, twelve-thirty. Coach Malone's curfew's twelve-thirty on Friday and Saturday." Jiggs had never before had any reason to consider the limits of weekend curfew.

Doc looked at his wife with his head cocked to one side, one eyebrow raised. Her lips were tight, but she shrugged her shoulders ever so slightly, as if to say, "Have it your way."

"Okay, you can go. Have a good time. Keep that curfew in mind."

Jiggs turned and ran across the parking lot towards Hegman's car. He stumbled in the gravel, almost falling as he ran. Hegman was leaning against the front fender of his gleaming black Ford hardtop, which had the words "High Velocity" written in script on the fender skirts. He was talking to Gil Burley, his best friend and favorite receiver.

"I can go."

"Good. Stick around until Jack and Ron get here." Just then Jack Miller, another senior, and Bjournquist walked up.

Down the Highway 40 hill from the field they rolled in second gear, pipes rumbling. At intervals, Bjournquist, who was chewing his everpresent quid of tobacco, would roll down the window to spit. It was against school rules to chew, even in games. However, Jiggs doubted anyone had bothered to tell Bjournquist, whose father and brothers all chewed. It would not have surprised Jiggs to learn Bjournquist's mother chewed.

"Hey, there go Gargoyle and Cheryl into the park." Hegman gestured at the familiar car of one of their teammates turning into the entrance to the state park.

"Those two spend so much time in the woods, they must be considering jobs in forestry," said Miller.

"Can you be a forest ranger if you never get out of the back seat?" asked Bjournquist.

They rode in silence for a couple of minutes lost in envious contemplation of Gargoyle Gordon's blossoming future in recreational forestry.

Hegman had blocked the springs of High Velocity so that it went down the road like a dog on a scent, nose down, tail up. Jiggs had the sensation of falling forward as they rode along. The moon was up and nearly full, lighting the gray pavement well beyond the beam of the headlights. Familiar farmhouses and yards along the highway were clearly visible even without their yard lights. Minutes passed.

"S'pose Gargoyle and Cheryl have finished their efforts at conservation?"

"Garg'll keep trying 'til he gets it right or it kills him."

"Or kills Cheryl."

Everyone laughed, but the conversation embarrassed Jiggs, because Cheryl was his cousin.

Soon the lights of Lake City appeared in the distance, sparkling across the level farmland in the cold air. The highway widened on the outskirts of town. Neon signs flashed at gas stations, motels and hamburger stands on either side of the road.

Leaving the highway, they dragged Central Avenue at a bumper-to-bumper, stop and go crawl. A carload of girls crept by going in the opposite direction. High Velocity's horn erupted. The noise on the narrow street, magnified by the solid rows of buildings on either side, combined with the lights from the stores' display windows and traffic reminded Jiggs of a carnival midway.

"Central eats shit!" Amid the barely muffled sounds of engines, loud radios, all the competing noise, three words unmistakably hollered directly at them.

Everyone in the car was immediately on high alert.

"Central eats shit!" This time it was obvious the taunt had come from a red pickup parked about three cars ahead of them to their right. Three guys, each wearing a black and white letter jacket from neighboring Northwest High School, were leaning against the truck grinning at them.

"It's just the Thompsons from over by Mooreville," said Hegman. Jiggs could feel the others in the car begin to relax. Bjournquist lowered his window and stuck his head out. "Central eats Northwest!"

As they rolled past their would-be tormentors, Bjournquist shouted, "Hey, Bill, ya bring the pickup so you can haul yer date home?"

"Your sister in town tonight?"

At the west end of Central Avenue, Hegman turned and headed for the Starlight, just a block north. The lot behind the ballroom was almost full, and they were forced to park at the far end. They were greeted by a blast of Buddy Holly serenading "Peggy Sue" blaring from the exits of the dancehall as soon as they stepped from the car.

"You can't chew tobacco in here," the ticket seller told Bjournquist. "Why do I have to tell you that every week?"

After a moment's pause, Bjournquist went over to the curb and spit his chew in the gutter, returned to the window and snatched his ticket. "You want to check and see if I got my lace panties on?"

The others smirked.

Inside the blare was ten times what it had been on the outside. In the semi-dark they wove their way among the jostling, bobbing dancers at the edge of the floor. There was no band, just a disc jockey from the local radio station playing records on a small brightly lit bandstand.

Jiggs stopped with the others near some booths, all of which were full, and turned to watch the dancers. His companions were busy greeting friends from other schools. No one bothered to introduce Jiggs to anybody, so he was left to contemplate the scene.

It was elbow to elbow on the dance floor, a whirling, laughing, sweating mass. *Jeez, they've even got girls dancing with girls.* Jiggs was relieved to see they didn't dance the slow ones together, but he still thought it looked weird.

Snaking in and out among the couples were the traps. Jiggs soon saw they were what kept things circulating. Four or five people, all boys or all girls, would join hands and wander among the dancers, occasionally encircling a couple. If the trap consisted of boys, the boy dancer would join the circle and the girl was free to choose a new partner from the trap. If it was a girls' trap, the process was reversed. Once in a while the old partner would be re-chosen, which sometimes generated mildly derisive comments about "love" from the unselected. Sometimes, instead of choosing, the person trapped would simply break the circle and walk away, choosing no one, thereby evoking derision of a less mild variety.

The more Jiggs watched, the more thankful he was that leaning against booths was favored over dancing among Hegman and his pals. *I must be the youngest person in the place.* In the midst of his musings, Hegman seized his hand and pulled him towards the dance floor. "C'mon, Junior, time to get your feet wet."

Jiggs immediately pulled back, only to have his other hand engulfed by Bjournquist's ham fist.

"Okay, I'll lead." Bjournquist hauled Jiggs in the direction he was already leaning in his effort to escape Hegman. They were joined by two others whom Jiggs didn't know. By the time they had covered ten feet they were a trap.

Jiggs' dread of dancing escalated to terror when confronted by the immediate prospect. "C'mon, Jim. Tell Bjournquist to let me out of this!"

"Don't be so damned conceited, Junior. What makes you think any girl would choose you anyway?"

This had the unintended result of giving Jiggs some hope, hope that was strengthened when the girl in each of the first two couples trapped chose one of the others. The second of the two chose Hegman, but only after stopping Jiggs' heart with a glance suggesting she had at least considered picking him.

Now if someone picks Bjournquist, I'm free. Jiggs considered the hulking giant in front of him. *It will take a brave girl to pick him. Especially if she knows him.*

Their pace quickened slightly as Bjournquist seemed to catch a promising scent. He shouldered his way through the crowd as if it didn't exist, dragging the others behind him like the tail of a kite. Jiggs' heart sank when he saw Bjournquist's intended quarry. They were headed straight for two girls dancing together. The odds of being chosen were about to double.

The trap closed just as the song playing ended, and the two girls pivoted slowly inside the circle as they sized up their alternatives. With each beat Jiggs' heart felt like a cactus was impaling his insides. He didn't think he closed his eyes, but his first signal that he had been chosen was his release from Bjournquist's calloused paw. Slowly the girl facing him came into focus. She was about the size of Bjournquist. Jiggs was a skinny 5'9". The girl's height combined with the high heels she was wearing caused her to be almost a head taller than he was.

Please, God, let the next song be a fast one. Jiggs thought he could fake a fast one, after which he would politely excuse himself and disappear. *This won't be so bad.* He tried to convince himself. *After all, she chose me.* He pulled himself together with some effort. "H ... Hi ..."

Brunhilda, as he later came to think of the girl, was gazing over the top of his head at something across the room, a feat she could perform without extending herself. She did not reply.

Before he could introduce himself, the music started. A slow one. Jiggs cast a look of betrayal heavenward. *I guess I'm supposed to take hold of her.* He tried to raise his arms, but discovered his shoulders had stopped working. *What will happen when I try to move my feet?*

Brunhilda solved both problems by grabbing him and pulling him towards her, hugging him with a suddenness that snapped his spine. Her right hand held Jiggs' left at arm's length and waved it up and down to the music like a pump handle. Her left arm snaked across his back and her hand rested at the base of his skull, pinning him against her with crushing force.

Jiggs' nose came to rest more or less equidistant between her torpedo-like bosoms, and there it remained, involuntarily buried in at least an inch of furry sweater. The fuzz from the sweater made Jiggs need to sneeze. Silently, he fought for control – anything to get his mind off his nose. *Better to smother than sneeze.* At least death would be an escape.

Back and forth Brunhilda dragged him, prying his arm up and down as if she was jacking up a car, his feet barely touching the floor. He feared to exhale in case his chest muscles were not strong enough to re-inflate against the force of her coils. Conversation was impossible.

On top of everything else, it became apparent to Jiggs after no more than a minute that they were dancing to the longest piece of popular music ever recorded. Somehow Jiggs' right arm had become wrapped around Brunhilda's ample back. Through her sweater he could feel her flesh where it bulged out below the restraint of the elastic strap of her brassiere.

Oh Lord. What if she thinks I'm trying to feel her up or something?

After a day and a half the song, whatever it was, ended, and Brunhilda put him down. Jiggs was in no condition to go another round with her and quickly excused himself. Brunhilda, of the same mind, headed in the other direction before he finished choking out his first word. They almost collided in their haste to get away from each other.

Turning and walking with feigned nonchalance towards the booths, Jiggs steeled himself for the next phase of the ordeal. There the authors of this treachery stood laughing.

"You looked like you could have danced all night and still have begged for more, Junior," said Hegman.

"It's a good thing you were centered on that woman, or you might have lost an eye when she put the clamps on you," Bjournquist observed.

Jiggs couldn't decide whether he was more dismayed by the experience or relieved it was over. He knew the rest of the team would be treated to a richly enhanced version at Monday's practice and tried to paint on a look of indifference so as to deny the four hyenas the satisfaction of seeing how he really felt.

After a few minutes Hegman, who had danced with one girl for two songs, announced that the experience had drained him emotionally, and they had better leave while he was still strong enough to travel. On the way out of Lake City, they took another lap on Central Avenue and then roared away.

Jiggs' place was Hegman's next to last stop. They turned into the lane and stopped beneath the yard light. Jiggs jumped out the moment the car stopped in order to shut up the dog. He noticed the kitchen light was still on.

"Good night, Junior," Hegman said. "You did alright."

2

December 1958

Jiggs disliked sanding. He especially disliked sanding tiny, narrow spaces. He hated sanding tiny narrow spaces in twenty degree temperatures.

What's Doc have against heat? Jiggs changed the paper on the sanding block and blew on his fingers for warmth. He resumed rubbing out the roughness in the base of one of a dozen bannister posts bordering the stairs up to the second floor.

It's the arctic version of the "Doc Morgan Bootcamp for Boys," Jiggs Morgan, lone boy in residence.

Across the stairs, Doc sanded his side, saying nothing as usual. Steam from his breath hovered in front of his face.

We have a furnace. The lamp, minus its shade, sitting on the otherwise barren floor illuminating their work said the electricity was on, just not the heat. Beyond its cone of light, darkness engulfed the room. Outside, the moan of the moving air.

They had gone riding a couple hours earlier. The sound of the wind rustling the cornstalks in the stubble fields they rode past had sharpened its bite, drawing the skin tight across Jiggs' cheek bones – so cold it seemed hot.

The horses liked it that way. Freckles, Jiggs' horse, frisked and pranced, ready to run. Jiggs often thought Doc was more horse than human.

Jiggs had gone through all his usual stages of suffering, beginning with *"Why did I ever agree to do this?"* and then, *"Five more minutes and I'm quitting."* Of course, he always kept going, ever reluctant to surrender to whatever ordeal Doc had arranged for the two of them.

Doc never insisted Jiggs join him. He would just mention whatever he was about to do and ask Jiggs if he wanted to come along. Jiggs always came. Inch by inch over the years the trials had lengthened as Jiggs' endurance grew. So far, he had never been the one to call "Time" despite his certainty that his Dad could withstand infinitely more than he. Whatever the activity. Riding in a snowstorm, stacking bales in the loft on a ninety-five-degree day, endlessly sanding the infinity of surfaces in the new house Doc had been building for the family for the last two years. Experience had taught Jiggs his dad would eventually suggest they take a break from whatever they were doing the instant before it became truly unbearable.

Doc's ancient radio still was capable of summoning the Grand Ol' Opry playing in faraway Nashville on a Saturday night. Jiggs tried to imagine the audience sitting in the theater listening, warm.

"Silent night, holy night..." Christmas at the Opry.

"Why don't you ever go to church with Mom?" Jiggs asked. "Is it just because you don't like Reverend Holmgren?"

Several years earlier, Reverend Holmgren, the local Lutheran minister, who also farmed, had hired Doc, to castrate his boar, a pig known to be extraordinarily bad tempered. When Doc showed up to do the job, the Reverend had inexplicably shut Doc in the pen with the boar, whose tusks the Reverend had never had clipped, with no easy means of escape.

According to the account Mrs. Holmgren gave to Jiggs' Mom, Doc, after somehow getting the job done, had come to the door asking for her husband. Upon being told that he was working on a sermon and could not be disturbed, Doc had handed Mrs. Holmgren a large plastic bag containing the two enormous testicles, saying she should give them to her husband, "He needs 'em."

As far as Jiggs knew, Doc had never mentioned the incident to anyone.

"No, my not going to church has nothing to do with the Reverend. It's more than that. I just don't believe in God, at least not the brand the Reverend's selling."

Years of Sunday school perfect attendance pins impaled Jiggs at the sound of his father's denial of God, but he said nothing.

"Do you believe in God?" Doc asked.

"I don't know. I think so. Something inside me makes me want to. Why don't you believe?"

"... all is calm, all is bright.,"

"Tough question. I suppose I've never seen any evidence that God exists."

"What about the world? The Reverend says proof of God, for those who need proof, is all around us."

"Which God? Jehovah? Allah? Vishnu? Zoroaster? There are lots of gods to choose from. If you ask me, most religions probably start out with good intentions, just trying to explain existence, but before long they're being used as an excuse for all kinds of horrible things, caste systems, crusades, inquisitions, sacrifices, jihads. The world may be evidence of something greater than mankind, but it doesn't tell me what."

CHRISTOPHER BRITTON   21

"... round yon Virgin, Mother and Child..."

"If that's what you think, why have you been sending me to church all these years?"

"How are you ever going to know whether you agree with something, if you don't learn what it is? Besides, your mom sees things a little differently."

Jiggs went back to thinking. The wind outside had died, and when neither spoke, the sound of the Christmas carol ringing in the cold night air made Jiggs feel a warmth on the inside he didn't feel on the out.

"... heavenly Infant so tender and mild..."

Doc put down his sanding block. "Let's call it a night."

Jiggs looked up, and they smiled slightly at each other. Their conversation made Jiggs a little sorry the time was over, despite the cold.

They turned off the radio and headed outside and down towards the old house. Jiggs could see Christmas lights reflected in the snow outside the living room window, so his mom was home from church, most likely watching the ten o'clock news, waiting for them to come in.

The fire in the kitchen fireplace had burned down. Only the embers glowed in the otherwise dark room. Jiggs went directly to the foot of the stairs leading up to his room.

"Night, Son." Doc looked up from the boots he was unlacing.

"Good night, Pop," Jiggs called over his shoulder as he climbed the stairs.

3

January 1961

If these ruts were any bigger, they'd swallow my truck.

Jiggs gripped the steering wheel with both hands as he bounced from one axle-wrenching frozen tire track to another on his way down Durward Westphal's quarter mile lane.

Ahead a barnlike white frame house loomed in the winter moonlight, and behind it the barn itself and several lesser buildings. Even though it was only five-thirty in the morning, lights were on in Durward's house. As Jiggs reached the farmyard a pair of headlights flashed onto his rearview mirror as another car swung off the road into the lane. *That'll be the Colonel.*

Jiggs was relieved to see the car behind him. In the two years he had worked for Colonel Clemons, a local farmer and livestock auctioneer, he had arrived at the site of an auction more than once at five-thirty, only to find the house dark and no Colonel, forcing him to wait in the cold.

Jiggs parked his truck in the far corner of the barnyard and was halfway to the house when Durward came out wearing bib overalls over his long underwear.

"Don't stand out there freezing something off," the old farmer yelled. "C'mon in and have a cup of coffee. You et yet?"

It was as hot in the kitchen as it was cold outside, and Jiggs shed three layers of jackets and sweatshirts.

"Seen you boys wrestle last night," Durward said, referring to the wrestling meet at the high school the night before. "You sure had your hands full with that boy you had. When they stopped yer match that time, I thought you were cooked."

Late in Jiggs' match he'd been on top, nursing a one point lead, when his opponent had thrown his head back and smashed Jigg's face. During the lull in crowd noise that accompanied the time out to stop the bleeding, Jiggs had heard Durward yell, "Let the boys fight. I never seen nobody bleed to death through the nose."

After the match Doc had put four stitches across the bridge and down the right side of his nose. This morning, Jiggs still couldn't breathe through the crust of dried blood. His right eye was also a couple shades darker than normal, although ice had reduced the swelling.

"Morning, everybody." The Colonel entered the kitchen. He shook hands with Durward and looked at Jiggs, but didn't say anything. He, too, had seen it happen.

Jiggs and the two men sat around the big table in the middle of the kitchen for half an hour, drank a cup of coffee and then another. Durward's wife, Mary, cleaned up some dishes, stirred an immense bowl of some kind of batter and poured it into a succession of pastry pans. Being there made Jiggs feel grown up, even though he only listened.

"Well," the Colonel set his cup down after draining the last dregs, "you an' Mary ain't ever going to get moved if we set here quacking all day. Let's get to it."

Durward had sold his farm and was retiring, moving next week to a house he'd bought in Walnut Grove, where the high school was located. In three more days, Mary and Durward, after fifty winters in the same house, would fight that treacherous lane for the last time

For the next three hours, Jiggs, Durward and the Colonel dragged out every piece of equipment and tool on the place, gave each a number and arranged them around the edge of the yard in a giant square, small items on tables. There they could be viewed by the crowd summoned to Durward's farm by newspaper ads and flyers the Colonel had sent out to be posted on bulletin boards in every gas station, grain elevator and café in a fifty mile radius.

"Geez." Jiggs, the record keeper, mumbled in frustration as he tried to keep notes of what Durward expected to get for each item and whether he would take less. He had to use two pens, keeping the spare in an inside pocket, alternating when the ink froze in the one he was using, always fumbling as he tried to write with gloved hands.

The sun came up. Pale yellow in a white sky across snowswept fields east of the Westphal farm. Jiggs loved sunrise. It was beautiful in a lonely way. He felt special just to be up and out at that time. Although he'd never been on a beach, he thought sunrises and sunsets must be like waves, timeless in their infinity.

About seven o'clock a carload of women arrived to help Mary fix the refreshments. Around nine, an hour before the sale was scheduled to start, the first buyers began to arrive. Actually, not all of them would buy. Probably more than three hundred people would come to the sale, but no more than thirty or forty would purchase anything. It was as much a social as a business gathering. They came to see their friends, drink coffee, lean against their pickups and talk about the market or politics or how the current teams weren't as good as when they were in school. Most kept their hands in their pockets. Only those with some specific need in mind when they arrived were likely to make a major purchase, a tractor or some other farm implement. For the rest, it was just a day at the beach – Iowa style.

Once they had hauled everything out and numbered it for inspection, Jiggs could take a break. When the auction started, he would walk along with the Colonel, keeping track of what each item sold for and who bought it. He would fill out numbered cards for the buyers to take to the house to pay Mary, who kept the cash box, and to get their receipt, so they could haul their purchase away.

Geez, I'm hungry. Jiggs was cutting fifteen pounds to wrestle at 165, and he didn't have them to cut. He imagined the dish of oatmeal without sugar he'd eaten four hours earlier being sucked out of his stomach immediately upon arrival by starving body cells screaming for nourishment.

Stamping the snow from his boots, he entered the kitchen where Mary and her friends had set up three tables with coffee, different kinds of baked goods and a huge pan of steamed home-made sausages. The aromas alone nearly made Jiggs faint. *The first bite may kill me.*

Jiggs took a sausage and a sweet roll and asked for coffee. The girl pouring was a stranger to Jiggs. She smiled, and Jiggs, who, with two sisters, had never been particularly shy around girls, said "Hi. What's your name?"

"Carol Westphal. What's yours?"

"Jiggs Morgan. You must be related to Durward."

She was cheerleader pretty, short dark hair cut in what his sisters referred to as a "pageboy," dark eyes, not too tall, with lots of curves and a friendly smile. She was wearing jeans and a sweatshirt that said, "Lake City Lions."

"Durward and Mary are my grandparents. I live over in Lake City. What'd you do to your nose?"

"Banged it up in a wrestling match last night."

"What's the other guy look like?"

Jiggs was tempted to tell her he won. *Nah, Don't brag.* "Not a mark on him."

"You're the one who's helping with the auction, aren't you?"

"Yeah."

"My grandpa just told me about you. He says you're a good wrestler."

Durward's opinion was news to Jiggs. All he ever heard from Durward and the other farmers was how much tougher they had been. *What else did Durward tell her about me?*

"Do you like wrestling?"

"I go to most of Lake City's wrestling meets, because I'm a cheerleader. It's okay, but I think I like basketball better. My boyfriend's a basketball player."

Boyfriend. Naturally.

Some other men had come in and Jiggs had to move away from the table. Carol turned away from him and began to pour coffee for someone else. As he ate, Jiggs glanced from time to time in her direction. He liked Carol's manner, no giggles.

After he finished eating, Jiggs still had half an hour before the sale started, but the food he'd eaten hadn't made a dent in his hunger. He knew if he stayed indoors, he soon would be taking seconds, maybe thirds, maybe fourths. *Discipline!* Coach Bucyk's litany at practice - *Discipline!* - rang in his ears. Jiggs retreated from temptation and went back out in the cold.

He was standing at the edge of a group that was talking about President Kennedy's inauguration the preceding week. Before Jiggs could hear what dire consequences were in store for the heavily Protestant, Republican farmers at the hands of the new, Democratic, Catholic president, someone tapped him on the shoulder. Jiggs turned around. There was Ronald Bjournquist looking down at him. Jiggs had grown five inches and put on almost forty pounds since they'd first met during Jiggs' freshman football season, but he still had three inches and fifty pounds to go if he was ever going to be as big as Ron. *Never happen.*

"Good match last night, Junior. Nice nose."

Jiggs grinned. He would always be "Junior" to Bjournquist and his friends.

Before Jiggs could say anything, Bjournquist said, "You know Charlene here, don't you?"

Charlene was Ron's wife, as short as Ron was tall, as light as he was heavy, except for now, standing there eight months pregnant, looking like she was about to give birth to twin elephants or, worse, another male Bjournquist.

Bjournquist put an arm around his wife. "Hey, Charlene, you better get inside. You don't want to get a chill. You want some help?"

"Ronald, I can still walk." Charlene gave her husband a nudge in the ribs that he probably couldn't even feel. "I'm pregnant, not crippled."

Jiggs marveled at the exchange. The concern and offer of help so far exceeded the amount of sensitivity Jiggs could have ever imagined Bjournquist being capable of.

"What're ya gonna do this fall? Yer goin' to college, ain't ya?"

"Sure." Jiggs shrugged. "Doc says I have to get enough education to support him when some hog chews his leg off."

"Where you gonna go?"

Ron had gone to Iowa State for a year and a half on a football scholarship until he hurt his knee and could no longer play. Since then he had farmed with his father and brothers. Jiggs wondered if he regretted not going back with or without football, but didn't ask. *No use poking at a sore.*

"Probably Iowa. Haven't decided for sure."

"Gonna play any ball?"

"You kidding? Give me forty of your pounds, then maybe I'd try. Not much market for one hundred ninety pound linemen in the Big Ten. Coach Malone says I ought to try baseball."

"I s'pose not." Bjournquist turned and spat, turning almost a square foot of snow brown with tobacco juice. "Wish I could give you forty." He rubbed his expanding girth. "Mars is closer to Earth than I am to bein' in shape these days."

"You see Hegman when he was home for Christmas?"

Jim Hegman, the Central quarterback, student body president and valedictorian the year Bjournquist graduated, was going to the University of Iowa.

"Saw him at a basketball game and said 'Hello.'" Jiggs replied. "He was with some girl who looked like Miss America. Did you see him?"

"Yeah. He called up and we went out, him and that girl, 'Karien' was her name, and me an' Charlene. We had a good time. He must be doin' pretty good down there."

Can't imagine Jim not doing good at anything he tries.

Just then Colonel Clemons called Jiggs. The sale was about to start.

"Gotta go to work, Ron. See you later."

"Yeah. Hey, if I don't talk to ya again, good luck in the tournaments."

"Thanks. I'll need it. Billings is back again."

The district wrestling tournament began in three weeks. The state tournament was the week after for those who won or finished second at District. Losing three years in a row at District to a guy named Jim Billings, Jiggs had never made it to State.

The auction lasted more than three hours. Everything went smoothly. Durward got the price he wanted or more on just about everything. For an hour after it was over Jiggs helped various buyers load equipment on their trucks.

"C'mon inside and get paid." The Colonel clapped Jiggs on the shoulder as they watched the last buyer bump his way out to the road.

Durward was in the kitchen and in high spirits when they entered. Apart from actually moving, the sale had been his last official act before retirement, almost like a farewell party at the end of a successful career. Instead of a gold watch, his neighbors had bought his farm tools and equipment at high prices. By so doing. they'd said, "Durward Westphal, you were a good farmer. You took care of all parts of your farm. If this is something you owned and used, we know it's something we can use and rely on."

Durward handed the Colonel a beer and asked Jiggs if he wanted a Coke, which he declined. Jiggs wished he could have a beer. It was another mark of adulthood, but even if Durward had offered one, it would have to wait until wrestling season was over.

Most of the women had already left, but the Westphal's daughter-in-law, Carol's mother, was still there helping Mary put the finishing touches on the kitchen. As Jiggs sat waiting for the Colonel and Durward to settle up, Carol Westphal, came in from outside carrying an empty wastebasket. Her cheeks were flushed from the cold air and her dark eyes sparkled. "So, does your high school wrestle against Lake City?"

"Nope. Central's too little for you big city girls."

She made a face at him. Jiggs was beginning to forget about her boyfriend. "I'm finished here except for getting paid. Would you like to go for a ride? I can drop you off at your house whenever you have to be home."

Carol looked at her watch and sighed. "I really can't. It's almost three o'clock now and I have an early date tonight ... but thank you for asking."

"Here's your dough." The Colonel handed Jiggs some money. Jiggs stuffed it in his pocket without looking at it. He was a little embarrassed by being turned down, even though he knew it had been a longshot. Now he wanted to get out of there. He stood up and said good-bye to everyone, wished Durward and Mary well and left.

Jolting his way down the lane and out onto the dirt road that ran past Durward's place, which wasn't in much better shape than the lane, Jiggs didn't know whether to be encouraged or discouraged. She had said no, but she looked at her watch like if there had been time enough, she would have said yes. *Probably just trying to be polite.*

Jiggs had more important things on his mind. *I'm hungry. Wonder what Mom's fixing for dinner.*

4

February 1961

Jim Billings was a great wrestler, a state champion as a sophomore and again as a junior, unbeaten both years. In this, his senior season, he was once more undefeated. His high school, Prairie City, was in Central's conference. Over almost four full seasons Jiggs had wrestled Jim Billings nine times, twice for the district championship. Jiggs was 0-9 against him.

As the District Tournament approached, Jiggs was wrestling better than ever. He had won all but two matches during the season, a 5-1 loss to Billings in a dual meet and a 6-3 loss to him for the conference championship over the holidays. Running in the morning, wrestling at night, the Central team, led by Jiggs' best friend, Beezer, a defending state champion, was undefeated and expected to send several members to State and come back winners. Jiggs was swept up in the spirit that was building as the team, the school, the whole community of Walnut Grove focused on the tournaments. To wear the plain gray T-shirt that said "Central Wrestling" had become a badge of honor. In the season's last dual meet Central shut out a good Keoqua United team, winning every match, six by pins, including Jiggs'. Central Wrestling was ready.

Throughout the three weeks preceding the District, as the pressure and intensity climbed, Jiggs retreated more and more inside himself, trying to concentrate all his thoughts on just one thing, beating Jim Billings. It would be Jiggs' last shot at Billings, whom Jiggs respected and admired; Billings, whose strength and speed and skill had so dominated Jiggs' own. This team was not going to State without Jiggs. He knew he had at least one great match inside him and was determined to have it against Jim Billings. He would bring every resource he could muster to bear on this one goal.

The days dragged and raced by at the same time. Finally, at the end of a long bus ride to Cresco, where the tournament was held, the District arrived. At the first weigh-in there were occasional greetings with wrestlers he knew from other schools as their teams passed each other, including a handshake with Billings "See you in the finals," was all Billings said.

To get to the championship round, Jiggs had to win three straight matches, which he did easily, so easily he could barely remember them. When his final match was called, he knew he had won three and so had Jim. Jim's preliminaries had been much tougher than his own. *Maybe all this winning is becoming old stuff to Billings, maybe he's looking ahead to State, taking for granted the District title will be his ... maybe ... maybe ... maybe.*

It seemed like the whole town of Walnut Grove was there, roaring as Jiggs walked onto the mat, fighting the urge to bounce, to dance, to provide some escape from the tremendous adrenal rush he was experiencing. He was saving it, saving it all for the whistle, channeling every ounce of energy he could summon for the explosion he planned.

Coach Bucyk stood toe to toe with him, slapped him hard on each cheek, fixed him with his stare. "Kick some ass," he snapped and stepped away.

There stood Billings across the mat, blond and freckled, built like a starving blacksmith, obviously cutting every bit as much weight as Jiggs. They jogged to the center circle, shook hands, backed slightly away and the whistle blew.

Jiggs immediately took a short step forward as if to tie up with Billings, and when Billings raised his head and shoulders ever so slightly to grapple with Jiggs' arms, Jiggs dove for his left leg, driving hard with his shoulder against Billings' thigh and simultaneously pulling back with all his might on his ankle, toppling him backwards to the mat before Jim could regain his balance and counter by trying to pry Jiggs' head and shoulders away from his body with a cross-face. Take down, two points.

Billings spun his shoulders away from the mat as he fell and attempted to sit out, jackknifing away from Jiggs without ever stopping. It was as if he had converted an off balance fall into a move of his own, but Jiggs caught him and cracked him back towards the mat, sliding his own body to one side as he dragged Billings past him. He knifed over the top of Jim's chest, seized a leg with one arm, Billings' head with the other, jerking them towards each other into a cradle and driving all of his weight against Billings' chest trying for a pin.

The crowd was screaming. Coach Bucyk, contorted like a jungle vine, was lying flat on his stomach just off the mat trying to show Jiggs where to bear his weight, as Billings writhed, bridging desperately to keep his shoulders off the mat to avoid a pin.

Only a two-time state champion could have done it, Jiggs thought later. Only the pride of someone who hadn't tasted defeat in over a hundred matches could have enabled Billings to survive that first period, to arch and bridge and twist furiously for ninety endless seconds, while Jiggs strained every fiber of his being, every ounce of the will that had made the season, especially the last month, a crusade, to put Billings away. When the period ended, Billings was still unpinned, but the score was 8-0 against him.

Even down eight, there were some in the crowd who believed Billings would come back, that he would draw upon his greatness and prevail. But Jiggs turned him over again in the second period for three near fall points and then escaped from the underneath position and took Billings down once more in the third period. When the knotted towel came flying out from the scorer's table to signal the end, Jiggs rolled off the winner, 14-0.

The temptation to shout, to jump for joy, to thrust his fist in the air in triumph was almost overpowering, but overjoyed and astonished as he was, Jiggs knew better. He knew Coach Bucyk would turn away if he showed up his defeated opponent. Nine times out of ten Jim Billings had beaten him, and Billings had never once shouted or jumped or gestured. Jiggs scrambled to his feet, and the ref held his arm in the air. He shook hands with Billings, who said, "Great job."

"See you again at State," Jiggs replied, and he walked into the waiting arms of his nearly delirious coach and the entire Central team.

"Shoot me now, Coach. Things aren't ever going to get any better."

"Next week they will, Jiggs," Coach replied, hugging him and slapping him on the back while his teammates milled around them. "Next week is State. Next week things will be even better."

Things didn't get any better for Jim Billings. An hour after losing to Jiggs, he had to wrestle the man Jiggs had pinned in the semi-finals to protect his second place finish and trip to State as district runner-up. Jiggs sat with Beezer and Coach Bucyk and watched in disbelief as Billings lost 4-0 to a guy who, most days, couldn't carry Billings' jock.

Later that night at the restaurant where the team and its accompanying caravan stopped before beginning the trip home, Jiggs talked to Doc for the first time since leaving for the tournament. "How do you feel about that last match?" Doc eyed Jiggs through the steam rising from his coffee.

"Happy, real happy ... except for one thing."

"What's that?"

"It was too easy, Pop. For me to beat Billings, it should have been war out there, but it wasn't. Maybe cutting weight got to him or something. I don't know. I just know it was too easy. "

Doc shrugged. "Probably it was just your day and not his. Don't sell yourself short, you earned this win."

Monday morning second period Ol' Man Gordon, the trigonometry teacher, was droning on about some of his beloved equations. Jiggs tried to listen and not think about either weekend, the one coming up or the one just past, or about how hungry he was, when there was a knock at the door. Mr. Gordon answered it, then turned and asked Jiggs to step outside and bring his books. He was excused for the rest of the hour.

Whatever the cause, Jiggs was thankful for the diversion. Coach Bucyk was waiting for him in the hall. He had a serious look on his face, but that wasn't unusual. Coach didn't crack many jokes.

"Jiggs, come down to the coaches' office with me. I need to talk to you."

Jiggs followed the coach in silence, not knowing what to think. His weight was okay, his grades were good, his conscience was clear. Whatever it was must be important to take him out of class.

They entered the office, a dingy, low-ceilinged room under the bleachers in the gym, furnished with a desk and chair, some lockers, and three folding chairs. Central's three coaches shared the space, but Jiggs and Coach Bucyk were alone.

"Sit down, Jiggs." Coach indicated one of the folding chairs, while he took the desk chair and swiveled it around to face Jiggs, their knees almost touching in the cramped quarters.

"Jiggs, ... Jim Billings died this morning."

The news hit Jiggs harder than Bjournquist ever had. He sat there looking at Coach, letting it sink in. It was true. Coach wouldn't joke about something like that, and, too, he knew all along deep in his heart something had been wrong. *It was too easy.*

After almost thirty seconds, he said, "What happened?"

"I don't know much, Jiggs. Jim Pierson, the coach over at Prairie called me. Apparently Billings got sick in the middle of the night. His folks called the doctor, but he died before the doctor got there."

The coach took out a piece of paper with a couple of words written on it. "They think it might be something called "hypertrophic cardiomyopathy" which means his heart muscle was too thick. I guess he'd been complaining of feeling weak lately, light-headed. They thought he was just worn down from the season and cutting weight."

"Well, that kind of explains a lot of things, doesn't it, Coach?"

It was Coach's turn to be silent, but only for a few seconds. "That's why I got you out of class, Jiggs. I knew that's what you'd think, that you only beat him because he was sick. But it's not true.

"In twenty years of wrestling, Jiggs, I never saw anybody more ready for a match than you were last Saturday night. That first move you put on him would have taken down an elephant. Geez, you were driving guys into the stands the whole tournament. Maybe the score wouldn't have been so lop-sided, but when you took the mat that night, you were every bit the wrestler Jim Billings ever was."

Jiggs stared at Coach. He believed everything except the last sentence.

"Jiggs, there's going to be a lot of talk about this, a lot of speculation. You don't have to believe me, but I'm asking you not to believe what others may say either. I'm asking you to find out for yourself how good you are, and the way you do that is by wrestling this weekend like you did last weekend. You do that, and you'll be state champion. Don't let it be decided off the mat. Don't do it for me, Jiggs. Do it for yourself." Coach Bucyk stood up and Jiggs stood too. "You have any questions, Jiggs?"

"I don't think so, not now. I need to think about it."

"Don't bother going back to Trig. You can sit here or go up to the library, whatever you want. Pick up your schedule when you're ready."

Wednesday afternoon Jiggs left school, drove to Prairie City and attended Jim Billings' funeral. He didn't tell anyone he was going, he didn't get excused from classes; he didn't speak to anyone while he was there. He just went and came back and attended practice as usual. No one asked where he had been. They just knew.

Jim Billings was the first dead person Jiggs had ever seen. It was the first funeral he ever attended. There would be many more.

After dinner that night, Jiggs and Doc went horseback riding. They'd gone about a mile when Doc broke his usual silence. "Rough week, huh?"

"Yeah, rough week. I went to Jim Billings' funeral today."

"I figured you did. How did that make you feel?"

"Selfish."

"Selfish?"

"Yeah. It made me see my whole reaction to his death was based on what it meant to me. Seeing him lying there, looking just like he looked in real life. Except he was dead. It dawned on me I was just feeling sorry for myself, because his dying made me look bad.

"Suddenly I began to feel sad for him, for the good person I think he was, who worked so hard and achieved so much and had so much to look forward to, not just wrestling, but life, and who now isn't going to enjoy it. It all made wrestling seem pretty unimportant. Does that make any sense?"

Doc turned and looked at his son and, for the first time, saw a man instead of a boy. He reached over and clapped a gloved hand on Jiggs' shoulder. "Yeah. It does."

Not long after they returned from the ride, Jiggs was in his room doing homework when his mom called up to him that he had a phone call.

He bounded downstairs to the kitchen phone.

"Jiggs," a girl's voice, "this is Carol Westphal. We met at my grandfather's sale a few weeks ago. Remember?"

Jiggs remembered.

"I just called to say I read about your win at District, and my grandfather told me today what happened this week ... and ... well ... that really is too bad. I'm sorry it happened. I hope you don't let it get in the way this weekend and that you have a great tournament."

For at least the fourth time that day, Jiggs had a lump in his throat, but far from heightening his bleak feelings, this one began to wash them away.

The 1961 Iowa State High School Wrestling Tournament was its usual pageant of color. Letter jackets, uniforms, pom-poms in every known hue and combination of hues were everywhere. Osage won the Class A Division for smaller schools, Central finished second; Waterloo West won Double A. Beezer took home his second title. The four wrestlers who qualified from Prairie City wore black patches on their uniforms in memory of their absent champion. Jiggs won his first three matches, lost in the semi-finals, but won the consolation to finish third. He was glad when it was over.

5

Late March 1961

The Morgan farm was in the valley of the Des Moines River – mostly hillsides too steep for cultivation, covered with hardwood, oak, walnut and elm. In addition to his horses, Doc raised Black Angus cattle on his ground. Horses and cattle meant fences.

Sometimes Jiggs envied town kids, whose chores were taking out the trash and mowing the lawn, and for whom a school bus was something other people rode while they walked over to a friend's house or played a pick-up game after school. At other times, like when he and Doc would stand watching a cow lick clean her newborn calf they'd just helped deliver out in a field somewhere, Jiggs envied town kids not at all.

Today, however, he was staggering up a hill too steep for the tractor to climb, struggling to balance a sixty-pound fence post on his shoulder and keep it away from his neck and cheek to prevent the creosote weather-proofing from burning his skin. Today he was longing for urban living.

Doc should have been a wrestling coach. If Coach Bucyk saw this, he'd have the whole team out here.

Just below the top of the hill, Jiggs dropped the post, the last of the day, with thud beside a small pile of black dirt from the hole Doc had begun to dig.

Jiggs inhaled and blew out his breath a couple of times, trying to catch up. "That's the one I've been looking for."

It was only forty degrees, but sweat poured into Jiggs' eyes. Without thinking, he wiped his forehead with the sleeve of his creosote stained sweatshirt, leaving an oily, black smear across his brow.

Doc looked up from the hole he was digging. He gazed at the row of fence posts lying at ten yard intervals more than five hundred feet down the slope to where the tractor and wagon were parked at the bottom. Despite the raw March wind, his shirt, too, was soaked with sweat. "If this ground was any harder, we'd have to blast."

Jiggs took a swig of water from a battered thermos and held it out to Doc. "Probably not thawed yet. Maybe you got too much of a jump on fence building season this year."

Doc changed the subject. "Given any more thought to what you're going to do next fall?

"Probably go to Iowa. That's where I've always thought about going. Marine recruiter gave a talk to the senior boys a couple weeks ago. He made the Marines sound pretty good."

"Yeah, like four years of wrestling practice." Doc had been in the Marines in World War II.

"I think Beezer's going to sign up." Beezer Griggs was Jiggs' best friend, although lately his interest in the Morgan family seemed to focus more on Jiggs' sister, Darcy, than Jiggs.

"After the recruiter left, Coach Bucyk talked to me. Said he'd been in the Marines, and that I should go in after college and be an officer if I was interested in that."

"Probably pretty good advice."

"Coach thinks I can wrestle varsity at Simpson, where he went. He even offered to take me down there and introduce me to the coach. They don't give scholarships."

"Is that what you want to do?"

"No ... I don't think I want to wrestle any more."

"Because of what happened with Billings?"

"Nah ... It's just that wrestling means giving up everything else. At college I don't even know what 'everything else' is. I might try baseball just to see if I can do it, but if I go to college, that won't be why."

"What do you want to be? That ought to figure in somewhere."

"Don't know. I'm thinking about journalism. I like English class. I like to read and write things. I don't think I have enough math and science in me to be a vet."

"What does the counselor at school say? Did you talk to him like we discussed?"

"Mr. Lundberg? He said journalists drink too much and are hard on their families, and I should think of something else."

6

May 1961

When Carol Westphal called Jiggs and asked him to her senior prom in Lake City, he was so astonished he blurted out, "What about your boyfriend?" The one time he had called her for a date after the State Tournament, she had turned him down. She was still "kind of going" with just one guy. But once again she thanked him for asking. Now she and the basketball player must have broken up. She had invited him to the biggest event of the school year – dinner, a dance, an all-night party. *Wow!*

On an earlier trip to Lake City right after the tournament, Jiggs had figured out where Carol lived and driven by her house – information more useful than he had dared to hope. After meeting Carol's parents and exchanging the corsage he'd bought for a boutonniere, they departed for Trevelyn's restaurant, Lake City's "finest," where the banquet preceding the dance was to be held. Once in the car and moving, Jiggs struggled to keep his eyes on the road. "You working this summer?" he glanced in Carol's direction for the third time in the first thirty seconds of their drive.

"I'm life guarding at the Country Club pool and working in the pro shop. How about you? Baling hay and working auctions?"

"No auctions in the summer. Farmers are all too busy. No, the coach got me a job working highway construction for a company out of Boone. I'm leaving on Wednesday, the day after graduation."

"Gee, I like my job better than yours. But, boo hoo, you being gone all summer."

Jiggs had been looking forward to being on his own and away from home with an eagerness so deep and wide the Pacific Ocean would have fit inside. But when Carol said "boo hoo," at the prospect of his absence, he was immediately kind of sorry to be leaving.

"I don't think my folks would let me go off for the summer like that," she added.

"You should ask. I'm sure there would be a spot for you shoveling asphalt."

"No, no. The Country Club needs me. I can't disappoint the Lake City gentry. Besides, like I said, I don't think my parents are ready to turn me loose on the highways and byways of Iowa."

Gentry. Jiggs knew what it meant, but had never heard it used outside some old novel.

"They're turning you loose this fall, aren't they? Where are you going to school?"

"Tucson. University of Arizona."

"Arizona? Why so far away?"

"There's more to it than this, but it can best be summed up in two words: 'sunshine' and 'golf.' I have a golf scholarship. Are you a golfer?"

"No." Jiggs laughed.

"What's so funny?"

"My dad says golf courses are a waste of good grazing land."

Carol shook her head as if such an idea was beyond her comprehension. "Where do wrestlers go to college? The University of Alaska? Some place they can major in suffering?"

Almost before Jiggs knew it, they were at the restaurant. Talking to Carol made him wish Trevelyn's was still another twenty miles away. As Jiggs parked the car, other couples were arriving and making their way through the parking lot. Carol's appearance sparked squeals of greeting from at least three hundred of her closest girlfriends followed in each case by an inquisitive glance at this unknown guy Carol was bringing to the big dance.

Everybody was telling everybody else how nice they looked. In Carol's case, they were telling the truth. Her mint green satin gown offset an early summer golf course tan. She had the darkest eyes Jiggs had ever seen, almost black. Cheerful and easy to talk to, it seemed the two of them had been friends forever rather than out on a first date.

Carol introduced Jiggs to everyone they met as they walked in, students and teachers alike. Mr. Dobson, the Lake City wrestling coach, said he'd seen Jiggs wrestle at State and asked if he was going to try it in college. *At least one person recognizes me as someone other than just "Carol's date."*

A display table had been set up filled with mementos of the Class of '61's four-year tour of duty at Lake City High School. Sports trophies, photographs, posters announcing class plays and pep rallies. Here, too, Carol was much in evidence. Not only was she a cheerleader, she was Homecoming Queen and the only girl on the golf team.

"Are you class president too?"

"No ..." Carol gave him a nudge in the ribs with her elbow. "... Treasurer."

Their seats turned out to be at the head table by virtue of her office. Carol dropped off her purse, and Jiggs shook hands with the principal and superintendent and several other class officers and their dates.

"If we don't eat soon, I'll have to feed myself left-handed, because my right will be disabled from all this hand-shaking."

Carol grabbed the hand in question. "Well, let's go get some food. You're going to need all your strength for dancing." They headed for the buffet hand in hand.

When they were about half way through the line, someone behind them said, "Well, look who's here. Carol Westphal and her date."

Jiggs turned. Three guys were walking towards them carrying plates heaped with food. As they neared, the tall one in the middle appeared to stumble, dumping his entire plate on the front of Jiggs' white sport coat.

"Oh, Jesus, I'm sorry." The voice said he wasn't at all sorry. "Here, let me wipe that off."

He took a napkin and rubbed hard on the front of the ruined jacket, grinding in the barbecue sauce and baked beans. Jiggs did not have to be told he had just met Carol's ex-boyfriend. On his way out the door to the car that evening, Doc had handed him twenty dollars he hadn't asked for. "Have a good time, but watch yourself. Stay out of trouble."

"What do you mean 'trouble?'"

Doc shrugged. "Who knows? Maybe you'll meet some people there who resent the fact this girl asked you to the dance. It's possible. Just keep cool and pay no attention to what anyone says."

Doc, the fortune teller.

After what Jiggs had already seen of Carol's high school career, it didn't surprise him to recognize the guy wiping food all over his chest was Gary Green, the star forward on Lake City's basketball team. *It figures.*

"Never mind," Jiggs stepped back, mad and embarrassed.

Green straightened, no more than three feet away, at least two inches taller than Jiggs. "Clumsy me."

"Forget it." Jiggs started to turn away and put his hand up as a signal for the obviously angry Carol to do the same.

"No. No, I can't forget it." Green put his hand on Jiggs' shoulder. The two boys with him laughed.

"Why, here's little Carol, the queen of the hop, and now I've made her mad, and she won't even introduce me to her date."

Doc's words ringing in his ears, Jiggs stuck out his hand before Carol could speak. *Stay cool.*

"I'm Jiggs Morgan. I recognize you. You're Gary Green. I've seen you play basketball. You're a good player. You guys had a great team. Pleased to meet you."

"How would you know, Country? You play basketball out on the farm?"

"GARY…"

"Shut up, Cunt."

The move that Jiggs had taken down Jim Billings with at the opening of their match at District had been made in slow motion compared to the speed of the blow that broke Gary Green's nose. A split second after it landed, someone from the side hit Jiggs behind his right ear, and he whirled in that direction, striking at his assailant as he moved, sensing his presence more than seeing it, driving him across the buffet table, which collapsed, smashing into the mirror covering the wall behind the table. Someone jumped on his back, blows rained down on him from all directions. A girl screamed.

Someone was stomping him, kicking his back and ribs. Jiggs thought he might die, but if he did, the guy he'd tackled was going with him. Jiggs' fingers dug at the guy's eyes, and he bit down hard on his hand.

No such thing as a fair fight. Another piece of Doc's advice.

"Which one of you is Morgan?" The desk sergeant spoke into a microphone from behind a clear Plexiglas window that looked into the room filled with teen-age boys in torn, stained formal wear, most of whom were sitting on benches, elbows on their knees, staring at the floor.

Jiggs, who had been standing alone at the far end of the room with his back against a wall, walked towards the window. It hurt to move. It hurt to breathe.

"Just wait, asshole," one of the boys muttered without looking up.

"Shut up in there!" The snarl of a cop who'd about had it with a bunch of idiot teenagers. Then in an only slightly lower voice, "Someone's here for you, Morgan."

Carol and her father were waiting for him. Carol was still wearing her formal.

"You're free to go, Jiggs" Mr. Westphal said. "Have you called your parents?"

Jiggs nodded. "My dad's on his way." It felt like someone's shoe was still lodged behind his right ear.

"Well, let's wait out in the parking lot."

Once outside, Jiggs turned to Carol and her father. "Mr. Westphal, Carol, I don't know to whom to apologize first. I'm..."

"Don't apologize, Jiggs." Mr. Westphal put his hand on Jiggs' shoulder, but took it off when Jiggs winced. "I know what happened."

Carol took Jiggs' hand and held it as the three of them stood together beside Westphal's car. Mr. Westphal, a lawyer, said he'd handle the charges and let Jiggs know what he needed to do.

Ten minutes later Doc arrived in his pickup. Jiggs introduced him to Mr. Westphal and explained what happened.

"How do you feel now?" Doc examined the scrapes and bruises on Jiggs' face in the dim light of the street lamp. "Where do you hurt the worst?"

"My right ear feels about twice normal size; the pain behind it makes it hard to swallow."

Doc took a closer look. "We'll stop on the way home and get some ice for it. See how you feel in the morning."

Before they parted, Carol led Jiggs away from where their fathers were standing. "Please call me tomorrow, Jiggs, will you? Let me know how you feel. Maybe we can go to a movie or something before you leave for the summer. You still owe me a date."

When they went to pick up Jigg's car, they found all four of the tires slit, so he and Doc rode home together. Neither said much until they were entering the house where Jiggs knew he would have to retell the whole story for his mom and sisters.

"Keep the ice on that ear when you get inside ... and Jiggs, if there's ever a next time, strike as hard as you can, but don't grab anyone. The moment you grab one man, you're defenseless against the rest."

7

Late August 1961

"Willetts will work you so hard you'll be too tired to get in any trouble," Coach Bucyk's words when he told Jiggs the job with the road crew was waiting for him The recollection made Jiggs laugh as he sat sipping a beer and waiting for supper in the only tavern in Colfax, Iowa. Coach had been right about one thing. Willets Construction Company drove him hard. For twelve hours a day, six days a week, the crew raced to accomplish as much as possible between rainstorms and before winter made work impossible. Jiggs dragged a sixty-pound jackhammer all over the state ripping curbs off highways built in the '30s, widening them for cars built in the '60s. $1.10 an hour, no overtime.

As for the "trouble" part, it wasn't really trouble, at least not Jiggs' trouble. Twice he'd seen men killed, one a motorist whose tiny economy car had been sandwiched between two semis; the other, a highway patrolman electrocuted when he stepped on a broken power line hidden in the grass at the scene of an earlier accident.

For the second time in his life, Jiggs had become "Junior." At seventeen, he was the youngest man on the crew.

Soon the others saw he knew how to work both hard and smart and that new guys kept theiri mouths shut. Once that happened, Gus, Mert, Will and the other crew members, men for whom the nomadic life of road construction was a full-time occupation, took Jiggs under their wing and vowed to make a "paver" of him.

He shared a hotel room with Gus and Will. The bathroom was down the hall. Jiggs now knew what it felt like to work all day in the hot sun after drinking ten beers the night before. More than once, rather than risk oversleeping, he had gone straight to the job site from whatever place he had been last the night before. When his new friends learned he was still a virgin, they took him to a whorehouse in Des Moines.

They parked in a shabby neighborhood in front of an old two story house painted green with a high peaked roof. The room they entered looked like Jiggs' grandmother's parlor except there were four women in sequined bathrobes sitting on the overstuffed furniture. As if only a mirage, Jiggs' three companions disappeared up the stairs at the far end of the room with three of the women before Jiggs was aware selections were being made.

The pudgy woman who remained was about Jiggs' mom's age. She wore high-heeled shoes and a black wrap-around garment half way between a robe and a dress that, like its owner, had long ago lost whatever sheen it once possessed. "You here for some fun?" She put out her cigarette in an ashtray on the table beside her and stood up.

"Yeah, ... I guess so." *C'mon Morgan, you're here. No hanging back.*

"Well, let's go then. I'm Sally. C'mon."

Once in the room, Sally took off her dress with a single tug on its snaps, folded it and placed it on top of a dresser. She lay down on the bed, nude except for her shoes. Jiggs' first real life naked lady.

Jiggs sat on the edge of the bed. *Should I say something? Just strip? What?*

Sally looked up at him. "You gonna fuck or not?"

Whatever ardor Jiggs may have felt for "losing his cherry," as Gus had so delicately put it an hour or so earlier when this adventure was first proposed, was quickly ebbing.

Sally, the wise working girl, reached over and gave his belt buckle a tug. "First time, eh?"

Between the two of them, they got Jiggs undressed.

"Aren't you going to take off your shoes?"

Sally finished putting the condom on him, Jiggs' ardor ebbing no longer. "The shoes stay on." She pulled Jiggs down on top of her.

It was the last thing either said until they stood dressing a few minutes later. Sally finished first and stuck out her hand.

"That'll be twenty dollars."

Don't pay more than ten. Gus's advice on the way in.

But haggling meant an argument, which meant Jiggs would remain there at least one moment longer than necessary. He handed her a twenty.

Shit. I worked a day and a half for THAT?

Jiggs had read too many adventure novels in which the heroine was chaste and pure, the way he dared to imagine Carol. Walking back downstairs into the parlor, he felt like he'd just kicked mud himself.

Every November, when the snows came and work ground to a halt for the year, some of the crew would head for Mexico, where it was warm and their money went further. They would stay, drinking, playing cards, shacking up and riding their motorcycles until money ran out or Spring came and it was warm enough in the North to resume paving. By the middle of July, Jiggs had traded his pickup for a used Triumph 650 motorcycle and made up his mind to ride south when winter came. School could wait.

College was the furthest thing from Jiggs' mind as he walked outside the bar after having supper with Will and Gus, his best friends on the crew. There was Doc leaning against his pickup parked just up the street. It was the first time Jiggs had seen anyone in his family in almost three months.

"Pop, what are you doing here?"

"Came down to pick up you and your bike. Summer's about over. School starts next week."

"Wait a minute, Pop. What're you talking about? I wrote and told you I'm not going. I even got my tuition deposit back and everything. I'm going to Mexico in a couple of months."

"I guess your mom sent in a new deposit when we got your letter."

"Well, tell her to get it back, if it's not too late. I'm staying here and working."

"Can't." Doc's usual quiet voice. In his entire life, Jiggs had never heard Doc yell. It was a hard voice sometimes, but never loud.

"What do you mean 'can't?'"

"I hear you've been fired."

"Fired. No way! No way Mr. O'Malley would fire me. I'm one of the best workers he has."

Doc shrugged. "It's just what I heard. Why don't you ask him? Do you know where to find him?"

"Yeah, I know where to find him." Jiggs eyed his father. *I bet you do too.*

Mr. O'Malley, the Project Superintendent, lived with his family in a large trailer he pulled from job to job behind a huge black Oldsmobile 88. The trailer was parked under some trees beside the Company's supply lot on the edge of town. Through the screen door Jiggs could see the light from a television.

Jiggs knocked. Mr. O'Malley answered and, upon seeing who it was, stepped outside.

"Sorry to bother you, Mr. O'Malley. This is my dad…"

"We've met."

Bingo. Suspicion confirmed. I should tell them both to go to hell. He didn't.

"Pop says I've been fired."

"That's right."

"Why … why? You don't have a better worker on the whole crew than me. You know that's true. Why fire me?"

"Son, you have a chance to do something none of your buddies on this crew ever had a chance to do. Take Gus, for instance. He's real smart, but he's got no school. If he'd gone to college, he could be bossing this whole job instead of busting his ass breaking curb. Same goes for you.

"I'm not going to let you blow that chance without even giving school a try. So you're fired until the beginning of next summer. If you want to come back and stay on after you've had a year of college, well … we'll see."

O'Malley stuck out his hand. "Just give it a fair shot, Jiggs, for Gus and Mert and me and all the rest of the poor dumb pavers who would like to trade places with you."

Jiggs looked at Mr. O'Malley, then at his dad, then back at Mr. O'Malley. *What now?*

Jiggs shook the older man's hand. "See you next summer."

It was less than a mile back to the bar where Jiggs' bike was parked. Jiggs spent the two minutes it took to get there struggling to suppress his impulse to scream. *No right. You've got no right. It's my life. Let me live it...*

Doc pulled up in front of the motorcycle and began to open his door.

"Don't bother getting out. I'm not coming home with you."

Doc took his hand off the door and shifted his weight around so he could face Jiggs. "What are you going to do?"

"Not go home with you. That's for sure."

"Can't make you. But, before you get out, tell me what you're thinking."

Jiggs paused. Even mad as he was, which was about as mad as he'd ever been, what he was thinking and what he was prepared to say to Doc were two different things. He bit his lip so hard it hurt. "I never figured you for a meddler, Pop."

"It's called being a 'parent.'"

"Yeah, well, maybe that ended three months ago."

"Mmm." A Doc sound, half way between a sigh and a laugh. "If you were drowning, would you not want me to throw you a rope just because you've been on your own for a while?"

"Hardly the same thing."

"Maybe, maybe not. Step outside your anger for a minute, if you can, and picture your life in ten years if you don't go to college. Do you think this Mexico trip will have the same luster in hindsight, when you're getting up and going to work every morning for a paycheck you've already spent? With a back that feels like it's on fire every time you pick up that jackhammer? Maybe with a wife, who's saying 'we have to do something different,' but you have no idea what that could be? There are different ways to drown."

"I'm going to Mexico, not Mars. How can you assume I won't go to college next year, just because I'm not going this year?"

"How can you assume you will? Things happen. Doors open; doors close. The longer you lay out of school, the harder it will be to go back."

"Guess that's a chance I'll have to take." Jiggs got out of the truck.

"Jiggs," Doc leaned across the seat and extended his hand through the open window, "you're right. School will still be there next year, but so will Mexico, and the year after that and the year after that. Think about it."

Jiggs met Doc's gaze. Somewhere buried deep beneath his anger was the suspicion he hadn't won this argument. "I'll think about it." He shook Doc's hand and walked away.

Two days later he rode home.

8

September 1961

The night before Jiggs set sail for the University, he and Doc were sitting on the porch having a beer "Why do you suppose fraternities exist?" Doc asked.

At Jim Hegman's suggestion, Jiggs had signed up for Rush, the buttoned-down, blazered, meat market of a week preceding the beginning of the fall semester, when freshmen could visit the University's fraternities to size up whether and which they wanted to join while being sized up in return.

"Never thought about it. They call'em "social" fraternities. I guess it's to give a bunch of guys who want to hang out together a way to do it."

"Why do they need a fraternity to hang out?"

Where's this going? "Probably don't. Probably the hanging out came first."

"Yes, and eventually they started looking for a way to set themselves apart."

"So?"

"Well, in which direction do you think they were trying to separate themselves from the rest of the students?"

"Separate themselves?"

"Above or below?"

Okay, I see. "Probably not below."

"Right. You ever read about caste systems, aristocracies, in school? That's how they get started. It's just a way for one group to set itself above the herd. You sure you want to be part of that?"

Jiggs wasn't even sure if he wanted to be a part of college. In the wake of his involuntary severance from Willlett's road crew, he was in no mood to please Doc, regardless of whether he agreed with him.

"I don't know. Hegman says it's okay. He seems to be doing all right."

"Well, if you don't want to wrestle, because you think it might preempt too much of college life, beware of fraternities. They might have the same downside as wrestling with none of the up."

Jiggs turned that thought over for a few seconds. "Guess I'll go down and take a look next week, then decide." He took the final swig of his beer, stood up and walked back in the house.

The strength of Doc's disapproval made him curious. "Mom," he asked at breakfast the next morning long after Doc had left on his first call, "What's Pop got against fraternities?"

"Oh, your Dad went to school during the depression. The frat boys were all the rich boys. Doc lived in the stock barns for six years and shoveled a lot of manure for his room and board. He has kind of a chip on his shoulder about fraternities, just like he won't join the country club now."

On the third night of the ensuing week, amid a bunch of would-be Greeks like himself having dinner at some nameless fraternity, Jiggs met Roger Hood. Everyone at the table was wearing wingtip shoes; there wasn't a white sock or wide tie to be seen. All were on their best behavior, striving to impress. Hood impressed Jiggs by eating twelve pieces of chicken.

He next saw Hood as he was unpacking in the tiny room assigned him at the Delta Tau Delta fraternity, where he'd pledged largely because it was the house Jim Hegman belonged to. As Jiggs put away his gear, he was reflecting that now he was one of the 'rich boys.'

"Morgan," a voice from behind him, "meet your new roommate."

Jiggs turned to find a couple of the actives, upper-classmen who had successfully weathered the semester long initiation process known as "pledgeship," standing in his doorway. Standing with them, Jiggs recognized the guy who liked chicken.

"Jiggs Morgan, meet Roger Hood."

Iowa was fresh from its second Rose Bowl victory in four years, and Hood was a football recruit. Jiggs had read about him when he committed to the University, first team all-state in Illinois, probable successor to the Hawks' senior All-American quarterback, at 6'3", 220 pounds, Hood looked more like a linebacker than a quarterback.

"We met somewhere the other night at dinner." They shook hands.

"Yeah, good chicken, huh?" Hood grinned, moved into the tiny room, and swung his enormous suitcase on to the vacant top bunk without apparent effort.

Jiggs was sure pledging Hood must be a coup for the Delts on the football-mad campus. The two actives continued to lounge in the doorway making small talk, mostly with Hood, as he and Jiggs apportioned the room between them.

After a few minutes of unpacking Hood took out an 8 x 10 portrait, beautifully framed, of the most lovely girl Jiggs had ever seen and set it on his dresser. She looked like a movie star.

"That your girl?" one of the actives asked.

"Yeah."

"Where's she going to school."

"Back home. She's still got a year of high school left."

"High school honey, eh?" The active smirked as he spoke.

"Yeah."

"Aw, do you love her?"

Hood straightened up from stowing some shoes in the bottom of the closet and looked at the two loungers. "I love to fuck her."

"Wh ... what?"

"I love to fuck her." Hood returned to unpacking.

Spoken like a paver.

Apparently the two actives were as astonished as Jiggs at Hood's version of love. Further conversation died before birth. In less than a minute both had disappeared.

"Nice to have a little peace and quiet while we unpack." Hood was laughing and nodding towards the empty doorway. He turned to Jiggs. "You like music?"

"Music ... sure, I like music."

"Good. My folks are bringing up my stereo next weekend. We can blow this place apart. What kinds do you like?"

"Ray Charles, Johnny Cash, Kingston Trio, stuff like that. Why? What kinds do you like?"

"All of that, but classical too. I'm going to major in music. Let me show you something."

Hood fumbled in his suitcase and with a reverence he had not displayed for his high school honey, he placed a small black case on the dresser beside her picture.

"Look at this." He opened the latch and lifted the lid.

The first thing Jiggs saw was a flash of blue velvet lining so rich and deep it distracted him from the case's contents, a pencil thin, tapered steel rod about fifteen inches long. It looked like a segment from a car's radio antenna.

"What is it?"

Hood removed the object from its case and held it up for Jiggs to inspect without offering to let him hold it.

"It's my baton." Hood almost whispered the words. "It's my baton. When I'm a senior, I'm going to be the student conductor of the University's orchestra."

Wonder whether he has the same kind of confidence about football. The way Hood said it sounded like conviction, not bragging. Jiggs decided he liked his new roommate.

9

November 1961

"Morgan, telephone for you, line three. Long distance." The duty phone pledge hollered down the circular stairwell.

"Make it quick, Morgan," the active proctoring Pledge Study Hall said, "You aren't supposed to have calls during study hours."

At the sound of his name, Jiggs hurried up the stairs, the proctor's overused snarl ricocheting almost unheard.

"Junior. This is Will Jeffcoat."

"Jeffcoat!" The name thrust Jiggs back on to the Willett's crew. "Where the hell are you?"

"I'm in Boone, but never mind that. Look outside the window."

"The window. Why the window?" From the phone booth where Jiggs was standing no windows were to be seen.

"Because it's snowing out, Junior. It's been snowing all over the goddamn state for a week. Willetts is shutting down and laying off. Me 'n Gus are headin' South a week from Saturday. I think Mert and Les are goin' too. Are you comin'?"

The following Monday night was "Pledge Night" at the Delt house. Pledges were required to dress in coats and ties for class on Mondays. At ten p.m., when study hours ended, they were herded into an otherwise darkened room, where they stood at attention, side by side, with a bright light trained on them. A line-up. From the dark behind the light the actives screamed curses on their unworthiness ever to bear the name of Delta Tau Delta.

"Morgan, you fucking pig's butt," Jim Torkelson, a sophomore, who took particular delight in harassing pledges, stepped in front of the light and stuck his nose in Jiggs' face, "Where were you at the mixer with the Pi Phis last Friday night? Don't you like your brothers? Don't you want to function with your brothers?"

"Yessir." Jiggs shouted his reply, but not too loud. He had known this was coming. Torkelson, who the pledges referred to as "Tears" after the night the drunken Hood dangled him by his feet out a third floor window making him cry, was the house Social Chairman. It was his job to arrange parties that no pledge dared fail to attend.

"Don't 'yessir' me, Fartface." With each "f," Tears showered Jiggs with spit.

All up and down the line similar one-way conversations were being screamed by actives berating various pledges for assorted sins. Here and there pledges were down doing push-ups, the standard sentence for run of the mill unsatisfactory pledge conduct. Jiggs numbed his mind to as much of it as he could, now and then tensing to suppress forbidden laughter at some unusually absurd awfulness going on elsewhere along the line.

"Where were you? Tears was really getting revved up. Jiggs could hear him breathing. "What was so important that you couldn't function with the hottest sorority on campus?"

"I went for a walk, Sir."

"Went for a walk!" Torkelson's scream rose above the surrounding chaos, commanding its attention, silencing the indictment of lesser sins elsewhere in the room.

"You went for a walk!"

It was true. It had been the day after Will Jeffcoat's call. Jiggs was trying out for the baseball team, and there had been a practice in the fieldhouse that day. Afterward, instead of going to the mixer, he had gone for a walk, trying to decide what to do about Mexico. He had come back to the Delt house still undecided.

"Give me fifty fingertip clappers, Pukeface!"

Jiggs dropped into the pushup position and began reeling off pushups, thrusting himself up with such force that he could clap his hands beneath him at the top of his cycle and catch himself on his fingertips as gravity took over and drove him back down.

Torkelson knelt beside him talking to him in a low voice. "I'm not letting you into this fraternity, Buttbreath. I'm making you my personal project, and I'm going to drive you out. Do you understand me?"

"Yessir." As he pushed, Jiggs watched his necktie alternately extend and collapse like an accordion against the carpet.

"Do you understand me?" More a growl than a shout.

"Yessir!"

After an hour and a half, most of the actives became bored and wandered off, but Tears and a couple of the other sophomores were still wound up. Instead of ending the line up and releasing the pledges, Tears yelled, "All right you dumb shits. I want every one of you lined up outside my room in one minute. Move!"

One minute later, twenty-six little sheep aligned themselves outside Torkelson's door awaiting whatever slaughter the nasty shepherd had in mind.

Tears and his roommate, Edwards, another pledge-baiter, barged past, stopping long enough to tell the flock to keep their mouths shut. They were followed by Overton, who bore the title "Pledge Trainer," carrying a pitcher of water, a glass and a bucket.

The door to the room closed behind the three actives for approximately five minutes while the pledges stood fidgeting, poking each other and laughing silently about things that had happened in the line up. Hood stepped over to the adjacent circular stairwell and mimicked hanging Torkelson upside down over the three story shaft to the basement.

Jiggs stood watching Hood's antics, reflecting. He thought of all they'd been through in their two months together. Jiggs knew the ordeal they were sharing was supposed to instill in them the kind unity he'd felt when he stood with the wrestling team at the big pep rally right before District the previous February or when he sat drinking with the other Willetts pavers at the end of another backbreaking day. Where they'd been and what they'd endured together was what made each group worth being part of. But now it wasn't working.

It was only the irrepressible Hood, the fiddle-playing, skirt-chasing, football throwing wild man, not the fraternity, he would miss if he left school. Four other pledges had already quit. It was as if they had dropped off the edge of the world. *Will Hood and I drop off each others' planets if I bail?*

The more confident he became of his ability to succeed at the University, to do the course work, to make friends, even to play baseball at that level, the less certain he was whether he wanted to be associated with guys like Tears Torkelson. *Maybe Doc's right.* But quitting? Jiggs had never quit anything in his life. Having withstood the bullride of Bjornquist's brutality during freshman football, Torkelson's screaming and a few pushups were like a carnival ponyride. The difference was that even during the worst of it, Jiggs had respected Ron Bjornquist. That, and he hadn't had an adventure waiting for him if he'd quit football.

What do you want to do if you stay? Jiggs had no idea.

Each night on his way back from baseball practice, he would cross the footbridge that spanned the highway out of town. Across the river dormitories and classroom buildings loomed, lights winking on in the dusk, students hurrying home from late classes for the evening meal. There on the bridge he would linger in the cold darkness, watching the lights of the big rigs disappearing up the hill to the West, changing gears as they went over the crest, gathering momentum and catapulting into the world. Jiggs longed to go all the places those trucks were going. *What to do? What to do?*

"Olson, get in here," a voice hissed through a crack in the door. Jeff Olson, the first pledge in line disappeared into the room. Sixty seconds of silence, then the sound of gagging and spitting, huge hawking sounds. Olson reappeared, rolled his eyes, and went to his room without a word.

Dick Kemmer was next, then Clark Calvin. Each time there would be silence, then the gagging and spitting. Jiggs was fourth in line. He went in when Calvin came out. All three actives were standing at the opposite end of the room by the bunk. On a table beside them stood the pitcher, now half empty, the glass and a cage full of white mice. The bucket was on the floor by their feet. Edwards had one of the white mice in his hands.

"Get over here and stand at attention, Pissant."

"Okay, Wartbutt," Tears said, "Here's where I begin to keep my promise to you. We're going to see if you've got the guts to be a Delt. Do you think you've got the guts to be a Delt."

"Yessir."

"Well, this is your opportunity to show it. All you have to do is bite the head off this mouse."

Edwards held up the mouse as Torkelson continued, "Just bite off the head and spit it in that bucket down there. Tears pointed at the bucket, and Jiggs looked down, glimpsing what looked like the blood-stained remains of a mouse.

"Stand at attention, Asshole. We'll tell you where to look."

"After you spit it out, you can rinse out your mouth with this water." Overton poured some water in the glass. "Spit it into the pail.

"Now, just to show you we're not bad men and to make the whole thing a little easier for you, we're going to blindfold you. You just stand there with your mouth open, and when you feel the mouse in your mouth, you just bite down hard. Got it?"

Overton stepped forward with a dish towel to blindfold Jiggs.

All Jiggs could think about was how Doc would look at this. He relaxed. "Keep your blindfold, Overton. I'm not biting the head off any mouse."

"What did you say?" Torkelson asked.

"I said, keep..."

"Shut up, Crotchcricket. We heard what you said. So you're not gonna bite the poor little mouse's head off, huh? I guess you don't want to be a Delt after all."

"It has nothing to do with wanting..."

"Shut up! Don't you say shit, you pubic hair. You know what you're doing, don't you? You're fucking over every one of your brothers out there in the hall. What about Olson and Calvin and Kemmer? I suppose you think it's okay that they went through this while you just skate, because you don't feel like biting a mouse today. That's some sense of unity you've got. Shit! You make me want to puke."

"Say what you want. I'm not biting the mouse."

"We'll see about that." Overton took over. He walked to the door and opened it. "All right, you skinks, we've got a little problem with your brother Morgan. I want all of you lined up in the front room in five minutes. One of you get the three who've already gone to bed. The uniform of the day is jock straps, nothing else. MOVE!"

In less than five minutes, they were reassembled in the living room. Twenty-five pledges in jock straps, Jiggs in his sweat-soaked coat and tie, Overton, Edwards and Torkelson dressed to go outdoors.

"Everybody out in the side yard."

There was a pause. A couple of the pledges looked at each other as if wishing someone else would rebel, so they could follow.

"Everyone out in the side yard. MOVE!"

Torkelson opened the front door and the pledges slowly trooped out.

"Line up side by side ... everyone but you, Morgan." He had to shout to make himself heard over the wind.

The pledges stood shivering in the wind, stamping their bare feet in six inches of fresh snow.

"Now, gentlemen," Overton said, "your brother Morgan seems to have lost his appetite for becoming a Delt. It's my responsibility as Pledge Trainer to get it back for him, and I need your help. When I say 'begin,' I want all of you to start pushing. Brother Morgan will stand over here with us, fully clothed and out of the wind and watch. When he gets hungry again, he can let us know, and we can all go back inside and get warm. All right, BEGIN."

Almost as one, twenty-five quivering bodies dropped to the ground and began to push. Jiggs watched in amazement. Surely someone would join him in drawing the line. Someone would say, "Fuck you, Overton. Fuck you, Torkelson. I don't feel like being 'trained' tonight," and the rest would follow. If they acted together, the actives would have to give in. They couldn't afford to lose an entire pledge class, and everybody knew it, pledges and actives alike. Surely, someone would stand up and say this game's gone too far and that, like Jiggs, they were done playing. But no one did, not even the fearless Hood. No one wanted to be the first to say he couldn't take it any more. So they pushed, groaning and collapsing with fatigue, all but naked in the snow.

As he stood beside Torkelson, who was cradling the mouse cupped in his hands, holding it up, offering it to him, Jiggs' last reason for not going to Mexico evaporated. He took a deep breath, glanced at Torkelson, who waggled the mouse at him one more time. Jiggs turned to the twenty-five pledges pulsing up and down in the snow like a keyboard on a player piano. "You can get up now, girls," he said to his former brethren and walked off into the dark.

10

April 1962

When Carol Westphal came downstairs in response to the message that someone named "Jiggs" was waiting to see her, she didn't recognize the man with the blond beard sitting in the Kappa Kappa Gamma living room. She glanced at the stranger as she walked through the room, thinking Jiggs must have wandered into the card room. The man stood as she walked past. Carol took a second look.

There beneath the beard and long hair, more blond than she had ever seen it, and inside a suntan the color of tobacco, she recognized Jiggs. Same broad shoulders, same blue eyes, same scar on his nose. He was wearing Levis faded whiter than his filthy white sneakers and a blue work shirt with the sleeves rolled up above the elbows.

"Oh, Jiggs, I didn't recognize you without any barbeque sauce."

Jiggs made a face and looked down at his shirt. "I hope it's okay to stop by like this. I was going through town and wanted to see you." He had hoped to stop last November when he and Will and Gus rode through Tucson, but it had been the middle of the night and the others were in a hurry.

"Of course it's okay. I'm glad you did. What brings you to Tucson? Are you on your way back to Iowa?"

"Yeah. Money's low. Gotta go back to work."

"I thought maybe I'd see you in Lake City when I went home for Christmas vacation, but my Grandpa told me what you'd done. He said you got down to the University with all 'them radicals,' those where his exact words, and you 'just went nuts.' Didn't anybody try to talk you out of going?"

Carol's question conjured the image of Jim Hegman the morning after the affair of the mouse, when he confronted Jiggs over his decision to quit the Delts and leave school.

"You know, of course, that nobody bites the mouse, don't you? That's why they blindfold you. They show you the mouse, move it all around your lips, but they stick a furry sock or something like that in your mouth to bite."

"Doesn't make any difference, Jim. The mouse was only the last straw. I'd have quit anyway, sooner or later, probably sooner. Torkelson's an asshole, but he was just playing the game. It's just not for me. Not now."

"You know you can quit the fraternity without quitting school?"

Jiggs gave Jim a look that said he was aware they were two different things.

"Have you told Doc about this?"

"Yeah."

"What'd he say?"

"He told me to keep my ears and eyes open and my mouth shut, but to have a good time."

"Well, Junior, I'm sorry you're leaving, but I guess the fraternity's not for everybody. I hope you come back to school. You have too much going for you just to work construction and ride motorcycles all your life." Hegman extended his hand and Jiggs shook it. "Look me up whenever you get a chance."

Saying good-bye to Hood had been tougher. During two months rooming together, they had become great friends, sharing much, including a few hours in the Iowa City jail for walking ahead of a meter maid putting pennies in all the expired meters. "Disturbing the Peace" had been the charge. "Public Drunkeness" would have been nearer the truth.

"Jesus, Morgan, you don't have to quit school. Screw the Delts. Let's get a place off campus. Who am I going to bitch to about the stupidity of football coaches, if you go?" Hood was currently running with the freshman third team.

Jiggs, afraid the lump in his throat would become tears, didn't answer.

"You can't leave before I've kicked your ass." Hood went on in reference to Jiggs' ability to outwrestle him despite Roger's superior size, strength and athletic ability.

"Got to leave before that happens. Before you get me arrested again."

When it finally became apparent Jiggs wasn't going to change his mind, Roger started to shake hands, but stopped and gave Jiggs a bone-crushing hug. "Be careful, you bull-headed pug." Hood's voice was raspy. "Write to me and come back next year. We'll get a place and screw every girl we can find. Fuck the Delts! Let's not let this friendship die."

"Mexico by motorcycle sounds pretty exciting to me." Carol's words pierced Jiggs' veil of memories.

"Sometimes it was. Sometimes it was just lying in a sweaty room in the rain watching lizards run up the walls."

"Maybe so, but I'd like to hear all about it anyway."

They walked out to the porch in the light, clear air of the Arizona spring and sat down on white lawn furniture. Carol produced a couple of cokes, and they sipped their drinks in silence for several seconds.

"Why did you go, Jiggs?"

"Probably the same reason you went to school in Arizona instead of somewhere in Iowa. I wanted to see what was on the other side of the hill."

"Did you ever get there, to the other side of the hill, I mean?"

Jiggs stared at Mount Lemon shimmering in the desert heat north of the City, remembering. *Turned out to be a mountain.*

The five of them, Gus, Will, Mert, Les and Jiggs, were still in Juarez, drinking and playing cards in a dirty little hotel two weeks into the trip, when Mert pulled a knife in an argument over cards. Gus, Will and Jiggs decided to head further west. Two days hard riding brought them to Ensenada, on the Pacific Coast seventy-five miles south of the border. The hotel was nicer. The ocean was nearby. Otherwise things weren't much different from Juarez.

On Christmas Eve, Jiggs was three beers into the afternoon in an almost empty cantina, but his thoughts were all in Iowa. He figured Carol Westphal was probably home from Arizona for the holidays. There'd be parties ... Mexico wasn't showing him much, but he knew he hadn't really looked. *I have to get out of here.*

"Goin' for a walk," he said to Gus and Will as he stood up. Out in the street, the late afternoon air was as cool and fresh as it had been stale and hot in the bar. As Jiggs took a deep breath, a procession of about fifty Mexican kids began to flow past, followed by some adults. At the front was a little girl riding a donkey being led by a boy. Both were wearing bathrobes.

In need of distraction from his homesickness and with curiosity piqued, Jiggs fell in at the tail end of the line. The children sang as they walked, occasionally stopping at houses along their way, a reenactment of Mary and Joseph's search for lodging. The people in the houses would turn them away, and they'd move on. Sometimes the people from the house where they'd just stopped would join the group.

About sunset the group came to a church. When they rang the bell, a priest came out and ushered them into a little courtyard. Jiggs' semi-drunkeness had worn off. He assumed he wouldn't be welcome inside, but the priest beckoned him in. There were piñatas strung from the trees and tables of food. At the far end of the yard was a nativity scene. The boy leading the donkey went right up to it. The girl got off, and they both knelt and everybody said a prayer. There was a big cheer, and a fiesta began.

All the religion Jiggs soaked up during childhood had become ever more dormant in the years since his talk with his father about Doc's lack of belief. This hibernation of faith made him feel like an interloper. He was headed back out the gate when the couple he'd been walking with took him by the arm, led him to the table and handed him a plate, motioning for him to fill it and join them and their family.

"Gracias," Jiggs nodded as he dished up, virtually exhausting his supply of Spanish. For the next few hours, he listened to people whom he mostly could not understand, and they listened to him with equal lack of comprehension. Nobody seemed to mind. Jiggs even danced.

Shortly before midnight, the priest celebrated a mass. Jiggs stayed for that too, his first Catholic service. It was beautiful, very simple, only candlelight. Standing there at the back watching, he was about as lonely and happy as he had ever been. At the end of the night the one thing he understood very clearly was how much of Mexico he'd been missing. The next morning, Christmas morning, Jiggs headed south. Will and Gus stayed behind.

By mid-January, he'd reached the tip of Baja, sleeping along the road, sometimes on beaches, under bridges if it rained.

"But what did you do? Just ride your motorcycle?" Carol asked.

"Loaf. Sightsee. It's great not being in a hurry. One morning I was camped at a little bay north of Loreto, and behind the beach was this cactus forest, hundreds of big cactus, like the Saguaro you have here. When I woke up, there was a turkey vulture perched atop each of the cactus for as far as I could see. They were all facing East, and they were holding their wings out as if they were drying them in the morning sun. They looked like the thunderbird carvings you see here in the Southwest. It was an amazing sight.

"I sat there all morning and watched birds fishing on the bay. Thousands of them, all kinds. A few times I went three days without seeing anybody. No towns, no people. No hurry. I read a lot."

"What did you read?"

"The best thing was *Les Misérables* by Victor Hugo. The same guy who wrote *The Hunchback of Notre Dame.* Do you know that book?"

"Vaguely. I've never read it."

"I have it in my pack. You can have it, if you're interested."

"What was so good about it?"

"To me it was about how one act of kindness can make an enormous difference; how easy it is to let life's cruelty towards you become an excuse for your cruelty to others."

"Acts of kindness like slugging some lout who calls your date a bad name?"

Jiggs met Carol's eyes. They were laughing.

As Jiggs talked about his adventures in Mexico, the mid-day heat began to wane. The porch, bathed in sunlight when they sat down, was now in shadow.

"What would you have done if your bike broke down out there in the middle of nowhere? What if you ran out of gas?"

"Did break down once south of Mulegé. First car that came along gave me a ride into town, dropped me off at a garage about as big as this porch. The owner, Jorge, and I took the engine all apart. Fuel pump was shot. Had to order a new one. I wound up staying in Mulegé for almost a month.

"The pump finally arrived, and we put the engine back together. I thought it would cost a couple hundred dollars. But when I went to pay, Jorge said 'setenta y cinco,' seventy-five dollars. I couldn't believe it. He'd lost three days' work just trying to get that part. I offered him one hundred, and he wouldn't take it. But he did let me take him and his wife out to dinner. I had met his wife, because they lived over the garage. During that month I met all their friends. It was the best part of the trip. His full name is Jorge Sanchez. His wife's name is Juana."

"What did you do for a whole month?"

"Fished, played baseball with Jorge's team, helped him at the garage sometimes, went kayaking down the coast for a few days with three Americans from Oregon I met at the garage. They had an extra boat."

"So, how do you feel now that you've done it?"

A Doc question.

"Fat."

"What do you mean?" Jiggs was anything but fat.

"I mean, I have so much and those people have so little, and I take so much of what I have for granted. It almost makes me feel guilty."

"How can you feel guilty about something that's not your fault?"

"Whose fault is it? God's? I could give away what I have, I suppose, even things out. But I'd have more in no time. The difference isn't so much in physical stuff, although there's plenty of that, but of opportunity. I'm fat with opportunity."

"Not if you work at Willetts all your life." Carol made a face at him.

Jiggs stood up and stretched and leaned against the porch rail instead of sitting back down. "I've talked enough. How about you? Do you like it here? Are you ever coming back to Iowa?"

Carol talked about her school year. It sounded to Jiggs like what he'd seen of college life during his few months at Iowa, except the weather was better, but Carol described it with enthusiasm. Obviously she liked it.

You get out of things what you put in to them. One of Doc's refrains. Last fall at Iowa, Jiggs just hadn't been in the mood to invest.

That evening they went to a Mexican restaurant in South Tucson, where Jiggs showed off by ordering in his recently acquired Spanish.

"How long can you stay in Tucson?" They had been talking for two hours.

"Leaving in the morning."

"Aw, c'mon. Stay another day. I want to show you the school. Somebody has to win you back to higher education."

"Like to stay, but I have a job waiting for me, I think. Won't wait forever."

"What are you going to do this fall, Jiggs? Have you thought about that?"

"Don't know for sure. Probably go back to school. Still don't know what I want to do, but I don't think it's paving."

"Why not come down here to school?"

Is she suggesting that for me or her? Jiggs couldn't tell.

"Love to, but things are a little less expensive in Iowa City. Besides, there's no way I could make the baseball team here." *Probably not at Iowa either.*

As they walked up to the door of the sorority someone inside began flashing the porch light on and off. "That means I have to be inside in two minutes."

Elsewhere on the porch several couples appeared to be vying for the World Kissing Championship. Jiggs wished he and Carol were competing.

"Jiggs," Carol took his hand and turned to face him, "thank you very much for stopping. This is the most we've ever talked."

She was so close to him now that their faces were the only parts of them not touching. Jiggs wrapped his free arm around Carol's waist and kissed her. "Don't stay gone all summer, Jiggs," she whispered in his ear. "Call me."

When Jiggs opened his eyes, Carol was disappearing in the door and the porch light was going off for the last time. He had planned to spend the night in Tucson, but suddenly he wasn't tired. He was twenty miles east of the City before the feel of her body against his began to wear off, so wide awake he rode all night, clear to El Paso, stopping only for gas.

When he finally arrived home two days later, he bought a new baseball glove. It had been his intention to send his old one to Jorge, but after thinking about it, he sent them both.

11

April 1962

The lane up to the house was rutted and washed out in so many places that Jiggs had to wrestle his bike up the hill. *This is more of a Durward Westphal lane than a Doc Morgan lane.* Jiggs reckoned he had shoveled and spread and rolled smooth enough gravel on those one hundred yards of driveway to pave ten miles of interstate highway. *Either Doc's sick or the tractor's broken.*

As he parked by the back step, he could see Darcy and Marie sitting at the kitchen table with Doc eating supper. They gave no sign of having heard him as he pulled up. He opened the back door and startled them. "Hello, everybody."

They stood to greet him, hesitating a moment as they did so. Marie and Darcy both glanced at Doc and then back at Jiggs as they lined up for hugs.

Jiggs knew Marie, only a year younger, would on many occasions have preferred strangling him to hugging. Now she was embracing him. "Oh, Jiggs, I'm so glad you're home."

"Me too, Jiggs. Me too." Darcy, only fifteen, clung to him in turn.

"Hello, Jiggs. Welcome back." Doc shook his hand.

Champ, Jiggs' ancient dog, danced at his feet, nuzzling him, demanding his attention. Jiggs stooped to pet her. "It's great to be back. Where's mom?"

Another exchange of glances.

"Sit down, Jiggs," Doc said. "We have some bad news."

Jiggs sat down.

"Mom died in February, Jiggs. February fourth..." Doc said.

"We tried to find you," Marie interrupted. She began to cry. "We tried everything, called the embassy, Mexican police, everything."

Dead. Jiggs just stared back at the three of them, too stunned even to ask questions. *Dead. Mom's dead.*

Darcy, too, had begun to cry. "Grandma and Grandpa were here for dinner, and Mom had just finished bringing out the last of the food and sat down, and we were about to say grace, and it ... it happened."

Doc didn't say anything.

Darcy took a couple of deep breaths, snivels.

Jiggs handed her a napkin. "What happened? What was it?"

"We didn't know. Daddy was trying to give her CPR, but that didn't work."

"So ... so she had this attack. Did she die right there?"

"Yes, she did. I called the doctor right away, but the weather was terrible. Marie was backing out the car for us to take her to the hospital, but Daddy said it was too late."

"She had an aneurism," Doc said. "We would have been too late even if it was a summer night and the hospital only ten minutes away. She died very quickly. We tried. There was nothing we could do."

"What's an aneurism?"

"It's where a blood vessel, in your mom's case her aorta, develops a weakness and balloons out in response to the pressure of the blood flowing through. The balloon fills up with blood. If it ruptures, you can bleed to death. Die of shock."

"I bet you're hungry." Darcy fled to the refuge of food, the Iowa antidote for all expressions of strong emotion. "Let me get you some stew."

Jiggs had always thought his mom should spell her name "Merry," instead of "Mary." Wherever she went, there was music. If none was playing, she would make her own, humming or singing the show tunes she loved, slightly off key, doing a little dance step now and then in the midst of her work. Upon learning of Jiggs' unlovely waltz with Brunhilda, she rolled up the rug, took him in her arms and walked him through the basics.

"Jiggs, you're picking up your feet and putting them down like you just walked out of a barn or something. Don't stomp 'em, slide 'em."

Jiggs slid 'em.

"Another thing, you're holding on to me with nothing but your fingertips. How're you ever going to steer me around without a good grip? Grab ahold. Girls don't break that easy. That's the fun part."

Doc, though seldom severe, was a serious man. Mary Morgan leavened his gravity, effortlessly coaxing laughter from her sometimes over-earnest husband, making a music all their own. It was a happy chemistry Jiggs had always taken for granted, could not have defined.

Darcy put a plate of beef stew in front of him and handed him a glass of milk.

Jesus. First Billings, now Mom. What kind of god lets such things happen?

Jiggs picked up a fork and began to eat. A robot would have enjoyed it more. It could have been steak, or caviar, and still have tasted like ashes.

"Is Mom buried in Lake City or Walnut Grove?"

"She's buried here," Doc said. "Up on that little finger of ground above the river east of the back pasture."

Jiggs knew the exact spot.

"Wow. So they let you bury Mom here. That's kind of surprising."

A few years earlier a salesman had come to the house selling cemetery plots. When Doc said he intended to be buried on the farm, the salesman told him it was against the law. People had to be buried in cemeteries, places sanctioned for burial. He even had a flyer with a copy of the state law on it. Apparently there were a lot of farmers who required convincing.

"It wasn't easy," Marie said.

"What did you have to do?"

"Couldn't have done it, if that pioneer family wasn't already buried back there," Doc said.

In 1872, between April and July, a family named Norgren had buried four children, six months, two, four, and seven, on the little plateau above the river where Mary Morgan now lay.

"Once the State learned there were already people buried there, it was easier to get them to let us add one. They designated about an acre as an historical burial site. Only owners of the land and their families can be buried there," Doc said.

"Dad had to set up a trust that would maintain the site for a hundred years," Darcy chimed in.

Jiggs put down his fork. "I'd like to ride back there after supper."

It was deep dusk when they rode out of the trees that grew farther up the hillside down onto the little flat open place nature had for some reason left like a balcony. One hundred feet below, a long bend in the Des Moines River gradually turned south again after having flowed almost due east for two miles on its way to the Mississippi. The trees were black against the almost night sky, unsoftened by any leaves this early in the northern Spring. It was cold, but there was no wind.

Doc and Jiggs approached the graves from the rear and rode around them, stopping in front. From atop his horse, Freckles, Jiggs stared down at the four small markers almost obscured by the tall grass. He had walked and ridden past them countless times without ever giving their presence much thought. Now, where the grass was lower, a new boulder sat bearing the inscription, "Mary Agnes Morgan, September 9, 1915-February 4, 1962. Beloved wife of Andrew Morgan. Cherished mother of Jon, Marie and Darcelle."

Jiggs dismounted, letting the reins drop to the ground, pushed his sweatshirt hood back off his head, and knelt on one knee on the damp ground. *Where was I on February 4th? Bird Bay? Mulegé?*

"I'm sorry, Mom. Sorry for not being there; sorry for not staying in touch; sorry for assuming you'd live forever; sorry for being so wrong. Two hours ago I wasn't even missing you, not really, and now it feels like there's this huge hole inside me. I hope you can hear this or somehow know how much I loved you." He lapsed into silence.

Jiggs didn't know how long he remained at the graveside. When he finally stood up and turned around, it was completely dark, Freckles was grazing twenty feet away, and Doc was gone. Jiggs had not even heard him ride away.

The next day he and Doc repaired the lane.

12

September 1962

During his second summer with Willetts, Jiggs had begun writing to Carol. When she wrote back saying she hoped he wouldn't work there a third summer, that was all it took to end his career in highway construction. By the end of July he was so anxious to begin school, he started marking the days off his calendar until the fall semester began. For the next four years he lived in a room he rented from Margaret Linder, the profane, snag-toothed cook at the sorority house where he got a job washing dishes and waiting tables.

His room was approved housing, which meant it was a place the University allowed students under twenty-one to live instead of a dorm or fraternity house. Approved status required Lindy, the only name by which any living person knew Margaret Linder, to sign a written agreement that no female guests would be allowed her boarder. But Jiggs gave Lindy, who had never learned to drive, a ride to work each morning on his motorcycle, lugging the heavy milk crates from outside downstairs to the kitchen before leaving for class. In return, Lindy let him do whatever he wanted in his room. The sight of the hump-backed old woman in a white cook's dress screeching,

"Get out of the way, you goddamned bozo!" at other motorists from the back of a motorcycle weaving in and out of campus traffic in the morning became a familiar sight.

"Lindy, you mind if Roger uses my room for a while tonight?"

Jiggs and Lindy were watching television and eating popcorn.

"Your goddamned friend is turning my home into a whorehouse. No wonder he never plays on Saturday. Nothing left for the game after screwing himself silly all week."

A knee injury at the beginning of spring practice his freshman year had dealt Hood's already floundering football career a setback. The knee recovered; the career never did. However, by the end of his sophomore year, he was first violin in the University's orchestra.

As much as she bitched about Roger's escapades and failure to contribute to the fortunes of her beloved Hawkeyes on Saturdays, Lindy loved him only slightly less than Jiggs, and she never said "no." Roger gave her tickets to the games, and by the end of Jiggs' first year in residence, Hood had his own key to the house. Many nights found him eating popcorn, drinking beer and watching *Combat* reruns alongside Jiggs and Lindy in her living room, a place off limits to all other women, before going home to the Delt house.

"For Christ's sake, when do you study, Hood?"

"I'm a music major, Lindy. I don't have to study."

"Music, bah. What the hell are you going to do with that? Teach? What'll you teach, fornication?"

Occasionally, Hood would try to talk Jiggs out of his monkish existence.

"C'mon. Get a date and let's go to the reservoir."

"Naw. You go, Rog. I need to catch up on my sleep."

"Sleep, shit. Rip Van Winkle's got nothing on you. This kind of life isn't good for you, Morgan. You're not having a wholesome, well-rounded college experience. You know what they say."

"No, Rog, what do they say?"

"Use it or lose it. It's like any part of your body; if you don't exercise it, it'll get weaker and have no endurance. It will begin to wither. You're not doing Carol any favors."

"Use it or lose it, huh? If that's the case, you must be in great shape."

"We're not talking about me, we're talking about you. Look at it this way. Do you sometimes think of doing it with girls you meet, besides Carol, I mean?"

"Sure."

"Well, the Bible says it's just as big a sin to think about it as to actually do it. You can look it up. So you may as well go do it. You're not going to be any worse off."

"Get out of here. I need a nap."

"Okay, I'm leaving ... but remember, you can't argue with the Good Book."

Jiggs stayed out for baseball, although it soon had become obvious that he was going to ride the bench forever. He had been making the cut on one team or another since he was eight years old. It still felt good.

"Why stay out?" Hood would ask when Jiggs groaned about not having enough time.

"I guess I just like taking showers with a lot of other guys. Why do you stay out for football?"

"That's different. I have to stay out to keep my scholarship."

"Bullshit! You don't need that scholarship. Besides, if you did, you could get it switched to music. Stop and think.

Every time you step on the practice field, you risk your future in music. You can't play the fiddle with a broken arm."

"It's a violin, not a fiddle, Moron."

"Violin ... fiddle ... what's the difference? It's too bad they don't give scholarships for taking showers. We'd both be stars."

So it went. They would laugh, open a couple more beers and toast the Athletic Department, the coaching staff, the Big Ten Conference, the NCAA, the Heisman Trophy, Babe Ruth, The International Olympic Committee, the list went on and on until the beer ran out.

"Lindy," Jiggs was sprawled on the battered, beer-stained chair reserved for him alone, watching two teams that meant nothing to him or anyone he had ever met battle it out in something called "The Blue Bonnet Bowl." "Why not come home with me for Christmas break rather than staying here by yourself? We've got plenty of room."

Lindy turned and stared at the nearly horizontal Jiggs, who had returned his attention to Baylor's unsuccessful effort to convert a third and two on its own twenty-eight. "Jiggs, Honey, you don't have to do that. Your family doesn't need me hanging around up there."

Jiggs straightened up and looked back at her. "You're wrong, Lindy. They do. I checked. Said they were sorry they didn't think of it themselves."

So Lindy began spending Christmases with the Morgans. It was Marie and Darcy's first turkey that year, and Lindy pitched in wherever needed. On the morning after Christmas, Jiggs had to hide the vacuum cleaner to keep her away from it. She talked Doc into taking her riding one afternoon, her first time on a horse. When Doc asked how the saddle felt once she was mounted, she replied, "A whole lot more comfortable than your son's goddamn motorcycle." Upon returning to the house, she announced to Jiggs and his sisters, "I feel like Dale Evans."

13

September 1964

During the two summers following Jiggs' return to the University, he and Carol spent so much time in each others' company that Jiggs' motorcycle could have made the trip between Walnut Grove and Lake City on its own. Movies, ballgames, horseback rides, if one or the other wasn't working or sleeping, chances were they were together.

"Do you know how I think of you? I mean when we're not together." Jiggs and Carol were sitting on the front steps of her house late one afternoon before Jiggs had to go off to his summer job, nightshift at a local packing plant.

Of course, there was no way for her to know.

"I think of you laughing. You always seem to be happy, with me, with everything. I know you can be serious. I mean, you're not laughing now. But my image of you is of your laughter. It's very musical, you know."

Carol shook her head in wonder. This was yet another example of the kind of thing she never thought about, unless Jiggs called it to her attention. She started to think about how she thought of Jiggs. He was strong and smart and cared for her, but what was her image of him? Carol knew lots of smart people.

She thought she was smart. But sometimes it was as if Jiggs detatched himself from life, stood back and looked at it as if he was a spectator taking notes. He picked up on things she tended to take for granted. He stretched her. If asked to name one word to describe her notion of him, it would have been "thinker."

Moving slowly at times, quickly at others, they progressed from exchanging stories about their pasts to exchanging ideas about their futures. These exchanges sometimes occurred on blankets during picnics, where Jiggs' idea about the pace of exchange varied from Carol's.

Jiggs considered himself a virgin. He had never been in bed with a woman, unless he counted the prostitute who wouldn't take off her shoes, a memory he preferred to suppress. On any number of occasions, he had been at the brink with various girls. In the backseats of cars. On couches watching television. Once even in a hayloft. Moral wrestling matches, lust versus virtue, points scored for body parts successfully touched and underwear removed. Jiggs had scored well in those bouts, but had never achieved a pin. It was different with Carol. Almost from the beginning, her answer was never "NO," only "Not yet."

Their only argument concerned geography.

"Why not transfer back to Iowa?"

"Golf's a lot better in Arizona. Why not transfer down to Tucson?"

"Baseball. I couldn't even ride the bench down there."

"Is riding a bench so important?"

"Is golf so important?"

"Oh, Jiggs, if we really like each other, our feelings will survive the test of separation."

Jiggs thought testing unnecessary, but he had to admit, he was unwilling to transfer to Arizona.

The Sunday before Carol was to depart for her senior year, there had been a barbeque. Marie was home from her summer job in Chicago, Darcy from summer school. Jiggs' old friend, Beezer, was home on leave from the Marines and clearly there to see Darcy, not Jiggs. Roger and Lindy had driven up from Iowa City, and Doc, who wasn't much of a Sunday picnicker, was there long enough to eat.

Jiggs and Carol arrived late, because Carol had a golf tournament that day. Jiggs caddied. Having had no hand in the preparations, they volunteered to handle the clean up. Jiggs was standing at the sink, elbow deep in dishwater, when he turned to Carol, who was drying.

"Hey, you."

Carol turned her head in his direction.

"I love you."

Carol's lower jaw dropped an inch and a half, but her lips were smiling a moment later as it climbed back up to its normal resting place.

"I love you, too, Jiggs, ever since you stopped to see me in Tucson, and, once I realized it, it seemed like there had never been a time when I didn't." She leaned over and kissed him. "There's nobody with whom I'd rather wash dishes." They resumed their washing and drying, not talking for a minute or two. "Jiggs, can I ask you a question?"

"Sure."

"Why did you choose this ultra-romantic moment to tell me?"

"Couple of reasons. I've felt this way for a long time. But I didn't want to first say it when you might think I was doing so just to try to talk you into something you weren't ready for. As we've been standing here talking and washing this mountain of dishes, it dawned on me that nothing I do with you ever seems mundane. Seeing that's so, how could I not tell you how I feel?"

A tear trickled down Carol's cheek. "Well, my love, those are the kindest, nicest things that have ever been said to me." She reached up and stroked his cheek. "We both know the time's coming, Jiggs. When it does, you won't have to talk me into anything."

The following Christmas vacation Carol didn't come home. Instead, she met her parents at her married sister's house in Tulsa. That was too much testing for Jiggs.

It had been an epic journey. Upon learning Tulsa, not Lake City, would be Carol's Christmas destination, Jiggs began to lay his plans. The fact that Iowa was under three feet of snow with more coming made his decision not to risk taking his motorcycle easy. Lindy had refused to ride home with him, pronounced him "a goddamned idiot" and took the bus instead. Early on Christmas Eve morning, Jiggs caught a ride into Lake City with Doc, walked to the south edge of town and stuck out his thumb.

Sixteen hours later, after two fruitless hours in the dark on an Oklahoma Turmpike on-ramp, he lost a shoe in a semi-frozen bog while retreating towards a truckstop called "Big Cabin." There, he practically highjacked a ride with the driver of an ancient Studebaker, who had stopped for gas and, upon returning from the restroom, found Jiggs in the passenger seat. As Christmas Eve became Christmas morning at a lonely intersection along State Highway 33, he spent another four hours without seeing a single car. He finally rode into Tulsa sitting next to a goat named "Sugah," in the backseat of an ancient Dodge belonging to George and Edna Williams, who picked Jiggs up and bought him breakfast because "a whole lotta folks" had been nice to George when he hitchhiked during "the Big War."

Now he was standing at the bottom of the steps of Carol's sister's house, with large red bow tied neatly around his neck by Edna before she and George lurched their way out of his life. The house was big and old. It looked as if it might have a hayloft. Jiggs took a deep breath. *Here goes.* There were some lights on and Ginny, Carol's sister, and her husband had small children who probably weren't lying quietly in bed on Christmas morning. Nevertheless, Jiggs tread softly as he climbed the steps in case no one was up. As he reached the door, he heard children's voices and Christmas music. He rang the bell.

Footsteps approached the other side of the door, a pause, then an excited voice, "Carol, come quick." More footsteps. "Look out the peephole."

"Oh, m'gosh! Jiggs."

The door opened, and Carol flew into his arms. Over her shoulder Jiggs saw not only Ginny, but Carol's parents and her brother-in law, Craig, all still in robes and slippers. He saw Mr. and Mrs. Westphal exchange glances at the sight of their daughter with her arms thrown around the neck of this vagabond who had just appeared at the door. Mr. Westphal shrugged, and they both smiled. "My gosh, Jiggs, where did you come from?" Mrs. Westphal said.

A dose of adrenalin akin to that which had fueled his last match with Jim Billings was the only explanation for what kept Jiggs going. He told the story of his journey during a second breakfast eaten without mention of the first, spent an hour in church wearing some of Craig's clothes and ate a Christmas dinner of such abundance that it had by itself probably driven up grain and livestock prices all over the Midwest. A game of catch in the snow with Craig and his son, Tyler, using Ty's new football followed, then another football game on television. By the time he, Craig and Mr. Westphal finished the dishes and rejoined the women in the front room, Jiggs was out on his feet. He had been quite prepared to go get a room somewhere, but the family wouldn't hear of it.

"If I have to heat this barn," Craig joked, "we may as well use all the rooms."

Jiggs was led to a small bedroom behind the kitchen that looked as if it had been a sun porch in an earlier life. There were windows all heavy with frost on three sides of the room. Jiggs was too tired to care about the temperature. He barely had strength to brush his teeth before falling into the small bed beneath a mountain of blankets. He was asleep before he landed.

"Move over. It's freezing out here."

Carol's urgent whisper, followed by a strong nudge and the feel of a pair of icy feet pressed against his legs, penetrated Jiggs' fog of sleep. At that exact moment, he became more wide awake than he had ever been.

"I figure if you can hitchhike seven hundred miles through the winter night to come see me, the least I can do is come thirty feet down some steps to repay the visit," she continued to whisper and began kissing his neck, running her hand up under his tee shirt and caressing his chest.

True to her vow at summer's end, Carol did not have to be talked into anything. This was no contest, however benign, this was surrender. There was no underwear to contend with only a flannel nightgown that disappeared so fast Jiggs could barely remember its presence. His own skivvies and tee shirt vanished with equal speed. Together, with an intensity wrapped in tenderness, they touched every part of each other. Fingertips, tongues, toes, eyes, ears, lips, legs, arms, breasts, thighs – all sending and receiving, swirling, pulsing, pushing, pulling, consuming, swallowing each other in a rhythmic embrace that had been three years in the making, the sound of their breathing so loud they later laughed in wonder they had not awakened the rest of the family.

"What happened to the covers?" Jiggs sat up at last.

"Funny," Carol propped herself up on one elbow beside him, "it doesn't seem cold in here any more. I have to get back up stairs before reveille." She bit Jiggs lightly on his right ear lobe.

Jiggs sighed. "This is the hard part. I'd give a million dollars to spend the rest of the night sleeping in your arms."

"Make it two, and I'll risk parental wrath." Carol swung her legs out of bed.

"Two? Where did I leave my wallet?"

"Oh, Jiggs, I'd pay to stay, but it can't happen this trip. If we ever were caught, you'd be hitchhiking back the way you came in less time than it takes to tell. Me too, probably."

She stood up and searched for her nightgown. Jiggs watched her move around in the cold darkness. To be lying in bed, having just made love with this lovely girl, watching her move lightly about, a sexy ghost floating above him, haunting him – Jiggs would have hitchhiked to the moon for her.

Finding the elusive garment in a far corner, Carol stretched her arms above her head and let the nightgown fall of its own weight down the length of her, shimmying slightly as it fell so as to align it comfortably. Jiggs thought it was the sexiest thing he had ever seen.

"I'll see you in the morning, Jiggs. Merry Christmas."

14

June 1966

Jiggs and Carol Westphal married at the First Presbyterian Church in Lake City on June 25, 1966, three weeks after Jiggs graduated.

Carol had graduated a year ahead of Jiggs thanks to his Mexican sojourn, and she came back to Iowa to teach school in nearby Cedar Rapids. Hood, too, had graduated, but, not wanting to become a music teacher, he had stayed on campus and gone to law school. Lindy relaxed her "No girls in the living room" policy for Carol and even bought a double bed for Jiggs' room. Carol's apartment saw little of her.

Having no idea what he wanted to do with his life, Jiggs took courses he thought he'd like. He majored in history, writing his senior thesis on the impact of Stonewall Jackson's death on the outcome of the Civil War.

Carol contemplated the future Jiggs had largely ignored for the last four years. "Why don't you go to law school? Roger loves it. He's really taking it seriously."

"Wait until the novelty wears off. Right now courses with books are all new to him."

Jiggs didn't know what he wanted to do, but he knew what he didn't want to do, and that was go to law school. Eventually, and with no particular enthusiasm, he entered an executive training program for a large insurance company. The six-month course would begin in mid-July, right after he and Carol returned from their honeymoon. Three days before the wedding Jiggs received his draft notice.

The bachelor party the night before the wedding wasn't much as bachelor parties go. Jiggs, Doc, Hood and Lindy, who had ridden up from Iowa City with Roger for the wedding, sat on the Morgan porch, drinking beer, listening to the Cardinal game and talking. Marie and Darcy were among Carol's bridesmaids and had gone with Carol and her friends after the rehearsal dinner.

"If I lived here, I would never leave," Lindy said, as she stood up and began to walk back into the house. "It's even prettier now than in the winter."

From half way up the hillside where the house sat, they looked south along the sweep of the valley. Even though it was almost nine o'clock, the evening light at the height of the midwestern summer enabled them to see the river winding southeast through the trees along the valley floor.

Hood had been unusually silent since dinner. "What are you going to do about that draft notice, Jiggs?" The notice ordered Jiggs to report for a physical in Lake City by July fifteenth. The two days since its receipt had been cloaked with gloom. "There's still time to enlist somewhere."

"Or you could go to Canada."

Roger and Jiggs both looked at Doc in surprise, half expecting to see he was being facetious.

"I agree with Doc." Lindy set down a tray filled with another round of beers and a refilled popcorn bowl.

I don't know how much you've thought about this Viet Nam situation, but I think it's one of the biggest damn mistakes this country's ever made," Doc said.

"Sort of stuck my head in the sand on this one, Pop. I kept thinking the thing would be over before I got around to graduating."

Doc never talked about his own military service, but when he took off his shirt, the scars from wounds he had suffered fighting in the South Pacific said all that needed to be said about what he'd been through. Around the Morgan house, the family stood up even when they heard the National Anthem on television, and Doc always stood for the Marine Corps Hymn. If anyone else had suggested he go to Canada to avoid service, Jiggs would have laughed in their face. *How could I ever face my dad, if I did that?*

"Don't you think going to Canada to evade the draft is disloyal, Pop?"

"Disloyal to whom?"

"To the country. To the United States."

"Bah. Viet Nam isn't this country's war. It's this government's war."

"I'm not sure I understand the distinction."

"Well, have we declared war, like the Constitution says we're supposed to? How about it, Roger? You're the lawyer? Does the Constitution say Congress is supposed to declare war before we fight one? Has Congress declared war?"

Hood didn't reply. They all knew the answer.

"Declaration or no declaration, do you see any threat to this country's security if the Communists do take over? Did you even know where Viet Nam was before this war? The word 'communist' is such a bugaboo in this country, but my guess is they're just another bunch of political crooks over there. If you look close at that bunch we're supporting, I bet you'd find they're just as unlovable."

Doc's voice was low and hard like Jiggs had heard it only a few times before. When he stopped talking, nobody said anything for several seconds. In the background Bob Gibson, the Cardinal pitcher, was mowing down Phillies like he had a machine gun.

"I'll tell you one thing." It was Lindy's turn. "Those goddamn politicians in Washington are lyin' to us..."

Jiggs glanced at Hood out of the corner of his eye. Lying politicians were an old Lindy refrain. She knew they were all lying, but she would never say how she knew. This time she had a reason.

"All this stuff about body counts, ten to one means we must be winning and all that. Jiggs, if you die, we lose. We lose every time one American boy dies over there, even if he took a hundred Vietnamese with him, because we're fighting for nothing worth having. Oh, Jiggs, Honey, I'm praying you don't go."

Lindy reached over and put her hand on Jiggs' knee and started to cry.

Jiggs was shaking. The two most loyal, conservative people he knew had just told him to break the law and hide. He took Lindy's hand. "Thank you, Lindy." He was half-ready to cry himself. "Thank you, Pop. I understand what you're saying. It means a lot. I don't know what I'm going to do. Carol and I are going to decide in the next couple of days, but I don't think I'll go to Canada. Maybe I should, but I don't think I can."

They resumed listening to the ballgame, trying to recapture its flow, searching for something else to talk about.

After a few minutes Lindy stood up and blew her nose. "I'm going to bed. Good night everybody."

Not long after that, Doc turned in.

Jiggs and Roger opened two more beers. "It's hot sitting here. Let's take the bike out for a ride."

On their way through Walnut Grove, they bought a case of beer. They roared along, enjoying the wind created by their speed on the sultry night. Twenty minutes and a beer apiece later, they were cruising down Hospital Hill on the west edge of Lake City.

"Hey, isn't there a big railroad trestle over there?" Hood pointed off to their right as he yelled to make himself heard over the sound of the bike. "Lindy and I saw it as we came through town this afternoon."

"Yeah. Longest one in the state. At least that's what people here say. Highest, too, I think." Jiggs had always wanted to go up there and look around, but never had.

"Let's check it out. There's a railroad strike, so there're no trains running."

Roger was right. There was a strike. Jiggs had read about it in the paper that morning. Without saying another word, he leaned the cycle into a hard right onto the River Road and headed for the bridge.

Other than at crossings, Jiggs had never ridden on railroad tracks before. He figured they couldn't be any rougher than Durward Westphal's lane. When he reached the tracks, he swung onto them and gunned the engine. Washboard roads were always smoother if you took 'em fast. *How different can railroad tracks be?*

The vibration of the bike rocketing over the railroad ties at sixty miles per hour reminded Jiggs of a movie he had seen about a jet pilot trying to break the sound barrier. As it neared Mach One, the pilot's plane seemed to be trying to vibrate itself to pieces. It was almost impossible to hold the old Triumph in a straight line. Jiggs had to do it though; he had to stay on course; he had to break the sound barrier for God and Country and Carol and Doc and Lindy – he gave the throttle in his right hand grip a vicious twist, and the bike catapulted forward, screaming past seventy, eighty, ninety miles per hour – up, up towards the invisible barrier just six hundred more miles per hour away. Jiggs was straining to hold steady and listen for the sonic boom he knew would signal success as his plane tried to shake itself apart.

"Jesus Christ," roared his co-pilot, "I can't hold on to the beer and the bike at the same time. Let's find some place to set the beer. "

Just as Roger spoke, a gap in the left guardrail appeared in the headlight's cone ahead of Jiggs' aircraft. It was a small safety platform. Jiggs slowed, banked left and glided to a perfect landing right beside it, just inside the rail.

"Sorry. I was trying to break the sound barrier. I forgot you didn't have anything to hold on to."

"The sound barrier, eh?" Hood glanced sideways at Jiggs as he dismounted with the beer.

An hour and a half and about ten "Fuck the Worlds" later, Hood rolled over and accidently knocked the remaining few beers off the platform into the river far below.

"Goddamn," Jiggs peeked over the edge, "we're out of supplies."

"I think we're going to have to make a run for it," Hood pulled himself onto his feet. "We can't hold out here any longer."

They staggered off down the tracks towards the end of the trestle where Jiggs had parked the bike. About one hundred fifty feet along Jiggs stopped. "Wait a minute. I gotta take a leak."

"Take that, you dirty Commies," he yelled as he began to fire into space.

"That'll get ... hah!" Hood's voice screeched to a halt. "Jiggs, trouble off to our left. I think there's a train coming."

"Train ... ah, screw the train ... dirty Commie trick."

"No shit, Jiggs. There's a train coming. We gotta get outa here."

"Screw the train." Jiggs continued to kill Commies.

"Morgan, am I going to have to bodily remove you from these tracks?" Hood grabbed Jiggs' right arm. "We gotta get back to that platform."

"Lemme go." Jiggs wrenched his arm away. "Can't you see I'm takin' a pee?"

"Jiggs, look!" Roger took Jiggs' head in both hands and turned it ninety degrees to the left so that his eyes were pointed towards the oncoming headlight. Just then the trestle began to vibrate.

"Holy shit, Rog! There's a train coming!" Jiggs whirled around and saw Hood sprinting away from him as fast as he could go without stepping into the spaces between the ties. Jiggs pounded after him, trying to tuck himself in and zip his fly as he ran.

"Wahh! Wahh!" Two blasts of a diesel horn at close range nearly blew Jiggs off the trestle. He stumbled but kept going. Behind him, frozen steel wheels sliding on steel rails screamed as the brakes of the train slammed on.

Up ahead, Hood had reached the platform and was looking out from behind the guardrail into the glare of the onrushing headlight. He gestured with his arm, encouraging Jiggs to hurry, and Jiggs could see his mouth moving, but could hear nothing but the roar of death behind him.

Eight feet from the platform, he dove headlong for its safety, slamming face first onto its rough planking with such gratitude and relief at his salvation that the iron hard boards might have been a satin pillow. He lay there retching over the side into the distant river as the freight cars rumbled past just two feet from the soles of his shoes.

"I guess they settled the strike," Hood said after the last car passed.

At noon, Marie came into Jiggs' room, where he lay sprawled on his bed in only his skivvies with no covers, his left eye and cheek badly scraped and swollen. She grabbed his ankle and began to shake him.

"Come on, Prince Charm ... oooh." She winced at the sight of his face. "That'll look good in the photos. C'mon, wedding bells in three hours."

Two weeks later, the day after returning from the honeymoon, Jiggs enlisted in the Marine Corps Officer Candidate Program. He figured his eyes weren't good enough to be a pilot, so he'd be a second-class citizen in the Air Force, and he knew he could never keep the white shoes he would have to wear in the Navy clean. The Marines had been good enough for Doc; they would certainly be good enough for him, if he was good enough for them.

II

WESTPAC

CHRISTOPHER BRITTON

15

August 1967

Okinawa – The Jewel of the Ryukyu Archipelago. The Island sat like a big beaver in shallow water. Its hump back jutted up in a mountainous spine, its sides covered with small patches of sugar cane and walk-in tombs of Ryukyuan ancestors, ending abruptly in the North with chisel-toothed cliffs where the Pacific and the China Sea slammed into the Island's bony snout. While to the south, the beaver's tail gradually flattened, tapering to the sea.

Here were former battlefields where some Marines walked in reverence, like pilgrims touring Mecca, while others threw beer cans out taxicab windows on ground their fathers died on. Here were Megatonic Maggie, the round-eyed stripper with the fifty inch tits, and Miss Cheeseburger, the oriental dancer who could pick up a sandwich off a plate on the stage using a body part never intended for that purpose.

So far, Jiggs had seen only the road from Kadena Air Base to Camp Hanson, the Marine base where he and two hundred fifty others had been waiting two days for a flight to Viet Nam, just three short hours flying time away.

"It'll be your last chance to talk to round-eyed women." Corky Taylor, Jiggs' roommate of two days, tried to entice Jiggs into going to some Army officers' club he'd heard about called "Sukiran." "They say every round-eyed woman on the island goes there on Thursday night."

"All ten of 'em?"

"No, teachers, nurses, wives of sailors out to sea. Dozens of 'em, hundreds."

"Hell, all right. Anything to get out of this room." Jiggs had been lying in the room since his arrival, writing to Carol, reading, watching it rain, getting up only for meals. It reminded him of the early part of his trip to Mexico, except it was clean.

An hour earlier word had been passed to report to Base Transit tomorrow morning at 0700 with all necessary gear. Tomorrow was to be the day. Tomorrow he would finally see the tiny country that had stuck its dagger in America's gut and been twisting the blade for the last three years.

Jiggs stood and pulled on a pair of blue kahkis and a white knit shirt and looked in the mirror. *Wonder when I'll next wear these.* Two hours later, he was leaning against a post holding a beer in either hand. Another full one stood open at his feet. He had bought the first round, and since then every time Corky walked past, he handed Jiggs another. Taylor could walk faster than Jiggs could drink, but Jiggs was determined to make a race of it. He was bored, tired of watching other people dance, impatient for Corky to wear himself out so they could leave.

A Filipino band was blaring American rock music, old and new, and strobe lights flickered red and yellow, as couples moved jerkily in and out of shadows, elbow to elbow, overflowing the dance floor, spilling among the tables nearest the floor. Sitting, standing, young people were everywhere, laughing, talking, drinking.

The path to the dance floor wound past where Jiggs was leaning. A slight, brown-haired girl stepped across it in his direction just as the band swung into "Hit The Road Jack," and a new rush of would-be dancers charged the floor, spinning the girl halfway around as they stampeded past. When she resumed course, she was looking right at Jiggs.

"Look both ways before you cross the street." Jiggs moved slightly to his right, uncovering a small piece of the pillar he was leaning against. "Come in out of the traffic."

"Thanks." The girl slid into the niche Jiggs had created. She extended her hand. "I'm Camilla Waron."

"Jiggs Morgan, Camilla. Pleased to meet you." They shook hands.

"Do you want a beer?" Jiggs held up one of his extras.

"I'd rather have a Coke."

Jiggs stepped away from his pillar towards the bar. People were standing three deep all along its length waiting to order. Seeing this, Camilla put her hand on Jiggs' arm. "No, wait. On second thought I'll have one of your beers."

They tried to talk as they drank, but the roar of the band prevented much communication.

"Would you like to dance?" Jiggs half-shouted, nodding towards the dance floor. Jiggs and Carol shared a trust borne of two years of successful long distance relationship while in college. Neither would begrudge the other an occasional dance with someone else. It was of Carol he was thinking when he asked Camilla the question.

Camilla nodded back. Jiggs set their beers at the base of the post. They threaded their way toward the dancers and melted into the melee. As they danced three feet apart, Jiggs took a closer look at his partner. Medium height, a slender, almost boyish figure. A wisp of her hair kept falling in front of her eyes, and she brushed it back with a wave of her hand almost as if the gesture was part of the dance. She had a fair complexion, blue eyes and an angular face. Jiggs compared her to Carol, his all time standard of feminine beauty. *Fewer curves.* "Winsome" was a word she made him think of, but that wasn't quite right – too much energy for winsome. Although not quite beautiful, she danced beautifully, lightly, moving as if the music flowed from somewhere inside her, while Jiggs tromped about, admiring her grace.

One song ended, the second one they had danced, and another began, a slow one. Jiggs saved all his slow dances for Carol. He was about to excuse himself when Camilla said, "It's hot in here. Let's find somewhere to sit down away from the noise."

Beats leaning against a post. Jiggs followed Camilla out of the bar.

There was a coffee shop right across the lobby, and they found a table overlooking a golf driving range that was lighted for night play. After they ordered, Camilla asked, "Are you a golfer?"

"Nope. My wife, Carol is. How about you?"

Camilla shook her head. "No. I'd rather read, or just walk."

My sentiments exactly. "I'd like to golf if you could hit the guy while he's lining up his shot. I feel the same way about figure-skating. If the girl could hold her focus once her partner throws her up in the air, knowing he might not be there when she comes down, that would be worth watching."

Camilla laughed. "That game's already been invented. It's called 'hockey.'"

From golf, they traversed a dozen subjects, where they came from, siblings, where they went to college, jobs back in the world, how they came to be on Okinawa. Like Jiggs, Camilla had two sisters, both younger, and grew up on a farm. Her parents had an apple orchard outside Winchester, Virginia. Camilla had gone to Duke, about which Jiggs knew only that it always seemed to have a good basketball team. She had taught for two years in Washington, D.C., before signing up to teach military kids on overseas bases. "I'm on Okinawa to teach high school English. "

"Friends, Romans, countrymen..." Jiggs began Anthony's funeral oration, which he had been required to learn in high school English. "Do you make your students memorize that? Do you make 'em read *Silas Marner*?"

"Shakespeare, yes; Marner, no. What's the matter? Don't you like the classics? You probably don't like poetry either. None of the boys in my classes like poetry."

Jiggs shrugged. "I like some poetry."

"What kinds do you like?"

There are different kinds? "The kind that rhymes, I guess. You'll have to teach me what I like."

"You already know. Maybe I can teach you what it's called."

Her voice was low and cool. Its sound bathed both the words she spoke and her listener with a sense of tranquility. Camilla talked like she danced, effortlessly, but without languor.

They drifted back into the bar when the coffee shop closed. The lights on the driving range had been off for more than an hour. The band was playing "We Gotta Get Out Of This Place," and everyone left in the bar, dancers and drinkers alike, were singing along. Jiggs' former perch against the pillar was open, and they resumed leaning, watching the singers, two hundred people joined in song, joined in momentary contemplation of the war, that, directly or indirectly, had brought them all together.

Last call had sounded. Corky came up to them. "Jiggs, I've been looking all over for you. Let's get a cab and head back."

Jiggs turned to Camilla. "Thanks for the evening. I enjoyed every word of it. Good luck with your kids and *Julius Caesar.*"

"Thank you. When do you leave for Viet Nam?"

Jiggs glanced at his watch for the first time since he met her. "In about six hours."

"Oh ... so soon." Camilla bit her lower lip. "You didn't tell me that." A film of mist clouded her eyes and her voice too. She touched Jiggs arm with her fingertips. "Be careful, Jiggs. God speed."

16

September-December 1967

Carol wrote to Jiggs every day; Jiggs wrote whenever he could, even if only a single rain or sweat soaked paragraph.

September 25, 1967
Dear Carol,

Here I am, a Second Lieutenant, fresh in country, the only thing greener than the oceans of jungle over which we sometimes fly, but through which we more often walk.

Fortunately, most of the people in my platoon have been here long enough to know what they're doing, so I'm not as much of a liability as I would be if they were as inexperienced as I. For the time being, I am keeping my mouth shut as much as possible and soaking up all I can. The feeling of responsibility is enormous.

The food over here is as bad as the weather. However, usually it's so hot, I rarely feel like eating much, so the two conditions complement each other.

I have been on several patrols but have experienced very little enemy contact. If, as some say, everything is relative, then I am relatively well and happy, but I miss you more than words can express. I've gone to sleep, or what passes for sleep around here, in some ditches little better than an Iowa hog lot and been comforted by your imagined nearness. Oink! Oink!

Please write whenever you can. Mail call is either the best of times or the worst of times, depending on whether there is a letter from you.

I love you, Jiggs

November 1, 1967
Dear Jiggs,

I watch the news each night half in hope, half in terror, that I will see you on the nightly horror show. I see the faces of the men jumping into and out of helicopters, wading through streams, or just walking in columns down roads or paths, and I think how each one of them surely has parents and a wife or girl and friends who all love them and worry about them as much as I worry about you. It makes me understand how anguished this country really is.

But enough of my anguish. I'm just glad I'm working. Having twenty-five first graders to teach every day is a much-needed diversion. We had a Halloween party yesterday. I dressed as a mean old witch. I told Roger what my costume was going to be, and he said it probably wouldn't require much acting. What do you think?

Well, Morgan, this is one witch with a sugar heart that's melting for you. I go through our album weekly, just wallowing in memories. Why didn't we take more pictures? Send me some of you and the guys you're with. Jim Linetti sounds like a good guy and so do the others you mention.

Stay safe. I miss you so.

Love – real love, Carol

November 10, 1967
Dear Carol,

Happy Marine Corps Birthday!

The fighting here is like a game of musical chairs. Week after week, we circle the same territory like children circling those chairs. From time to time there will be a burst of violence like the scramble for the chairs when the music stops, and those who don't find adequate cover leave the game, while the rest of us resume our endless circling. The only prize is that, if you can keep finding a chair for thirteen months, you don't have to play any more. But the game goes on, and your friends must continue to play.

First platoon (mine is Second) had a couple of guys who couldn't find chairs this morning. Last night they set out Claymore mines for booby traps to guard their position. If I haven't told you, Claymores are terrible little devices that blast out thousands of steel balls, like ball bearings, in an arc, cutting down everything in their path, up to and including medium sized trees.

Nothing happened last night. So this morning they decided to blow the mines in place rather than disconnect them. Unfortunately, they didn't check them before detonation. Someone (guess who) had crawled up in the night and turned one of the mines around, pointing it back towards the platoon's position. When they touched it off, it killed the two guys who were going around disposing of them.

I'm sorry to write about such depressing things, but that's the only thing of note that's happened since yesterday's letter, and it so typifies the days and nights here that it would be dishonest not to write about it. It's not meant to scare you. I know you're already scared. Me too. Rest assured I'm being as careful as possible. I have no wish to be a hero.

All I want to do is come back to you! Knowing you are waiting, thinking about our life together, how much lies before us – I think about these things all the time – you are my strength.

Please keep writing every day. Tell me about everything that's going on. Nothing is too small or insignificant. Your folks, Doc, my sisters, Hood, Lindy, the kids in your class – everyone. I need to hear about them all. You are my lifeline to sanity. I read your letters dozens of times.

I love you so much, Jiggs

P.S. Don't have your kids play musical chairs anymore.

"Sir, can I talk to you?"

Jiggs looked up from the pile of sandbags where he was sitting writing a letter to Carol. David Leslie, a Private in Second Platoon, was standing at attention in front of him. Even though Jiggs was sitting and Leslie was standing, Leslie wasn't much taller than Jiggs.

"At ease, Pvt. Leslie. You know better than to stand at attention out here."

Leslie, the smallest man in the platoon, was also the youngest. His nickname was "Saucers," because he had the biggest, roundest, brownest eyes anyone in the unit had ever seen. They reminded Jiggs of the eyes of big-eyed little kids he'd seen in a series of paintings in a gallery somewhere. Staring out of his small, unwhiskered face above his baggy utilities, Leslie looked more like a tiny waif than a Marine rifleman.

In the month he had been with the platoon, Leslie had done nothing to dispel Jiggs' impression of him. Often the smallest or youngest Marines were the boldest, striving to prove their size or youth was no handicap, but not David Leslie. He did what he was told, but there was a hesitance about him, almost a meekness. Jiggs wondered how he ever came to be in the Marines.

"I'm sorry to bother you, Sir..."

"No bother. What's on your mind?"

Leslie looked around to see if anyone was within earshot.

"Sir, I think there's something wrong with me." Leslie paused but Jiggs didn't say anything. "I'm so scared, sometimes I can hardly breathe. My heart will start to race, and I can't get any air, and my brain just blanks out like there's this fire red wall in there and nothing else. I think I'm going crazy. I think I'm a coward."

As Leslie talked, Jiggs studied the boy. If this wasn't a con, he wondered how much it cost Leslie to make such an admission. What was he going to ask for? A medevac? Transfer to the rear? Leslie was tentative as he spoke, but that was probably because he had no idea how what he was telling Jiggs would be received. This was probably already the longest conversation he had ever had with an officer. When he finished speaking, he began to bite his lower lip so hard Jiggs thought it would bleed.

"I don't think you're going crazy, Pvt. Leslie. Everyone out here is scared. I'm scared. Everyone in this platoon is scared. Any guy who says he isn't is more scared than the rest, because he's even scared to admit it.

"Out there," Jiggs pointed down the hill towards a tree line five hundred meters beyond the wire, Charlie's scared too."

"That's what I keep trying to tell myself, Sir. I watch the other guys do their jobs, and, somehow, they overcome bein' afraid. Everyone does. Except me."

One night on patrol two weeks earlier the platoon was dug in, when, about midnight, Jiggs was checking lines. As he approached one hole along the perimeter, he heard low mumbling and stopped to listen. It was one of the Marines in the nearest hole praying. As Jiggs began to listen, the barely audible worshiper asked God to protect not just himself, but the whole platoon and to give "the Lieutenant and the Platoon Sergeant the wisdom to keep the platoon safe." Silently, Jiggs joined in that prayer. Calling out the password in a loud whisper and receiving a reply, Jiggs came to the edge of the hole. It had been Pvt. Leslie praying. Jiggs was sure of it. The other man in the hole was asleep.

"I thought I heard someone talking over here, Leslie," Jiggs hissed. "No talking unless absolutely necessary. Understand? When you do have to talk, whisper." Leslie nodded his understanding, and Jiggs crept on.

Now Jiggs was remembering that prayer as Leslie stumbled on about his feelings.

"Out on an operation ... I can barely make my legs work." Leslie was taking quick, shallow breaths now in between phrases, becoming more upset at the thought of his fear. "...and it's getting worse. I have to force one foot ahead of the other ... It's like my brain has lost control over them ... like they know they've ... used up all their safe steps ... and the next step will ... blow them away.

"Sometimes ... just walking along ... I'm crying ... like now." Leslie was clearly on the verge of tears. "I dunno why ... I try to stop ... but I ... can't. I haven't fired ... my weapon ... since I came here."

This last revelation took Jiggs by surprise even coming as it did in the midst of Leslie's otherwise unsurprising confession. There had been no lack of opportunities to fire.

"Why not?"

"That's ... that's the main reason ... I'm telling you this, Sir. I'm afraid someone's gonna get hurt because of me. My hands shake so much, I keep my rifle on 'safe' all the time. When we make contact, I don't do anything ... I just burrow as deep as I can and freeze ... and pray it stops. Nobody should count on me...I can't count on myself. If it was just me, ... well, that'd be one thing ... but we're supposed to support each other ... and I'm just panicking. I'm a coward."

The halting earnestness with which Leslie spoke, his visible upset to be revealing his own failure, made Jiggs think Leslie wasn't bullshitting. "'Coward' is a hard word. Telling me this took guts, didn't it?"

"Yes ... yessir ... I guess so."

Jiggs wanted to help him without giving up on him, without letting Leslie give up on himself, but he didn't want to endanger the platoon by ignoring Leslie's undependability. Jiggs believed the only thing that kept any of them going was that no one wanted to be the first one to quit.

"I believe what you're telling me, Pvt. Leslie, and I appreciate you telling me and your reason for telling me. But don't be too quick to give up on yourself. This place, Viet Nam, combat, takes time to get used to, and your experience here is something you'll probably think about all your life. Probably fifty years from now you won't like thinking about it ending like this."

"No sir. It's just that I ... I don't want it to end even worse for someone else on account of me."

"Seems to me," Jiggs searched for the right words, "that getting a grip on yourself is all in the way you look at things. You believe in God?"

"Yessir."

"Me too. I'm not real religious, but when it comes down to it, I believe more than I even realize. Do you know the Twenty-third Psalm? The real one?"

All Marines knew the Corps' version that stated the reason the Marines walked in the Valley of the Shadow of Death without fear was because they "were the meanest motherfuckers in the Valley."

"Yessir, I do."

"Well, all I can tell you is that sometimes when we have contact, somewhere deep in my brain, the words to that Psalm start scrolling through, and it slows me down enough to do what needs to be done. It's made me start thinking about those words and what they mean ... about 'fearing no evil.' I figure God made me love life and not want to leave it, but those words showing up just when they do, when I need 'em most, is His way of reminding me that He gave me this life, and if He takes it away, it's because He knows better, and I'll eventually find out why.

"Meanwhile, I'll just try to do what I have to do the best way I can. Right now, that's taking care of this platoon. It doesn't keep me from being afraid, but it calms me down ... helps me take that tough next step you were talking about a minute ago."

Jiggs had been looking at his boots as he talked. He didn't know whether confiding like that to one of his troops was a good idea. Even though what he said was true, he felt uneasy using God, however indirectly, to try to keep someone fighting a war, even if his main goal was simply to salvage the boy's self-esteem.

"Leslie," Jiggs looked directly into the boy's face and held those enormous eyes with his own. "If you care enough about this platoon to tell me what you just told me, you care too much not to stay and do your share. Think about these things for a couple of days ... maybe talk to the Chaplain ... if nothing helps, come back and see me. Okay?"

Leslie began to draw himself up to attention, caught himself and appeared to relax a little. "Yessir." A wan smile flickered and disappeared across his face. "I will."

Jiggs watched his back as he walked away.

"What did Leslie want, Sir?" Staff Sergeant Lefler, Jiggs' Platoon Sergeant, walked up as Leslie vanished around a corner.

"Oh, the same thing we all want, Sarge, to go home."

December 19, 1967
Dear Jiggs,
        Congratulations on making First Lieutenant. Christmas is almost here. My folks are having Doc and

your sisters and Lindy over for Christmas dinner. The
first big snow has fallen, and school is closed today,
because of the weather. So I'm just sitting here in my
pajamas writing and watching the snow continue to fall.
Wish you were here to watch it with me. Then I
wouldn't need the stationery (or the pajamas).

I got Doc a painting of two Indians on horseback
on a snowy night for Christmas from the two of us. I
knew you wouldn't get a chance to shop. Do you think
he'll like it?

Sometimes I worry about him now that Darcy is
away at school, and he's all by himself in that big house.
I know he's not old or sick or anything, but he must be
lonely. He never goes anywhere, except on calls.

Roger is all set to graduate in June. He says he's
going into the Navy and will be in JAG. I guess it's all
arranged. Lindy had us both over for dinner last
Sunday. I showed her the pictures you sent me, and she
showed me the pictures you sent her. I'm glad you're
writing to her. She thinks of you like you are her son.
You ought to hear her talk about the President – she
thinks he's a "GODDAMN A-RAB."

Jiggs, it will be a lonely Christmas without you,
but not half so bad as I am sure it will be for you. At
least they've announced the "cease fire" for the
holidays. That's the second best present I could have.
Everyone here loves you and wishes for your safe
return – especially me.

I love you, Carol

17

January 1968

A dry day. Jiggs had abandoned hope of ever again seeing a day without rain in the Republic of Viet Nam. The irony was that Second Platoon was moving for the first time in its endless wanderings along a paved, or at least what once had been a paved road – long segments of ancient asphalt, bleached a pale gray by the sun, crumbling at its edges, here and there disintegrating into chunks, weeds growing up through the cracks. How many times during the last three months had the Platoon waded in shin-deep, boot sucking mud through days of perpetual rain, days when an asphalt road would have been every man's wet dream?

As the Platoon rounded a bend in the road heading east, a small village appeared about half a mile ahead, baking in the tropical heat. To the platoon's left a panorama of fields and rice paddies stretched away to the foot of some hills more than a mile to the North. To its right, about two hundred meters across some rice paddies there was a tree line paralleling their line of march. Jiggs was nervous about that tree line, although he thought an ambush unlikely. There was a stream behind the trees that would impede any attacker's retreat if the platoon counterattacked.

Zip! ZIP! ZIP!

As the point fire team came within twenty meters of the village, the Platoon began to take fire all along its line. What sounded like corn popping in those trees Jiggs had worried about, told the Marines all they needed to know about where the rounds were coming from. Diving for cover, they rolled over the left edge of the pavement behind the three-foot bank that elevated the road above the adjacent marshy field.

Jiggs was approximately two-thirds of the way back in the column.

"Return fire," he bellowed. "Casualty report." He looked around for Sgt. Lefler, his Platoon Sergeant. "Get Sgt. Lefler up here."

Shouting ranged along the line, some distinguishable, most not. "Sgt. Lefler report. Sgt. Lefler report!" Echoes in both directions as casualty reports came in. Nothing in the first or third squads.

"Second squad – one flesh wound – Pfc. Williams," Buskirk, Jiggs' radioman, who was right behind him shouted. "Doc's with him."

"Right behind you, Sir." Sgt Lefler crawled up behind Jiggs, who was peeking over the edge of the bank trying to assess enemy strength by counting muzzle flashes, wishing he had a periscope.

"Tell Braily to get his machine gun up asap and rake the entire line," Jiggs told Buskirk. "Pass the word."

Before Buskirk could turn around, the stutter of the M60 announced that Braily had figured things out for himself.

"I figure about fifteen of 'em. What do you think, Sgt. Lefler?"

"Twelve, maybe fifteen. No mortars, or they'd be arriving by now." The din was increasing. Jiggs could barely hear Lefler.

"Those trees peter out as they reach the village," Jiggs thought out loud as he looked back and forth from his map to what could be seen when he looked over the bank. "If you take the first and third squads, leaving me the second and Braily, do you think you can get back around that bend in the road, cross it and come up on their flank?"

"Sounds good to me." Lefler glanced at the tree line and back to his right towards the curve in the road they had just rounded.

"You'll drive 'em into that stream behind their position." Jiggs traced what he envisioned on his map. "Pop smoke when they start to withdraw, and I'll call in some..."

"Lieutenant! Lieutenant!" Someone yelling louder than the sound of the fight.

"Jesus Fucking Christ, look at the vil."

Jiggs looked. There toddling along the road towards the Platoon, no more than a few feet from the near end of the cross-fire, was a tiny Vietnamese child, smiling, waving its arms for balance as it headed out to see what all the noise was about. Behind the child, perhaps fifty meters away, still back among the hooches, was a screaming woman sprinting to recover her baby. What was happening in an instant unfolded slowly, like time lapse photography in Jiggs' mind's eye. He could see the woman was going to lose the race.

"Cease fire!" Jiggs dropped his map. "Stop firing!" He shouted again and again as he began to run stooped low behind the row of Marines plastered against the side of the bank returning fire. "Cease firing!"

Before Jiggs had taken five steps in the direction from which the child was coming, one of the Marines ahead of him bolted out of his position up onto the deadly road and ran bent over towards the child. Marine fire diminished and then ceased altogether. Enemy fire continued to zip just overhead. Then, as the woman and the Marine reached the child, enemy fire also stopped. The woman grabbed the baby, and the Marine grabbed the woman and dragged her and the baby off the road, rolling and landing on his back at the base of the bank with his human cargo on top of him.

"HURRAH!" An immediate cheer erupted from the Marine line as forty grunts who were in the business of risking death daily saluted, resuming fire a split second later.

The Marine who performed the rescue sat up from his fall, and Jiggs saw it was Saucers. As Jiggs turned back to find Sgt. Lefler again, the Marine fire fell off once more, because no return fire was being received from the tree line. The fight was over. It was silent. Nothing moved.

That night, after the Platoon dug into another tree line just two clicks east of the vil, Jiggs went looking for Saucers. He found him eating a can of C-rats he had just heated over a piece of burning C-4.

"You walked in the 'Valley of the Shadow' today Pvt. Leslie."

Saucers looked at the ground, and Jiggs thought he was probably blushing beneath the multiple layers of camouflage paint and crud he'd accumulated over the last three days.

"Aw, the shooting had pretty much stopped by the time I got there, Sir."

Jiggs shook his head. "Not when you stood up and jumped out on the road, Leslie. The bad guys were still shooting, and you didn't know what they were going to do. Good work."

Jiggs patted Leslie on the shoulder and walked away.

That night Jiggs wrote Carol he'd seen two miracles in one afternoon: Saucers' rescue and the VC ceasing fire before Saucers dived off the road. "Maybe there is a god," he concluded. Three days later, Major Davis, the battalion XO, after reading Jiggs' after action report, chewed Jiggs out for letting the enemy escape.

18

January 1968

The rear. Hill 410, where Second Platoon returned at the end of its patrols, was a barren, pock-marked welter of tents, sandbagged bunkers and a few tin-roofed hooches. The structures crouched on pilings driven into the hillside to prevent them from slipping off the slope or sinking into the sea of mud that had covered the hill ever since Jiggs arrived. Its name was simply the designation on the map signifying that particular point of ground was four hundred ten feet above sea level. The place lacked any geographical distinction for which it might have been named other than its elevation.

Although surrounded by jungle, the place would never be called "Shady Grove." There wasn't a single tree inside its perimeter or within five hundred yards outside of it. All trees had been blasted away by incoming mortars or bulldozed away by the engineers to provide clear fields of observation and fire. Any person in whose honor the dreadful scab of earth might have been named would have been insulted.

Still, 410 was not without its charms. The bunkers were inviting. Although populated by rats and often containing six inches of water, such small distractions were as nothing when

Charlie decided to remind the cooks, supply sergeants and other REMFs that there was a war going on by lobbing a few mortars into their midst. Then, too, there were the showers once a week in the unlikely event you happened to be in camp when they were working. Like the bunkers, their drainage was imperfect.

This was disconcerting at first, because, when you pulled the chain to start their flow, you received an arm-numbing electrical shock. The fact that the bather was standing on a concrete floor in three or four inches of water left over from previous bathers at the moment of receipt, made one think such showering might be unsafe. However, so far no one had died, and the Battalion Commander had ordered whatever caused the shocks not be repaired. Marines tended to take shorter showers when usage depended on hanging onto a chain that made their teeth ache. Clean water was in short supply.

But 410's best feature to Jiggs' way of thinking was the wire. 410 was surrounded by miles of concertina wire, which, while not impenetrable to unwelcome visitors, was impossible to ignore. A night on duty guarding perimeter lines, however unpleasant, was somehow much more restful knowing he was encircled by three rings of razor sharp wire coils that would ruin Charlie's clothes if he wasn't careful.

For Marines from Da Nang or Saigon or even nearby Quang Tri, who had occasion to visit, coming to 410 meant coming to the front. For Second Platoon, coming to 410 meant going to the rear. Jiggs thought about how the war was kind of like the poem about the blind men and the elephant. One's impressions of what the war was like depended on what part of the elephant one touched. Today he was tight-roping along the planks that cobwebbed 410, trying to hurry through the rain and not slip off into the bottomless mud in the dark as he made his way to Larry Nelson's hooch carrying a case of beer.

Larry was a squid, the battalion chaplain. He had been an enlisted man in the Navy, serving as a corpsman with a Marine Advisory Unit early in the war, before the U.S. troop build-up. At the end of his enlistment, he left the service, attended seminary and was ordained. Then he re-enlisted, went to Navy OCS and volunteered to come back to Viet Nam and serve with the Marines. Larry was a quiet guy, who seemed like he needed to help people to be happy. Jiggs thought he was insane for having come back to the war, but they had become friends, and he was happy for Nelson's insanity.

Jiggs had once asked Larry why he chose to become a minister rather than a doctor.

"To keep a promise to God. When I was over here the first time as a corpsman, I saw some awful wounds, terrible suffering, and I noticed that even when there were no drugs available to control pain, when the chaplain came by and talked to guys, the word of God seemed to take the edge off what they were going through. The time came when I had some kid dying before my eyes, and I vowed, if he pulled through, I would become a chaplain, and he made it. Before I finished my tour, I had made that promise more than once. I decided I wanted to ally myself with the power that took over when medicine ran out of gas."

Jiggs and Larry had spent a lot of hours hashing over why God ever let all that suffering happen in the first place. It all seemed so random to Jiggs.

"How can we know what's 'random,' Jiggs? We can't begin to know everything God knows. But if one looks at the way the world works, birth, death, the seasons, it's hard not to conclude a plan exists. The evidence is too compelling for me not to believe just because I don't have all the facts."

Today was Larry's birthday, and he was having a few friends over for cocktails. The tent Larry shared with five others was pitched over a wooden frame that rested on a platform, just like the few more permanent structures on 410. It was dank and musty and dark. The cots were situated at odd angles from the sides of the tent, positioned so as to be out from under the leaks in the roof. Each resident had a locker in which a light bulb burned constantly in an effort to slow the inexorable march of mold. Compared to where Jiggs spent most nights, it was lovely.

Jiggs came up the steps and entered Larry's hooch. Five or six other officers, captains and lieutenants, were already drinking. Jiggs put the beer he brought on the floor, took one for himself and greeted Larry, who offered him some beef jerky. Jiggs recognized a couple of Larry's roommates, officers who occupied various staff positions in the battalion office. There were three others he did not know, and there was Randy Yakitan.

It had been Jiggs' misfortune to go all the way through OCS and Basic School in the same platoon with Yakitan. Almost nine months of listening to Yak's loud-mouthed bullshit, boasting, complaining, gold-bricking. He was a big bull of a man, 6'4" and at least two hundred thirty pounds, but he was lazy and dumb. He had been Jiggs' frequent opponent in pugil stick fighting in OCS, the one on one battles with padded staves that the Corps used like cudgels to teach trainees to be aggressive and cagey in the face of direct physical challenge. Yak got the aggressive part, but his only tactic was to rush his opponent and try to overwhelm him with his size and weight. The first time they fought, Jiggs, whose wrestling footwork served him well in these matches, side-stepped Yak's initial charge, tripped him as he lunged past and slugged him on the back of the head as he went down.

Yak had been embarrassed, but he never adjusted. In innumerable skirmishes after that, he took every fake Jiggs threw, swinging at the air and getting smacked in the head or jabbed in the gut for his failure to recognize what he was seeing. This same failure of recognition had earned Yak a ticket out of the bush and into a staff position after less than two months of patrolling. Someone with some authority had seen what Jiggs and every enlisted man in Yak's platoon already knew. Yak was going to get people killed unnecessarily, or be killed by one of his own men just to keep that from happening. So now Yak was in the S-2 shop, Intelligence. Maybe he would pick some up.

"Happy birthday, Lar." Jiggs raised his bottle in his friend's direction, and Larry introduced him to the two guys he was talking to.

"Jiggs, we were just talking about dysentery, said Larry, the former corpsman. "That's something you know about, isn't it?"

Jiggs' interest in the subject had lately been increased by personal experience. He was about to reply, but was distracted by the sound of Yak regaling another group with some imagined exploit, and instead just rolled his eyes and stayed silent.

After a few minutes, Larry turned to Jiggs. "Just got some new pictures from home." He had shown Jiggs pictures of his family on other occasions, and Jiggs had shown Larry pictures of Carol.

"Show me."

Larry took an album wrapped in plastic off a shelf above his rack and opened it. A pretty blond woman, whom Jiggs recognized as Larry's wife from earlier photos, sat on the floor of a living room playing with two small children, both girls, equally blond. Two or three others drifted over and were looking over Jiggs' and Larry's shoulders as they browsed. Four or five pages from the end of the album, Larry closed the book.

"Hey," said a voice from behind Jiggs, "there's still more pictures." The voice was Yak's.

Larry smiled. "Those last ones are private, just for me."

"C'mon. Band of brothers. Share and share alike."

Larry shook his head as he re-wrapped the album and replaced it on the shelf. "I wouldn't show those pictures to my brother."

It was obvious the unseen photos were intimate pictures Larry's wife had sent him. It was obvious, too, that Yak knew it.

"You show me yours, and I'll show you mine," Yak half-whined.

Jiggs wanted to say no woman in her right mind would ever send Yak her picture fully clothed, let alone naked, but he kept his mouth shut. Larry ignored Yak, and the conversation turned to other things.

About twenty minutes later, Jiggs and Larry, a UCLA grad, and a couple of the others were discussing whether the Bruins could win another national basketball championship. Suddenly Larry yelled, "You son of a bitch!"

As he spoke, Larry yanked a K-Bar, a Marine Corps fighting knife, out of the tent post next to where he was standing and in one motion threw it. It happened so fast Jiggs did not instantly understand what was going on until his eyes, following the flight of the knife, saw Yak look up from the last few pages of Larry's album at the sound of Larry's voice and move his head slightly to the right.

That slight movement saved Yak's life. Larry could not have thrown and stuck that knife one time in a thousand, but he did this time. Maybe because he was drunk. The point buried itself in another post just behind and to the left of Yak's head.

However, as the blade zipped past him, it sliced Yak's left cheek completely through. There was blood everywhere. Yak was pressing the side of his face with his hand in disbelief, contemplating how it was that he could put his fingers in his mouth without opening it.

What good's a knife if it's not sharp? One of Doc's lines.

Two guys were holding Larry, who had lunged in Yak's direction, intent on finishing the job.

"Somebody better get Yak over to the aid station," Jiggs said to Mark Wilson one of Larry's roommates. "He's going to need a few stitches."

Jiggs bent over and picked up the album from the floor. There was blood on the cover. He wiped off as much as he could and handed it to Larry as Wilson and another lieutenant led Yak out the door into the rain.

Jiggs watched them leave. "Well, Yak probably won't do that again."

"I suppose the shit's going to hit the fan now," Larry said.

"What do you mean?"

"I mean that Yak's going to bring me up on charges for this."

"For what? Him getting drunk and falling down and hitting his face on the corner of that rack?"

Jiggs glanced at the others who had seen what happened and was met with nods. "Maybe one of you ought to catch up with Wilson and make sure those guys saw what we saw."

"I'll go," grunted Jack Shea, another of Larry's rooommates. "Yak never could hold his liquor."

Within a couple of minutes everyone had left the tent but Jiggs and Larry.

"Wow, Lar. You kind of went all Old Testament there."

"You think that story will hold up?" Larry asked.

"I think Yak may see things just the way the rest of us did," Jiggs said. "If he doesn't, he'll have to admit what he was doing. Dumb as he is, Yak's smart enough to know there's no way he can come out of this looking good if he makes a stink ... Besides, the scar will make him look tough. He'll probably tell everybody back in the world he got it going hand to hand with a VC regiment."

"Hope you're right. Jesus, I don't know what came over me."

"Ah, it's the heat and all this rain. Everyone's irritable."

Jiggs stayed for a few more minutes helping Larry try to clean up the blood, without much success. The occupants of the tent were just going to have to live with the stain. Jiggs and Larry joked that they hoped it wouldn't affect the property value.

Jiggs made his way back to his own tent far more sober than he had expected to be that night. *There's war on both sides of the wire. Depends on where you touch the elephant.*

19

January 1968

Jiggs was not an apprehensive flyer. But he hated helicopters – a sad fact in a place like Viet Nam, where the insect-shaped machines were as numerous as taxis in mid-town Manhattan. Helicopters were big, slow targets, superb at plunging and exploding, incapable of gliding. *Noisy, fragile, flammable* – Jiggs reflected on his disaffection as he sat strapped into a seat molded into the outside of the fuselage of a chopper. He was headed for the hospital ship anchored several miles off the coast, where two of his men were recuperating from wounds.

He hung by his seatbelt, suspended above the rice paddies and jungle that lined the Qua Viet River. The aircraft banked to its right towards the South China Sea.

Forcing away the thought of himself as a bulls-eye for any sniper, Jiggs struggled to concentrate on the beauty hundreds of feet below – the shimmering white where the beach delineated the junction of explosive green land and sapphire blue sea.

Far out on the water, beyond the range of any weapon in the enemy's arsenal, bobbed a white speck, like a hat on a sailor's head. Gradually the speck grew and grew and grew, until it became the biggest ship Jiggs, a child of the prairie, had ever seen. The chopper flew directly over the fantail of the enormous albino boat, paused, then allowed itself to drop, landing with a thump on a bright red cross painted dead center on the helipad. By virtue of his external accommodations, Jiggs was the first one off. Unbuckling his seatbelt, he jumped to the deck and ran, stooped over, out from beneath the radius of the rotors that continued to whirl.

He was greeted by a swarm of tiny Vietnamese children, each bearing some grizzly mark of war.

"Hey, Marine, you got smokes? You got candy?" They scampered to keep up with Jiggs' much longer strides. He paused, feeling his pockets for some Lifesavers from one of Carol's recent care packages. *Why didn't I scrounge some more treats in anticipation of this?* Finding the almost full pack of candy, he stripped off the wrapping and knelt to distribute the individual pieces. They didn't go far. An orange one to the boy with only one eye; cherry to the little girl, the edge of whose facial burns peeked out from beneath a swath of bandages, lime for a tall girl whose right arm ended just below her elbow, lemon to a girl whose outstretched palm had only its little finger remaining. The smallest of the fifteen or sixteen children clustered around him was a one-legged boy who had hobbled up to the group on crutches no longer than Jiggs' arm.

"This is for you." Jiggs extended the last piece, pine-apple, through the sea of outstretched arms, to the boy, who let go of his right crutch, balancing on it under his armpit, reached for the candy, popped it in his mouth and smiled.

When Jiggs stood up, the children understood the candy counter was now closed. Almost as one they turned to see what other potential donors might be coming their way. Jiggs watched the flock scurry over to two troops who were unloading some crates from the chopper's side hatch. The tiny boy to whom Jiggs had given the last Lifesaver stumped along behind the others, game to keep up.

"They'll pick you clean, if you let 'em, Lieutenant," laughed the pilot, who had just threaded his way through the children without stopping, having signaled with a wave of his hand that he had nothing for them.

"What a tragic sight," Jiggs muttered, speaking around a lump in his throat.

"They're the lucky ones," the pilot replied. "At least they're getting some care."

There it was, the Vietnamese definition of "luck." You may be maimed by napalm at the age of five, but among all those who suffer, you are one of the few to receive care. So you can go back to what? More napalm? Another atrocity?

Jiggs wondered if any of these children had been injured by something done by his platoon. It was certainly possible. Or, maybe the children his platoon hit were among the "unlucky" ones.

"Yeah," Jiggs said, "They're real lucky."

Jeremy Kaufman was at the far end of a large ward. Jiggs was surprised to see three empty beds between Kaufman's and that of the nearest patient. *Can the war business be slowing down?*

Jiggs walked up to Kaufman's rack. "Lance Corporal Kaufman, I brought you some mail." The military mailmen hadn't gotten the word that Kaufman was vacationing away from Second Platoon aboard a local cruise ship. It was quicker just to bring it out to the ship than return it to an uncertain fate in the maw of the Marine mail system.

"Thank you, Sir." Kaufman pushed himself up into a sitting position against the metal headboard. He did a one-armed shuffle through the three envelopes Jiggs handed him, his other arm being encased in plaster. He had been accidentally shot by Mike Beringer, who neglected to put his rifle on safe before coming over to sit next to Kaufman, his best friend, when the platoon fell out for fifteen minutes while on patrol ten days earlier. When Beringer put down his weapon, Bang. Accidental discharge.

"Where's Pfc. Sanchez? I thought he was in this ward too?"

"He was right next to me." Kaufman set his letters aside. "But he got an infection. He told me they were moving him to somewhere in Japan. His rack was empty when I woke up this morning."

"Maybe his war's over."

Kaufman and Jiggs exchanged looks that said they both hoped so for Aurelio Sanchez' sake.

"What about you, Kaufman? How are you holding up?"

"Stomach still hurts if I move much. They're giving me something for that. Arm throbs like hell. Doc says that means it's healing. Hope it heals slow. I still got three months to go." The same round that had broken Kaufman's arm had deflected off the bone down through his side, missing all major organs or arteries, but leaving a nasty hole as it left the area.

Kaufman was a good man. The Platoon could use him. *I hope it heals slow too, Kaufman.*

"Sir, could you do me a favor? I got this college application for next fall, and I gotta get it postmarked by tomorrow to make the submission deadline. I filled it out, but there's an essay part, and I don't know a comma from a coffee stain. Would you look at it and help me touch it up before I send it?"

Fifteen minutes later, Jiggs was half seated beside Kaufman on the bed as the two of them went over Kaufman's essay entitled "The Best Teacher I Ever Had." He had selected one of his drill instructors at Paris Island.

"Oh, Oh. Here comes the Fish."

Jiggs looked up at Kaufman's exclamation. Coming down the aisle between the racks was a Navy Lieutenant.

"Look out for this guy, Sir..."

Before Kaufman could add anything, the Lieutenant arrived. He was wearing a chaplain's cross on his collar and a nametag that said, "Lt. Norman Trout." "No visitors during Sunday services, Lieutenant. You'll have to clear out."

Clear out?

Jiggs ungritted his teeth. "Can I talk to you privately for a moment, Lieutenant?" He stepped towards Trout, who was standing by the foot of the bed.

Trout turned back towards the aisle. "We can talk on the way out."

Jiggs followed him until they were far enough away not to be overheard by Kaufman.

"This is good, Lieutenant." Jiggs stopped. Trout kept walking. "Lt. Trout," Jiggs said in a louder than normal voice. "Just a minute."

Trout turned and took a couple of steps back. "You need to leave here, Lieutenant. We can talk outside."

"Lt. Trout, I have a chopper leaving in half an hour. There's no telling when I'll get a chance to get back to see my man back there. I'm helping him with a college application. Any chance you can bend whatever rule it is that requires me to 'clear out?'"

Trout looked at Jiggs without saying anything, turned around and walked away.

He didn't say no. Jiggs went back to Kaufman.

"He letting you stay, Sir? That surprises me. The other day he came in and started talking to me about converting. I told him I wasn't interested, but he just kept on. I think he might be one of those padres who killed a few heathen in order to save 'em." Kaufman was Jewish.

Jiggs did not have a good feeling about Lt. Trout. "Yeah, you may be right. Anyway, let's wrap up this application in case he comes back."

Five minutes later Jiggs heard the tramp of feet coming from the direction of the entrance to the ward.

Kaufman nodded towards the door. "Fish is back. He's got company."

Lt. Trout walked up to where Jiggs was standing beside Kaufman's bed. He was accompanied by two Marine enlisted men, a corporal and a pfc., both wearing armbands signifying they were on duty as ship's security.

"Corporal, arrest this man." Trout pointed at Jiggs.

The Corporal hesitated. "You ... you want me to arrest a Marine officer, Lieutenant?"

"You heard me. Arrest him. He disobeyed the direct order of a superior officer."

Jiggs wanted to laugh. "Go ahead, Corporal. You heard the Lieutenant."

The Corporal looked from Jiggs to Lt. Trout and back at Jiggs.

"Get on with it," Trout hissed.

"Okay. Sir, you're under arrest."

"I'm your prisoner, Corporal."

"Corporal," Trout spoke through compressed lips, "isn't it customary when placing someone under arrest to place them in restraint?"

Before the Corporal could answer, Jiggs thrust his hands out. "Go ahead, Corporal, put me in irons."

Open-mouthed, the Corporal reached for the handcuffs on his belt and placed them around Jiggs' wrists.

"Are you going to make me walk the plank, Lt. Trout?"

"Take this man to the brig, Corporal. I will write up charges after services."

Jiggs nodded farewell to the amazed Kaufman and walked out between the Corporal and the Pfc. Lieutenant. Trout led the way. As the four of them neared the end of the first passageway outside the ward, a Marine major stepped out of an adjoining compartment directly into their path. It was Lee Hammersmith, with whom Jiggs had played baseball while in training at Quantico. "The Hammer" had been a captain back then.

"Jiggs, how the hell are you. What are you doing here?"

"I'm on my way to the brig."

Hammer looked at the two Marine enlisted men, both of whom looked like they wished they were somewhere else. Then Hammer looked at Lt. Trout. "What's this all about?"

"This man has been insubordinate and disrespectful. He disobeyed a direct order, and I've had him arrested. I intend to bring him up on charges."

"What? You arrested ... you ... what order did he disobey?"

"I ordered him to vacate the Recovery Ward during Sunday services. He failed to do so."

"You had two of my Marines put a Marine officer under arrest?" The concept was having a hard time gaining traction in

Hammer's brain. The job of the Marine detachment, which Hammer commanded, aboard the ship was to provide security, but the notion of a Navy officer arresting a Marine officer, especially one only a single grade below him in rank, for anything less than open mutiny, was inconceivable.

"Barkin, Milliken," Hammer spoke to the two enlisted Marines, "I'll take custody of your prisoner. You two are relieved. You can go back to the Department."

"Aye, aye, Sir," both replied, but the Corporal hesitated. "Er, Major, can I get my handcuffs back?"

"Handcuffs!" Hammer whirled toward Jiggs, who held up his manacled wrists. "Jesus Christ, yes. Get those cuffs off him.

"Did you order Lt. Morgan cuffed?" This to Trout.

"I believe that is standard procedure when someone is to be arrested and taken to the brig."

Hammer drew a deep breath, deciding what to do.

"Corporal Millikan, take your cuffs back. We're not going to the brig."

Trout stepped between Jiggs and the Corporal. "Major, this man is still under arrest..."

Ignoring Trout, Corporal Milliken unlocked the cuffs, and the two enlisted men disappeared down the passageway with a great story to tell their pals.

"That's right, Lieutenant, and I'm taking him straight to the Captain. A serious case like this, insubordination, disrespect towards a fellow officer, offenses so severe that the prisoner must be restrained, should be dealt with at the highest levels. You're to come with me so you can explain the magnitude of this crime and your prompt response in detail to the Skipper. Let's move out." Hammer turned and walked away at a pace that forced Jiggs to almost run to keep up. Trout straggled behind.

The Captain's office was a room behind the bridge. Hammer barged through the personnel calmly steering the ship and confronted the seaman sitting outside the office. "Major Hammersmith to see the Captain. Is he in?"

The seaman pushed a button and announced the arrivals. "You can go on in, Sir."

"You two wait out here. Lt. Morgan, can I have your word that if I leave you alone with Lieutenant Trout, you won't attack and kill him?"

"Yessir."

Hammer disappeared into the office, closing the door behind him.

Jiggs turned to Trout. "Lieutenant, with all due respect, I think you've overplayed your hand. How would it be if, when we go in there, we both say it was just a misunderstanding that we've resolved between ourselves, and we're sorry for the bother."

"Getting nervous, Lt. Morgan. You Marines think you run things. Well, you don't run the worship of God. You can't interfere with that and get away with it."

Jiggs blinked in disbelief.

After no more than three minutes, the office door opened and a voice from the inside said, "Gentlemen, step in here, will you?"

Once the door closed behind them, Jiggs stood at attention in front of Captain's desk. Trout stood beside him, unbraced. Hammer sat in a side chair to their left. The Captain didn't waste time on introductions. "At ease, Lt. Morgan. Lt. Trout, tell me what happened."

"Sir, this Lieutenant was in the Recovery Ward as Sunday services were about to begin. I instructed him to leave. There was a discussion during which he echoed my order in a sarcastic way. Rather than argue with the man, I had him removed. The opening hymn had begun to play over the intercom, and I didn't want to cause a disruption."

"Did he threaten you?"

"No Sir, not directly."

"Indirectly?"

"I saw that he was armed."

Jiggs was studying the Captain's face. He could see his eyebrows begin to lift at Trout's answer, but, whether because of some effort at control or gravity, they settled back into their normal configuration without ascending to their peak. "Well, there is a war going on you know, Lt. Trout."

The Captain turned to Jiggs. "What's your version, Lt. Morgan?"

"Sir, I was seated with one of the men from my platoon who was medevaced out here. I was helping him with his college application, which has to be in the mail by tomorrow. Lt. Trout approached us and told me that Sunday services were about to begin and to "clear out." Those were his exact words.

"I admit I was a little surprised by his choice of words and the attitude they carried with them, but I asked to talk to him privately. When we were out of earshot of my troop, I asked him to make an exception. I mentioned the application deadline, that I didn't have much time before my chopper was leaving and I didn't know when I'd be able to be back. Lt. Trout walked away without replying to my request. I assumed he'd had second thoughts, so I resumed helping my man. Next thing I knew, the Lieutenant showed up with two MPs and arrested me. As for my being armed, Sir. I doubt that was of very grave concern to Lt. Trout. As you can see, when he had me arrested, he did not have me disarmed." Jiggs patted the holstered .45 pistol on his chest.

"You have anything else to say, Lt. Trout?"

"Only that the man Lieutenant Morgan was visiting was as entitled as anyone else in the ward to hear Christian service without interruption. That, and I was shown further disrespect at the time Lt. Morgan was placed under arrest."

"Oh, how so?"

"Sir, Lt. Morgan asked me whether I intended to make him walk the plank."

Jiggs thought the Captain was going to laugh, but he stifled it, saying only, "Well, you probably frightened him."

"Sir," Jiggs said, "if I may. Lance Corporal Kaufman is Jewish. The services weren't for him. We were at least thirty feet away from any other patient."

The Captain leaned back in his chair, looked down at his steepled fingers and pursed his lips. "Lt. Trout, I don't ordinarily reprimand officers in front of other officers, but I'm going to make an exception. Are you out of your goddamn mind? Do you think we're sailing around out here just so you can proselytize the Marines? We are here to serve and support the combat troops who are fighting this war. That mission does not involve blind insistence on a bunch of chickenshit rules. Do I make myself clear?"

"Yessir."

"Very well. You're dismissed."

Trout fled.

The Captain turned to Jiggs. "Lieutenant Morgan, I half think you baited Lieutenant Trout, but maybe it would have been hard not to. Anyway, I'm sorry for your inconvenience." He stood and shook Jiggs' hand. "You're dismissed. Be safe."

"I think that went well," Hammer grinned once they were off the bridge, "but I'm afraid you missed your flight. There's not another until morning, unless there's an emergency.

Who're you with? I'll have them informed that you've been shanghaied for the night. You can bunk in my cabin. There's an extra rack."

That night Jiggs spent his most comfortable night in five months. He and Hammer nearly emptied a bottle of Jack Daniels Hammer kept secreted in his seabag in violation of the naval reg. prohibiting alcohol aboard ship. They discussed inviting Lt. Trout, but decided merely to toast him instead.

The next morning, Jiggs stopped at the ship's store and made sure he had candy for all hands on his walk out to the chopper.

20

February 1, 1968

Jiggs remembered looking down on Da Nang from the air as the plane delivering him to the war maneuvered to land. The City looked like a big grimy wart on the skin of the country. *So this is Viet Nam.*

It had felt strange to actually see it, to be just minutes from actually putting his feet on it, after seeing and hearing it depicted, debated, marched against and maligned for so long. Viet Nam was more familiar to Jiggs than some states. He had certainly seen and heard more about Viet Nam than he had seen and heard about Vermont or Delaware.

I wish I was in Vermont or Delaware right now. Jiggs paused, listening. *Even Da Nang would do.*

Don't think about fucking Delaware or Vermont. He cursed himself as he resumed moving, inspecting each spot of ground for possible booby traps before placing his foot on it. Jiggs crept with the concentration and deliberation of a diamond cutter, twisting to avoid contact with branches, silently bending aside those he couldn't avoid.

He tried to force himself not to think about Carol's letter in his pack and how much he wanted to sit down right there in the mud and read it for the tenth time and take out his paper and write her a long reply and tell her how much he loved her and how writing to her transported him out of this shithole for a time. Jiggs strained to see through the green curtain drawn a foot in front of his face, to see where his squads were, to hear the silence of their stealth and know they were moving carefully and well.

Don't think about anything except where the next step leads, Jiggs, where your men are. Concentrate.

The company had been moving on a sweep through this nameless valley for three days. It had rained the entire time. Jiggs no longer noticed the rain. It was a given. To his left and right the First and Third Platoons were on his flanks, moving with equal caution through the steaming emerald wilderness, their lines extending to the base of the steep, jungle encrusted hills at either edge of their line of advance. Jiggs' Second Platoon was straddling the trail that ran the valley's length, moving parallel to its course towards a village reportedly at the lower end, where the trail intersected with another that wound into the hills.

Search and destroy. Search and destroy. That was the litany; that was the mission. Search for all signs of hostile activity reported in the area, make contact with and destroy the enemy and all his resources. There had been no signs, no contact, no resources destroyed but their own.

Concentrate. Jiggs silently laughed at the notion. He remembered how he used to tell himself to concentrate when he was hitting in baseball, how he would call "time out" at the slightest discomfort, the tiniest distraction. If a fly buzzed around him as he took his stance, if a bead of sweat was about to drop into his eyes, if some part of his uniform suddenly began to bind, he would step out of the batter's box and shoo away the fly, wipe away the sweat, pluck at his uniform to realign it, so when he stepped back in, he could focus all his attention, concentrate all of the strength and intelligence he was capable of on hitting the baseball about to be thrown in his direction at ninety miles per hour. *Concentrate.*

As he moved, he imagined what it would be like trying to hit knowing he was probably wearing a couple of leeches somewhere on his body, or with his ass bleeding from a month of dysentery, or so tired from carrying around nearly sixty pounds of gear and the continual responsibility for the lives of forty men in hundred-degree heat without more than an hour or so of sleep, or all of the above. *Probably I would be in a slump.*

The muzzle velocity of an AK-47 rifle was 1600 miles per hour, and that was just one of the pitches in the repertoire of his opponent, who was trying to throw a little death and dismemberment his way. *I wish I could call "time" and step out of this box and never step back in.*

Shortly before 1500, Jiggs sidestepped through a maze of ferns and vines and almost stumbled over Corporal Gorman, the second squad leader, crouched at the base of a tree with his hand up as a signal to halt. Presumably, the same signal was being given all along the second platoon line, because ahead the vegetation thinned and a large clearing loomed. Jiggs estimated it was nearly two hundred meters wide and three hundred meters long. Strewn throughout the clearing were the charred remains of the village. It had been burned to the ground.

Jiggs reconnoitered the clearing with his binoculars. Through the entire open space nothing moved. There was no sound.

"You thinking what I'm thinking, Sir?" Gorman whispered.

Jiggs nodded. "Trap City."

If they stayed on line, virtually the whole platoon would be in the clearing, a large open space with no cover, surrounded by trees and undergrowth, an ambush waiting to happen. Jiggs knew they couldn't detour around it. Regimental Intelligence would want them to sift the ruins for some sign of what happened. Maybe a supply cache would turn up.

He could send a squad around either side to flush out anyone there, but they'd be spread thin. Or, he could wait until the flank platoons went through and closed behind the ruined village before going through.

"Buskirk," Jiggs motioned for his radioman, who stepped up to where Jiggs and Gorman were standing, "raise Company for me."

A moment later, Buskirlk handed him the receiver. Jiggs talked as he stared through the vines into the clearing. "Alpha One, this is Four, over."

The familiar voice of Jim Linetti, the Company Commander, who was with First Platoon on the left, crackled over the receiver. "This is Alpha One. Go ahead. Over."

"One, we're at the vil. Except the vil's gone. Burned up. We could use some flank security before we go through there. Over."

"Affirmative, Four. Sit tight. We'll take the port. Five will take the starboard. We'll close west of the clearing and pop smoke. You verify and come through."

Word was passed and the platoon hunkered down to wait in the rain. Jiggs sat with Gorman and Buskirk. Both men looked like zombies. The black and olive drab camouflage paint had blended and run together in the sweat and rain into a puke green pallor that covered their stubbled faces. Jiggs knew he looked the same. The three of them sat quietly in the mud as naturally as they might sit on a carpet in someone's living room to watch a football game on television.

"How much time you have left, Buskirk?" Jiggs knew his radioman was getting short.

"Twenty-seven days and a wake-up, Sir," the Lance Corporal immediately replied.

"What are you going to do?"

"Going to school. University of Nebraska."

"A Cornhusker. What are you going to study?"

"Haven't decided. Maybe construction management. Always liked to build things."

"Luck with that."

"Thank you, Sir."

Jiggs hated to see Buskirk leave. The two of them had shared some great ditches. Buskirk could probably get WHO-AM in Des Moines on his PRC-10. He was a magician with the radio.

Jiggs had made up his mind to train Saucers to replace Buskirk. In the two months since they had their talk, something had clicked for Saucers. He was still quiet, but he was no longer meek. He even looked bigger. Because he was small, he was ideally suited to slip into the Vietnamese-sized tunnels and bunkers the platoon would find. But tunnels were lonely places, whose owners often left surprises that made the price of occupancy, however temporary, impossibly high. There was no flank security in a tunnel. Saucers volunteered.

When food arrived from home, no one in Second Platoon hoarded it. Tradition decreed it be passed around until it was gone. However, the chain of distribution rarely reached above the squad leaders, not by design, but by circumstance. Yet, when

David Leslie received a case of beef jerky from home, he made sure Jiggs received a handful. On another occasion, when Jiggs happened to be in the area while some of second squad were talking about their lives back in the world, Leslie had shown Jiggs a picture of his girl. Saucers was no ass-kisser, but he had become an important member of the team. He had managed to swallow down his fears, and little things he did showed he thought Jiggs had helped him.

At 1630, a yellow smoke grenade was hurled into the far end of the clearing signaling all was clear. Buskirk verified the color so they could be sure they weren't walking into Charlie's smoke. Word was passed, and Second Platoon moved out, entering the clearing in a wedge-shaped formation with Second Squad in the lead.

Fog was beginning to settle in, and from where Jiggs stood with Buskirk in the tree line, the forms of the Marines retreating away from him in the mist quickly became silhouettes, floating like ghosts in the hazy rain. There was now no particular need for silence, but no one spoke, the squad and fire team leaders automatically communicating with their troops by hand signals on the infrequent occasions when communication was required. Like a great team, every man knew his job in every game situation and could execute without being told. It was just another walk in the woods for Second Platoon.

It was phony dark when Jiggs took his first step into the clearing. The towering hills to either side, the low overcast, the February monsoon, all combined in a premature dusk. Jiggs was lulled by the ease of movement in the clearing after three days of the jungle resisting his every step, and by the comfort of having two platoons of heavily armed Marines guarding his progress. Two hundred meters beyond the vil was another clearing, where they would be extracted at 0700 the next morning. They were almost home again. From some long ago English lesson, the words of an ancient poem came floating into Jiggs' mind, the title lost to time.

The curfew tolls the knell of parting day,
The lowing herd winds slowly o'er the lea,
The plowman homeward plods his weary way,
And leaves the world to darkness and to me.

That's us, just a bunch of weary plowmen on our way home from a day in the fields cultivating death.

KA-BOOM!

A thunderous explosion to Jiggs' right split the air, its concussion staggering him, its heat momentarily evaporating the rain. Booby trap. Someone had stepped...

KA-BOOM!

An identical explosion to his direct front shook the earth, mingling with someone's screams. Just to Jiggs' left, Gorman began to sprint toward the sound of the screams. Jiggs sensed the movement more than saw it and whirled to yell, "Hold..."

KA-BOOM!

The third explosion within five seconds ripped across the clearing, this one behind the main body of the platoon on ground it had already crossed, on ground where a moment before Corporal Gale Gorman lived, before he and thirty cubic feet of earth vanished, flattening Jiggs and Buskirk with its blast, showering them with human debris.

"Mines," someone was yelling, the sound of despair. "Oh, God, we're in a fuckin' minefield!"

Someone else was screaming, beseeching by the formless sound of his agony help that could not come. Second Platoon was frozen in place.

The sounds reached Jiggs as if they were coming from far away, as if he was coming off a mountain or in a descending airplane, and the pressure in his ears was yet to equalize, blocking most of the sound. In almost twenty years of sports, no blow Jiggs had ever received, not even some of the tremendous hits the mighty Bjournquist had laid on him, no blow could begin to compare with the one that leveled him from the mine that had killed Gorman. Like a steam iron chasing a wrinkle, the blast had pressed all the air out of him.

Now he lay, alive, that much he knew, nearly deaf, listening to the faint sound of Sgt. Lefler yelling for everyone to hold their positions and to the dim, unidentified voice screaming from somewhere beyond. Jiggs gasped and sucked at the sodden air, struggling to re-inflate. He was crumpled on his right side in an L-shaped configuration that allowed him to take a visual inventory of his body parts, although none of them had begun to feel or move. Jiggs wondered if the absence of sensation meant he was paralyzed. Gradually, however, probably within less than a minute although it seemed much longer, feeling began to return. Jiggs rolled off his right arm onto his stomach and tried to raise his head. The vertigo was tremendous, but he forced it up, and little by little it began to clear.

"Lieutenant! Lieutenant! Where the fuck is the Lieutenant?" Someone, probably Sgt. Lefler, was shouting.

"Over here." The sound of Jiggs' own voice was faint. "Buskirk, you all right?"

No reply. Jiggs peered through the semi-dark, trying to focus eyes that felt as if they were reels spinning in a slot machine. Twelve feet away, half way between Jiggs and the crater that had formerly been Gorman, Buskirk lay face down in the ooze, his head at an angle to his body that left no doubt there was no longer a working relationship between the two. One of Buskirk's legs was missing, and his radio hung by one strap.

Good-bye, short-timer. Someone else's going to have to build all those buildings for you.

"Alpha Four, this is Alpha One. Alpha Four, this is Alpha One. Do you read me. Come in, Alpha Four, over." Jim Linetti's voice sounded in the gathering darkness. Buskirk's radio still worked.

Jiggs leaned in that direction, intending to start towards it but caught himself. *Remember where you are.*

Ever so cautiously, he wiggled out of his own pack and dragged himself to one knee, being beyond careful to bear no weight on any ground where he had not already been. Well to his right and fifty feet ahead of him, he could just make out the familiar form of Sgt. Lefler.

"Sgt. Lefler, I'm over here. I'm all right. Stay where you are. Everybody stay where you are. Pass the word." Jiggs could barely hear himself yelling.

Shouts echoed left and right as Jiggs' order passed along the platoon line. Nobody was tempted to disobey.

Hollering back and forth, Jiggs and Sergeant Lefler and the two surviving squad leaders exchanged casualty reports and laid their plans. Word was passed for each man to turn around in place and lie down, first taking out his bayonet and very gently probing every inch of the ground on which he was about to bear weight, the object being to detect, but not detonate, any more mines. If one was encountered, pile up some dirt to mark it. Then go around. Assume there is another right next door until the blade of your bayonet tells you otherwise. In that way, inch your way back out the way you came, feeling ahead of yourself for trip wires. Go slow. Be patient. Good luck.

Sawyer, the corpsman, had already made his way to Lance Corporal Karnewski, the wounded man in the third squad. PFC Wollman, the casualty from the second explosion was dead. Numbly, Jiggs watched as the spectral forms of the second squad, the men nearest to him, most of whom had already turned to the rear, knelt and with surgeon's care began to poke, all but one.

Somebody laughed. "Hey, this is like finger fuckin' the ground."

"You better hope she don't come."

"Shut up!" Jiggs snapped, his ears a little better. "Pay attention to what you're doing. No grab ass!"

Jesus, you might deplore their taste, but you had to admire their nerve. Nobody but another grunt would believe it, not the families back home who loved them and thought they knew their sons and brothers and husbands, not even the Marines in the rear, the clerks and cooks and fat-assed staff officers like Yak, who wrote up the troops for dirty boots or not saluting the moment they came in from the field.

As second squad crawled back in his direction Jiggs thought for the umpteenth time about the two different wars and the luck of the draw that put him and his men in this mess and guys like Yak at a club somewhere having a beer. He was about to turn and work his way over to Buskirk's body and the radio, when he noticed a single upright silhouette out well beyond where the second squad was inching along. He was sure it was a Marine. There was nothing more than two feet high in the whole clearing except this one stationary form frozen in the twilight.

"Callman," Jiggs shouted to a member of the squad he recognized, "who's that standing out there? Who was out by Wollman when he got it?"

Lance Corporal Callman stopped stabbing the ground, raised himself onto his right elbow and squinted over his left shoulder. He was silent for a few seconds. "Jesus Christ, it's Saucers!"

It was Saucers. Two months of being brave had used up his last reserve of courage. When Wollman blew up behind him, spinning him around to see fragments of his friend falling to earth, David Leslie's frightened feet had taken the last step they would ever take in combat. He stood paralyzed, watching in an unseeing, uncomprehending way as Jiggs turned the platoon around and got it started back towards the trees. Shivering in the rain, he heard the whistles, then the yells of the Lieutenant, as they tried to get his attention.

David Leslie eyed the ground in front of the toes of his boots. What manner of device waited beneath its plain, brown wrapper, speckled with puddles in every indentation? Which were his boot prints and which were low places left by little yellow men digging a hole and placing a bomb in it, carefully arming it, covering it up so its trigger lay just below the surface, laughing as they finished their work about how some day David Leslie would step on it and blow his legs off?

Jiggs hollered himself hoarse and received no response of any kind from the figure rooted sixty meters in front of him.

Suddenly, a wailing cry every man in the clearing that afternoon would remember until the day he died, pierced the rain. "Please help me. In the name of God, someone please help me!"

It frightened Jiggs to hear its ring, to think about the terror that had driven its pitch somewhere up beyond the range of voices of sane men. Jiggs was afraid Saucers would start to run.

"Stay where you are, Leslie. I'm coming to get you!"

Digging into his pack, Jiggs withdrew a ball of parachute cord, tied one end to his belt and the other to his pack that he was leaving behind. Then he picked up his bayonet and began plowing, holding the hilt in the very tips of his fingers, letting it sink in the mud almost of its own weight. Concentration was now no problem. No safecracker ever felt for the click of tumblers any more attentively than Jiggs felt and listened for the contact of that bayonet blade with anything other than wet dirt. *With this kind of concentration, even I could bat .500.* Trouble was, in the game he was playing, it was very important to hit 1.000.

Each time he would pull himself ahead, he would turn and unroll the cord behind him, not pulling it tight, but letting it lie slack along his course. Jiggs intended to walk back, and he wanted to know where he'd been.

Every few seconds he would look up to check on Leslie, to make sure he hadn't decided to come to meet him. In Leslie's condition, Jiggs had no confidence in his ability to feel his way out, should he suddenly decide to try. But Leslie remained motionless, a statue. *This war's answer to the fuckin' Iwo Jima Monument.*

After twenty minutes, he had covered approximately fifteen meters, a fourth of the way to where Leslie stood, when he either felt or heard a slight metallic "ting." For the moment, his heart stopped and his eyes squeezed shut. He felt the sweat gush from already overworked perspiration glands.

"Um ... hello there..." he said out loud to himself, opening his eyes, happy to find he was still alive. He swallowed the sour tasting bile that had welled up in his throat and was burning the roof of his mouth. He veered left.

Inch by inch, he crept along, while Leslie stood petrified before him, a pillar of salt like Lot's wife, who had looked at sin once too often. Jiggs shook his head to rid himself of the image. No more Bible, no more religion. Even during Leslie's miraculous about face in the two months following their talk,

Jiggs had felt guilty about using Leslie's belief in God to keep him with the platoon. Leslie didn't belong here, and Jiggs knew it. *Hell, I don't belong here. No one in the platoon belongs here, but Saucers...*

Ever since the boy had joined the platoon, Jiggs had known Leslie had belonged less than himself, less than all the rest. He could have gotten him out. Right then, right after they talked, he could have gone and started the paperwork – unfit for combat – and David Leslie would have been in a chopper leaving 410 the next day.

Once at Iowa, in a course on Modern European History, Jiggs had heard a professor deliver a lecture condemning the way both sides in World War I had used God in their propaganda. Jiggs felt the sting of that long ago indictment and regretted what he had said to Leslie. What gave him the right to use God to keep a terrified boy in harm's way?

An hour passed. Jiggs glanced at his watch. Nearly 1800. He felt relieved. There had been no more explosions behind him. The rest of the platoon must be safe in the trees by this time.

Twenty feet from Leslie, Jiggs' bayonet once more told him to take evasive action, and he veered again. Now he was fifteen feet from the boy. Holding his bayonet in his right hand, Jiggs groped ahead with his left, feeling the mud, testing the air, when he felt something brush the back of his hand as he drew it back towards himself.

A spasm of fear stabbed at his stomach. *What was that?* He couldn't see, and he wasn't going to wave his arms around on a voyage of discovery until he could. Little by little he probed the arm's length of ground between his head and whatever it was his hand had touched, then he moved forward.

It was a wire stretched about a foot off the ground. *How did Leslie manage to avoid tripping over it? Which way does it go?* It was too fine, and Jiggs couldn't see either end in the gloom.

There was a low bush about six feet to his left, and Jiggs decided that was probably the anchor, so he went right, probing the ground and groping the air as he went. Six feet or so in that direction he came to an old c-ration can attached to the wire. Resting just inside its rim, too fat to fit down inside, was a grenade, also American made, with the pin out, the spoon held down between the rim and the lethal little pineapple delicately balanced on the lip of the can, waiting for the slightest jar to send it toppling. Jiggs took another sip of bile.

He couldn't just pick it up and throw it. Usually the VC removed the fuse, so as soon as the spoon flew up, it would explode, no three second delay. Jiggs kept rubber bands around his own grenades, a precaution against a loose pin. He was about to borrow one of those and use it to hold down the spoon, when he was struck by the thought that the gook who put it there had a sense of humor. Here were all these pressure plate mines buried throughout the field, and the guy who buried them probably imagined all these dumb-ass Marines blowing themselves up and jacking off their bayonets trying to get the hell out of there. Why not throw in a different kind of boobytrap, one they wouldn't be looking for given their other distractions. Might be good for a laugh.

That kind of humor made Jiggs want to look at the other end of the wire before he touched the grenade in front of him. *Is it really just tied to that bush?* Sure enough, a few minutes later, Jiggs found himself staring at another can tied to the other end of the same wire with another unpinned grenade on its brim beneath the bush. Wondering how either failed to trigger from the concussion of the earlier explosions, Jiggs slid the rubber bands off two of his own grenades. He put one band around his wrist and slowly, deliberately, with the kind of grasp he would have used to pick up a baby, picked up the grenade. Gently, ever mindful of the fish on the other end of the line, he inched the remaining band over the hinge and spoon and around the body, doubling it to increase the tension, leaving no possibility of slack. Holding the grenade tightly against his chest, he crawled on two legs and one arm back to the first grenade he had found, banded it and set both down on a little pyramid of mud he scraped up with his bayonet to mark their location. Once he had Saucers out of there, the platoon could use them for target practice.

Jiggs stopped and took several deep breaths. It seemed like he'd been fucking around with those grenades for three hours. The mute Leslie stood rigid and shivering less than fifteen feet away. Jiggs fought back his impatience. The temptation simply to walk over and get the catatonic boy and beat it the hell back down the cord was almost overwhelming.

Passing where the wire had been, Jiggs began to talk to Leslie in a low voice, the way he'd heard Doc talk to skittish animals so many times when he was treating them.

"This is a rough one, huh, Dave? We're almost out of here now ... you and me, we're going to walk right down that cord and out of this awful place together ... you and me, Dave ... you and me."

"You and me ..." Infield chatter on the diamond of death. Jiggs kept it up as he sifted his way right up to the toes of Leslie's boots. As he came near, he warned the boy, "Stay still." Jiggs wanted to check out the ground a couple of feet to either side just as a precaution. Leslie said nothing, but Jiggs thought his great eyes flickered, a glimmer of understanding floating in those oceans of suffering. Jiggs put his hand on Leslie's ankle,

just to touch him, just to let him feel that he was not alone, that help had arrived, that someone was going to take care of him.

A breeze had come up as Jiggs worked his way out to the boy, thinning the fog, and the rain had slowed to a sprinkle. There was more light now than when Jiggs started. He was relieved. He had been worried the fog, if it worsened, might prevent the choppers from landing next morning for the company's extraction.

Finishing his exploration of the dirt in a three-foot radius around them, Jiggs stood up for the first time in almost two hours.

Crack ... crack ... crack, ... crack...

An automatic weapon sounded, and a sniper round in the back drove David Leslie into Jiggs' arms. More rounds snapped past and into the mud around them.

Jiggs dove for the ground, dragging Leslie with him. Before he even landed, the perimeter of the clearing erupted with savage fire from one hundred fifty Marines who for more than an hour and a half had helplessly watched a lone man do the Viet Nam version of a broken field run through death to save someone whom they all knew, but for the grace of God, might have been any one of them. Trigger fingers squeezed out accumulated fears and tensions, and from the second platoon area an M-60 sprayed the treetops for snipers, its tracers lacing the twilight with the machine gun's fiery stitch. From somewhere in what Jiggs figured must be third platoon's area, another M-60 added its deadly stutter to the choir's song.

Jiggs thought he was hit. His left calf felt like it had a horrible cramp, and his left side at the bottom of his rib cage was on fire, but he had no time to investigate. The round that struck Leslie's back had come tearing out his right breast, leaving a three-inch hole in its wake. Air bubbles were perco-lating up through the blood in Leslie's wound like it was some kind of thermal mud pot.

Jiggs cradled him in his arms. Saucers was gasping for breath, and each time he exhaled, blood foamed out his chest, the wound making a raspy, sucking sound as Leslie's damaged lungs fought for air they could no longer hold.

Jiggs was frantic. He knew he had to plug that hole immediately or Saucers would die. He would probably die anyway. But with what? Jiggs tore at his left boot, failing to notice that it, too, was soaked with blood, fumbling with the laces with his free hand, holding Leslie with the other, telling him to "hang on."

Saucers coughed blood as Jiggs tugged at his sock.

"Sir," the boy spoke in an unintentional whisper.

"Don't talk, Dave. Save your strength," Jiggs jerked his sock free, even more intent now on what he was doing than he had been coming through the mines. "Everything's going to be all right," he lied, twisting the filthy rag of a sock and inserting it in the wound, trying not to jam it, trying to make a seal, something, anything, to help Leslie breathe.

"Sir..." Leslie gasped and convulsed, closing and opening his eyes as he relaxed a little. They were filled with tears. "Sir ... I'm sorry."

"Never mind. Never mind." Jiggs, using Doc's bedside manner, hugging the boy even tighter. "You're okay now. You're okay now."

David Leslie was okay now. He was completely relaxed. He had stopped breathing, no longer in the Valley of the Shadow of Death. He was lying across Jiggs' lap, dead.

Jiggs Morgan was too empty to cry. He struggled to his feet with Saucers still in his arms. His whole left side from his shoulder to his toes felt like someone had beaten it with a bat, but he didn't care. *"One thing more! One thing more!"* Coach Bucyk's litany of discipline rang in his ears. *"You can still do one thing more!"*

Untroubled by the thought of snipers, surrendering himself to fate, Jiggs tight-roped back down his parachute cord, limping towards home. Halfway back, he was met by Sgt. Lefler and Sawyer, the corpsman, but Jiggs silently nodded for them to turn around. David Leslie was a burden he would have to bear.

You and me, Dave…you and me.

21

February 4, 1968

Saturday morning. Outside, the drifts in the yard were brimming at Carol's window sill and snow was continuing to fall. Inside, Glenn Campbell on the stereo, a second cup of coffee and *Up The Down Staircase*, a book about some other teacher's travails, for Carol a busman's holiday.

Carol, still in her pajamas, curled up under a blanket in her one easy chair and searched for the page she'd been reading when she fell asleep last night.

Weekends were tough, no classroom full of six year olds for distraction, something she was in particular need of at the moment. There had been no letter from Jiggs in a week. That had never happened before. If only she knew where Jiggs was, what he was doing at that very moment.

Less than ten pages later the doorbell rang.

"Just a minute." Carol ran for her robe.

Tugging the belt tight around her waist, she stood on tiptoes to peek through the window near the top of her front door. There stood a Marine officer in a khaki overcoat with captain's bars on the shoulder. Carol's knees buckled. Her face started to crumble. She sucked in her breath so hard her throat burned.

In the movies, the soldiers only showed up at your door when someone died, otherwise a telegram.

Carol looked at the doorknob as if it was red hot. She didn't want to touch it, to open the door to the confirmation of her worst fear, to the explanation for the absence of letters, but she had no choice.

Carol opened the door a crack. "Hel ... hello."

"Mrs. Morgan? Carol Morgan?"

"Yes."

"Mrs. Morgan, I'm John Danko. I served with your husband in Viet Nam. I have word of him. May I come in?"

Carol opened the door a few more inches. The Captain was big, taller than Jiggs, thicker. Danko. She remembered the name from Jiggs' letters. A good guy.

Carol tried not to stammer. "Please."

She took a step back, and Captain Danko entered, taking off his hat as he did so. He had red hair and freckles, not Carol's image of the Marine on the recruiting poster, but unnoticed by her amid this moment of near panic.

"Mrs. Morgan, Jiggs has been wounded, but he has not been killed."

Carol tensed herself even more tightly at the news. She felt as if she was going to disintegrate, to collapse into a pile of a million tiny pieces.

"Wounded..."

"Yes, Ma'am. I'm afraid I don't know where or how severely. I have a telegram saying only that he was wounded. Because Jiggs is my friend, I wanted you to hear it from someone who knows him."

Carol nodded at his words, saying nothing, convulsing inside her suddenly rigid shell.

"I am in charge of the Marine recruiting office here in Cedar Rapids. When the message came in, I tried to get more information, but so far have been unsuccessful other than to learn that Jiggs is in Kue Hospital on Okinawa. I have an address of the Marine Liaison Office at the hospital for you. If and when I learn more, I will let you know immediately."

Danko paused, looking at Carol standing silently facing him, tears streaming down her cheeks.

"Maybe it would help if you sit down." He nodded towards the chair where Carol's blanket lay rumpled beneath her open book.

Carol didn't sit down as much collapse on top of the blanket when her legs decided they were too numb to carry her any farther. The image of Jiggs lying in some hospital bed fifteen thousand miles away from anyone who loved him, from her, Carol, the person who loved him most, really loved him, seared her brain. She wondered if Jiggs was scared.

It was nearly impossible for Carol to think of Jiggs being scared. Mad, happy, sad, puzzled, disappointed – all these feelings, yes, she had seen all these. But scared? No. The fact that Carol had never seen Jiggs frightened made the possibility that he might be frightened now, that he might be fearful about the rest of his life, all the more excruciating for her. Carol had been frightened for Jiggs ever since he went to Viet Nam, ever since he joined the Marines. But that vague, subconscious dread with which she'd been living for the last two years wasn't a patch on the fear that ached through her as she thought of him lying alone in some hospital bed so far away. She looked up at Captain Danko, who had remained standing.

"Mrs. Morgan, I think that my having come in person may not have been a good idea. It may have frightened you more than a telegram. I'm sorry if that's the case. I had hoped to assuage your fears, let you know personally on behalf of the entire Corps that everything possible is being done on Jiggs' behalf, no half-stepping.

"Before I leave, is there anything I can do for you? Any questions I can answer?"

In an effort to summon speech, Carol sucked in and exhaled one of the biggest breaths she had ever taken. "No ... no. Thank you for coming. I mean it. I've been so worried anyway and then to see you there ... I do appreciate you being here. I guess I do have a couple of questions. Where is Okinawa? I mean, I know it's somewhere out in the western Pacific, but I have no idea where."

"It's part of Japan, down at the south end. It's been administered by the United States ever since World War II. There are several Marine bases there."

"What's the time difference? Can I call?"

"Not sure. I think they're fifteen hours ahead of us. I will get you that information. I don't know whether there is phone service available to patients. Mostly it's radio phone, which isn't very satisfactory for personal calls."

Captain Danko departed.

Instead of just burrowing back into her chair with the book she knew she could no longer read, Carol got dressed. As she did so, she looked around the apartment. There was so little of Jiggs in the place.

She had some calls to make, but couldn't face them yet. She grabbed her purse, went out the door, came back in and put on her coat, hat, gloves and scarf and went back out, heading for her car to drive she didn't know where.

An hour of creeping along snow-swept highways later she pulled to the curb in front of Lindy's. If the car had been a horse, it would have been said, "it's a good thing the horse knows the way," because Carol didn't remember the twenty-five miles she'd covered between Cedar Rapids and Iowa City. All she knew was that here was the bed she and Jiggs had shared more than any other, and she had Jiggs' key.

4 February 1968
Dear Carol,

By this time, I'm sure you will have been informed that I've been wounded. Don't worry. It's nothing serious – no bones or organs, just my left calf and side. I'm on Okinawa now. Charlie started some big offensive over the Vietnamese New Year, and I guess we're taking lots of casualties. I got moved here because they need all the beds in country for those.

So, you see, in a way I'm lucky – to be out of Viet Nam, I mean. But I've come to one conclusion, where this war is concerned. We're all unlucky. If you can tell me one reason I, or any other American should be over in that shithole country fighting, I'd like to know. Can you figure out any way America would be worse off if we quit fighting right now? I once read about some Indian who surrendered to the cavalry saying, "I will fight no more forever." Johnson and his so-called "experts" ought to follow that guy's advice, at least where Viet Nam's concerned.

Sorry to sound so pissed off, but I've seen too much evidence to the contrary to keep kidding myself that anyone in Washington knows what they're doing.

I think about coming home and how the war
will be over for us then, but it won't be, because it will
still be going on unless something unbelievable
happens like McCarthy getting elected. For a lot of
people, I don't think this war is ever going to be over.
It's just going to be different.

Please write to me all you can. Your letters are
my one bright spot.

Love, Jiggs

Carol finished reading the letter and lowered her hands
to her lap. She bit the corner of her lower lip, looked up from the
sheets of paper she was holding and gazed out the window.
Outside, the February wind was scouring the nearby houses and
trees. Overhead gray clouds stirred. Carol's apartment was
small, and she had tried to make it cozy, filling it with warm
colors and soft furniture. She shivered and looked back down at
the letter resting in her lap. It contained no new sentiments.
Jiggs' ideas were the same. Nevertheless, his letter made her feel
cold, as if it had somehow opened a door and let in the wind.

22

March 1968

While Carol pondered Jiggs, Jiggs was pondering baseball.

What would you rather do, Dummy? Jiggs limped back to the hospital's officers' ward. *Play baseball or go back to Viet Nam?*

It wasn't that simple. Jiggs had been recuperating on Okinawa for over a month. For the last two weeks, he had been allowed to come and go as he pleased once the doctors checked his daily progress. Four days ago he had seen a poster at some Marine O Club advertising tryouts for the Okinawa Marine baseball team. He had played for the base team at Quantico during the latter phases of his training. He thought he could probably make this team, even with his limp, which was getting better every day. Marine baseball wasn't the Big Ten. *But do I want to?*

What he wanted to do was get as far away from the war and the Marine Corps and politicians and snipers, and himself as he could. He was about to be returned to duty. Tryouts were two days away. Do well, and he wouldn't have to go back to the war, the Platoon, 410, or wherever the hell the Platoon was these days. But at this point things became confused.

Where is Second Platoon anyway? Jiggs had had a note from Jim Linetti ten days earlier saying the Company was still on 410, but expected to be moving out of the area shortly. He didn't say where. The fact that he cared where his platoon was and how it was doing was at the root of his dilemma. *Is it still my platoon?* He hated the idea of someone else commanding "his" platoon, risking "his" people's lives. No one else could care so much.

He wrote to Larry Nelson about his quandary. Larry, who was still back on 410, replied that Jiggs had been wounded trying to save someone he had persuaded to stay in the war and asking Jiggs how it would feel if he did any less. Maybe not the answer Jiggs wanted to hear, but an honest one.

"Smells like poultry," Hood used to say whenever they saw some timid behavior where bold was called for. "Cluck, Cluck." For Jiggs to be laying on a soft rack with clean sheets in Okinawa, eyeballing round-eyed nurses and thinking about playing baseball, while Second Platoon was catching hell somewhere in the rain smelled like poultry.

Jiggs stood in the doorway of the Marine Liason Office at Kue. Major Al Carpenter looked up from his desk and nodded Jiggs in.

"Major, I'm going to be released from the hospital shortly and, if possible, I need to know what my next assignment is going to be. How can I find out?"

"What do you want it to be, Jiggs?"

Jiggs sighed. There it was, the question with the real answer not among his choices.

"If I can go back to my old platoon, that's what I want to do. But if that's not possible, I would prefer not to start all over with some new platoon."

"Jiggs, I don't know for sure, but you've been away from your platoon for more than a month. I think there's a new lieutenant in place. Besides, just because you can walk around – you know as well as I, that doesn't mean you're fit for combat. And there's the fact that you've been written up for a Silver Star for your attempt to save that kid. My guess is that you're going back to battalion staff at 2/4, maybe in the S-2 shop, at least for the time being. If an opening occurs, you might get a company after a while ... or you might get another platoon, depending on whether your health is good enough. I've talked to Colonel Katkavage, the Battalion CO, and that's the way he's thinking."

Great. Virtue rewarded. A desk next to Yak.

Jiggs rose. "Thank you, Sir. That helps."

Two days later, Jiggs tried out and made the team. Cluck, fucking Cluck!

February 10, 1968
Dear Jiggs,

I don't know whether to laugh or cry. Cry to know you are hurt, laugh to know you are out of danger, at least for a time.

I wish I could be there to take care of you, to bathe you and fluff your pillow and bring you a beer and all the other things nurses do and some that they don't, or at least they better not. I have some medicine for you called "love," that is guaranteed to make you well. I'm storing it up and when you come home, I will administer massive doses.

I told Doc you've been wounded, and he seemed to take it okay once he was assured you were all right. Darcy came up from school to be with him.

Roger knows and says he's already sent you some books to read when you're not pinching nurses. I told Lindy, and she took it very hard. Lindy's aged a lot this year, Jiggs, and I think it's because she's so worried about you. Please write her a cheerful letter to convince her you're okay. You're the only one she'll believe.

It's late, and I have to turn out the light. I hate to stop writing, but I will go to sleep with dreams of you.

Take care of yourself, Morgan.

I love you, Carol

23

March 1968

Death, taxes and Officer of the Day. Jiggs had been out of the hospital and on full duty status only two weeks and already he was OD, out making his midnight rounds of the base.

"Corporal, what are those lights off to the right of the road up ahead? Pull over and stop this side of 'em so our lights will be on whatever it is."

The lights they saw were the headlights of a small red car that had run off the road and into an embankment. There was a young woman, who at first glance looked like an American, standing beside the car. As Jiggs and his driver approached, she waved for them to stop.

It was Camilla Waron. Jiggs recognized her as soon as he got out of the Jeep, but he did not identify himself. If she recognized him, she gave no sign. He was twenty pounds lighter than when she'd last seen him, and now he was limping. *No reason she should recognize me. School teachers on Okinawa see lots of guys.*

"The driver's still in the car." Camilla gestured in that direction. "He's unconscious, more drunk, I think, than hurt. But I can't get him out of there."

Jiggs walked around to the driver's side and opened the door. The young man in the driver's seat had fallen over to his right and was lying half way across the front seat. He had a bloody nose, but it was obvious the impact had little to do with his loss of consciousness. He was snoring.

"Never seen anyone bleed to death through the nose." Durward Westphal hollered in Jiggs' brain.

The sleeping man stirred only slightly as Jiggs shoved him aside, slipped behind the wheel and started the car. He put it in reverse and attempted to back away from the bank, but the front wheels had gone into a shallow ditch at the base of the embankment and the car wasn't powerful enough to pull itself out. The engine kept dying.

Jiggs got out of the car. "If we get a chain and pull you out, can you drive this guy home?"

"Do you mean, am I sober enough?"

Jiggs looked at her and shrugged. "Take it any way you like."

Camilla recoiled at the tone of his reply. "I prefer Coke, Lieutenant Morgan. Remember? You're the only person I know who drinks two beers at one time."

His abundance of beers at the time they met floated into Jiggs' memory.

"I can drive, Lieutenant, but before you run off for the chain, tell me what you're doing here. I thought you were in country defending me. Why are you limping?"

"I was transferred back. I'm stationed at Camp Courtney now."

"And the limp? Were you wounded?"

"Got hurt playing baseball." Jiggs had no wish to discuss his wounds or their circumstances.

"Baseball?" Camilla's tone asked, "What are you doing playing baseball in the middle of the war?"

Jiggs was on the point of responding that it made a whole lot more sense than killing people, but didn't. *What's the use?* Why get into a philosophic discussion with some woman he hardly knew, especially standing on the side of a road at 0100 in the Okinawa damp and headlights' glare?

"Yeah, baseball. That's what I'm doing here ... playing baseball."

"Excuse me, Lieutenant." Jiggs' driver pointed to the front of Camilla's car. "That ditch the front wheels are in isn't very deep. If the lady can drive, you and I might be able to push her out."

Camilla got in and Jiggs and the Corporal wedged in front of the small car in the space between the bumper and the embankment where the two weren't quite touching. Standing with their backs to the car and their feet against the bank, they gripped the underside of the bumper.

"Hope she gets it in reverse," the Corporal muttered, evoking an image of the two of them pancaked against the bank.

When Camilla let out the clutch, they heaved against the front of the car, pushing back and lifting at the same time. That was all it took. Without great effort, the car rolled free.

Camilla got out, raised the hood and peered inside, checking the radiator.

"Nothing appears damaged." She closed the hood and turned towards Jiggs and the Corporal.

"Thank you, Corporal Jackson. That was a good idea."

Jiggs liked the way she didn't have to be told the car was all right and the way she thanked Jackson by name and how she must have recognized his rank from his insignia, because the Corporal's nametag bore only his last name. Most of the women he'd seen interact with enlisted men had been the wives of new officers, only recently mindful of and still uncomfortable with the idea of rank. Rather than say something wrong to some troop, they usually said nothing at all. *She seems perfectly at ease.*

"Jiggs," Camilla said, using his first name for the first time, "thanks for stopping. I'm glad to see you again. I'll bet your wife and father are glad to know you're safe."

Jiggs nodded, but said nothing. She didn't sound finished.

"Hope you don't mind my saying this," that voice so relaxed, betraying no hint of anxiety over whatever she was about to say, even while half-apologizing for saying it, "but somehow you don't seem the way I remember you."

Then she smiled. "Probably just my imagination. Anyway, my roommate and I are having a party next Saturday night and you're welcome to come. I'd like you to come. Bring some of your friends, if you want. It's nothing very organized. I mean nobody will be 'with' anybody. It's just a bunch of people we know. Here's the address." She wrote it on a piece of paper and handed it to him.

"Glad to help." Jiggs held the car door open for her. "Uh ... about the party ... I'm pretty sure we play that night, so I probably can't make it, but thanks for the invitation."

"Well, come if you can." She drove off, her companion still snoring beside her.

"Killing time," an expression Jiggs had heard a thousand times, but never considered before his return to Okinawa. Throughout his life, he had always been so swept up by the moment, good or bad, that, with the exception of his brief earlier visit to Okinawa spent waiting for a flight to the war, he had never had the sense of emptily waiting for future events. Even while patrolling out of 410, there had been so much to think about, so many precautions to take, so many other people to look out for, that he never had the sense of prolonged waiting.

Now Jiggs was killing time. He was just waiting for days, weeks, months he knew he would never get back, to pass, in order to arrive at something, the end of his time on Okinawa, that required nothing of him except patience. Occasionally Hood had used the expression "throwing cards at a hat," and Jiggs was tempted to try. In the midst of his ennui, *Zhivago* arrived.

The novel had been in the care package of books Hood sent him while he was in the hospital. In the empty days and nights between games, practices and meals, Jiggs had sat alone in his room writing letters to Carol, Doc, Lindy, Hood, reading in between – killing time. From the moment he opened the front cover until he finished the last word of the collection of poems at the back of *Dr. Zhivago*, Jiggs wrote no letters.

The odyssey of the gentle Russian doctor captivated him as no other story ever had. Zhivago's life so perfectly expressed Jiggs' own feelings, it was as if he was seeing with Zhivago's eyes, breathing with his lungs, feeling with his heart. As he read, the walls fell away, and Zhivago's anguish and his own became one. Why wouldn't the world leave him alone? Why couldn't he make his harmless way without being torn from his family, without being shot by strangers, without having become a killer?

More realistic, perhaps, than the dreamer Zhivago, Jiggs knew the system. He knew whom to salute, whose jokes to laugh at, when and how to move and act efficiently and aggressively, despite his feelings. Jiggs knew how to succeed, but more and more he came to hate himself for continuing to try, for even being part of a system, the objective of which seemed to be the infliction of one's will on others.

He closed the cover at the end of the final page and stared at the ceiling, listening to the cold rain pound the roof above. "Son of a bitch," he sighed to Carol twelve thousand miles away. "Why do things happen this way?"

March 13, 1968
Dear Carol,
    Hood's books finally arrived safe and sound. Among them is a copy of *Dr. Zhivago*. No wonder the Russians banned it – it's about a man who just wants to be left alone. I'm surprised Johnson hasn't banned it or at least the Corps. Somebody better tell the Commandant.
    Glad to see Nixon says he's got a way to end the war if he's elected this Fall.
    What utter bullshit! He's real smart keeping it to himself. I'd hate for his secret to get out and have someone else end it early and spoil Dick's election chances.
    Speaking of chances, I received a letter from Larry Nelson, that Navy guy I met at 410. He's still there. He told me Jim Linetti was killed by a grenade two weeks ago. Meanwhile I play baseball.
    I tried to write to Jim's wife, but I couldn't because most of the stuff I was saying wouldn't have been any comfort. How could I say that her husband was one of the best men I ever knew and in the next breath say the grenade that killed him was probably stolen from us and might even have been thrown by one of us, fighting to secure ground we probably abandoned the next day and will surely abandon eventually?

Carol, I've just stopped and read what I've written. I'm sorry I can't summon more cheer, but if I don't tell you how I feel, who can I tell? Nothing that's happened makes me love you less. Just the opposite – you're the only one I care about.

I guess I'll bring this to a close and go to sleep. Maybe things will be a little better in the morning. Ha, Ha.

Love, Jiggs

The game Saturday was at Kadena Air Base, which was the only field on the Island with lights. Kadena was also the base where Camilla Waron lived.

The Marines won both the game and the brawl in the fourth inning. John Kelvecchio, their second baseman, who, Jiggs figured, would probably be in prison within six months of his return to civilian life, slugged the Air Force first baseman for tagging him too hard on an attempted pick-off and both benches emptied. It was an important game, as games go. Going in, both teams were undefeated and tied for the league lead. Air Force was the defending champion. There was a large crowd, mostly Air Force, but the Marines in the stands made the most noise. A couple of players from Air Force had carried bats into the fight, although no one was hurt. Jiggs never left the bench.

"Afraid I might hurt my leg," he explained, as the exhilarated warriors filed back in to the dugout after the umps regained control. No one questioned that. They had all seen the fresh scars on his leg and side. He was the only one of them who had been in combat. They respected where he had been and what had happened to him.

The truth was, he didn't fight because he didn't give a shit. The thought of the fight, particularly the sight of the bats, depressed him more than ever. *Now even games are fucked up.* He didn't think he could bear the triumphant bus ride home or the empty room waiting for him once he got there. On the way out of the dressing room to the bus, he told Paul Stromberg, the coach, that he'd catch a cab later and walked off into the dark.

Camilla Waron glanced away for a moment from the people with whom she was standing and saw Jiggs in the open door. Without saying anything, she left the group and came across the small, crowded room towards him.

"Hi, Soldier. You come here often?"

"First time." Jiggs looked around. "Where's the bar?"

He followed her into the kitchen, where she handed him a Heinekin. "Your brand, I believe. It's stuffy in here. Let's go outside."

It was a warm night for late March and there were as many people outside as in, scattered in groups about the yard.

Jiggs and Camilla leaned against the front fender of a small blue car parked behind the house. "Glad you could come. No game tonight?"

Jiggs shook his head. "Played here ... at that ball diamond over by the base gym. Know where that is?"

Camilla knew. "How'd you do? Was it a good game?"

"I suppose. We won. There was a fight ... I'm pretty tired of fighting."

"You didn't hurt your leg playing baseball, did you, Jiggs? You hurt it fighting. That's why you came back to Okinawa, isn't it?"

Jiggs nodded, staring at the ground, saying nothing.

"What happened?"

Jiggs took a deep breath and slowly began to tell Camilla about Saucers and the minefield.

Camilla stood just to his right, almost touching him, turning her head slightly, looking at him across her shoulder, lips pursed, thinking about what she was hearing. Now and then she would ask a question, but mostly she just listened, soaking up not only the words, but the sadness and anger the words contained.

"So that's what happened. Five guys dead in the rain in a burned out vil not one American in a million even knows existed and fewer care." Jiggs flipped a twig he'd been twisting as he talked into the air and watched it fall to the ground.

"Did you have to write the families of the men who died?"

"Don't know if I had to, because of being medevaced, I mean, but I did."

"What did you say?"

"I lied. I told them about their sons' and husbands' courage and loyalty and capacity for friendship – those parts were true. But then I said their deaths were not wasted, that they died for something they believed in, fighting for their country. That part was the lie.

"The truth is not one of them died fighting 'for his country.' If they died for anything, it was each other."

"Each other?"

"Yeah. That's what keeps you going out there, the other guys, the feelings you have for people with whom you've shared fear and danger and hardship, for people who have probably saved your life and whose lives you've saved. You develop a kind of 'us against the world' mentality, and the last thing you want to happen is to let one of those other guys down."

"Well, do you think that's a bad thing, that kind of friendship and loyalty?"

"A bad thing? No. In some ways it's the greatest thing in the world, but the price you pay to get there, the toll it takes, is terrible. To get there, you have to lose all your faith in everything else."

"Is that where you are right now, Jiggs?" Camilla touched his shoulder with her fingertips.

"Pretty much."

"What about Carol? What about your family?"

Jiggs straightened and shuddered. "It's like I'm watching them across a chasm."

"What do you mean?"

"Well, I see Carol, my dad and sisters, even myself, but none of us are as we used to be. We're blurred, out of focus. There I am before I went to the war – playing ball, going to school, getting married. But now I see myself, my family, through the eyes of the person who goes down to the beach and stares across the sea in the direction of the war and wonders whether anybody he's come to love is dying as he sits there, as he plays baseball. We were eating, drinking, being merry back then, but we didn't know that tomorrow we were going to die, not just individually, but collectively, and for nothing. How could I have been so fucking ... sorry ... blind?"

The vision of Jiggs sitting wounded in the mud and rain cradling the dying Saucers in his arms branded Camilla's brain. "Mmm," she murmured, wanting to say more, to ease Jiggs' self-indictment, but unsure what that could be with this man she knew so slightly.

"Whatever I'm doing," Jiggs went on, "whatever else I'm thinking, somewhere in the back of my mind that sniper up in the tree watches me sitting there on that bunker talking Leslie into staying, imagining even then me crawling out to Leslie, choosing to wait to kill us, to play with us by letting us hope. I keep seeing those kids on the hospital ship and wonder whether I put them there. Did anything I've done kill any children?

"It makes everything I did before the war seem hollow, but here I am playing baseball, terribly afraid that I'll just go back and resume my mindlessness. All the joy has been wrung out of me."

Hours had passed. The guests had gone home long ago. Someone had turned out all the lights. Jiggs and Camilla stood side by side in the dark for a long time without talking.

"Jiggs," Camilla's voice was low and slow, cooler than the night air, "at the end of your talk with Leslie, you left the door open, didn't you? You didn't turn him away? You only asked him to be sure he didn't have it in himself to stay."

"No, I didn't turn him away."

"When he was out there in the minefield, are you sorry you tried to save him? Whatever the outcome, wouldn't you be even more troubled, if you hadn't? By going out there, weren't you being the kind of friend you just talked about?"

So fucking what? They're all dead, aren't they? Callman, Buskirk, Jim Linetti, Saucers. They're all dead, and thousands more just like them. Jiggs wanted to scream, "You don't know. You weren't there? You're no more a member of this fraternity of death than all the people back in the world."

But he didn't, because he could see Camilla was weeping, that she had begun to understand.

They were silent as Camilla drove him out to the back gate of the base. Just past the guard shack, Camilla pulled onto the shoulder. Across the street two tiny Okinawan cabs waited for a fare.

As she came to a stop, Camilla put her right hand on Jiggs' arm. "Jiggs, I've never experienced anything half so terrible, but I know about chasms. You need someone to talk to and so do I. Do you think we can be friends? I'm afraid you'll think you shouldn't because you're married."

The notion that he might allow a friendship with Camilla Waron or anyone in the world somehow to interfere with his marriage to Carol had not occurred to him.

"You being married shouldn't prevent our being friends, Jiggs. Nothing will happen. You won't let it ... and neither will I ... nothing you'll be sorry for later."

Jiggs paused with his hand on the door handle. "I could use a friend."

24

April 1968

The rain that washed out practice earlier in the afternoon was still coming down in waves. Umbrellas being a Marine Corps' taboo, Jiggs was drenched in the ten seconds it took him to sprint from the door of his quarters to Camilla's car as she pulled up to the curb.

"Wait 'til I tell you what happened this afternoon," Camilla said as Jiggs folded himself into the tiny car and she put it in gear.

Jiggs wiped the rain out of his eyes but said nothing.

"Some of the other teachers and I are taking a life-saving class after school. You know, water safety."

Jiggs nodded.

"Anyway, we're all in our swimsuits at the shallow end of the high school pool, when the door to the boy's dressing room bangs open and the whole boys track team, all naked, exploded through it up by the deep end, racing for the pool. Three or four of them, including two of my best students, were in mid-air jumping in before they realized they were not alone. They folded up like accordions when they saw us."

Camilla glanced across her shoulder at Jiggs.

He was staring straight ahead.

Camilla abandoned the rest of her story. "Jiggs, are you okay?"

"Yeah, just preoccupied, I guess. Sorry to be such poor company."

"Why don't you tell me about this baseball team? What position do you play?"

The sentry at the main gate buried deep in his poncho waived them through, and Camilla turned left back towards Kadena, where they planned to have dinner.

They had driven no more than a minute or two, Jiggs yakking about baseball, when they approached a tiny Okinawan girl wearing a yellow rain coat and hood and yellow galoshes walking along the side of the road. She was carrying a plastic sack that was billowing in the wind and rain. As they drew abreast of her, a gust seized the bag and blew it out of the girl's hand. As it tumbled in the breeze, papers came scattering out, whipping away from the girl who began to chase them and then stopped and began to cry. Camilla skidded to a stop, hopped out without a word and began chasing the fugitive papers. Seeing what she was up to, Jiggs followed her lead. *What the hell? I'm already soaked.*

When he had recovered all the soggy schoolwork he could find, he returned to where Camilla was kneeling, talking to the little girl and trying to put the papers she had collected back in the bag without smearing their content or allowing them to dissolve in her hand. Jiggs handed her what he had rounded up. "Good luck salvaging this mess."

Camilla looked up at him. Her hair, which had been in a ponytail, was hanging in her face, and she had to push it aside to see. "The important thing's to try." She handed the bag back to the girl. "I'd like to offer her a ride, but I don't know where she lives, and she can't tell me."

Jiggs looked around. "She must live nearby, but putting her in your car might be misunderstood. Oh, here comes Mama, I think."

An Okinawan woman with an umbrella was coming towards them through the rain, taking rapid little steps as she tried to avoid the worst of the puddles. As she reached them the little girl spoke to her, and the look of concern on the woman's face broadened into a smile. She bowed towards Jiggs and Camilla. "*Arigato. Ariagato.*"

Camilla bowed in return. "*Döitahimashite.*"

After a further exchange of nods and smiles, the woman put her arm around the girl, and they turned back in the direction from which the woman had come. Jiggs and Camilla got back in the car.

"What'd you say to her?"

"I said, 'you're welcome.' Not hard to pick up some of the common words, if you listen. I seem to have the knack."

Jiggs looked at the little girl and her mother in his side mirror as they retreated away from him, still seeing Camilla in his mind's eye, kneeling in the rain, trying.

"The knack, huh? Do you have the knack for any other languages?"

"Yes, sort of."

"Which one?"

"Polish ... and Russian, and French."

"My god, Polish and Russian. Those aren't languages you expect from the girl next door. How do you happen to speak those?"

"My folks are from Poland, but Grandpa Baturovich was Russian, and he lived with us while I was growing up. Conversation at the dinner table was interesting.

"How about you? Any second languages?"

Ignoring the smattering of Spanish he'd picked up in Mexico, Jiggs shook his head. "Barely conversant in English."

"Right. I've noticed how much trouble you have making yourself understood." Camilla rolled her eyes at him.

Jiggs smiled, his first of the evening.

April 15, 1968
Dear Jiggs,

Tell me more about this baseball team you're on. Are you catching? Roger wants to know if they throw curves in that league. If so, he wants to know if you're hitting them.

I spent Easter weekend with Doc. He took me for a four-hour ride. Ouch! I rode Freckles. He was a real handful. Doc says nobody's been on him since the day you left. The snow's all melted, but it's still too wet to get into the fields. The trees have budded, but there are very few leaves. We did see a robin though.

That night we went into town, and I met your friend, Ron Bjournquist, and his wife, Charlene, and their kids. They were in the restaurant. They both asked about you and asked me to say "Hi" for them. Ron says if they can't start planting soon, they might as well not bother. Charlene says he says that every spring.

Bobby Kennedy seems to be building lots of momentum towards the Democratic presidential nomination, especially now that Johnson says he won't run. That was good news! Maybe there's reason to hope an end to the war is in sight after all. There are so many problems in America, like what happened to Martin Luther King, that it's hard to see why we should be in Viet Nam trying to solve someone else's problems.

So much for the 'Carol Morgan World View.' The truth is, Jiggs, it's hard to think about anything except you coming home, being home. Matter of fact, I'm kissing you right now, do you feel it? How about this? Or this? You haven't forgotten what this feels like, have you? (This paragraph has been brought to you by Iowa's horniest woman.) So hurry home, Big Boy, the national debt's a drop in the bucket compared to the amount of catching up we have to do.

Love, Carol

Because of his speed, which at least one of his coaches had described as "sub-glacial," Jiggs had been a catcher almost from the moment he first stepped on a baseball diamond at the age of eight. In college he had also practiced and sometimes played first and third base, but Jiggs loved to catch. He called every pitch, his calls determined the defense, shading it according to speed and location. When he was catching, Jiggs was the quarterback.

However, to save wear and tear on his wounded leg, Jiggs had not tried out as a catcher. When it became apparent he could start at third, he hadn't even mentioned he could catch. Now he was glad he hadn't, because a huge Black Lance Corporal named J.D. Jones had won the position and become the rock on which Paul Stromberg, the coach, had built a good team.

With a detachment that would never have been possible behind the plate, Jiggs watched from third as J.D. made miraculous diving stops of pitches headed for the backstop, threw out runners with electrifying throws that often arrived before the runner began to slide. At six-four, two hundred thirty pounds, J.D. intimidated opposing hitters just by standing beside them between pitches. His hustle drove the rest of the team to play up to J.D.'s obvious standards. On the Okinawa Marines, J.D. Jones was clearly "The Man."

Although unwilling to admit J.D. was a better catcher, Jiggs knew that J.D. was the better man for the team. Jiggs no longer cared enough to play with such fire. He went through the motions at third base. He played steadily and hit well. No one could accuse Jiggs of not hustling, but he wasn't playing in overdrive like J.D. Jones.

In late April, in the last inning of the last game of the Marines' first time through the league, against a Navy team from Japan, J.D. went down. He was blocking the plate against a runner only slightly smaller than himself, who was trying to score what might be the winning run from third on a ground ball to short. Just as the throw arrived, they collided like two trains on the same track. Jiggs heard the collision ninety feet away at third. He figured Pete Ramierz out in centerfield probably heard it too. Probably the Commanding General up in the headquarters building half a mile away could hear it, had he been listening.

When the dust cleared, both men were sprawled across the plate, the ball was back at the screen, J.D. had a broken leg. Jerry Sherrill, the back-up catcher, caught the last two outs, and the Marines went down in order in their final at bat while J.D. was on his way to the infirmary. The Marines had lost their first game and much more. For once, the rest of the team was as quiet as Jiggs after the game.

Camilla had begun to attend games back in the sore arm weather of early spring, when the temperature rarely rose above sixty and the rain swept back and forth across the Island like the strokes of a broom. It was seldom enough to rain out even a practice, but more than enough to make playing unpleasant and watching miserable. Sometimes Jiggs would glance into the stands on such days, see her sitting there alone, and wonder what on earth compelled her to come. They were not lovers. They tried so hard not to be it was sometimes laughable. At movies neither rested an arm on the armrest between them, they never went to dances together, although they'd see each other there and sometimes dance, but never slow.

"You're going to miss J.D.," Camilla said. They waited for pizza at a tiny Okinawan restaurant, where "they make pizza just like in Iowa City," Camilla had promised.

Jiggs doubted she was right about the pizza, but she was right about J.D. "Yeah. I don't think Sherrill can handle it."

"Can you catch, Jiggs?"

Jiggs nodded.

"Are you going to do it?"

"I don't know. I'm not up for it."

"What are you up for these days, Jiggs?"

"Another beer." He held up his empty glass to get the waitress' attention.

Camilla smiled. "I must remember to ask you that question sometime when you have a full glass."

"I know I'm not up for the kind of leadership catching takes. I've had enough of being responsible for anyone besides myself for a while."

Instead of replying, Camilla took her first bite of pizza. She was the only person Jiggs ever knew who liked shrimp and green olive pizza.

After a while, Jiggs began telling her about Lindy, and how the profane old woman had mothered him and Hood. Even now no week passed without a letter from her filled with clippings about her beloved Hawkeyes and telling him to come see her when he came home.

"Speaking of letters," Camilla began to fish around in her purse, "I received one today. Want to see a picture of my folks?"

Jiggs took the snapshot she handed him and held it under the small lamp that sat at the end of the table. A couple standing in front of a knotty pine wall stared back at him. The woman was taller than the man and had dark hair, while the man had gray hair and wore glasses. He had only one arm.

Jiggs looked up at Camilla, who was also bent over studying her parents' images in the dim light. "What happened to your father's arm?"

"He lost it in the war, in Poland."

"Were you born in Poland?" Jiggs did some mental math. "You must have been. You were born during the war."

Camilla shook her head.

"No. My dad came to the United States after the war. His name was 'Waronowski.' He likes to say he left his 'owski' in 'Krakowski.' He was in the Polish underground, but his group was anti-communist, so he had to get out when the Russians came in. First, he went to England and later he came here, to the U.S. I mean, to Virginia. He was tortured by the Germans. That's what happened to his arm. He escaped, but he couldn't get any medical care, and his friends had to amputate it."

Jiggs looked with deepened respect at the stocky man in the photograph with the light from the flashbulb reflecting off the lenses of his glasses. *Of course.* Camilla's tranquility, usually so light-hearted, her gentleness without ever seeming meek or submissive. *Why haven't I ever wondered what her parents are like?*

He looked up again, about to ask once more about her birth, but she anticipated him. "I'm adopted, Jiggs. Joe and Ulla adopted me. I don't know when or where I was born."

"But surely there are records ... didn't the agency know?"

"There wasn't any agency. A man, probably my real father, and an older boy and I were walking down this dirt road where my folks, Joe and Ulla, I mean, lived in 1948. My folks think I was about three.

"They were sitting on the porch of their house, and the man came up to the fence and asked if he could leave me with them while he and the boy walked to this country store that was about a mile down the road. I was little and would get tired, he said, but he couldn't carry me on the way back, because he would be carrying groceries ... Except he never came back ... He just left me there. That's my chasm, Jiggs."

Camilla started to cry. "He didn't even tell them my name."

The snapshot lay on the tablecloth in the pool of light beneath the lamp where Jiggs dropped it when he took Camilla's hands. She had been leaning forward with her head bowed as she spoke. Now Jiggs' forehead was almost touching hers across the table.

"I hardly remember anything. I know they looked for my father, if that's who the man was, but he and the boy were never found."

"So you just stayed with this couple?"

"Yes. Eventually they adopted me. I went to their citizenship ceremony and we had a little ceremony when my adoption papers were signed. I was ten. Every September 4th we would have a great celebration in honor of my arrival on that date, and that became my birthday."

"Is 'Camilla' the name they gave you?"

"Yes. It's what they intended to name their first daughter."

Wow.

Camilla dabbed her eyes with a napkin Jiggs handed her. "The thing I keep coming back to is, what was my dad going through that was so bad he decided to leave me? What happened to my mom? Who was she? I wonder about that all the time."

"Seems like your dad stumbled on some good people to care for you."

Camilla picked the photograph up off the table and stared at it. "The best."

25

April 1968

Jiggs had not been back to Kue, the hospital where he had recuperated from his wounds, since receiving his final clearance to return to full duty. He dreaded returning now. There were five steps up from the street to the plaza leading to the front entrance, five steps that felt like a thousand. He felt as if he was about to dive into a polluted pond. On the plaza patients in hospital gowns, robes and footwear ranging from paper slippers to unlaced boots sat in the sun, reading, talking to other patients, staring. There was lots of plaster, and, here and there, an uneven number of limbs.

Jiggs made his way through corridors lined with beds that spilled out of overstuffed wards. More than once he had to stop and turn sideways in order to make room for a gurney and its attendants to rush past, threading their precarious way through the clogged arteries of the giant hospital. *Business is booming.*

As Jiggs neared his destination, he slowed his already slow pace and took several deep breaths. He stopped just before the doorway of the room he was looking for and took another one. He would rather have crawled back across the minefield where Saucers died than turn the corner and walk through that door.

Inside, the room was a familiar scene. Two rows of white sheeted beds sticking out at right angles from opposite walls like teeth with gaps between. Jiggs walked down the aisle between the rows. In the sixth bed on his right lay Larry Nelson.

Larry was asleep. Jiggs stood at the foot of the bed looking down at him. Larry's head lolled to one side, his mouth open slightly. He was snoring. Jiggs forced himself to look for what he knew he would not find. The outline of Larry's body beneath the sheet flattened out half way between Larry's waist and where his knees should have been. Larry's legs were gone. *How can he sleep so peacefully?* Having seen it for himself, Jiggs wasn't sure he would ever sleep peacefully again. He wanted to throw up.

Instead, he pulled a chair over to the side of Larry's bed and sat down, closing his eyes, taking more deep breaths, trying to purge himself of the image of Larry's newly-acquired void, to will back a vision of his friend of former days, but the old Larry was gone. After several minutes Jiggs opened his eyes. Larry was lying wide awake, staring at him.

"Jiggs, is that you?"

"Yeah, Lar, it's me. How're you feeling?" *Stupid fucking question.*

"Been better. One of these damn drugs they're giving me is blurring my vision. It's like I'm looking at everything under water. You look a lot better that way."

Jiggs laughed in spite of himself.

"I just found out you were here. How long have you been here?"

"I don't know. Week or ten days, I guess. I lose track. I got hit on the eighth. What's today?"

"Seventeenth."

"Seven or eight days then. The first few were all a blur. Lots of good drugs – visions. They tell me I'm going home ... I mean back to the States in a few days. It'll be a while before I get all the way home."

A dozen questions were floating around in Jiggs' mind. *How'd it happen? Where were you? Have you talked to your wife yet? Is there anything I can do for you? Anything at all?*

Jiggs suppressed all but the last two. Larry seemed in a half-decent state of mind, but somewhere inside there had to be buttons of despair just waiting to be pushed.

"Is there anything I can do for you, anything at all?"

Larry stared at Jiggs in silence for several seconds.

"Jesus, Jiggs, I was going to make a wisecrack about the two things I need most, no one can get for me. But I can barely even think about it to myself, let alone say it out loud. Jesus, Jesus, Jesus, what am I going to do? You're a smart guy, Jiggs. What am I going to do?"

Larry started to cry and turned his face away from Jiggs.

The suddenness of Larry's mood shift tore away the last vestige of whatever fortification against grief, anger and sorrow, Jiggs had managed to construct since learning of Larry's wounds and starting to think about this visit. Jiggs, too, started to cry.

He stood up and stepped to the edge of the bed and touched Larry on the shoulder.

"I know a couple of things you're going to do. You're going to get your benefits. You're going to draw down on the account you've accumulated with your grateful fucking nation. You're going to collect every penny's worth with interest."

The words just came tumbling out of his mouth.

"Therapy, rehab, counseling, prosthetics, whatever there is, you're going to get it. You're going to collect on your investment in your friends, in your family, because this didn't just happen to you, Lar. It happened to all of us, everybody who loves you."

At that, Larry turned his head back in Jiggs' direction. Jiggs snuffled and wiped his eyes with the back of his hand. "See, now you have me seeing as if through water too."

Larry gave a little half laugh.

"Have you talked to Sandy yet?"

"No. She knows I got hit, I'm sure. But she doesn't know the extent of it. I've started half a dozen letters to her, but tore 'em up before they were finished. I don't know how to say what I need to say."

Jiggs didn't know Sandy Nelson beyond the little Larry had told him, but he could not imagine she would want to learn of what happened other than in the most straightforward, direct way possible.

"Well, you've been around Marines long enough to know the best tactic is usually to go right at 'em. Hey diddle, diddle, right up the middle. Don't bother with a lot of fancy maneuvers. If it was good enough for Chesty Puller, it ought to be good enough for you. It's not as if you can keep it a secret. The longer you wait, the harder it's going to be for you and the more she's likely to feel hurt you didn't seek her love and support sooner."

Larry rubbed his hand over his face and ran it up through his hair as if he was clearing off a cobweb. "I suppose you're right." He looked away. "I mean, I know you are. I just ... I just don't know where I'm going to find the words..."

He paused and turned back towards Jiggs. "Will you help me write the letter?"

Talk's cheap, Morgan. It was easy to tell Larry to write to his wife, to tell her that he'd had his legs blown off, with its implication that their lives together and those of their children were never going to be the same; that Larry might never again walk beside her or stand holding her in his arms; might never lift his daughters above his head and toss them laughing in the air or stand to greet and shake hands with their boyfriends.

Jiggs thought of his half dozen failed attempts to write to Jim Linetti's wife after Jim was killed. "Yeah," he said, "Where's your paper?"

26

May 1968

Seabees had stacked a huge pile of large three-cornered gray concrete forms along the water's edge on the southwest corner of the Island. The massive blocks towered over their car as Jiggs and Camilla pulled up, parked and got out. Jiggs looked up at the massive heap. He had had no idea there was such a place on the Island. *Wow!*

Camilla was already climbing, picking her way up. Jiggs hastened to join her, and together they reached the top, where they found a relatively level spot and sat side by side nestled in the angle of two of the manmade boulders. Thirty feet below the water of the China Sea lapped against the base of the wall and the sun turned the underside of some high, feathery clouds a pale gold from somewhere behind the western horizon as darkness gathered.

"Those clouds look like ears of wheat," Camilla said, after a couple of minutes of silence, speaking as much to the sea and air as to Jiggs.

Jiggs nodded. "Makes me think of God ... the splendor, I mean."

Camilla turned her head slightly towards him. "Do you believe in God, Jiggs?"

That question. Jiggs remembered when Doc had asked it one night a thousand years ago. How many times had he asked it of himself in the time since without coming any closer to an answer?

"I think I used to, back when I still liked myself."

"What do you mean by that?"

"Well, I used to take a kind of personal inventory, and I could see I'd really been blessed. I was intelligent, healthy, surrounded by a family that loved me, sufficiently good-looking not to make people want to run screaming into the night, not a great athlete, but a decent one ... I had all that it took to do well in life as I knew it. It would have been harder for me to fail than to succeed.

"Some people had more of one thing or another than I did, but I had more than my share, especially in combination. Once I began to see that, I began to wonder, whom do I thank for all this? Surely there must be a plan. Who else but God could plan on such a scale? I was filled with gratitude because I had so much, without ever thinking about those who had less."

Camilla sat looking across her shoulder at him, her head bent slightly towards him, intent on what he was saying.

"But now I see how blind I really was. Until I had seen them, I never stopped to think what all the disadvantaged of the Earth must be saying. What do those kids on the hospital ship, alone and blind and with noses burned off and limbs blown away by a war they have no way of understanding, think? What are they saying? 'Plan, hell!'

"If there is a god, he's left me filled with guilt over the plate full of blessings I'm carrying around, while much of the world goes begging, and angry over being used to kill people.

What I used to see as a plan, I now see as randomness, chaos. Now I ask, who should I blame?"

Camilla turned her gaze back towards the water and sat in silence for a time watching the sky darken. The first star appeared. "Does it make it any easier to think of those poor children without any hope of salvation?"

"No, it doesn't. But I'm not sure I'm looking for an easy answer. Do you believe in God?"

"Yes."

"Why?"

"Because I choose to. Because I have faith. I see the chaos, Jiggs, but beneath it all I see the birth and renewal of the Spring, the withering of the Fall and Winter. For me, the rhythm of it all transcends the chaos.

"There are lots of things that happen that I don't understand, but I don't think God intended the chaos. It's simply a by-product of His gift of free will. Each person gets to choose. Some make bad choices, but if you choose God's way, you're blessed no matter what else happens. I don't think the bad things are any more reason not to believe than the good things are reason to believe. Life itself is all the reason I need."

What choice did those kids on the hospital ship make?

"Cam, you talk of choices and salvation, but what about the people who make bad choices, prodigal sons, who then are saved anyway simply by doing an about face? Seems to me there ought to be some price to pay for bad behavior."

"Jiggs, I'm no theologian. If I were, I would say that the prospect of damnation every day prior to repentance is the price of bad decisions, and the promise of forgiveness in the event of sincere repentance is the incentive to forsake evil. But I'm not staking my faith on scientific analysis. I'm humble enough to know there are things that 'surpass my understanding,' but my instincts tell me God exists, and I'm prepared to trust them in face of the logic of others."

The few people Jiggs had ever heard try to explain their faith had usually done so in a half-apologetic tone, as if to say, "I know this doesn't make any sense, but..." There was no such suggestion of apology in Camilla's voice, nor any hint of self-righteousness, another theme Jiggs had detected in the voices of many believers, starting with Doc's old nemesis, Pastor Holmquist. Camilla's explanation was an answer to Jiggs' questions, nothing more, spoken, as always, in her strange low musical voice.

"I understand what you're saying." Jiggs tossed a pebble he'd been playing with into the water. "I just struggle taking the first step."

A clear sky at the time of their arrival at the seawall had become a cold rainy one shortly after dark, forcing them to clamber down in haste. "Jiggs, will you drive?" Camilla tossed him her keys when he looked up at the sound of her voice.

Now she sat, half mesmerized by the slap of the windshield wipers and the rings around oncoming headlights, chewing on her lip, stewing over what she was about to say.

"Jiggs, something's come up. A guy named Pete Fellows is going to stop by this evening." She and Jiggs had talked about going to a movie.

Jiggs shrugged his assent to the implicit change of plan without asking who Pete Fellows was.

"Pete's a guy I used to date, a pilot. We used to go out whenever he was on the Island. He's in the Air Force. He called late last night saying he'll only be here today and wants to see me before he leaves."

Only recently had Camilla given up hoping Pete would call or write. She wanted to see him, to learn why he had waited so long to get in touch after their last time together. But she had not called Jiggs to change their evening's plans. Camilla wanted him nearby when Pete showed up, not to make either man jealous, but to protect her from herself, from accepting whatever excuse Pete came up with. She suspected any future with Pete would be filled with excuses.

Jiggs glanced across his shoulder at Camilla. "No problem. Drop me off at the back gate. I'll catch a cab."

"No. No. I told Pete I had plans. He says he just needs to talk to me for a few minutes, but doesn't want to do it over the phone or in a letter. I said okay, but I want you to stay."

Jiggs nodded. He would be a poor friend to object to this guy's visit after all the time Camilla had given their strange friendship.

Once inside her tiny house, Jiggs helped Camilla off with her coat and she headed for the kitchen to make coffee.

Jiggs went into Camilla's room, hung up her coat and threw his over the back of her desk chair. Apart from the bed, dresser and desk with two shelves crammed with books, the room was filled with the purchases Americans in the Far East felt compelled to make. Speakers capable of filling Carnegie Hall with sound occupied two corners diagonal from each other, a stereo receiver and tape deck sat on the desk. An oriental screen and big bowl-shaped wicker chair lined with a thick cushion, a "papa-san" chair, completed the furnishings. On one wall was a black and white poster of a beach in the moonlight at low tide. Superimposed over the scene were the words of *Desiderata.*

Jiggs flipped on the FM radio on the receiver, which was tuned to Armed Forces Radio, plopped into the papa-san, and stared at the ceiling listening to the song that was playing. He loved this tiny room. It seemed filled with the same warmth Camilla had shown him since the first night they met. It even smelled like her. The unknown scent she wore, fresh and light, that sometimes came to him as she walked past, made the room almost a living extension of her.

As Camilla came in carrying two steaming mugs, Jiggs stood up, went over to his jacket and withdrew a box from one of the pockets. Opening it, he took out a reel of tape. "I brought you something for school."

"Oh what is it? Is it something you recorded?"

"One way to find out."

Camilla took the tape, went over and threaded it through the tape deck, and turned it on. The lights on the gauges came on, and as the reels began to turn, Jiggs' voice filled the room.

"Hello, everybody. I guess I ought to introduce myself. My name is Jiggs Morgan, and I'm a friend of Miss Waron's.

"A while ago, she told me she was having trouble convincing some people in her classes, especially you guys, to give poetry a chance. She said some of you thought it was for sissies.

"Well, I began to think about that. I thought to myself, 'Hey, I like poetry. Does that mean I'm a sissy?'

"Of course, I didn't want to think so. So I began to think about why I liked it. I don't know anything about meter or rhyme schemes or any of that stuff. Even if I did, it probably wouldn't make me like it any more ... maybe less.

"I finally decided what I liked was the sound ... better even than the words ... I liked the sound, kind of like music. Stop and think. Most of you probably like one kind of music or another, don't you? Is there anyone out there who can honestly say you've never heard a song you liked?

"Well, poetry, at least for me, is kind of like the lyrics of a song without the music. Like some songs, when I just read the words to see what they're saying, that by itself may not mean much, but when I listen to the sound of the song or the poem, it's very different. It's as if it has a secret life which is only revealed when read or sung out loud."

Jiggs looked at Camilla out of the corner of his eye as he listened. She was sitting on the edge of her bed, intent on what she was hearing.

"Naturally, I don't like all poetry," the voice on the tape continued, "just like I don't like every song. But some poems can really make me feel something – pride, sadness, happiness, any one of dozens of emotions. These poems I like aren't about sissy stuff either. I'm not talking about 'tiptoeing through any tulips.' I'm talking about things I like, or maybe things I don't like, but have experienced or thought about myself, things like sports or nature, the wilderness, America, war and ... yeah, love too. You know, if love's for sissies, then there are sure a lot of sissies around.

"Let's take sports as an example. How many of you have ever heard the expression, 'it's not whether you win or lose, but how you play the game?' Probably most of you have heard that. Where do you think it comes from?

"A poem? You guessed it. Grantland Rice a great sports writer, a friend of guys like Babe Ruth and Jack Dempsey and Knute Rockne, wrote:

> When the one great scorer
> Goes to write against your name,
> He'll write not whether you won or lost,
> But how you played the game."

There was a pause before Jiggs continued.

"This illustrates one of the real appeals of poetry, at least for me. It has a way of being more memorable than just saying, 'it's important to be a good sport.'

"That's sports. What about the wilderness? You can ask, 'have you ever been outside on a quiet, snowy day?' Or you can ask, as a poet named Robert Service once did, 'Have you known the great white silence, not a snow-gemmed twig aquiver?'"

Jiggs' deep voice on the tape seemed to quiver, and Camilla felt a chill and shivered as she heard the words spoken.

"And of the horrors of war a poet named Siegfried Sasson wrote:

I'm back again from hell
With loathsome thoughts to sell;
Secrets of death to tell;
And horrors from the abyss.
Young faces bleared with blood,
Sucked down into the mud,
You shall hear things like this,
'Till the tormented slain
Crawl round and once again
With limbs that twist awry
Moan out their brutish pain,
As the fighters pass them by.
For you our battles shine
With triumph half-divine;
And the glory of the dead
Kindles in each proud eye.
But a curse is on my head,
That shall not be unsaid,
And the wounds in my heart are red,
For I have watched them die."

Camilla continued to shiver. She glanced at Jiggs for the first time since the tape started to play. Is a curse still on Jiggs' head, she wondered?

"Of love, a fellow named Richard Lovelace wrote while he was, himself, in prison:
Stone walls do not a prison make,
Nor iron bars a cage;
Minds innocent and quiet take
That for an hermitage:
If I have freedom in my love,
And in my soul am free,
Angels alone, that soar above,
Enjoy such liberty."

"The freedom to love is the freedom of angels in flight, despite whatever cages imprison us. Nice thought, don't you think?"

Camilla stole another glance at Jiggs. "... freedom in my love..." This Marine, she decided, had been sand-bagging when he told her he didn't know what kinds of poetry he liked. Camilla was sure his last two examples were not random choices.

"The people who wrote these words weren't sissies. Rice is one of the most famous sports writers of all time; Sassoon fought in the trenches during World War One, sometimes hand to hand, for years and was wounded several times; Service lived and worked in Alaska during the gold rush and was a war correspondent during World War One; Richard Lovelace was a captain in command of troops during the wars of Seventeenth Century England.

"So you see, there have been some great things written, poems that have given people real inspiration at times when they've most needed it. Let me close by reading you one that my drill instructor, surely no sissy, put up on the barracks wall in

Marine Boot Camp. Judge for yourselves whether this was written by a sissy."

Jiggs then read Kipling's "If." When he finished, he said, "The only thing I can add to that is to say that you must not be afraid to like or love somebody or something because you're afraid of how others will see you. The courage to pursue your personal values despite the snide remarks and teasing of others, that, too, is the measure of a man. Thanks for listening."

Jiggs' voice vanished, but the tape reel continued to silently turn. Outside the rain had picked up, and the sound of it on the Quonset roof seemed to sever the little room from everything else in the world and set it adrift on a sea of their own making.

For a time, neither spoke. Jiggs was staring at the floor lost in some private world where he had been throughout the recording

Finally, Camilla said, "Where did that come from?"

Jiggs answered without looking up. "Something you said. I don't even remember exactly what, made me start thinking about poetry. I knew I had always liked it ever since my mother read me nursery rhymes, and you got me started thinking about why. I like the sound of it being spoken. It's as if the voice is a musical instrument itself, and the words are notes. It makes me think so intensely about what I am hearing. I really get wrapped up in it."

Camilla watched him. At last she was seeing the man she thought she'd met the night before he went to war. She was both happy and sad. When Jiggs finally looked up to find her staring at him, she smiled a small smile and shook her head. "What am I going to do about you after you're gone?"

Over the sound of the wind and rain, they heard someone knocking at the door. The Quonset didn't have a bell.

"That will be Pete."

"You sure you want me to stay?"

"More than ever. Just wait in here."

Camilla went out and closed the door.

Jiggs heard her open the front door.

The quarters Camilla shared with her roommate, Annie, were very small. The living room was just one thin door away from where Jiggs sat, no barrier to overhearing, however unintentional.

"Hello, Pete. Long time no see."

A pause, and then a male voice, "That's why I wanted to see you tonight. I'm going home tomorrow, and I need to apologize for something."

There was no response from Camilla.

"I'm married, Camilla. That's why I stopped calling you. I'm sorry. I never intended for things to go so far."

"If you didn't intend for things to go so far, Pete, why'd you ever start?"

"I'd been overseas for six months. A long time. One night the thought of having a little fun just became too much, and I took the ring off. That's all I thought it would be, a night of fun for a change."

No response from Camilla. She wasn't making it easy for him.

"Anyway, I met you, and it was fun, but by the end of the evening, I knew you weren't a 'one-night girl.' After that, I was afraid to tell you the truth, even though I wanted to, because I knew it would mean not seeing you again, and I didn't want that. I liked you too much."

"You mean you liked me too much not to lie to me."

"Listen, Camilla, I don't blame you for looking at it like that, but at least understand that I did stop, and I do feel guilty."

"Yes, Pete, you stopped, and I'm guessing you made your decision right after the night when you decided things had gone ... how should I put it, 'too far.' Trouble is, you forgot to tell me we had gone 'too far' or why you should be feeling guilty."

"I'm telling you now."

"After five months of silence, why bother? You can't think my learning that you were married the whole time makes me feel better? All it does is let you kid yourself into thinking you've somehow atoned for your dishonesty."

"Sorry you feel that way, Camilla. It's not what I intended. None of it was."

A couple seconds of silence followed. Then, "Well, you've said what you came to say. Now, I think you should go. Good-bye, Pete. "

The outside door opened and closed. An engine coughed to life above the sound of the rain. In the living room, no stirring. Then, after a minute or two, the sound of water running somewhere, probably the bathroom.

When Camilla re-entered the room, her eyes were red, but she wasn't crying.

"Could you hear any of that?"

"All of it. I'm sorry."

"He was wearing his ring tonight. I never saw that before. If he didn't want such things to happen, he would never have taken it off in the first place. Why did he have to tell me now? To soothe his conscience at the expense of making me feel used? Great guy, huh?"

"Yeah. You really know how to pick 'em."

"Hold on a minute, Jiggs. Don't go counting yourself in with Pete. It's the lie that hurts so much. You told me about Carol within five minutes of the time we met, and you always wear a ring. I chose to be your friend, and you've never taken advantage of our friendship." She stopped, leaving unsaid her certain knowledge it would no longer be a matter of "taking advantage."

Jiggs just listened. The conversation was such an extension of his own thoughts. *Is the question whether I'm lying or to whom?*

"Let's talk about something else." Camilla picked up a book. "So you're a big-time poetry jock, eh? I know what we should do."

They spent the rest of the evening reading poems back and forth to each other from the English teacher's inexhaustible supply, and Jiggs went home at midnight.

27

June 1968

Okinawan time, once so slow, began to speed ever faster as Jiggs' and Camilla's friendship deepened. At the end of the school year, Camilla's housemate, Annie, returned to the States. Camilla stayed, but the end of their time together was in sight.

On a night early in their last month together, Jiggs and Camilla were alone in the quiet house. Jiggs didn't know what time it was, but knew it must be after midnight as he stood in Camilla's room puzzling over a diagram of a record turntable he was trying to assemble. He hadn't started until almost eleven, because there had been a game.

Now he was nearly finished. Camilla had been unusually quiet, studying the instructions with him, making an occasional suggestion when things refused to work the way the manual promised.

Between them, they had eight years of college and two degrees, and it had taken them over an hour to assemble a piece of equipment Jiggs knew Doc could have put together in twenty minutes, probably without the manual. *Handiness must skip generations in my family.*

As the project neared completion, Camilla came in with two cups of fresh coffee and set one on the dresser in front of him.

"Are we ever going to get that arm to balance?"

Jiggs fiddled with the counterweight, trying to find the right spacing, so the needle would neither bounce across the record nor bore into it and drag.

"Try it now. Put on some record you're willing to sacrifice to science."

Camilla took an album from the top of a pile. The clear and haunting notes of Simon and Garfunkel's "Bridge Over Troubled Waters" filled the room. Jiggs listened carefully for several seconds to make sure the needle was tracking properly, then picked up his coffee and retreated three steps across the room, where he leaned back against the desk beside Camilla's bed.

Camilla came over and stood beside him as they listened to the song together. Halfway through, Jiggs said, "Sounds good." Then, with a little flourish of his arms in the manner of a magician having just successfully completed a trick. "I think we've got it!"

Camilla smiled at his theatrics. After a few more seconds, she asked, "Jiggs, how do you think you'll remember me?"

Jiggs didn't answer, the need to remember her with its implication of long separation being something he did not wish to think about.

"I mean, will you think of me, of us, as we are now, or will we age in your mind until I become a shriveled up little old lady pottering about my parlor making sure the doilies are straight on the arms of all my chairs?"

Jiggs thought for a moment. "Probably I'll remember you as one of those cat ladies whom the neighbors reluctantly have to report to Public Health for her own good. Then a couple of guys in ice cream suits with soothing voices will come and try to talk you into going with them to a place where everybody will be very nice to you.

"'But… but who will take care of all my children?' you will ask, gesturing towards the three hundred cats lounging in your living room. The men will exchange a glance they think you don't see and then assure you that your 'children' will be well cared for.

"What about you, Camilla? How will you remember me?"

"Remember you?" Camilla shrugged. "I'll just name one of my cats after you, that's all."

In this way they maintained their distance while becoming ever closer. Sometimes Jiggs accompanied Camilla on her forays into the City's bazaar. There she careened like a pinball from one booth to another, ducking beneath the awnings to bargain with tiny, ancient ladies in their language, asking questions about everything from pickled octopus to pottery and pins, buying seldom, but always earning their welcome.

On the way back to Camilla's place after one such junket, they were driving along the coast when they spotted some dolphins cavorting close to shore. "There I am in my next life," Jiggs said. "Next time around, I'm going to be a dolphin."

"Not me," Camilla, the girl captivated by cirrus clouds and vapor trails, was quick to reply, "not me. Next time I will be a bird."

As she spoke, Jiggs realized he had known what she was about to say before she said it. The recognition scared him a little.

Once at Willetts, the crew had been loading a huge ready mix tank onto the back of a flatbed truck using some rollers and the truck's power winch to drag the tank aboard. The cable became tighter and tighter, straining to overcome the thousands of pounds of resistance and pull the unwilling tank up the ramp. Without warning a metallic whine sang in the air as the cable snapped, unable to bear the tension any longer. It recoiled like a steel whip, striking the driver across the face, blinding him.

Jiggs could sense that the slightest impulse between Camilla and him could sever that taut line stretching back to all his commitments in the world, blinding him forever. Camilla seemed to sense it too and changed the subject.

"Jiggs, why did you catch tonight? What made you change your mind?"

Good question. In the two games following J.D.'s injury, one of which they lost, it had become obvious that Jerry Sherrill couldn't control opposing runners.

After the second game, Jiggs told Paul Stromberg he would try catching, if Paul thought it would be easier to replace a third baseman. Stromberg thought it would. It felt good, better than Jiggs expected. The mentality of sacrifice Jiggs had always responded to so well, both in wrestling and when catching, washed back over him. The leadership that went with the position settled naturally upon him. Before the first inning was over, he was more into the game than he had been all season.

Unlike J.D., Jiggs had never been a holler guy, especially not now, but he was capable of influencing the intensity of a game. His occasional gestures, a word of encouragement, a wave of a fist in salute of a particularly good play by an infielder, a particularly good pitch – he was good at the little things that made others play harder. When he picked an Army runner off first for the last out of the second inning, he could feel the team take off. They came trotting into the dugout chattering their congratulations, confident they were once again unbeatable.

"I don't know, Cam," Jiggs emerged from his reverie. "Maybe Joe Waronowski taught me how to quit feeling sorry for myself. Maybe his daughter did. She's a teacher, you know."

"The credit's yours, not mine, Jiggs. Everybody gets the blues. You certainly had plenty of reason. But healthy people work their way out. You've always looked pretty healthy to me." Camilla leaned away from Jiggs and looked him up and down with one eyebrow raised, as if she was appraising him. Jiggs made a face.

Billing's death, his mom's death, fraternity hazing, even a whore who wouldn't take off her shoes, Jiggs knew he had always bounced back, but Saucers had been different. Saucers was only the tip of an iceberg - Larry Nelson, Jim Linetti, Buskirk, the hospital ship, all the others. Behind the face he was making, Jiggs knew he had lost all his resilience in a very dark place. The patient listening and occasional insights of the girl beside him, expressed mostly in questions asked in that energy at ease voice, the low range of a clarinet, had been what he needed when he needed it. *You saved me from myself, Cam.*

Jiggs rested his palms on the edge of the desk behind him, where he felt his forgotten cup of coffee. He took a sip and made a face. "Bleah, coffee's cold and I'm old."

Camilla laughed and shook her head and sighed. "It really isn't fair, you know." She didn't say what, and Jiggs didn't ask.

Jiggs was suddenly tired. He slapped his thighs. "I'm beat. These guys are still third baseman's legs, not catcher's. They're going to ache in the morning. I have to get going."

"You can stay here tonight, if you want to. Now that Annie's gone, you can use her room."

Jiggs' cable back to the world ratcheted a click tighter. He looked at Camilla and shook his head slowly from side to side. In response, Camilla took a deep breath and smiled.

Camilla drove Jiggs to the gate where he could get a cab. When she stopped he got out and walked around to the driver's side where he knelt on one knee beside her door. Even kneeling he was taller than she was sitting there.

"Good night, Jiggs." Camilla put her hand on top of his where they rested on the edge of the door.

Jiggs reached out and touched her cheek with his fingertips. "Has anyone ever had a friend like you?" He stood and walked away.

28

June-July 1968

12 June 1968
Dear Carol,

    I still cannot believe Bobby Kennedy's dead. Now who are we going to get, Humphrey versus Nixon or Rockefeller? Some choice.

    I look at myself and what I'm doing here, which is nothing, and I tell myself that just sitting sullenly by while the war rages on is disgraceful. I suppose I could burn my uniform on the steps of the headquarters building in protest, but it wouldn't do any good. I'd just get carted off and hassled unmercifully. Maybe my rotation would be postponed. I'm sure that kind of exercise of freedom of speech is some kind of crime in the Corps.

    I'm more interested in finding something that will make a long term difference, a job that will help prevent more Viet Nams in the future. My cynical side tells me there are no such jobs. Hope I'm wrong. Any suggestions?

The team is playing well again after a let down when J.D. (that catcher I wrote about) broke his leg. Now I'm catching, and I'm enjoying the game more. The weather has warmed up and it's more fun to play. My leg's okay.

Well, my love, we're in the home stretch now. The "word" is that tours may be shortened from thirteen months to twelve. If so, I'll be home in August. Seems like I have been away forever.

I hope your summer is starting well. How will you spend three months off? How many rounds of golf can one woman play in that amount of time? Whatever the number, I wish you nothing but birdies and eagles.

I love you, Jiggs

Before he went to Mexico, the closest Jiggs had ever been to a wave was going to a *Gidget* movie. In Mexico and again in San Diego, where he'd been stationed briefly before being transferred to Viet Nam, he'd tried surfing and loved it. Everything he knew about the ocean fascinated him – the empty, prairie-like horizons, the sense of a vast unseen world masked just beneath its glassy furrows, the microcosms of the tide pools and the feeling of forever conveyed by the endless repetition of the waves, as countless as the sand.

"You know, I can't believe I've never asked you this, but where did the name 'Jiggs' come from? Is it a family name or something?" Camilla interrupted Jiggs' wave-watching as they sat on a beach well up on the sparsely inhabited northern part of the Island.

"Not exactly. I don't think I've ever mentioned it, but my dad was a priest..."

"A priest?" Camilla's eyes went wide, then narrow.

"Yeah, and a scholar. Before he met my mom and left the church, he was doing some research in an abbey in northern England, and he came across this ancient account of a lost prince named 'Jiggs,' the second son of some king, one of the Henrys, I think. This prince was kidnapped by an enemy of the king and trained to become the greatest swordsman in the world. Despite his captor's best efforts, he became a brave and honorable man who fought for the poor and oppressed. My dad was so taken with the nobility of character of this little known prince, that he decided, in the unlikely event he ever had a son, he would name him 'Jiggs.'"

Camilla rolled her eyes. "Kind of like Robin Hood, I suppose."

"Exactly. So, it's a very brave and revered name of ancient lineage."

"Don't forget 'intelligent' and 'handsome.'" Camilla poked Jiggs in the ribs. "Where do you come up with this stuff?"

"So you doubt me?"

Camilla dipped her head as she looked at him over the top of her sunglasses, but said nothing.

"Okay, okay, the truth is, my name is 'Jon Charles,' but for some reason when my sister Marie was just beginning to talk, 'Jon' came out 'Jiggs,' and it stuck. "

"So, if you have a son, are you going to name him 'Jiggs?'"

"Don't know."

"Don't you and Carol ever talk about it?"

"Oh, we've talked about names we like, but I don't think we've picked any."

"What names do you like?"

"I like 'Yogi' for a boy and 'Babe' for a girl."

"You know, I think I liked you better when all I got from you was straight answers."

"I like 'Justine' for a girl's name. So does Carol, or at least she did the last time we talked about it. For a long time, we liked 'Joel' for a boy's name, but then Carol had a kid named 'Joel' in her class the first year she taught who made her want to pick another name.

"Hell, after being in country for a while, you begin to wonder if you should even have kids, if that's what they have to look forward to."

"Oh, come on. If your folks had thought that way during World War II, you'd never have been born. Even when things were at their worst, did you really wish you were dead? If so, why did you work so hard to stay alive? It's like the old joke about life being so full of misery and it's way too short."

"Instinct, I guess. Human nature, the hope that things will get better, who knows?"

"See, and things did get better, didn't they?"

"I don't even know what 'better' means. 'Better' for whom? Me? Better for the guys who are still on 410?"

"What are you going to do when you get back to the States? Are you going to protest?"

"Something. Something to help stop the war. I want to go back to school, but I have to figure out something I can do to help get us out of there.

"What about you, Cam? Have you heard back about next year yet?" Camilla had applied to teach at a base in Europe in the fall.

"Not yet. I'm getting worried. But if I'm not accepted before I get there, I'm going anyway and take my chances.

There's always someone who doesn't show up for these overseas teaching jobs."

"So, are you just going to go on roaming the world bringing the joys of *Julius Caesar* and *Paradise Lost* to armed forces offspring thirsting for knowledge?"

"I think I'm going to go get my Master's at some point, probably after one more year of teaching. Maybe I'll have shaken my wanderlust by that time."

"Want to know what I'd do if I was you?" Jiggs looked up from the shape he'd been drawing in the sand with a stick. "I'd see what I could do with all those languages. How many people have your gift, Cam? None I've ever met. Most are like me, can barely speak English."

Camilla laughed. "Right. Just a poor illiterate farm boy."

"I'm serious. You see those pictures of places like the U.N. on television, and there are all these guys with earphones sitting around changing whatever language someone at the podium is speaking into a dozen others. I think that might be a really good job. You'd probably meet some interesting people, maybe get to travel some."

Camilla made her thoughtful face, eyes squinting slightly, lips puckered, calculating. "Maybe. I never thought of it. I want to get married, have a family someday. Translating might be a good job for that, probably no homework, no papers to grade at night."

On the afternoon of July Fourth, the Marines ended their season with a win over Air Force, clinching the season's championship. Because of the holiday, there was a big pre-game celebration, with generals giving speeches and throwing out first pitches. It was the biggest crowd of the season. Jiggs went 0 for 4 and was glad it was over. That night at midnight, Camilla flew home.

The end of their time together loomed large as they sat waiting for their farewell pizza four hours before Camilla's departure, neither saying much. Camilla was feeding the jukebox. She had played "Stranger On The Shore," the song they always played there, three times.

"Jiggs, what do you think of our continuing to write to each other?" Camilla knew vows to write were seldom honored, but if Jiggs was comfortable with it, she wanted the option. She couldn't bear to think of him just being swallowed up by the world without her ever knowing what became of him, without learning what he thought about things, at least now and then.

The question made Jiggs pause. He, too, had been dreading the prospect of their complete disappearance from each other's lives. *Where does having a pen pal like Camilla fit in the puzzle?*

"I'd like that," he said after a moment.

From the restaurant they drove to the seawall and sat for a time in the dark, watching the stars and listening to the waves, saying very little. Then, when it was time, they drove to Kadena, and Camilla checked in for her flight.

Twenty minutes until boarding. They waited together not far from the gate, but away from the other passengers waiting to board, out of words. Camilla took an envelope out of her purse and handed it to Jiggs.

Opening it, Jiggs found a piece of stationery to which Camilla had taped a "Peanuts" cartoon. Charlie Brown was standing on the pitcher's mound, his baseball cap covered with snow. Lucy, dressed in a winter coat stood facing him "The season's over, Charlie Brown," she said. Below that, Camilla had written, "The saddest words..." and her name.

Jiggs bit his lip. "I promised myself I wouldn't cry. I have some mail for you too."

He reached in his pocket, took out an envelope and handed it to her. As Camilla began to open it, her flight was called to begin boarding. Inside was a letter that read:

Cam,

Since the first time that I met you,
Was it just ten months ago,
It has been as if I've always known you,
So easily time has flown.
We have learned about each other
Each gentle, laughing hour,
The time's been like a garden,
Each minute like a flower.
Now uncompromising circumstance
Is forcing us to part.
I will feel your absence mightily,
Both in my mind and in my heart.
Who knows what the future holds?
I've been wrong each time I thought I knew.
But I know whatever else it brings
Will include some thought of you.

Cam, I thought my good-bye should involve poetry, even though I'm no poet. I have tried and tried, but what you see above is the best I can do. You must know, however, that despite their clumsiness, those lines are heartfelt. Wherever our paths take us, please know it is my most profound wish to always remain as good a friend to you as you have been to me.

Be well always, Jiggs

"Oh, Jiggs..." Camilla's voice was breaking as she spoke his name, "you are a poet. I love it."

For the first and last time in their months of friendship, she was in his arms.

"Good-bye, Camilla," Jiggs said. "You have helped me so much. Remember, if I can ever help you, find me. I will help you no matter what."

Camilla's eyes were brimming and the tears were trickling down her cheeks in a steady stream. "Glad I didn't make any unkeepable promises about not crying." She blinked back the tears and put her forehead against Jiggs' chest.

The last boarding call for her flight sounded and she looked up once more, eyes still swimming. "I'll remember you, Jiggs."

She turned and walked through the gate and out of the terminal toward her plane without looking back. Jiggs watched through the window, eyes swimming, until her plane lifted off and disappeared into the night, heading back to the world.

III

WINNETKA

29

July-October 1968

During the months following Camilla's departure and the end of the baseball season, Jiggs was given a desk in one of the battalion offices, but little to do. Inside the desk he found a Bible left by some previous occupant. For the first time in his life, he read it cover to cover. It was amazing how hesitant people were to interrupt when they saw what he was reading.

What do I believe? Jiggs spent a lot of hours thinking about that question. Ever since his trip to Mexico, he had known how much more he had than most. He had come home with an impulse to give something back, but apart from sending Jorge, the guy who fixed his motorcycle, a couple of baseball gloves, he'd never acted on it. He thought God had been talking to him when the Twenty-third Psalm started running around in his head just when he needed it most. What else could it have been? He had used that fact to persuade Saucers to stay in a war he had known was wrong. Jiggs couldn't explain all the death he had seen, but the more he reflected, the more convinced he became that Saucers' death was retribution for that misuse and for having ignored God's message to start paying off his blessings.

But which god? Doc's question.

Jiggs had taken a History of Religion course at Iowa. What he remembered best was the fact that every civilization had one – a religion. Despite some pretty shocking differences, most had a lot in common. Christianity, Judaism and Islam all traced back to the same roots. Jiggs thought the same god was pulling the strings for everybody; the differences could be explained by the different environments in which the various faiths evolved. Ever since his days in Sunday School he had wanted to believe. The more he thought about it, the more it seemed faith did not require a leap, more like a short step. The Theology of Jiggs. He began to pray.

It had been a long flight - ten hours to Hawaii, four more to California, with a four-hour layover in Honolulu in between. Jiggs thought time had stopped. His cab ride from the air base in San Bernardino, where he landed, to the Los Angeles airport for his flight to Iowa had not exactly been a "Welcome Home" parade. Rush hour traffic was more stop than go - plenty of time for looking around. When other motorists saw Jiggs sitting there in uniform, they hollered their hellos.

"Hey, Baby-killer..." "Hey, Butcher, you put on a clean uniform for the car ride?" and the old all-purpose standard, "Hey, Asshole, you suck!" came rolling through the open windows of the cab, accompanied by a mooning, a couple of spittings and some middle fingers.

Omaha, where Jiggs spent the hours from midnight to five a.m., had been another story. Seeing his uniform, the waitress at the airport coffee shop, a woman old enough to remember more popular wars, asked where he was coming from.

"Try the steak and eggs," she said when Jiggs told her. "They're the best thing on the menu."

It had been Jiggs' best breakfast in a year. The check she handed him at the end of the meal said, "On the house. Welcome home!"

It all depends on where you're touching the elephant.

In anticipation of Jiggs' homecoming, Carol had not returned to teaching in September. Having completed his WesPac tour, Jiggs was eligible for an early release from active duty, which he hastened to accept. Their next stop was undecided. When Jiggs emerged from the jetway into his arrival gate in Des Moines, Carol took flight, coming to a perfect landing in his arms.

"Oh, Baby, I'm so glad you're home!" She half-whispered, half-exclaimed amid kisses, hugs, caresses, and more kisses, as the other passengers flowed around the obstacle they created in the midst of the stream. Arm in arm they walked to the luggage carrousel, where they picked up Jiggs' seabag, a newly issued deep khaki green when he departed thirteen months earlier, but now bleached almost white by the Southeast Asian sun and rain.

"What do you want to do first?" Carol thought she already knew the answer to her question.

"Let's find some place where I can put on civilian clothes and then take a walk in a park somewhere."

It wasn't what she'd expected, but there would be plenty of time for that. Carol had read articles about the difficulties some couples experienced when soldiers returned to a world where a loud noise didn't necessarily mean someone was trying to kill someone else. Jiggs had had an eight-month transition, but Okinawa must be a far cry from the seventy-five mile per hour world he was re-entering. A walk sounded like a good idea.

The park they eventually chose was Gallatin State Park, just a few miles up river from Doc's farm, almost all the way home from Des Moines. Jiggs had spent the hundred-mile drive north mentally pinching himself to make sure he wasn't dreaming, that he was really home. *Now for the surprise.*

They were walking, holding hands, along a stretch of riverbank they had walked a hundred times before.

"I think I've decided what I want to be when I grow up."

Carol stopped walking and turned to look at him. "Are you serious?"

"Yep. I want to be a minister…"

"A what?"

"A minister, a clergyman. Actually, I want to be a missionary to some third world country. Haven't decided which part of the world yet, Africa, I think."

If Jiggs had said he wanted to become an undertaker or a ballet dancer, Carol could not have been more surprised. Jiggs was looking at her with his "What do you think?" look. Apparently he was serious. She didn't have an answer beyond, "Do they have golf courses in Africa?" Instinct told her that should not be her threshold response.

"I … I don't know what I think, Jiggs. It's nothing I've even thought of. It's not one of the careers we've ever talked about. Where did this idea come from?"

Jiggs flashed on Camilla helping the little Okinawan girl in the rain, telling him the important thing was to try, on Larry Nelson allying himself with a power greater than the forces of mankind, the children on the hospital ship.

"Lots of places. You know how unhappy I've been about the war, not just my part, but everything about it. That, and the inequalities I see, not just in wealth, but in opportunity, in justice, in everything. I want to do something that will make people's burdens more bearable, be a voice for them sometimes when they are incapable of saying things that need to be said."

"But Jiggs, I don't hear anything about God in there. Can't you do those things without becoming a ... a minister?" She had difficulty even saying the word.

"To begin with, I think I've always believed in God. I haven't always admitted it, even to myself, but when I look back on my life, I recognize that at moments of crisis, there I was, talking to God, even if only in my mind. Somewhere down in my core, God got in without my even knowing it."

Jiggs slowed and scooped a handful of stones from a patch of gravel along the riverbank. "True, I haven't paid much attention. When I have, it was often negative attention, but there have been moments when I've had glimpses of a genuine peace of mind faith has brought to others." He skipped a stone across the water. It was so quiet they could hear the plinking sound as it bounced along the surface. "The more I look at the world, the more I see God's hand. The universe, the seasons, birth and death, despite all the misery, there is a system, there is an underlying plan.

"I spent the last couple of months reading the Bible, really getting into it. It's a blueprint for what I believe, what I want to help achieve. I want to awaken people to that fact. I want to try."

They walked on a while in silence. Jiggs continued to feed rocks to the river.

After almost ten minutes passed and Carol hadn't spoken, Jiggs stopped again and stepped in front of her. Facing her, he took both her hands in his. "Carol, I thought you'd be happy about this. Me at last finding something I really want to do, instead of doing something I care nothing about just to make some money."

"I know you think you've found something, Jiggs. But being a minister, there has to be more to it than just believing in God. You ... as far as I know, the only time you were in a church after high school was when we got married, and maybe one time you told me about when you were in Mexico."

Carol bit her lower lip while searching for the right word. She didn't want this to become an argument, not on Jiggs' first day home.

"People talk about the ministry being a 'calling.' You and I have been together now for almost five years, and we've never even mentioned God until today. Now you're telling me you're hearing this call so loud and clear that you want to give your life to it? I'm surprised, that's all. I'll need some time to get used to the idea, to get used to the idea of being the wife of a pastor. I've never seen myself that way."

It was a lovely warm Indian summer day. For once, the Iowa autumn had been gentle, and the trees were still wearing their cloaks of many colors. When Jiggs had suggested they go to Gallatin Park, Carol thought that would be the perfect place to really celebrate Jiggs' return. It was vast. It was a weekday. Finding privacy would be no problem. There was a blanket in the trunk. She brought it with them on their walk, a fact not unnoticed by Jiggs. But their conversation had been double-edged. Carol's lukewarm response to Jiggs' ambition was as unsettling for him as the fact of that ambition was for her. The blanket remained folded under Carol's arm.

That night, after eating more than daily recommended portions of the feast prepared by Darcy and Marie and repeatedly toasting not only Jiggs' safe return, but Darcy's recently announced engagement to Beezer, Jiggs' and Carol's year-long yearning reasserted itself, and they went to bed early.

When Jiggs awakened the next morning, Carol was lying on her side, her head on her pillow facing him, wide awake.

"Jiggs, I've been thinking some more about you wanting to help people. Why couldn't you be a coach? You've played sports forever; you're smart, and articulate. You'd be helping kids. You'd be a natural."

Jiggs had thought about that. "I don't know, Carol. If I was coaching some sport for a living, it wouldn't be a game any more. Besides, football, wrestling, even baseball, they all involve forcing an outcome on someone else, war in a test tube. I'm pretty tired of trying to force anybody to do anything."

Those articles Carol had read about the difficulties couples encountered while trying to readjust to each other after wartime separation had discussed problems of malaise. They hadn't mentioned zeal. Jiggs had never been one of those testosterone soaked jocks who lived and died according to the outcome of their most recent game, but the man lying beside her, who had just rejected something he had loved all his life because it involved mere competition, was not the guy who broke Gary Green's nose for calling her a bad name.

"Time," she told herself. "Give this time. He hasn't even been home twenty-four hours." Besides, she didn't know exactly why she thought this was such a bad idea. She wondered what Doc would say when Jiggs told him. She propped herself up on one elbow and kissed Jiggs and the fun began again.

The day after his return, Jiggs and Doc went for a ride. As soon as Jiggs had walked through the gate, Freckles recognized him, coming up and nuzzling him by way of welcome. Nevertheless, it took almost a mile of sidestepping and head tossing for the gray horse to remember he wasn't driving when Jiggs was on his back. Eventually the two of them reached an agreement, and it became possible for Jiggs and Doc to have a conversation.

"Glad you're back in one piece. I guess those wounds don't give you much problem, if you can still play ball."

"Nah, they're fully healed. I don't even think about them most of the time. You were right about the war though."

"What do you mean?"

"Remember telling me we had no business being in Viet Nam and suggesting I go to Canada?"

"I remember."

"Well, you're right, we have no business being there. I thought for a while I should have taken your advice. But I've come to think that if the U.S. was there, I'm glad I was too, because it opened my eyes to a lot of things."

"Hard school. What kinds of things?"

"What war's really like, the suffering it causes. A person could read every book ever written about war and not have as clear an idea of what it's like as one night spent in the bush being shelled and knowing the bad guys are coming up the draw, one day spent in a military hospital, would give'em. They ought to give everybody who's been there a Purple Heart. We've all been wounded, regardless of whether you can see the scars."

Doc grimaced, remembering some of the wounds, seen and unseen, inflicted on him in the South Pacific. "What good does it do, the discovery of that fear and savagery?"

"Well, I figure that's what led you to tell me to think about going to Canada."

"I suppose so, although I still believe there are things worth dying for. Viet Nam just wasn't one of 'em."

"Maybe. But something needs to be done to pare down the list."

They rode single file down a gentle slope to the tiny cemetery overlooking the river, where Jiggs' mom was buried, and dismounted.

Doc took a swig of water from his canteen and handed it to Jiggs. "So, what's next for you? Given that any thought?"

"Yeah, Pop. I'm going to become a minister. I'm going to enroll in the seminary in December."

Doc had been looking directly at Jiggs when he asked his question, but on hearing Jiggs' reply he shook his head slightly and looked down at his boots.

"Well," Doc nodded in the direction of his wife's grave next to where they were standing, "that would have made her happy."

"A minister! A minister! Morgan, are you out of your goddamn mind?" The unambiguous Hood.

Roger had come down to Lindy's for the weekend from Great Lakes Training Center near Chicago, where he was stationed at the legal office. The four of them, he, Lindy, Jiggs and Carol had been to Iowa's game with Wisconsin earlier in the afternoon, a loss, and were now back in Lindy's living room.

"Yeah, Rog, a minister. I want to become a missionary, do some good in the world."

"Do ministers drink beer, ride motorcycles and pee on Commies?"

"Do drunken, whore-mongering football players play the fiddle and conduct orchestras? You mustn't stereotype people, Rog. Didn't they teach you that in law school?"

Hood opened his mouth, about to argue, but changed direction. "Well, Morgan, I never understood you before you went in the Marines, and from what I've seen of the Corps, I'm sure you've not been simplified." Hood tipped his bottle of beer in Jiggs' direction. Jiggs tipped his back.

Jiggs did not think for a moment that Hood thought he was making a wise choice, only that Roger was prepared to concede it was none of his business. It was ironic that of the four people closest to him in the world, excepting Camilla, now teaching somewhere in Germany, Lindy, the most profane and blasphemous among them, was the only one who approved of his decision.

"Jiggs, Honey, it's a hard, goddamned world, and if you can do some good that way, do it," was all she'd said when Jiggs told her his intentions earlier that day.

Sunday morning before leaving Lindy's, Jiggs and Roger were playing basketball at the basket Lindy had let them put up on her garage when Jiggs lived there. As usual, Hood was beating Jiggs.

"My God, Morgan. You play like a wrestler." They were both out of breath and sweating.

"Can't imagine why." Jiggs grinned. He had expected to lose. "Speaking of wrestling, want to try your luck? All these years, no wins for Roger. Who knows? You might get lucky?"

"Three times. That's all you ever beat me." Hood held up three fingers just in case Jiggs didn't understand what he was saying.

"That's because you wouldn't wrestle any more."

"I was afraid I might hurt my hands. Violinists can't be too careful, you know."

More likely your pride than your hands. Jiggs didn't say what he thought. He had something else he wanted to talk about. What if something happened to him, and one of Camilla's letters, assuming there were any, came to Carol? Jiggs wanted to guard against unnecessary heartache.

"Rog, I need you to do me a favor."

"Sure, if I can."

"If anything ever happens to me, something bad, like I get killed in an accident, I want you to write to a person whose address I'll give you and tell her what happened. Will you do that?"

Hood hesitated, thinking. Jiggs could see he was just on the point of asking for an explanation, but then he didn't. Hood being Hood, Jiggs figured he assumed the worst, that Jiggs was having an affair, and so he didn't ask. He was Carol's friend too. It would be easier not to know for sure.

"Sure. I guess so."

Jiggs went over to his wallet sitting on Lindy's back steps. He fished out a slip of paper and handed it to Roger, who opened and looked at it. Then he re-folded it and put it in his own wallet.

"Thanks, Rog. It's not what you think it is. Can we just leave it at that?"

"Sure. Play one more before we go?"

As Carol and Jiggs were driving back to Walnut Grove from Iowa City that afternoon, the subject of Jiggs' career choice came up again. "Jiggs, I think I've figured out why I've been so leery of your wanting to become a minister. It's not just my uncertainty about whether this is something you'll really be happy doing. You've pretty well convinced me of that. But, I have a feeling that being the wife of a minister is kind of like what they say about being 'Caesar's wife.'"

"What's that?"

"It means that she must be above suspicion."

"What is it you're afraid you'll be suspected of?"

"Nothing ... and everything. You know ministers are expected to be good examples, and my guess is their wives are too. If you do this, we, both of us, are going to be held to a higher standard of conduct than the people in your congregation by those very people.

"You know me, I like to have a good time, and I'm definitely not the kind of girl who goes to church teas and rummage sales. Even if I'm not openly disapproved of, I'm afraid I'll have this sense of being scrutinized all the time, and that I'll hate it ... and that they'll hold my conduct against you."

She's right.

"Carol, I think there's a lot in what you say, at least in terms of the scrutiny. But, I don't think the same rules will apply doing missionary work. Those people have so little. If you're helping them, they're not going to care if you have a beer on the veranda at the end of the day."

"That's another thing, Jiggs. I really don't want to go live in some underdeveloped country, or in a slum somewhere. I'm a country club girl, Jiggs. There's no way around it. I'm prepared to take my chances with wagging tongues if being a minister is what you really want, but living with the natives or like the natives isn't my cup of tea and never will be."

No golf. Without saying what he understood, Jiggs said he understood. That decision seemed a long way off.

30

January 1969

To most Marines, hair length was the sole criteria of "hippiedom." Hair much more than an inch long equaled "Hippie," no other facts required. Untouchables in India had nothing on a flowerchild aboard a Marine base. To be shunned would have been a blessing, to be harassed the norm. Jiggs was now experiencing the opposite side of that coin. Sitting in class at Princeton Theological Seminary, he felt he'd taken an overnight journey to Jupiter, a place where the bulletin board sagged with protest literature against the war, and a guy in the row in front of him was wearing a coat that had once been an American flag. Jiggs watched his classmates wander in and find seats. *This bunch would starve a barber.*

Enrollment in divinity school continued to be a draft deferment, so almost every seat in the large amphitheater-like room had a student in it. The only ones empty were on either side of Jiggs. In a way, Jiggs was glad for the avoidance. Although hardly the most gung-ho of Marines, he was happy to see that the Corps was no more intolerant and narrow-minded than the very persons it was so unwilling to tolerate.

Acceptance will come. He turned his attention to the lecture that was about to begin. *Can't force it.*

The professor was Harold Meeker, a man who appeared to be in his mid-fifties, balding; he was the only one in the room with less hair than Jiggs. His subject was "Introduction to Spiritual Discipline," a required course for the first year class. It was Jiggs' favorite. Professor Meeker was the best teacher Jiggs had ever experienced.

A Howard Meeker lecture did not drone. The words came carefully chosen, cutting like razors through the calluses left on Jiggs' brain by sixteen years of education concentrating almost exclusively on the "what" of things, occasionally on the "how," almost never on the "why." Jiggs' notes from Meeker's lectures were filled with questions Meeker posed, examples Meeker gave, references Meeker made to various writers and thinkers from Ernest Hemingway to St. Augustine and Socrates. Meeker's words wrapped themselves around Jiggs' mind and twisted it like a damp cloth, wringing out ideas he never knew were there.

Jiggs wished he could take only Meeker's course, so he could wallow in this new world. It made the shock of going back to school after a three-year vacation filled with learning experiences of its own easier to absorb. But he was taking Greek, and the origins of the saying, "It's Greek to me," had become apparent early in his first hour of instruction. There was no time for wallowing.

"Spirits," as Meeker's class was known among the students, was Jigg's last class of the week. Carol would finish teaching at four. They would have two full days of having no place they needed to be except with each other. Not even Professor Meeker's magic could prevent Jiggs' mind from wandering forward to that prospect as he sat there. *How am I ever going to make myself study?*

As Jiggs passed the lecturer's podium on his way out of class, Jeff Evans, the owner of the coat made from the flag, stepped in front of him. From the beginning of orientation three weeks earlier, Evans had made himself the leader, or at least the loudest spokesman, for those in the class actively involved in the anti-war effort. Brecause of Evans and a couple of others like him in the peace organizations at the school, Jiggs had thus far postponed acting on his own determination to join some organized opposition to the war. Evans assumed Jiggs' Marine Corps experience must mean he approved of everything the U.S. had done in Indo-China in the last six years. He never bothered to ask.

Now Evans was standing between Jiggs and the door to the weekend. "I bet the class Marine here's never seen a coat like this one." His voice was obviously intended to reach everyone still in the room. He held his lapel out from his chest between his thumb and forefinger as he spoke.

"You'd lose," Jiggs replied. "I've seen several close friends covered with the same material."

"Serves 'em right." Evans preened for his audience.

There had been a time when Evans' remark would have triggered all of Jiggs attack systems. The words fanned emotional embers that had been banked so low since he left Viet Nam that Jiggs thought they were out. The impulse to strike flashed through him like an electric shock, but passed in an instant, and sadness took its place.

"If that's what you really think, what are you doing in a place like this?"

Un-phased, Evans appeared about to hurl some further provocation, but a companion pulled him away. Those who had paused on their way out to witness the fun when Evans first spoke, departed, leaving Jiggs to collect his thoughts.

"You handled that very well," a voice from behind Jiggs said.

Jiggs turned to discover Professor Meeker standing at the podium putting away his lecture notes.

"Thanks. That guy's hard to like. I suppose I asked for it though by not ignoring his first remark."

Meeker shrugged. "Don't be too hard on yourself. Sainthood's not part of our theology. Do you have time for a cup of coffee? I'd like to talk to you."

The student lounge was deserted on this Friday afternoon. Jiggs cleared away the empty Styrofoam cups left by earlier loungers. Professor Meeker set down two cups of coffee and took a seat across the table.

"So, what do you think of seminary so far?"

Jiggs reflected for a moment. "I guess it's about like I should have expected, but didn't. I thought there would be more of an effort made to deepen our faith, the students', I mean. But I haven't seen any of that ... at least not so far ... and, as you saw back there after class, friends have been hard to come by."

Meeker looked down at his coffee as if the words he was searching for might be floating on its surface. "Do you think part of the seminary's job is to strengthen your faith? What made you decide to come here in the first place?"

In the hour that followed, Jiggs related in a general way his Marine experience, the conclusions he had reached, and his determination to make a positive difference in the world. He talked about Viet Nam in a non-specific way, saying only that he'd had a "bad experience" there. He didn't want to relive those days and nights even one more time. *What's the point?* They had happened. He was here now. *That's enough.*

Somewhere during Jiggs' narrative, Meeker asked, "Did you work your way through all this depression by yourself, or did you have help? Who was with you during that time on Okinawa?"

The question startled Jiggs. *Am I so transparent?* Did he bear the stamp of Camilla's wisdom and grace so prominently that it was discernable in casual conversation? He had heard nothing from her apart from a Christmas card that said, "Back to school for Master's at Columbia next September. Job translating at the U.N. to pay the rent. Great Idea! Thanks. Merry Christmas, C." The return address had been from some Air Force Base in Germany. Jiggs wanted to talk about her, to give her the credit she deserved at least as much as he wanted to avoid the details of the war, but he suppressed both. Like the war, Camilla had happened. *That's enough.*

"I had friends, later family, people who loved me."

The Professor nodded as if he understood. He gazed at Jiggs in silence for a few seconds, and Jiggs had the impression what Meeker understood was that there was more than Jiggs was willing to tell, not only about how Jiggs' spirit had been wounded, but about how it had been healed.

Meeker finally ended his silence. "I have a son over in Viet Nam right now. He's been there a month. He's only nineteen. He got drafted."

In the space of a single sentence, the Howard Meeker Jiggs was looking at across the table morphed from caring professor to concerned father.

"What's your son doing over there?" *Where is he touching the elephant?* "It makes a difference."

"Carrying a rifle, I guess. He talks about 'patrolling' in his letters."

Jiggs sighed to himself. *Not much room for comfort there.* "What's your son's name?"

"Tommy ... Tom. He says he's outgrown 'Tommy,' although his mother and I still think of him that way."

"Well, he'll be in my thoughts," Jiggs said. He had been going to say "prayers," but his image of himself using that word in that way bespoke a piety he knew he did not possess.

Meeker sighed. "Thank you. Sometimes it's hard for me to think of anything else."

31

May 1969

Despite the stigma of his military service, Jiggs began to make a few friends. Sports had always been one of his foremost sources of friendship, and his baseball skills opened some doors once softball season arrived.

The level of play in the school's intramural softball league was such that it wasn't even called an "intramural" league. It was a 'Fellowship' league. It was a league where an ex-catcher could be a shortstop, where The Dugout Disciples, Jiggs' team, consisting of five guys and five women, several of whom had never played before, was relatively respectable. That suited Jiggs. He wore shorts and sneakers and never dove for a grounder just out of his reach unless it threatened the beer he usually had parked behind his position.

So it was with more than a little surprise when, during a game against some upper classmen midway through the season, the opponent's pitcher was combative, argumentative, and obnoxiously competitive from the first inning on. Arguing umpire's calls, clumsily attempting to interfere with infielders fielding ground balls when he ran the bases, his constant yells of encouragement to his own team were almost as disagreeable as his protests of plays that went against him. Unlike anyone else on the field, this guy was wearing a baseball uniform, including cleats. Even his teammates seemed embarrassed by him.

Jiggs tried to ignore him. It didn't take more than a glance to see the guy was a bozo, not a ballplayer. Ignoring him became impossible in the fifth inning. Jiggs was playing second base. With two outs, Bozo was the base runner on first. There was a ground ball to the shortstop, who underhanded it to Jiggs for the force out at second base - three outs, inning over. Jiggs stepped off the base a couple of feet into right field, intending to trot back to the Disciples' bench with one of his friends who was playing centerfield. At least two seconds after the play was over and more than three feet behind the base, Bozo slid hard into Jiggs, raking Jiggs' calf and ankle with his spikes. The impact was not enough to knock Jiggs off his feet, but when he looked down he saw his sock beginning to turn red. Bozo was still lying there.

"Nice slide."

Bozo looked up at Jiggs standing over him. "If you don't want to play hard, don't play."

It was all Jiggs could do not to go down hard with his knee onto Bozo's face or chest, but he gritted his teeth, turned away and trotted back to the bench.

Carol surveyed Jiggs' wounds from the bleachers where she was sitting behind the fence. "That guy ought to be thrown out of the game."

Jiggs shook his head, no, but didn't say anything. Carol could see he was angry, but figured this was just another provocation the new Jiggs was choosing to ignore. She had heard about the confrontation with Jeff Evans and the flag coat.

32

June 1969-January 1970

The summer following his first year at seminary, Jiggs began to volunteer at CHOP, Children's Hospital of Philadelphia. For four hours every Wednesday evening, Jiggs shared supervision of the playroom with another volunteer, visiting kids in their rooms, playing board games, reading stories, pushing wheelchairs, talking. Children would come and go. The average stay was only two days. Jiggs would see them one time, and they would go home. He seldom knew why they were there. Despite the hour commute each way, Jiggs looked forward to his time there more than any class.

Tony Capini didn't go home, and Jiggs knew why. The reason was in "Volunteer Notes," the briefing sheet containing any special instructions the volunteers needed to know before starting work each night.

Room	Patient	Age	Comments
111	Anthony Capini	5	Cardiac patient, keep quiet, no strenuous play

Jiggs first met Tony while proving to a group of youthful skeptics that even someone as old and creaky as himself could not only stand on his head, but walk around the room on his hands. Tony had joined the audience after Jiggs began his demonstration, and when Jiggs glanced around from his inverted stance, there was the roly-poly five-year-old teetering upside down, about to dissolve his attempted headstand into a back pancake. Jiggs' co-worker, who, moments before, had been reading a story to another group that had included Tony, was rushing to catch the would-be acrobat before landing.

The first time Jiggs took Tony for a ride around the grounds, as soon as they were out the door and away from the overseeing eyes of the nurses, Tony held up his hand and ordered a halt. Jiggs stopped, and Tony got out of the wheelchair, walked around and took Jiggs' hand and led him to the front.

"Get in."

"Why?"

"My turn to push."

"Can't happen, my man. But I'll make you a deal. When your doctor says it's okay for you to push me, I will ride wherever you want to take me. If that's fair, let's shake."

Tony stuck out his hand, and a deal, the conditions of which were never satisfied, was struck.

During the first three months Jiggs worked at CHOP, Tony became his special friend. They played for the "World Candyland Championship." Tony won. They read every *Winnie-the-Pooh* book Jiggs could find and dozens of others. They drew pictures of everybody at the hospital. In Tony's pictures of people, he always drew their hearts.

Jiggs managed to visit Tony every Monday afternoon, the day he knew Tony's parents couldn't make it. One time he took Carol. She had a great time, but when Jiggs asked her to come along on his next visit, she declined. "Tony's a great little kid, Jiggs, and it's great you can do what you're doing, but I can't. I hate hospitals. They depress me too much."

Tony was not getting any better. Nobody told Jiggs this; he could see it. By late November, the boy's energy had diminished noticeably. He no longer talked very much, but his expressions, the looks he would get in his eyes as he listened to the stories gave him continued eloquence.

When Jiggs visited the hospital on the afternoon of Christmas Eve, it was even more quiet than usual. Most of the rooms were empty, because everyone who could possibly be released for the holidays had gone home, and only emergencies were coming in until after the new year began.

Tony did not even sit up in bed when Jiggs entered his room, but his black diamond eyes shone when he opened Jiggs' present. He insisted on immediately putting on the sweatshirt Jiggs gave him with the picture of Tigger from *Winnie-the-Pooh* on the front.

Jiggs read a couple of stories and they talked about Santa Claus.

"What do you want from Santa, Tony?"

"To go home."

The impossibility of that simple wish and the courage with which Tony bore its obvious denial was more than Jiggs could bear. Sitting on the edge of Tony's bed, Jiggs began to cry. Tony patted his knee and, in his most grown-up tone of voice, he told Jiggs he "had to be brave."

On the way out of the hospital, Jiggs stopped at the chapel for the first time. He entered intending to pray, but spent most of his time wondering why God made children suffer. The following Wednesday, when he reported to the playroom at six o'clock and glanced at the Volunteer Notes, he learned that Tony was no longer a patient, and Jiggs knew Tony didn't have to be brave any longer. The knowledge was no comfort.

Instead of having dinner at the hospital cafeteria as he usually did, he went for a walk. Coatless, he wandered between the piles of shoveled snow along the frigid, jarring sidewalks that wound through the hospital campus. A raw wind sanded his cheekbones and nibbled at the edges of his ears with frosty fire, but for a time he was oblivious to the cold.

Jiggs kept telling himself God had really given Tony a gift by allowing him to escape life as a bedridden invalid, a witness only to the many joys he could never share, but he remained unconvinced. What had Tony done in the first place to deserve a life from which escape was a blessing? Given a choice, would Tony have chosen escape?

After thirty minutes, the knife edge of cold penetrated Jiggs' armor of grief and drove him into the nearest building, one he had never been in before. There was no waiting room or reception desk at the entrance. Jiggs wandered a maze of unmarked corridors populated by doors to anonymous rooms, without seeing anyone.

Finally, he came to a lounge furnished with several couches and easy chairs in worn condition arranged in a random way in front of a television. The television was on, but there was no one in the room. There were three vending machines against the far wall, one for hot drinks, one for cold, and a third for snacks. Scrounging in his jeans' pocket, Jiggs found a dime and bought a cup of coffee.

He was sitting on the arm of one of the sofas inhaling the steam when a young girl appeared around the corner. About nine or ten years old, Jiggs guessed. She stepped into the room by first thrusting her right hip forward then dragging her left foot somewhere ahead of her right, while at the same time her head and shoulders kept turning away from the direction she was trying to walk. Her left elbow was pressed tightly against her hip, but her left forearm and hand kept waving uncontrollably out from her side. *Some kind of palsy.*

The anguish Jiggs was already feeling seared even deeper as she lurched past him. "Hello." He nodded as he spoke.

The girl turned her whole body to look at him. She was momentarily pretty, and then a spasm twisted her features as she made an incomprehensible effort to reply to Jiggs' greeting.

Jiggs smiled and the girl resumed her painful way towards the vending machines. When she arrived, she put her right hand up to insert her dime into the slot for a snack, but she missed. Jiggs had seen it coming. When the coin clicked against the metal side of the machine, it was as if it was clicking against his heart. She tried again and missed again and again.

Jiggs watched hollow-eyed. Should he offer to help her, or would that somehow be the worst thing he could do? Did she need to do it herself? She evidently came in with no expectation of help.

On her fourth try the girl dropped her coin on the floor. Very slowly she bent her head forward to look at the money lying at her feet. The deliberation with which she bent her head, as if forcing herself to look over the edge of a cliff, made Jiggs realize that for this girl, the money lying just beyond the tip of her toes might as well have been at the bottom of a well. He reached in his pocket and found another dime as he walked towards where the girl was standing. He reached to insert his own money and then stopped, as if noticing for the first time the coin on the floor.

"Oh, did you drop this?" He picked up the dime and handed it to the girl. She smiled as he put his own dime in the machine and bought a candy bar he didn't want to complete his charade.

Once more the girl tried to insert her dime, and this time she succeeded. As she turned away from the vending machine with a pack of potato chips, Jiggs stuck out his hand. "Hi, my name's 'Jiggs.' What's yours?"

"Eln." The girl exhaled loudly, struggling to form the sounds she wanted to make with uncooperative lips. Jiggs shook her left hand.

"Ellen," Jiggs guessed.

"Uhhh." The girl nodded.

"Well, I'm pleased to know you, Ellen. Do you live here?" Jiggs knew CHOP had a care facility for patients with cerebral palsy, where they lived and learned how best to cope with problems of everyday life that would later confront them, like vending machines.

"Yuhh." Ellen again nodded, as she tore the potato chip wrapper with her teeth. "Yuh wuk heh?" She moved her hand in the direction of Jiggs' volunteer nametag pinned to his shirt.

"Yes, I do." Jiggs explained in what part of the hospital he worked. As he was finishing his explanation, a middle-aged woman in a white lab coat came into the room.

"Hello, Ellen." The woman had waited until Jiggs finished speaking. "I was wondering where you disappeared. Hadn't you better be getting back to the group?"

Ellen said something that sounded like "Okay" and started for the door.

"Bye, Ellen," Jiggs said, and the girl turned and said in the clearest pronunciation Jiggs had heard her manage, "Good-bye." Her success with the word obviously pleased her, and she smiled again as she turned away.

"I'm Dr. Skalsky, Mr. ... Morgan." The doctor squinted to read Jiggs' nametag. "What are you doing in this part of the hospital?"

Jiggs explained he had gone for a walk without stopping to think how cold it was and had ducked into this building to get warm.

"Why? Is it against the rules for me to be here? If so, I'm sorry."

"Well, we just need to know who's here. It doesn't sound as if you came in through the main entrance. It's not against any rules, although from the infrequency of visitors here, one might think so."

"I don't even know what building this is. What is this place?"

"This is the Rehabilitation and Therapy Facility for the Cerebral Palsy Center here at CHOP. I'm the Director here. I was sitting in on a therapy session before I came looking for Ellen. Would you like a tour? Do you have the time?"

During the next thirty minutes, Doctor Skalsky showed Jiggs some exercise rooms, a swimming pool and several therapy pools, classrooms, a typical living quarters and a room Dr. Skalsky called the "Problem Room." "We try to simulate everyday problems and work out solutions together that will enable each student ... we prefer 'student' to 'patient' here ... to deal with problems within their own capabilities."

"Yes. I just saw an example of what you're talking about. Tell me a little about Ellen, that girl I was talking to when you came in, can you?"

"Hmmm. What can I tell you about Ellen? Her last name is 'Kelso.' She's an orphan, or at least completely abandoned by her parents, neither of whom she's ever known. She is a ward of the State. She's been here almost three years now. She is neither the most nor the least severely challenged of our students, but she's very bright and determined to do whatever she can to cope. She's a very lonely, loveable child."

As Jiggs walked back to the playroom, it occurred to him that since seeing Ellen and meeting Dr. Skalsky, he hadn't thought more about Tony's death.

33

May-September 1970

May 7, 1970

Dear Larry,

I need to vent. Correct me if I'm wrong. Nixon was elected on his promise to end the war. Eighteen months have passed and the war is still going on. Ten days ago Nixon broadened the conflict by invading Cambodia, a neutral country. Five days later American soldiers killed American citizens for protesting the very war Nixon promised to end. Nixon is a war criminal and should be hanged.

There, I feel marginally better. Sorry to begin with such negativity, but ever since Kent State, I've been able to think of little else. How are you faring? Is your new church living up to your expectations? I hope your congregation doesn't hold your military service against you the way many of my classmates seem to hold mine against me.

How are the new legs working out? Can you get around without too much struggle? How's the family?

How old are the girls now, ten and twelve? How do they like their new home?

Sorry this is so short, but the schoolbooks beckon. Drop me a line whenever you can and let me know how you're doing.

Your friend, Jiggs

May 22, 1970
Dear Jiggs,

You're correct in your facts, but wrong in your conclusion. While I believe the policy to be mistaken, do you think Nixon broadened the war just for the sake of broadening it, rather than in the belief that by taking away North Viet Nam's Cambodian sanctuaries, he could ultimately shorten the war? I certainly wouldn't vote for him, but neither would I hang him. Neither would you, I suspect. Taking away his power is one thing; taking away his life is another. The latter should be left only to God.

Turning to your other questions, when I think of all the ways my life could have turned out after the loss of my legs, I fall on my knees (figuratively speaking) and give thanks for Sandy and the girls, all three of whom have done everything humanly possible to encourage me and keep me from despair. Consequently, the Reverend Nelson is thriving in a full and friendly church, a second ministry among other disabled vets, a new sport (bird watching) and, most important of all, the opportunity to watch my two lovely daughters grow and become kind, generous, interesting people. Lucky me.

Of course, there are problems. Can you imagine life without problems? My jump shot has not come back, preachers don't get paid much (a fact you're about to learn), and now and then I have something called "phantom pain" where my wheels used to be. But there are so many good things going on, that the bad things are bearable.

Your letter didn't say much about your plans. Drop me a line and let me know what's in store post graduation. I continue to be astonished at your career choice. As I've said before, nothing you ever said or did when I was around suggested that's the direction you would take. Bravo.

If you ever get anywhere near California, come see us.

Regards, Larry

Control of the anti-war activities at the school by Jeff Evans and his crowd had not prevented Jiggs from marching locally as part of demonstrations arranged by groups outside the school.

Jiggs and Carol lay in bed, talking about Jiggs' next foray into protest. "I don't think I'll flunk out if I take a day off to send Nixon a message about how much he's disappointed me." Jiggs stretched and yawned as he prepared to get up. "There's an organizational meeting tonight."

Carol brightened. "Do you really think there's any chance you might flunk out?"

"Suppose there's always a chance."

"I better get my champagne glasses and feather boa out of mothballs, just in case. We can celebrate our return to wanton living."

Jiggs folded his hands in mock piety. "Lord, please watch over your servant, Carol. She really wants to be a good Christian woman, but she just likes to drink and smoke dope and screw so much that ... HEY, OUCH..." He rolled away from her, laughing and trying to cover his head to protect himself from the blows Carol was raining down on him with the pillow they'd been sharing.

Sometimes such laughter made Jiggs feel guilty. Guys were still dying over there. This next march would be a big one. Jiggs was determined to be a part of it, even if doing so meant confronting Jeff Evans, whose animosity towards Jiggs remained undiminished.

There were more than twenty people in the room when Jiggs and Carol walked in. As they entered, the buzz of pre-meeting chatter suddenly stopped. The abrupt onset of silence elsewhere in the room caught the attention of Evans, who was standing near the front talking with two of the coordinators of the planned descent on the Capitol. Several campus groups were combining to organize transportation and support for those from the seminary who intended to make the trip and be heard.

"Well, well," Evans came hurrying towards the door to confront Jiggs before he could find a seat. "What're you doing here, Morgan? This isn't the VFW."

Carol, who was ahead of Jiggs, paused at the sound of Evans' voice, but Jiggs nudged her into motion and, a step inside the room, they turned towards the back.

"Not so fast, Morgan. Not so fast." Evans, loud as always, came up behind Jiggs and put a hand on his shoulder. "We don't want you here. Go away. You're not welcome."

Jiggs turned around when he felt the hand on his shoulder. Carol put a restraining hand on his arm as he turned, but he smiled and shook his head at her, letting her know that he was in control.

"Just go on with your meeting, Jeff. We want to be part of what's happening here tonight as much as you."

"This is a private organization, Morgan," Evans hissed, "and we don't want you in it. Go kill some peasants or whatever it is you like to do."

Evans will never change. Jiggs turned away and nodded to Carol to head for two empty seats in the corner. It was a public meeting. It had been advertised on every bulletin board on campus for two weeks. Before Jiggs took his first step, Evans grabbed his shoulder, hard this time, and jerked him back around and spit in his face.

Carol gasped. So did several others. Jiggs stood motionless staring at Evans for a long moment, then just shook his head and went over and sat down, as one of the other students came up to Evans and said, "Jeff, you're way out of line, man."

Silence reigned. After a few seconds, Evans stomped out of the room, and the meeting began without him.

Carol didn't know if Jiggs was right or wrong not to have retaliated when Evans spit on him. At what point was turning the other cheek no longer a viable option? In the year since Jiggs' return, she had listened as he rejected a coaching career because of the competition, she had heard about the incident involving the flag coat, she had watched him walk away from Bozo's spiking; she knew he was different. But until this moment, she had never appreciated how much.

The campus was eerie. From corner street light to corner streetlight nothing moved. Their footsteps echoed off the walls of buildings as Jiggs and Carol walked through the night, sounding as if some invisible person was following them. Jiggs carried a small cooler Carol had packed with sandwiches and fruit. Carol carried a thermos of coffee. They might have been going to a football game on Saturday afternoon, except it was four-thirty a.m.

As they drew near the library parking lot, the sidewalks became more heavily populated. In ones and twos and threes, people quietly made their way to the large charter buses standing in the lot with their engines idling. Jiggs and Carol boarded the first bus they came to. Jiggs handed the driver their passes, and they found seats together about two-thirds of the way back. Stowing their carry-ons in the overhead rack, they settled in. Jiggs was asleep by the time the bus was full and pulling out of the parking lot, making its way south to Washington.

They were crossing the Susquehanna River north of Baltimore when Jiggs awakened. It was still dark in the bus and no talking could be heard. Out his window he could see the sky beginning to lighten in the East. Jiggs hadn't seen a sunrise for some time. It reminded him of working the farm sales with Colonel Clemons. *Wonder if the Colonel's still auctioneering.* It seemed like a hundred years ago.

"What do you think this day will bring?" A familiar voice from across the aisle asked. Jiggs turned away from the window and looked across the still sleeping Carol to discover Howard Meeker sitting there.

"Professor Meeker, what're you doing here?" *World class stupid question.*

"Same thing you are. My wife and I decided it was time to walk our talk, so to speak, and let the Administration know it's not just you youngsters who oppose the war."

"They know. Nixon knows, he just doesn't give a shit." Jiggs winced as the offensive word slipped out. "Sorry about that."

Meeker appeared un-phased. "Can't quarrel with the sentiment."

"Is your son back in the States yet?" Jiggs was always hesitant to ask about family members he knew were in country, because maybe they'd been hit, but he figured if Meeker's son had become a casualty he'd have heard about it at school.

"No. He has about three months to go," Meeker replied.

"Ninety-four days," the woman sitting on the far side of the Professor piped up, leaning forward for the first time so that Jiggs could see her face in the half light.

"Jiggs, this is my wife, Evelyn. Evelyn, this is one of my students, Jiggs Morgan."

"We've met."

It was true. Evelyn Meeker was Dr. Skalsky, whom Jiggs had met the preceding January, when he unknowingly wandered into the Cerebral Palsy facility at CHOP. Since that time, Jiggs had transferred from the playroom to the CP unit, where he worked with children like Ellen, practicing their routines with them under the supervision of the therapists, helping the kids outflank uncooperative bodies. He had spoken with Dr. Skalsky nee Meeker, on any number of occasions. She had never given any indication she had any connection with the school.

"Hello, Dr. Skalsky. It's a small world, I guess."

Professor Meeker looked back and forth between Jiggs and his wife. "How do you two know each other?"

Evelyn Skalsky explained. When he heard about Jiggs working at the hospital, Meeker regarded him in silence for several seconds, much the way he had months earlier when Jiggs had told him of his post-Viet Nam depression.

However, no more was said of Jiggs' work at the hospital during the bus ride. Instead, Howard Meeker asked, "How do you like the seminary now that you have a year under your belt? You seem to be doing alright."

Jiggs shrugged. "I'm learning a lot about Christianity and little or nothing about faith. We dissect God the way we dismembered frogs in high school biology. We're learning all the parts, but very little attention's being paid to the appreciation of the whole." Jiggs paused and looked at the Professor, then went on. "It seems like I'm being taught to sell God like someone else might teach me to sell insurance. God is no more alive in my classes than that insurance policy or some frog floating in formaldehyde."

"Jiggs, most people come here because they've already been inspired by the beauty and mystery of the faith. It's to be hoped what students learn here helps perpetuate that inspiration in a way that propels them into a lifetime of service. Maybe we're not doing as well as we could with that, but, as I think I told you when we first met, coming to seminary to obtain that inspiration in the first place is putting the cart before the horse."

The day dawning outside the bus was bright and sunny. Carol awakened as it became lighter. Jiggs introduced her to the Meekers, and they shared the coffee Jiggs and Carol brought.

"Ohhh." Professor Meeker twisted and stretched in his seat. "Pre-dawn bus rides are for the younger..."

"Pig!" Someone in the front of the bus yelled out an open window at two policemen standing beside their cruiser parked on the shoulder of the road. A chorus of oinks and other unpleasant sounds followed from some of the other passengers. The two policemen continued to stare at the flow of traffic without any visible reaction. They knew it was going to be a long day.

It was only eight-thirty, but people were everywhere, walking along the sidewalks, heading for the Mall. The police had put up barricades to keep traffic off of Independence and Constitution Avenues. The bus threaded its way around the Capitol to RFK Stadium to let out its passengers.

The parking lot looked like a sea filled with steel whales. Row upon row of buses stretched all around the silent stadium memorializing the foremost proponent of the movement that brought them there. An endless line of newcomers queued up nose to tail, waiting to disgorge their occupants, eager to swim in the ocean of protest beginning to rise.

Several campus organizations had cooperated to arrange the charters from Princeton. Nominally, Jiggs was there as a member of "Seminarians Against the War," but he had no intention of marching with that group. He just wanted to be part of the throng, to add his presence to the mass, so that when the cameras surveyed the scene and the commentators made their crowd estimates, he would have made his contribution to this expression of the people's wrath. Carol tagged along to keep him company, disappointed that the cherry blossoms weren't in bloom.

The atmosphere along the Mall was anything but wrathful. Here and there speakers harangued gatherings, but more often it was a musician with a flute or guitar who commanded attention. Families in the crowd were having picnics. Jiggs and Carol had some fried chicken when they stopped to chat with members of a group called "Iowans Against the War."

More like a folk festival.

Frisbees buzzed through air filled with banners announcing the presence of hundreds, perhaps thousands of groups as disparate as "Methodist Mothers For Peace," union locals and a group calling itself the "Young Trotskyites."

Jiggs was wearing a Marines Corps' utility jacket so worn that its camouflage pattern had almost disappeared into itself. He hadn't had it on since Viet Nam, and he'd debated with himself whether to wear it. *Will it add anything to be identified as a veteran against the war?* Would the jacket earn him the enmity of other protesters the way his military service had alienated so many of his classmates?

Who cares? It meant something to him to see other veterans protesting, maybe it would mean something to somebody else to see him. He was no stranger to dealing with enmity. However, enmity was not what materialized.

"Hey, Bro, you been there?"

"Yeah."

"No more war, Man! No more war."

"Right on."

"Hey, Marine, over here."

"How's it goin'?"

"Fine. When were you in country?"

"Sixty-seven. You?"

"Sixty-five and sixty-six. Wow, can you believe we're still fightin' over there? It's still going on, Man. It's still going on."

"That's why I'm here."

"Yeah, me too. That's *really* why I'm here, for those poor sons a bitches who are still over there."

About eleven-thirty an electricity began to buzz through the crowd. It was half an hour until the march was to begin, and groups began to form around their banners, soon children would be hoisted to their fathers' shoulders, blankets would be folded and put away. The army was preparing to move.

As noon approached, Jiggs and Carol were near the front of the crowd, at the end of the Mall nearest the Capitol, in the vicinity of a group of Viet Nam Veterans Against the War. At twelve o'clock a great wave of noise erupted, bells rang, whistles blew, sirens blared, shouting everywhere. One of the veterans near Jiggs blew "Charge" on what looked and sounded like a NVA bugle, and the front ranks started for the Capitol. In the vanguard just ahead, a group of students walked chanting the battle-cry of a generation, "One, two, three, four, we don't want your fucking war!"

Jiggs loved Washington, D.C., the Washington Monument, the Lincoln Memorial, the Jefferson Memorial, the White House, the Capitol. Despite having seen them several times while in OCS at nearby Quantico, his first glimpse of these shrines during each new visit never failed to stir him. No amount of disillusionment with government could completely dull the edge of excitement instilled by some long forgotten school teacher's indelible imprinting of both the facts and myths of his heritage on his mind. He remembered his first walk up Capitol Hill four years earlier, thinking about walking on ground where men like Lincoln, Clay, Roosevelt and Harry Truman, a Jiggs' favorite, had actually been. He felt like he was in church.

Now he was walking up the same slope, this time to tell by his mere presence the successors of Lincoln and Roosevelt they were wrong, to tell the men and women of Congress what he and many of his three hundred thousand companions had learned through bitter experience, that America was killing people, its own and others, for no reason thaving anything to do with the principles that made this hill such hallowed ground.

Despite everything that had happened to him in the last four years, Jiggs' respect for the place where he was standing made protest difficult. His stomach turned over and his feet felt like lead. It was as if he was climbing Mt. Everest instead of a low rise in a tidal plain on the Mid-Atlantic coast of North America. Jiggs thought about Doc, the veteran of Iwo Jima, suggesting he go to Canada, of Lindy weeping and cursing the body counts, of David Leslie and Buskirk, and Gorman and Wollman and Jim Linetti, legless Larry Nelson and dozens of others. Jiggs thought of the children on the hospital ship and marched on.

Half way up the Hill, the government had thrown a makeshift chain link fence around the Capitol to prevent the mob from invading the building itself. If it had really been a mob, the fence would have been worse than nothing; it would have only antagonized those bent on destruction. *But this isn't a mob.* The crowd was not bent on destruction. Those walking point stopped at the fence, and Jiggs and Carol, who were fifty yards back, soon were forced to halt as the line backed up behind its leaders.

Some people stood milling about in place, waiting to see what would happen next. Others, feeling the compression of the multitude behind them continuing to forge ahead while the front of the line was no longer moving, peeled off to the left and right, rapidly spreading along the fence line throughout its length. Jiggs and Carol remained on their original line of march and slowly filtered forward through the press of bodies ahead of them.

Isn't anybody going to say anything, do anything? Television cameras and microphones had been set up at the fence, now just twenty feet from where they were standing. Wasn't there going to be any gesture, any symbol tying together the efforts and sentiments of more than a quarter of a million people who felt strongly enough to be there?

As he drew nearer the front, Jiggs saw a tall, skinny youth with shoulder length brown hair, also wearing faded jungle utilities, step to the microphone. The young man held up a handful of medals. "I'm giving these back. I'm ashamed of what I had to do to get them." With that, he threw the bits of ribbon and brass over the fence where they clinked on the stone steps. Bystanders applauded.

He was succeeded at the microphone by another man brandishing a handful of decorations, who gave a brief speech about why he was doing what he was about to do. Then he, too, threw his medals over the fence. For fifteen minutes, Jiggs watched, shaken, as man after man stepped up, spoke, and then threw away the tokens of recognition they'd received for their gallantry and pain. The white marble steps on the other side of the fence were now splashed with color, red, white and blue ribbons in a wide variety of combinations, golden and silver stars shining in the sun, here and there a heart-shaped medallion. Boys, draftees, who had suddenly become men in jungles and rice paddies, and grizzled middle-aged warriors, officers and enlisted from other wars, unpracticed and self-conscious, mumbled their messages of guilt and regret into the microphones and moved on.

Carol tugged at Jiggs' arm. "Let's get out of here. This is creepy."

"Let's wait a bit." Jiggs withdrew his hand from the pocket of his utilities. Carol looked down and saw he was holding his Silver Star and Purple Heart along with some other, lesser awards.

"Jiggs, please," Carol stepped in front of him so she could face him. "don't go up there. I know it was awful, but you earned this honor trying to save a life, not take one. Don't throw it away. Please ... please don't go up there."

Jiggs stared at Carol and past her, up the steps a few feet away to where the parade of excoriation continued. He knew she was wrong; he knew his award had been earned in the service of an unjust cause, but he could not entirely suppress his pride at having met the test. Years of striving, of competing for medals, trophies, championships, to make the cut, had so thoroughly ingrained the need for recognition that he hesitated to turn his back on his accomplishment, however dubious it now seemed.

"Jiggs," Carol was hugging him now, "please ... please put them away."

He felt like a robot whose guidance system had gone haywire, receiving conflicting signals from different sources. Which must he obey? He closed his eyes and took a deep breath. Then he relaxed and dropped his medals back in his pocket and buttoned the flap

"Let's go."

Hand in hand they made their way back through the crowd. Eventually they reached a point where it began to thin. There, off to their left, fifty yards away and retreating from him on a diagonal path, Jiggs noticed a slightly built, brown-haired woman. He saw only her back, but his heart leapt. She was walking with an older man who had only one arm.

34

May 1971

Carol looked up as Howard Meeker sat down beside her. "Dr. Meeker. I didn't know you were a softball fan."

"Softball's all right. This is the first game of any kind I've attended since Tommy finished high school. I heard some of the students talking about the games, and it was such a nice day, I thought I'd come out and take a look. It's on my way home." Meeker looked out at the field for the first time. "I guess Jiggs must be playing. Let's see, which one is he? Does he like to play?"

"Huhh!" Carol's attempt to keep from laughing at the Professor's question turned into a snort. "He's the shortstop. He loves to play any sport ... except golf. If I had a nickel for every game I watched him play, I'd be a rich woman."

Together they watched the first couple of innings, remarkable only for the fact that the opposing pitcher's extraordinarily competitive behavior stood out like a fart in church.

"That fellow out there pitching doesn't seem to have gotten the word that this is a friendly league," Meeker said, following yet another loud argument over a routine call.

"You noticed. I think he's the guy Jiggs calls 'Bozo.' If he's the one I think he is, he spiked Jiggs last year well after a play was over - drew blood. Strange guy."

"So he's always like that?"

Carol nodded. "This is the second time I've seen him play, and he's been like this both times."

"Interesting."

Things became more interesting in the fourth inning. Bozo led off and managed to get to first on a walk. The next batter hit a ground ball to the second baseman, who tossed it to Jiggs coming across the bag from short to force Bozo, the runner coming from first. Jiggs caught the ball while moving forward and in one continuous movement fired a rocket towards first in an attempt to complete a double play. An instant before Jiggs released the ball, Bozo veered slightly to his left, as if to force Jiggs to alter his throw, except he was too late. Jiggs was playing on instinct, his momentum too great for any reaction. The throw hit Bozo, no more than fifteen feet away, right in the tip of his nose, and his face exploded.

Bozo went down as if struck by lightning. Immediately there was blood everywhere. Before anyone could reach him, he rose briefly to his knees, but in less than a moment collapsed face down on the grass and didn't move.

A woman nursing a baby three rows down from where Carol and Howard Meeker were sitting screamed. She stood up and hurried down the steps, breaking into an awkward run when she hit the ground while simultaneously trying to shift her child to her shoulder and button her blouse. By the time she reached the fallen player, presumably her husband, the umpire and several of the other players were kneeling over him, and one of them appeared to be rendering some kind of first aid. Another left the group and ran looking for a phone on which to call for help. Jiggs was not among those showing concern. He had returned to his position between second and third and sat sipping his beer as he watched the commotion.

Eventually an ambulance arrived. Bozo was put in a neck brace and wheeled off the field on a stretcher, passing just beneath and to the left of where Carol was sitting at the end of the bleachers. Bozo's mouth was agape, and Carol could see he was missing teeth. Both his eyes were swollen shut, and his nose was pulp. The woman with the baby had been sobbing throughout and was still weeping as she climbed into the ambulance, her child still in her arms.

The two teams decided to call the rest of the game, a decision on which Jiggs voiced no opinion. When it was announced the game was over, he trotted into the bench, picked up his bat and walked around the fence to where Carol and Professor Meeker and were waiting.

"Hi, Babe. Hi, Professor Meeker. What brings you out to the game?"

"Too nice a day to stay indoors, I guess ... at least until that all happened." Meeker nodded out towards where the game's last play had occurred.

"Wow, what a terrible thing." Carol said.

"Want to go get something to eat?" Jiggs asked.

Howard Meeker gave Jiggs a funny look. "Just a minute, Jiggs. I'm curious. How does what just happened make you feel, especially since you're the one who threw the ball?"

"I think it's too bad the runner didn't get out of the way. Screwed up the whole game."

"That's it? I'm a bit surprised. Carol says he spiked you last year."

"That's right, he did."

"Does that have anything to do with your apparent lack of remorse?"

Howard Meeker was the one person at the school above all others whom Jiggs did not want to disappoint. He looked at his professor and friend for a couple of long seconds. "Look, Professor, that guy tries to hurt people when he plays. He did it to me. I didn't intend to hit him, but I did intend to make sure he didn't spike me again by giving him something else to think about."

"But now that you see what happened, aren't you sorry about how badly he was hurt?"

Jiggs shook his head and opened and closed his eyes as if trying to clear it. "No. I'm not. Guys like that, they've got it coming. Too many of them never get what they deserve. The persons I feel sorry for are his family. The guy's a jerk."

"Gentlemen," Carol interrupted, "enough with the philosophy of revenge. Let's go get something to eat. We can discuss this further at the restaurant ... if we must."

Professor Meeker looked at his watch. "Thanks for the invitation, but what I just saw and heard leaves me without much appetite. Another time." He walked off.

Later, as they were having a cup of coffee and some dessert, Carol came back to the incident. "Help me understand something, Jiggs. Since you got back from the war, I've seen you ignore some enormous provocations, and show compassion for people far less in need of it than that guy you maimed today. How do you choose?"

Jiggs thought about it for a few seconds, then he told her the story about when Larry Nelson sliced up Yak, and of his own lack of sympathy for Yak's disfigurement. "Like I told Professor Meeker, I have a hard time giving a shit about guys like that.

They deserve the consequences of their behavior, however unintended. He's the one who wanted to 'play hard.'"

35

July, 1971

Colonel and Mrs. Rodney Lincoln
Request the honor of your presence
at the marriage of their daughter
Karien Michelle Lincoln
To
James Grant Hegman
on Saturday, July 17, 1971
at Two O'Clock P.M.
at First Presbyterian Church
of Lake City, Iowa

Jiggs was using the invitation as a bookmark. As the plane leveled off and headed west, he glanced at the hand-written note Hegman had added below the engraving.

Jr., come a couple of days early and play some basketball. We need a wrestler to dive for loose balls.
Jim

P.S. Hood says he's coming.

Must be a big wedding. Hegman, three years older, had often acted as sort of a mentor to Jiggs. On the scattered occasions they'd seen each other in the years since college, they would have a beer and update each other on their lives, nothing more. Jiggs supposed Hood made the guest list because he was a fraternity brother.

Doc and Darcy were waiting for him at the gate as he entered the terminal.

"Where's Carol?" Darcy demanded by way of a greeting.

"Working woman ... couldn't come ... couldn't get time off. Glad to see you too."

Jiggs hugged Darcy and shook hands with Doc. "I figured I better come anyway just to make sure Pop hadn't been run over by some bull. I still can't afford to support him."

Doc grinned. "You should have stayed and worked and sent Carol. She's nicer to me."

Throughout their wait for Jiggs' suitcase and on their way to the car, Darcy yakked about everything that had happened in Walnut Grove, which wasn't much. As they paused to unlock the door, Doc asked, "Do you want to drive, Jiggs? You remember how to get to the park?"

Darcy stopped talking.

"Park, ..." Jiggs repeated, thinking he was missing a joke. "What park?" He glanced from Doc to Darcy. Neither was laughing.

"Get in," Doc tossed Jiggs the keys. "We'll tell you on the way."

Grimes, Granger, Madrid, Luther, Boone, Stratford, tiny towns, old familiar names, each with its grain elevator poking the sky, quiet, tree-lined streets, interrupting only for a moment long straight stretches of two lane highway down which Jiggs had careened in pickup trucks and on motorcycles during a former life. Fields of young corn and soybeans shimmered in the heat, row on row. It made Jiggs a little sad to think he was no longer a part of it. Nothing they told him on the way home eased his mood.

"What's this about a park?" Jiggs asked as they cleared Des Moines.

Doc grimaced and looked as if he was seeking a place to spit.

Darcy, sitting in the backseat, leaned over between them. "There was a bill introduced in the legislature last session to make a new state park on the river east of Walnut Grove."

She paused.

Jiggs said nothing, waiting to hear their obvious objection to the proposal.

"If it passes, they'll take our place."

"What?" Jiggs' head jerked around to stare in disbelief at Darcy. Doc, who was sitting in the front passenger seat, said nothing and stared straight ahead. "The whole farm? Everything? House and all?"

Jiggs thought his father the most complete man he had ever known. He'd seen Doc bitten, kicked, bucked and scratched by nearly every known species of "domesticated" animal in North America and never once seen him retaliate. Pain, cold, heat, frustration – Doc withstood them all with quiet humor. Even the emotional blow dealt him by the death of his wife, he had silently endured. Never once had Jiggs heard him raise his voice, but the hard edge that crept in when he wanted emphasis never left any doubt in the minds of listeners that he was a man who meant what he said.

Doc was a scientist who would sit at the dinner table after the dishes were cleared and recite "Annabel Lee" or any one of dozens of other poems he knew by heart. He was the father who, when Jiggs started to date, cautioned on one of their long rides, "If a girl gives herself to you, she has given you her greatest gift, the gift of herself. Would you repay such kindness by boasting of it with your friends, when you know it would hurt her?"

Not only had Doc built the family's home, he had "built" the ground on which it stood. The Morgan farm was on the north side of the road. Immediately adjacent the road was a small pasture at the base of a steep hill. Doc had rented a bulldozer and cut a huge stair step in the hillside facing down the narrow valley. There, with the help of the entire family, he had built the house now threatened. Jiggs remembered sanding floors, painting walls, carrying lumber, pouring cement. He remembered moving in the year he was fifteen. The new house had a shower; the old place had only a tub. Jiggs thought he'd gone to heaven. He couldn't remember ever taking a bath again.

Doc had lived on the farm sixty years, his entire life minus time out for college and World War II. He'd lived in the new house, the one he'd built with his own hands, twelve years. His children grew up on that ground, his wife died and was buried there. He was like one of the oaks on the hillside above the river. Jiggs feared he would not survive being uprooted. "So, what happened to this bill? It hasn't passed, has it? What're the chances? How do you try to stop something like this?"

"It's being studied by some committee right now," Darcy replied. "Walt Shields, the editor of the Lake City paper, thinks it has a good chance to pass, although maybe not right away. He says it'll be several years before we'd have to move."

At the mention of moving, Doc stirred for the first time since the conversation began. "While I'm alive," his voice hard enough to cut glass, "nobody's living in that house but me and my family."

Karien Lincoln looked exactly like the kind of girl Jiggs would have imagined Jim Hegman marrying. "Like Miss America," was how Ron Bjournquist had once described her. Jiggs did not disagree. Tall and willowy, with dark hair and sparkling blue eyes, she seemed to flow down the aisle towards the altar, her deep summer tan a fine contrast to the shimmering white satin she was wearing.

Karien danced with Bjournquist at the reception. Jiggs and Hood sat watching, sipping beers Roger had smuggled up from the hotel bar, saying he didn't trust any punch in which sherbet was floating. Karien Hegman's grace seemed to communicate itself to her barnlike partner, and Bjournquist danced with a lithesomeness he had not possessed for years, or perhaps ever. Jiggs thought Karien danced like Camilla.

"No flies on the bride!" Hood banged the empty bottle he'd just finished on the table for emphasis and fished another out of the pocket of his coat.

"No, no flies." Jiggs agreed. "Do you think Hegman's really going to bring her back here to settle down?"

"Sounded like he was serious last night." Hood was referring to Hegman's announcement at the bachelor party that he was going to take a job with First Iowa Bank in Lake City beginning in September.

If it had been anyone other than Hegman, Jiggs wouldn't have given the plan to return much chance of success. At the party, he had met several of Hegman's friends, guys who had flown in from the East. City boys. Good guys, smart, friendly in their way, but so completely lacking anything in common with Ron Bjournquist, Jack Miller, Gil Burley and the rest of Hegman's Walnut Grove friends, most of whom had never left home, except for the war, that it was as if there had been two different parties going on in the same room.

Except for Hegman. Hegman had held the party together. Jiggs had watched as he moved among the others, joking with some, reminiscing with others, talking about everything from farm prices to international monetary regulation.

Midway through the evening enough beer had been drunk for serious bragging to begin, the upshot of which was an arm wrestling contest, which Bjournquist won easily with his right arm even though he was left handed. Hegman had beaten Jiggs in an eye-popping, bicep-cramping battle that had lasted more than two minutes. "Not bad for a spaghetti-armed preacher." Hegman rubbed his elbow following the match.

"I'm still morally superior," Jiggs replied, silently wondering whether he'd done any permanent damage to himself.

"Where are you going to set up shop when you're ordained, Junior?"

Jiggs shrugged. "Don't know. If I can talk Carol into it, I want to be a missionary. She wants to go back to Arizona, where she went to school, or California. For the sake of Hood's soul, I should probably live near him," Jiggs nodded towards Roger, "so it can receive the intensive care it needs."

"Ever think of coming back here?" Hegman asked.

"Sometimes. Hood says he's coming to Des Moines once he gets out. Already got a job lined up. I'd like to be close to Doc. I don't know how much longer he can keep practicing. Right now he's very unhappy about this new state park they're talking about down in Des Moines."

"Don't blame him much," said Bjournquist, who was walking past. "Do you?"

Jiggs shook his head. "No. I just don't know what he can do about it."

Jiggs turned back to Hegman. "What made you decide to come back anyway. Seems like you'd have lots of choices."

"Haven't found any place I like better. To really be on the prime career track in New York, where I am now, you have to give up about everything else. Everything's business. You either live in an apartment in the City or waste hours commuting. Might as well not have a home. Nobody goes pheasant hunting in the Fall; nobody knows how any of the local school teams are doing unless they have a kid playing on one. I'm a product of my upbringing. Business shouldn't get in the way of life.

"Besides, if you're really good at what you do, maybe you can get somewhere quicker here, where the track isn't quite so crowded"

Hegman stopped talking, but Jiggs didn't say anything.

"Hegman! Hegman! Hegman!" The revelers were crowded around Bjournquist, who was demanding Hegman arm wrestle him for the "World Championship."

"They smell blood." Hegman rolled his eyes.

"Why do you think I let you win?" Jiggs grinned. "Bjournquist will maim you."

"Shit, Junior, you never 'let' anyone win … none of us ever did." Hegman turned away and then turned back. "Think about coming back home, Junior. I'll give you a rematch."

When the dancing began at the reception the next night, Jiggs and Roger were making plans to drive to Iowa City the next day. Jiggs wanted to see Lindy and celebrate her recent retirement at the conclusion of the semester just ended.

"Jiggs, would you like to dance?" It was the new Mrs. Hegman.

"Jim tells me he's responsible for you learning to dance," Karien said as they found an open space on the crowded floor and began a slow one.

Jiggs shook his head at the memory of his bout with Brunhilda. "He might be giving himself too much credit. Did he tell you what happened?"

Karien nodded.

"I think I learned in spite of that experience, or maybe in self-defense."

"Whatever your motivation," Karien smiled, "you learned pretty well."

Jiggs was surprised by the compliment. No one had ever praised his dancing before.

"Thanks..."

Before he could continue, Karien went on. "Jim also told me to convince you to come back here when you're ordained."

Jiggs leaned back an inch or two so he could look Karien in the eye. "What about you? Do you think Lake City, Iowa, is the place dreams are made of?"

"Place doesn't make much difference to me," she shrugged. "I'm an Air Force brat. I've lived lots of places, none of which I call 'home.' That's why we decided to get married here. I don't like New York City any better than Jim."

One of Hegman's half dozen uncles cut in before their conversation could go farther.

"Don't forget about Iowa, Jiggs," Karien said as they parted. "Thanks for the dance."

Jiggs returned to his table thinking Karien Hegman was a lot more in step with her husband's career than Carol was with his. He found Bjournquist busy telling Hood how to get rich farming.

"More land. Only way to make the equipment pay is buy more land."

"How are you going to pay for it?" Roger asked. "Land prices are out of sight."

"Simple," Bjournquist, the tipsy giant, waved his finger at Hood, "borrow the money. If the bank wants more collateral, use the land you already have."

"What if farm prices go down?" Hood persisted, sounding like a lawyer. "It's happened before you know."

"Won't happen again. Government won't let them. We can feed the world. Half the world doesn't have enough to eat."

Jiggs listened, half amused, half amazed to hear Bjournquist talking about something other than sports or the weather.

"Why do you suppose they don't have enough to eat?" Hood's cross-examination continued.

"Bad soil, bad weather, poor farming practices, lots of reasons."

"Yeah. So they can't grow their own. How come they're starving? Why haven't they been buying it from us right along?"

Bjournquist hesitated, and Hood answered his own question. "Because they can't afford to pay for it, Ron. That's why."

"Government will pay for it now. That's what foreign aid's all about."

"Butter instead of guns, huh, Ron?"

Bjournquist nodded. "Exactly."

Hood glanced up and saw Jiggs had returned. "Well, Ron, good luck. You're the farmer, not me. Just remember, don't put all your eggs in one basket.

"C'mon, Morgan, let's drag Doc away from all the local widows and go watch the Cardinal game. It comes on in half an hour."

"About time you goddamned A-rabs came to see me." Lindy hugged them both as she walked up to her porch between Jiggs and Roger.

They sat there shelling peas from her garden. "Do you know the three of us haven't been together like this, just the three of us, since before your wedding, Jiggs. What year was that? 1966?"

"Yeah, 1966."

"That was such a sad time." The old lady shook her head. "I was so scared for you to be going to the war, Jiggs ... and then you, Roger, right after that ... But you both came back to me. The Lord answered my prayers."

"Yeah, five years, and the goddamned thing's still going on. How unbelievable is that?" Jiggs shook his head, staring at the bucket where they were throwing the empty pods. Hood and Lindy exchanged a glance over the top of Jiggs' bowed head, and Lindy cleared her throat. "Well, it's over for us. When are you and Carol going to get busy and make me a Godmother?"

"You sound like Carol's mother, Lindy. Starving students can't afford kids ... can barely afford the cost of contraception."

"Abstention is free," Hood volunteered.

"How would you know?" Lindy slapped her thighs and stood up. "Hey, you guys still drink beer?"

Lindy wouldn't let them take her out to dinner, insisting instead on cooking for them. They wound up staying the night and taking her out to breakfast.

On the way back north to Walnut Grove after dropping Lindy off, Hood looked at Jiggs, who was driving. "You know, Morgan, you don't sound like any preacher I ever knew."

"What do you mean by that? I can't imagine you've known too many."

"Maybe not. But the ones I knew seemed to have a lot more optimistic outlook than I hear coming from you. Sometimes, it's like you're still out on that trestle yelling 'Fuck the world!'"

"You mean I'm not going around spewing sweetness and light like some born again bliss ninny?"

"That's kind of an exaggerated characterization."

"Aw, Rog, I know what you mean, at least I think I do. You're right. Sometimes I have a hard time being happy, especially lately. I think I'm just sick of school, of learning about God, but not doing anything on God's behalf. Did you ever feel that way about law school?"

"Well, to begin with, it was a very ungodly place, but, yeah. I was ready for it to be over a long time before it was over."

"I agree duration's probably the only similarity between seminary and law school," Jiggs said. "Anyway, I appreciate the attitude check. Just a little over a year to go. Once I'm out of school, let me know if nothing seems to have changed."

36

September 1971

The Pennsylvania hillsides were wearing more colors than a football crowd. An early frost had triggered the onset of autumn, then retreated, leaving a succession of warm, balmy days in its wake. Jiggs sat cross-legged silently scanning the distant hills, while in the foreground the children of the CHOP CP Unit played and basked in the early afternoon sun. Carol sat beside him reading a magazine.

"C'mon everybody!" Dr. Skalsky began to shout. No one paid any attention. "C'mon, make the Games Committee feel needed. One organized game before we eat ... just one."

Still no one heeded her call.

"Jiggs," Evelyn Skalsky walked over to where he sat, "how do you get people's attention in the Marines?"

You don't want to know. Jiggs pursed his lips and whistled a whistle that stabbed the consciousness of everyone within one hundred yards. Carol winced and went on reading.

The game was a potato race. Carol chose not to play.

Students could use any body part to propel their potato. All others had to use their noses. The only potato left by the time

Jiggs reached in the sack for his was a lumpy little marble, a miniature football with mumps.

"Hey, Ellen..."

Ellen Kelso, the girl Jiggs had first encountered in the recreation room at the hospital the night he wandered in after learning Tony Capini died, turned at the sound of her name. "Ellen," Jiggs said, "I got your potato and you got mine." He made a weak attempt to take the large potato she was holding while handing her the gnarled dwarf he'd been left with.

"Nuh." Ellen began to squeal and laugh as she shielded her potato from Jiggs' grasp. "This ... muh put... at... oh." She held it in two hands like a running back trying not to fumble. "Ya gota pea instud of ... a putatah."

"You two stop arguing." Evelyn Skalsky interceded. "Jiggs, you have to take whatever you drew."

A look of triumph flashed across Ellen's face.

"You're holding up the game. Everyone else is ready to start. Is everyone in the starting circle?"

Stragglers hastened in.

"All right ... Get on your marks... Get Set ... GO!"

Chaos ensued. Students in wheelchairs tried to push their potatoes with their feet; those afoot with whatever body part seemed most promising. Parents and volunteers inched along, butts up, noses down. The potatoes' lack of symmetry made progress in a straight line impossible, even if the students had otherwise been capable of that kind of navigation.

Onlookers cheered, potatoes collided, contestants groaned in frustration.

Jiggs had no intention of winning, but if he had, the tiny potato he'd drawn would have dashed his hopes. It was so small, he could barely get his nose on it, and so gnarled that it refused to roll even six inches in a straight line. Within moments of the start, he was dead last, just behind Ellen, who had elected to compete on her own, and was having a tough time.

Jiggs zigged and zagged across the lawn, rooting along with his by this time grimy nose like a hog in pursuit of a truffle. Up ahead, the leaders of the pack were already crossing the finish line. Within no more than two minutes, he and Ellen were the only two racers left on the course. Ellen was slightly ahead. Jiggs was spurring her on by calling out that he was about to pass her.

Now the focus of the onlookers became the race between the two of them. Without exception, the entire crowd adopted Ellen and yelled encouragement as she made her halting, painstaking way to the finish line just ahead of Jiggs, who finished with a desperate, headlong dive slightly ahead of his stubbornly uncooperative spud.

As he stood up, Ellen gave him a tremendous hug amid the cheers of all assembled, and Evelyn Skalsky, pretending to be a television reporter interviewing competitors, stuck a rolled up newspaper in front of his face as if it was a microphone and asked him how it felt to finish last.

"Well, I had some equipment problems out there on the field today, but those are about to be solved." With that, he ate his potato.

"And what about the winner?" The microphone moved over to Ellen.

"Uh won bya nose." Ellen laughed and everyone applauded.

"I think that about wraps everything up here at the track. Let's eat."

"Do you want to eat with my wife, Carol, and me?" Jiggs asked Ellen as they made their way towards the picnic tables.

"Shuh." Ellen smiled.

Carol joined them at the table, where the three of them helped each other to fried chicken, baked beans, jello and cake. Sitting on Morgan's blanket as they ate, Jiggs asked Ellen about school, where he knew she excelled.

"What's your favorite subject these days?"

"Social stu ... dies." Ellen struggled to make her lips and tongue form the words.

"Oh, that was always one of my favorites, too," Jiggs replied. "Why do you like social studies?"

"For ... eign lunds ... uh like... ta see how other ... peo ... ple live. I want to tra ... vel."

"If you could go anywhere, where would you go?" Carol asked.

"India."

"India, why India?"

"Uh wannta ride un ... an ... ele ... ele ... phant."

"Jiggs has ridden on an elephant." A veiled hint of sarcasm crept into Carol's voice. "Tell Ellen what it was like riding on an elephant, Jiggs."

Jiggs slowly finished chewing the bite of chocolate cake he had just taken. Carol's sarcasm did not escape him. The Marine baseball team had flown to Thailand to play a team at an Air Force base there. Jiggs had sent Carol a picture of himself and a teammate aboard an elephant in Bangkok, accompanied by two beautiful Thai girls. Despite his explanation that the girls came with the elephant, which was true and which Carol believed, the elephant ride had provided her with endless ammo for long term teasing.

Jiggs rolled his eyes at Carol for resurrecting this old chestnut, but was happy she was in a joking mood. He turned towards Ellen. "Yeah, I rode an elephant in Bangkok, Thailand, once when I was in the Marines. Do you know where Thailand is?"

"Yuh." Ellen nodded.

"This was a pretty skinny elephant. Sitting on his backbone was like sitting on a bunch of rocks." Jiggs paused and then added for Carol's benefit, "Another problem was that there was nothing on the elephant to hold on to ... there were no reins, no mane, and, of course, you couldn't wrap your arms around its neck like you could a horse."

"How did ya ... keep from ... falling ... off?"

"Oh, the elephant wasn't going very fast, so I wasn't in any real danger of falling, but just to be safe, I held on as tight as I could to the person in front of me." Jiggs glanced at Carol as he finished his description. She made a face at him.

Not long after they finished eating, Ellen went off with a couple of girls from her class. Jiggs lay in the sun staring up at the sky. The blue was so sharp, he could shave with it, and the streaming sunshine warmed his spirits.

"Ellen's a nice girl, isn't she?" he said to Carol, who had resumed reading.

"Mmmm."

"Did you know she's an orphan?"

"I think you've mentioned it before."

Jiggs propped himself up on one elbow "What would you think of adopting her? Not right now, of course, but after I graduate."

Carol put down her magazine and shook her head. "Never, Jiggs. Never, never, never!"

"Why do you feel so strongly against it? She needs help, and we can really help her. She already knows and likes us. She's a wonderful little girl."

"Jiggs, I know she's a wonderful little girl, but she's not our little girl, and she has enormous problems. I don't want them to be my problems, and, if we were to adopt her, that's whose problems they would mainly become, because you'd be off working, while I would have to deal with her disabilities all day long. I just don't want to do that."

"You want a problem free life, is that it?"

"C'mon, Jiggs. That's not fair, and you know it. There'll be lots of problems, but I don't want to go out looking for them. If Ellen was my child, I'd gladly do everything I could to help her, but she's not. I want to have my own children and be able to concentrate on helping them."

Jiggs regarded Carol across the blanket, considering his reply. "Don't you ever look at these kids and wonder, 'Why them? Why me?' Don't you ever think maybe you ought to do something to even things out a little? There's nothing about adopting Ellen that would prevent us from having kids of our own."

"That's where you and I differ, Jiggs. I don't think I 'owe' anybody anything. I didn't bargain for my 'blessings,' as you put it, nor did I have anything to do with other people's handicaps.

"You seem to think you do ... that more than anything else seems to me to be the reason you've decided to become a minster. That's great if that's what you want to do with your life. I'll go along and help where I can, but I'm not going to sacrifice myself in a one-woman effort to ease the world's pain, Jiggs. That's just not me."

Jiggs lay back down. The sun was still streaming, but he had begun to feel the autumn chill. He was still thinking about what Carol said, when Evelyn Skalsky announced it was nearly time to pack up and return to the hospital. Jiggs helped carry the picnic supplies back to the bus. As he did so, he watched Ellen Kelso playing with her friends.

37

October 1971

Jiggs loved his desk. It was small and green, a metal desk with a linoleum top Doc bought for him the day before he started junior high school. Nothing fancy. It had been his companion from that point on throughout his education. Its drawers contained some of his most treasured mementoes, yellowed photographs, sports awards, clippings, a couple of poems he'd written. His struggles with *Julius Caesar* and *Silas Marner* he joked about with Camilla had been waged there. Occasionally it had been his pillow in the midst of some endless term paper or final week. In Jiggs' mind, his desk was no longer a green metal object with a linoleum top, but the sum of all the experiences he had had while sitting there, like a favorite baseball glove.

"Wish I could draw on some of that experience to help me with this sermon," Jiggs muttered to himself, as he stared at the barren branches of the trees outside the high window above the desk. The yellow legal pad in front of him was as empty as the branches dancing in the autumn wind. Homiletics – "Preaching," the students called it, a four hour, third year roadblock of a course designed to help future ministers learn the fundamentals of communicating the word of God from the pulpit. By most, it was regarded with the same dislike and terror they had harbored for oral book reports in seventh grade.

Jiggs was in the minority of mankind that didn't mind standing up and talking to a group, no matter how large, but only if he had something to say. "What can I say about God and faith that hasn't already been said better a thousand times before?"

Carol looked up from the book she was reading. "I doubt your first sermon is expected to plow much new spiritual ground."

Jiggs continued to stare into space. Across his field of vision, a solitary bird flew so high it was only a V-shaped line against the blue. It reminded him of Camilla, the girl who would be a bird in her next life. A lone wild bird. Soon it was out of sight, leaving behind only an idea.

As Carol helped him on with his robe, he felt like a candidate for knighthood. Thus attired, he lined up behind the choir as it assembled in the Narthex, where it sang the Prelude. Falling in step behind the singers alongside Dr. Keller, the school's Chaplain, they processed down the center aisle between the ranks of worshipers. Jiggs could not feel his feet touching the floor. The choir and the congregation were singing "Rock of Ages." The words of the ancient hymn echoed and rang up among the beams of the high vaulted ceiling as if the sound was too big for the room, ballooning out the walls and roof in search of escape from confinement. Jiggs' heart, filled with emotion, felt much the same.

After reaching the chancel, standing with bowed head for the invocation prayer and taking his seat to wait his turn in the order of worship, Jiggs glanced at his watch. The last twenty minutes of the hour were to be his. Thirty-five minutes to go. It was like the curse of wrestling at the higher weights Jiggs had lived with in high school. You came out of the dressing room all pumped up and then had to sit around for an hour while the little guys wrestled their matches, as the force of your own vitality built to an unbearable level. For big matches, Jiggs couldn't watch. He would go behind the bleachers and burrow deeper into his mental preparation until his bout was called.

He was deep in that cocoon when he heard the first notes of the Doxology and reflexively stood as the offering was borne to the altar by two ushers. As the music died away and the ushers turned and departed, Jiggs stepped up to the pulpit and looked out over the congregation, determined to take command.

"The scripture lesson for today consists of passages from three different books of the Bible, as noted in your bulletin. Please take your Bibles and turn first to Proverbs, chapter 15, verse 33 at page 914. We will read just that verse and then skip to Luke, chapter 6, verse 38 at page 98, and then to John, chapter 13, verse 5 at page 165. Please read in unison with me."

> *The fear of the Lord is the instruction for wisdom,*
> *And before honor comes humility.*

> *Give, and it will be given to you; good measure, pressed*
> *down, shaken together, running over, they will pour into*
> *your lap. For whatever measure you deal out to others, it will*
> *be dealt to you in return.*

> *Then He poured water into the basin, and began to wash the*
> *disciples' feet, and to wipe them with the towel with which He*
> *was girded.*

"May God add his blessing to this unison reading of His word. Let us pray.

"Father, let your words be like chimes ringing in our souls, the sound of their message slicing through the egotistical shell with which we surround ourselves, enabling us to embrace your offer of salvation. We make this prayer in the name of your Son, our Savior. Amen."

As Jiggs spoke these words, words he had rehearsed at least a hundred times, he prayed a silent prayer, "Lord, don't let me screw this up." Behind closed lids, he rolled his eyes at his own irreverence.

He opened his eyes, glancing at his notes to make sure they were arranged just the way he wanted them before raising his bowed head. Looking out at the congregation, he took a deep breath. *Here we go. Rock and roll.*

"Before I decided to become a preacher, I spent some time in the Marine Corps, an organization that attaches a great deal of importance, in the words of its own Hymn, to 'keeping its honor clean.' One of the Corps' favorite sayings is, 'When you're a Marine, it *is* hard to be humble.' Upon reflection, I see now that none of us were trying very hard to be humble back then.

"But regardless of our efforts, regardless of the importance God obviously attaches to humility – 'Before honor comes humility' – there is a great deal of truth to the Marine's saying. It is hard to be humble. Preoccupied with our own cares and ambitions, we live our lives in front of an invisible mirror, constantly checking our own reflections for ways in which we can meet those cares, fulfill those ambitions.

"Of what does 'humility,' as God would have us practice it, consist? What does 'humility' mean?

"God has given us both an explanation and an example. 'Give and it shall be given to you.' 'Give,' a simple four letter word. Give, not necessarily material wealth, but, first and foremost, of yourself, of your time, of your attention, of your caring. Do this. Abase yourself, and honor will be yours in the eyes of God.

"I do not mean 'abasement' in the sense of degradation, but merely the recognition of how microscopic is the place we each occupy in God's universe. In short, God wants us to put aside our mirrors.

"Lest we miss God's point, he has given us an illustration. In Jesus' time and place, sandals were the footwear of choice. Most of the streets and roads were dust. Washing one's feet was a necessity usually performed by the meanest slave. Yet here was God's own son on the very eve of his crucifixion, washing the feet of his disciples. Even in this moment of utmost turmoil, Christ put aside his own burdens and knelt to perform the task of a slave, to put the cares of others above his own. 'Give and it will be given to you.'"

As Jiggs had written this part of the sermon and as he now delivered these lines, he was thinking of Camilla, of the simple, unassuming way she had let him know she cared for the rude and wounded stranger he had become upon his return to Okinawa from Viet Nam.

Too bad. There was no way he could use the best example of unselfishness and humility he'd ever encountered to illustrate his point. He'd considered it. He'd written her into and then out of the sermon, recognizing that the mere mention of such a great friend whom he had somehow failed ever to talk about would only spark fires of curiosity, if not suspicion, in Carol. Once kindled, they might never be completely extinguished, no matter how unfounded.

"Well, if she was such a good friend," he could imagine Carol saying, and rightly so, "how come you never talked about her before?"

So he talked about Jim Hegman instead. Jiggs spoke of how Hegman, the all-state player, the senior quarterback, the star, had taken no part in hazing the lone freshman on the team during that long ago football season, of how Hegman had helped introduce Jiggs to things, pool, dancing, the fraternity, things Jiggs might use. The fact that Jiggs turned his back on some in no way diminished the value of the introduction. Hegman, who Jiggs had seen carried off the field in triumph on the shoulders of his teammates, and who, an hour later, helped the towel boys and team managers pick up dirty towels and sweep the floor of an otherwise empty locker room.

"I went to Jim Hegman's wedding last summer back in Iowa." Jiggs began to wrap up. "Jim's done okay for himself. In college, he was the starting quarterback his last two seasons, All Big Ten his senior year, a finalist for a Rhodes scholarship. He has his MBA from Harvard now, and in the words of one of his buddies from high school, the girl he married looks like Miss America.

"So, he's continued to soar, but to no one's surprise, the night before the wedding he sat around with a bunch of us who had known him longest, teammates and friends, most of whom had never left the farm, men with whom Jim might be expected to no longer have anything in common – but do you know what? It was as if Jim had never gone away, because throughout the evening he spoke only of others, asking questions about their lives, listening, reminiscing about experiences they had shared.

"That night and at the reception the next day, I met people from all over the country who had interrupted their far away lives to come to that tiny Iowa town to celebrate Hegman getting hitched. There must have been twenty people there who told me they thought of Jim Hegman as their best friend. Twenty people with stories of how Hegman had shoveled their snow, hauled their water, showed up to listen when their marriages fell apart, sent them a book he thought they would enjoy, all unasked.

"Three years older than I, Jim was more like a big brother to me. He probably isn't my 'best' friend, if friendships can be graded. But I have seen in him the qualities the Bible talks about, the willingness to give of himself for the sake, not of himself, but of others. And he has been honored, not by awards and degrees, but by the friendship of those to whom he has given.

"How nice it would be if each of us was thought of by twenty others as their 'best friend.' Could we but achieve that, then, according to this," Jiggs held up a Bible, "it would be fair to believe that we would be numbered among God's best friends as well. 'Before honor comes humility.'"

Jiggs gave the Benediction. At his final words, the organ began to play the recessional, and Jiggs stepped down from the pulpit and joined Dr. Keller, who, without turning in Jiggs' direction, muttered "Nice job." Together, side by side, they retreated down the center aisle and outside the Chapel, where they stood shaking hands and greeting the congregation as it filed out behind them.

Jiggs felt good, not because of the grade he thought the sermon had earned, or the compliments he was receiving from his listeners. He felt good because he'd finally said the one thing he'd wanted to say ever since he decided to enter the ministry, ever since Camilla Waron by her friendship had revealed to him the well-publicized but underappreciated secret that love, the thing most worth having, is best obtained by giving it away.

38

November 1971

Howard Meeker reached into a small refrigerator under his bar, pulled out two beers and handed one to Jiggs. "I invited you for dinner tonight, not just because you'll be graduating and gone soon, Jiggs, but because I want to talk to you about what you're going to do following graduation."

Little late for that.

Howard, whose friendship with Jiggs had evolved to first names once Jiggs finished the last course he would ever take from the older man, knew exactly what Jiggs was going to do. Apart from Carol, no one had been more involved in Jiggs's decision. He had come to Howard in the midst of his wrangle with Carol when the chance to work for United Presbyterian Missions in Tanzania after graduation had showed up at the beginning of his third and final year. Carol continued to be adamant in her refusal to have any part of missionary life. Both Howard and his wife, Evelyn, with whom Carol had become friends, had long talks with her about her feelings. Jiggs had thrown in the towel after Howard reported no progress and asked Jiggs how much appeal the Tanzania opportunity would have knowing that Carol would be profoundly unhappy.

"I do know of another position," Howard had said at the time, attempting to soften Jiggs' obvious disappointment. Carol's initial reaction to Meeker's alternative hadn't exactly been a warm embrace.

"'Winnetka!' Jiggs, is Winnetka where I think it is?"

"Well, it's not in Arizona."

"It's in Chicago, isn't it? Somewhere around Chicago?"

"Northern suburb."

"Why are you even talking about a church in Chicago? I thought we had agreed on somewhere in the Southwest."

That wasn't the way Jiggs remembered it.

"You've always said you wanted to live in the Southwest – just like in college. That's never been my castle in the clouds."

"But Jiggs, Chicago is windy, cold, dark, old. Ugh."

"Don't forget bad for golf."

"Bad for everything. We grew up in the Midwest. Do you want the news you listen to most intensely each night to be the weather? You know what it's like."

"Never minded the weather that much."

"You never mind anything much. Why Winooka ... or whatever it's called, anyway?"

"A Presbyterian church there is looking for a youth pastor. Something I'd like to do. I've been there a couple times. The baseball team stayed there when it played Northwestern. It's a little upscale, but I liked it. I'm pretty sure it has a golf course."

"Yes. I bet it's open at least six months a year. Oh, Jiggs, can't you at least try to find a church in a warmer place?"

Like Tanzania? Struggling to remember that he was trying to build a bridge, not burn one, he said only, "Carol, there are lots of warmer places I'd rather go, but as I recall, those places were deal breakers for you.

"This opportunity in Winnetka is the best thing I've seen come through the placement office in six months. The pastor there, a guy named Moorfield, is a friend of Howard Meeker's. He and his wife are coming to visit the Meekers in a couple weeks. If we're interested, Professor Meeker will take us all out to dinner. I think I have a real shot at this."

"If we're interested…"

"Listen, give it a chance. Please. You might like it. If you can honestly say you hate it after having seriously considered it, well, then we'll go somewhere else."

At dinner three weeks later, Carol had been seated next to Harry Moorfield. He was tall, taller than Jiggs, with wavy blond hair and a tan that looked like it had grown up in Hollywood. When Jiggs heard him ask Carol if she'd played any golf while she went to school in Arizona, Jiggs could have kissed him. Mrs. Moorfield, who was sitting next to Jiggs, leaned over in his direction. "Harry loves golf."

The meal went very well after that. It was followed by a three day visit to Winnetka a week later. Jiggs met with the members of the search committee, both individually and as a group. Carol and Harry Moorfield played golf. On their last day in Winnetka, Jiggs, with Carol's approval, accepted a call to become Youth Pastor at First Presbyterian Church of Winnetka following his ordination.

It had been Howard Meeker who started that ball rolling. Jiggs even suspected Howard of priming Moorfield to ask Carol about golf.

What's left to talk about?

Howard recognized Jiggs' puzzlement. "Not the position in Winnetka," he said, glancing through the open door into the living room, where Carol and Evelyn were sitting looking at photographs spread out on a coffee table, "your 'career,' not your 'job.'"

"I'm not sure I understand the difference at this point."

"There isn't one for people who are in the right career." Howard walked over and closed the door. "But I may as well tell you up front that I don't think the ministry is the right career for you, Jiggs."

Jiggs' look of bewilderment did not go away.

"I think that about a lot of students that come through after I get to know them. I think it about myself. That's why I teach rather than preach, but I seldom bother to tell students what I think about that. They need to find out for themselves."

"Why are you telling me then?"

"Because you've become my friend. Because where you're concerned, my care is not so much for the ministry as for you as a person. Like the rest, you, too, will have to find out for yourself. You have more gifts than most. Maybe it will take longer; maybe I'm wrong, but I don't think so. Anyway, as you go out and answer your first call, I hope you will think about what I have to say."

Jiggs waited. *What exactly is that?*

"There are different kinds of love, Jiggs. Different kinds of compassion. You love your wife, your family. You feel compassion for people you know, that little girl, Ellen, in Evelyn's program, those children on the hospital ship you told me about, your friend who lost his legs. These are lovable, sympathetic persons to you. They've earned your love by being something to which you can relate. You're pretty good at individual love, Jiggs."

Howard paused and sipped his beer. Jiggs had forgotten his own beer.

"But to truly minister the word of God, to feel, not just mouth, the Word, you have to be in love with God himself. Through him or her or whatever, you must feel love and compassion for all God's creatures, even the most unlovable, the most undeserving - people like that player who spiked you, the one you hit with the throw."

Jiggs opened his mouth to say something, but closed it when Howard held up his hand.

"I think you know what I'm talking about, Jiggs. Your idea of being 'God's best friend' that you talked about in your sermon a few weeks ago and of becoming the best friend of all mankind in the process is what a great minister needs to achieve…"

"Do you think this kind of love can be acquired, Howard, or do you have to be born with it?"

"I think it can be acquired by those with the capacity, Jiggs. But, sadly, I think you lack the capacity."

Jiggs was unused to being told he lacked an ability.

"I've thought about it a lot," Meeker continued. "Somewhere in you there's a hardness. I don't know why or where it came from, but it keeps you from forgiving people for their humanness."

"Don't you think you're drawing a pretty big conclusion from one softball game?"

"It's not just that game, it's life. It's the government and the war and the presidents, Johnson, then Nixon ... you've been hating those men for so long."

"Yes, but..."

"'But,' that's the problem, Jiggs. Don't you see? There are no 'Yes, buts.' There are no exceptions to God's love. Assume they are terrible men, although they probably aren't. Assume what they've done or allowed to happen is terrible, which it is.

You must still love them while at the same time hating what they've done. There are no skills we teach at this school that can help you do this. It has to come from inside yourself."

Jiggs considered what Howard had just said. "Howard, I know I'm pretty good at hating the sin, but not so keen on loving the sinner. I'm certainly not all the way there yet where Nixon's concerned, but despite my lapses, I'm getting better. I appreciate your candor. I really do. It's something I need to work on, but meanwhile I've gone pretty far to back out now."

"Jiggs, I'm certainly not suggesting you give up the ministry just on the basis of my opinion. Few ministers I have ever met have this quality I think you're lacking. It's just that I happen to think you're capable of achieving a true greatness in some other field, something that may not be within your reach in the ministry.

"Go on out to your first church. Do your very best. Prove me wrong. Just remember that the true yardstick isn't stained glass and big congregations. The true measure is the ability to reach somebody who needs reaching, no matter who they are or what you think of what they've done, no matter how repugnant. Look inside yourself as you go along. If you're not doing that, then maybe I am right. Maybe then you need to start thinking about doing something else."

39

January 1972

"Jiggs, this is Marie."

Marie. Bad news. Darcy was always the good news messenger.

"Doc broke his leg. He's in the hospital."

"Whoa, is he okay? I mean, how bad is it?"

"Bad enough. It's his upper leg. He had to have a pin put in. He's in a cast up to his hip and won't be able to walk, even on crutches for at least two months, likely more."

"How'd it happen? Some bull get him?"

"No. Apparently he'd been up in the loft throwing hay down for the horses. As he came down the ladder, one of the rungs broke and he fell. He says he was carrying a pitchfork. Lucky he didn't land on that."

A dozen complications raced through Jiggs' mind. Knowing Marie, he was pretty sure she'd already thought of them.

"What now?"

"Well, at least it looks like the stock's taken care of. Darcy and Beezer were about to drive out from town last night to get 'em fed when Ron Bjournquist called. Said he'd heard about

Doc, and he'd take care of the chores until Doc was back on his feet. Pretty nice."

"I'll say..."

"That leaves the question of who's going to feed Doc, among other things. He's going to need someone full time for a while. You're in New Jersey, I'm in Seattle. Darcy and Beezer don't have any room. She and I talked about them living with him at his place, but with them both working and the baby, that's no solution."

"Guess we'll have to hire someone."

"Yes, unless..."

"Unless what?"

"What about Lindy? Didn't you tell me she's retired? Do you think she'd come up and do it? He probably won't be the easiest patient, but he already likes her. Plus, she's tough and won't take any crap off him."

Lindy. Maybe.

"She might. Whenever I talk to her, she says she's looking for something else to do. Far as I can see, she just takes care of her house and plays bingo. She stopped taking in boarders a long time ago. Let me call her."

"Jiggs, one more thing. Are you still getting mail there in New Jersey?"

"Yeah. One more day. Why?"

"Oh, Darcy sent you something. I was wondering whether you'd received it yet."

Something? "What did she send me, Marie?"

"Oh, it's almost too upsetting to talk about. It's a newspaper clipping. Apparently that bill for the new park has passed, and the governor says he's going to sign it. I gotta go. I'll be late for work. We can talk about that when you let me know about Lindy."

40

January 1972

"Hello, anybody home?" Jiggs stood in the receptionist's office of First Presbyterian Church of Winnetka. A half empty coffee cup with lipstick on the rim was sitting on the desk, and there was a piece of paper in some kind of fancy typewriter unlike any Jiggs had ever seen. He scanned the desk for a bell, but found none. The door to the inner office, Rev. Moorfield's office, was closed.

Jiggs glanced at his watch. Three-fifteen. *Too late for lunch.* He decided to wait.

Sitting there, he went over his recent communications with his new employer in his mind.

They knew I was coming in this afternoon.

Five minutes passed. Ten. Jiggs remembered the way over to the Youth Department from his recruiting visit and decided to go on up without waiting further.

As he stood up, a tall middle-aged woman with dark red hair walked into the office. "Oh, hello. May I help you?"

"Hi. I'm Jiggs Morgan, the new Youth Minister. I spoke to Dr. Moorfield by phone a couple of weeks ago and let him know I'd be coming in this afternoon. My wife and I just arrived in town yesterday."

As Jiggs spoke, the woman looked down at the blotter on her desk, which also served as a calendar for the month.

"Mmmm. Dr. Moorfield didn't say anything to me about it. He's not here right now."

Golfing in January? "Is he expected back this afternoon?"

"I'm not sure. He might be back in around five, before he goes home. I go home at four-thirty. I'll leave him a note saying you came by."

Welcome aboard, Jiggs.

"I thought I might wander over to the Youth Department and begin to get an idea of things I need to do first. Will that be okay?"

The woman, she hadn't bothered to introduce herself, although the nameplate on her desk said "Marlys Davidson," hesitated. "I suppose it wouldn't hurt anything. There's no one up there. You know the way?"

"I think I remember. Thanks." Jiggs turned to go.

"Just a sec. Before you go, spell your name for me, for the note. I'm Marlys Davidson, by the way. I'm sorry. I should have introduced myself sooner. I think I was on vacation when you visited here last fall. I'm the Church Secretary."

"Ohhh! You startled me." A young girl sitting across the otherwise empty room from the door stood up when Jiggs entered. She smiled slightly as she spoke. "I wasn't expecting anyone this early."

"Hi. I'm..." Jiggs' attempt to introduce himself was buried beneath an avalanche of words streaming from the girl.

"I mean, it's just a couple of other kids who're coming. We don't hurt anything. I came up early to do some work on my article for the Bulletin. It's usually so quiet up here during the week. I come here a lot actually."

She paused for breath.

"What are you writing for the Bulletin?" Jiggs asked.

"An article about the new Youth Minister. He's supposed to be coming sometime this month, but I don't know for sure."

"So the new Youth Minister's a man?"

"Yes. His name is Jon Morgan, and this is his first church. He just graduated from seminary, Princeton Theological Seminary in New Jersey, I think. I'll have to check my notes. I interviewed Dr. Moorfield about him a few days ago."

"What else do you know about this new minister?"

The girl made a face like she was straining to remember an answer for a test. "Well, he's married. I can't remember his wife's name, but it's in my notes. She likes golf. Dr. Moorfield said Mr., I mean Reverend, Morgan was in the Marines and was in Viet Nam. I don't know where he grew up. Dr. Moorfield didn't know that much about his childhood."

"Sounds like how he grew up might be important information about a guy who's here to help you and your friends with the process. Maybe you ought to interview him. When does the Bulletin go to press? Maybe he'll arrive in time."

The girl turned her head away ever so slightly as if a new idea had just occurred to her. Without turning her head all the way back, she looked at Jiggs out of the corner of her eye from beneath an arched brow. "Maybe he already has."

Jiggs threw up his arms. "You got me! I'm Jon Morgan, but most people call me 'Jiggs.' What's your name?"

"I'm Susan Karochek."

"Pleased to meet you, Susan." They shook hands.

"What's this get together you mentioned that's going to happen later on?"

"Oh, it's just me and three or four other kids from the old youth group. We come up here after school on Mondays and talk, sometimes we play a game."

"The old youth group…"

"When Rev. Terry was here, she was the last Youth Minister, Westminister Youth Fellowship used to meet every Wednesday. A lot more kids came then. But even though there were no more activities after she left, a few of us just kept coming. Nobody stopped us. We switched to Mondays, because mostly we wanted to talk about our weekends."

"Susan, would you care if I sat in on today's meeting, if the other kids are okay with it? I promise not to say anything, but I'd like to meet them, to hear what's on your minds."

"I think that would be neat."

41

March 1972   - August 1972

"Make haste slowly," Doc was fond of saying.

Good advice, but like most good advice, hard to follow. Jiggs had been waiting for years to start making a difference. Now that he had the bit in his teeth, he wanted to run, but he also had the reins in his hand, and he forced himself to hold back.

He interviewed all five of the teen-agers he met on his first day at work, the day he met Susan Karocek. He talked to them about their experiences during his predecessor's tenure, what they thought the purpose of a youth fellowship should be, what activities they would enjoy. He discovered that Program Committee Chairpersons are always hungry for speakers, and soon word of his energy and enthusiasm had spread through every organization in the church. On this particular day his host was the Presbyterian Businessman's Club, a Wednesday breakfast meeting in a private room at a local restaurant.

Jiggs was among the first to arrive. He was standing talking with several other early birds. A man, who had introduced himself as "Gene Smallwood," was describing his recent trip to Hawaii.

"Joan and I did something a little different this trip."

"What was that, Gene?" someone asked.

"We visited this Buddhist temple way up in a mountain valley on Kauai. It was beautiful, but the remarkable thing was the way it was built. There are no nails or screws or glue. It's held together completely by fittings sculpted into the wood itself. Here, I brought a picture of it." He took out a small snapshot and handed it to Jiggs, who was standing beside him.

The building was beautiful. Its light-colored wood seemed to glow in the sunlight, radiant against the green hillside in the background. Its roof sloped gently in all four directions, curving up near its edges like the very tips of a bird's wings in flight. One of the entrances was open, and inside a statue of the Buddha could be seen.

Jiggs nodded in appreciation and handed the picture to the man beside him, who had just walked up to the group.

In response to Jiggs' proffer, the man drew back and held up his hand, palm out, fingers vertical, rejecting.

"I don't need to see that."

Jiggs eyebrows went up. "What...?"

"I don't need to see any heathen temple." The man turned and walked away from the group. Jiggs handed the picture to one of the other men. Everyone in the group was grinning.

"Now you've met 'By the Book Basil,'" said Gene Smallwood, "an Old Testament man in a New Testament time."

Jiggs glanced around at the retreating figure. "Wonder what he thinks of the Taj Mahal?"

"Left to his own devices, he'd probably tear it down. Basil takes the commandment against having no other gods very literally," Smallwood said.

"And all the other commandments as well," added someone.

"How do people get that way?" Jiggs and Carol were laying in bed, books on their laps.

"You mean so rigid like that?"

"Yeah. Unwilling to even appreciate beauty, if it doesn't have a Christian origin. Afraid to even look at it. The guy reminded me of that knucklehead on the hospital ship, the one who had me arrested, 'Fish,' or something like that. I think I wrote to you about him. Those kinds of people are almost caricatures of what Christians should be."

Carol turned her head towards Jiggs. "You know, how big a step is it really, when you're taught to worship a god who drowns the whole world for being out of step with his teachings - even animals who can't know what those teachings are or what they're being accused of? Sounds to me like ol' Basil whatshisname is just playing it safe."

"C'mon, those stories were like parables. They're from a culture that was really primitive. Times change. Behaviors change."

Carol shifted onto her side so she was facing Jiggs with her whole body. "So what happened to Noah is no longer relevant?"

"Not literally."

"Then why put it in the Book? Why call it the 'Word of God?'"

"Because its an object lesson."

"What's it teach?"

"The importance of adherence to God's word."

Carol recoiled slightly. "Jiggs, I rest my case. Once you accept that there's a supreme force, whatever you choose to call it, one that insists you play the game its way or risk death and eternal damnation, it's not a big step to becoming Basil or Fish, someone you're calling a 'fanatic.'"

"Yeah, but you can't just take one story in isolation from all the rest as a basis for your actions. The New Testament tempers a lot of that ancient harshness."

"Like what? Where does it say, pay no attention to what happened to the folks who didn't have a ticket on the SS Noah?"

Jiggs thought for a moment. "Nowhere, of course, not in so many words, but the New Testament is certainly a kinder, gentler take on things. The Golden Rule for example."

Carol shook her head. "I don't begin to know the Bible that well, Jiggs. I just think if you let yourself believe any of this stuff, it becomes easy to believe there's no room for mulligans."

"Sounds to me as if you don't believe any of it."

"I guess I really don't. I think the Golden Rule's a good rule to live by. That's about it ... You look surprised."

"I just assumed that, at bottom, you believed in a god."

"That's a pretty big assumption."

"I guess I figured that having been raised in the Church..."

Carol reached over and brushed Jiggs' cheek with her fingertips. Her voice, which had sounded dismissive to Jiggs, changed. "Jiggs, my love, we both grew up in churches. Before you went to Viet Nam, it might just as easily have been you saying the things I just said. You've told me what happened over there. It sounds too awful for me to even comprehend. What I can't understand, despite more hours spent thinking about it than you probably imagine, is how that experience turned you in the direction it did. How could one's faith in a god that lets things like that occur be anything but weakened?"

"Carol, those things were done by men, not God."

"Men created by God, an all-powerful God, who, according to your belief, nevertheless allows such things to go on all the time. I'm sorry Jiggs, but at some point you and I came to a crossroads when it comes to faith. You went right and I went left. Let's leave it at that."

Carol reached back and set her book on her nightstand and turned out her light. Then she turned back and kissed Jiggs on the cheek. "Good night, my love."

Doc Morgan was staring out the window from his favorite chair, his broken leg propped on two pillows on a stool, when the phone on the table beside him rang.

"Hello, Pop. It's Jiggs. I'm glad to finally be talking to you, instead of just getting bad news reports. You must be glad to be home."

"Yes, although I'm being forced to live under a reign of terror."

"A reign of ... oh, you mean Lindy."

"Yes, that's who I mean. I thought she was my friend, but she's turned on me. I haven't been sworn at this much since the Marine Corps."

"Well, I suspect it's a benevolent tyranny. How's everything else going?"

"Not so great. Darcy sent you that clipping about the park, didn't she?"

The park. The ever-looming shadow. Jiggs had racked his brain how he might help Doc fight against it. It was often the subject of Jiggs' prayers. Evidently, those prayers weren't being answered. "Yes, that was disheartening. Is there organized opposition, anything I can help with?"

"We're getting organized. Three other affected families and I have pooled our resources, and we're hiring Roger's law firm in Des Moines to figure out the best way to go about it. We're probably going to file a lawsuit. I think we should have done it earlier, before the bill passed."

What a nightmare. "I wish you luck with that, Pop. Let me know if there's anything I can do. Are you feeling all right apart from the leg?"

"Yeah. I'm okay. Listen, Lindy's in here waving a fist full of pills at me and brandishing a glass of something. They've got me on a bunch of anti-biotics to fight the possibility of infection. I have to hang up now and get dosed, before she turns mean."

YOUTH YAK
By Susan Karocek

Hey, Teens, think you're in shape? Join the Youth Department's Thursday evening bike rides along the Lake. Reverend Morgan says he needs to lose a few LBS!!! He needs our help to keep him exercising. There will be a hot dog roast after the ride (Just salad for you, Reverend).

Where: Davidson Park (Meet at the bandstand)

When: Every Thursday at 5:30 p.m.

How Far: 10 miles round trip

HELMETS REQUIRED!!

How does a preacher measure success?

By the end of October, when the time changed and it became too cold to ride in the late afternoon, the number of regulars showing up for the rides had swollen from the original three or four to more than twenty. Most also came to the Monday Fellowship Meetings, along with several more to whom Jiggs' bicycle ministry did not sing a siren song.

In the minds of some, the increase in numbers in the Youth Department was at best a mixed blessing.

"Something needs to be done about all the noise coming from the Youth Department."

It had been ten months since Jiggs began work. He was sitting in a meeting of the church's Session, the monthly meeting of the Elders, who governed the church. It was only the second meeting of the Session Jiggs had been invited to, the first having been purely for the purpose of welcoming him aboard shortly after his arrival. No reason had been given for the invitation on this occasion. As the meeting droned on, Jiggs doodled on the pad of paper in front of him, wondering what was going on with Camilla wherever she was in the world, when the words "Youth Department" brought his head up.

Bob Ladewig, the Minister of Music, was speaking. "The noise coming from that room on Monday nights is deafening." Because of the success of his music program, Ladewig was an icon to many in the church, despite an arrogance that made General Patton seem humble. Jiggs thought he was a bully.

Nice of you to bring it up in Session, Bob, without ever mentioning it to me.

"Precisely what noise are you talking about?" Jiggs asked.

"There's all this yelling and shouting. I don't know what's going on in there."

"Is what you're complaining about the sound of kids cheering on their friends in some kind of game?"

"How should I know?"

"Well, have you ever looked in to find out?"

Jiggs sensed more than saw a couple of smirks among the Elders.

"Why should I? You're the one who's supposed to be in charge over there."

"Do any of the choirs practice on Monday nights, Bob?"

"No."

"Any Music Committee meetings that night?"

"No. What is this, Twenty Questions?"

"Then what exactly is this 'deafening noise' from the Youth Department disturbing?"

"I was working late last Monday trying to get some things caught up, and the noise was so loud I couldn't think."

"I tell you what, Bob. On those rare Mondays when you work late, let me know, and I'll silence any cheering or singing, and, if I work late on Wednesdays when the choir rehearses, I'll let you know, and you can give me the same courtesy by silencing your bunch. How's that?"

Jiggs heard a couple of gasps mixed among the murmur of unsuccessfully suppressed laughter.

Pompous fucking windbag.

"Now, now, there's no need for sarcasm, Jiggs." Harry Moorfield, who presided at Session meetings, held up both his hands in a gesture that said, "Calm down." "I think you made your point."

"You really settled Bob Ladewig's hash." Gene Smallwood, who was one of the elders, turned away from the coffee urn during the mid-meeting break and handed Jiggs a styrofoam cup of coffee, then poured one for himself.

"It made me mad that he didn't say anything to me first, if he had a problem with the noise, before bringing it up in Session."

"Oh, I think Bob's just jealous of your success. The Music Department's all anyone's talked about around this church for years. The life you've breathed into the Youth Department's casting a bit of a shadow across Bob's bask in the limelight"

"It would have been hard not to improve the Youth Department."

"I know. It was just a sign on the door when you showed up. But you've done way more than put up some pictures and sing "Kumbaya" during the time you've been here."

"Thanks."

"A word of caution though." Smallwood looked around to see if anyone else was near enough to overhear. "Even though sometimes Bob's a fool and deserves some come-uppance, you didn't exactly show him any unconditional love in there. You might even have taken a step backwards in terms of your program's success. Bob has lots of allies in high places.

"I'd guess it's important to try to get along in your business, even with those who aren't trying to get along with you. I read something somewhere about 'turning the other cheek.' Ever hear about that?"

Smallwood grinned as he spoke and shook Jiggs' hand. "Anyway, keep up the good work with your noise-makers."

Not one of your finest moments, Morgan. Jiggs was driving home following the Session meeting. The radio had come on when he started the car. He turned it off. He wanted to think. Gene Smallwood's words rang in his ears, or were they the words of Howard Meeker? *"Somewhere there's a hardness in you, Jiggs."*

Jiggs knew it wasn't just Ladewig's failure to come to him about the noise. It was ten months of his walking past Jiggs in corridors without responding to Jiggs' greetings, of Bob's objection to the increase in the Youth Department's appropriation during the mid-year budget meetings.

"I fail to understand why the Youth Department should receive a bigger percentage increase than the Music Department," Bob had said in that meeting. "The Music Department is the backbone of this Church."

"Maybe it's because the Youth Department has had no budget for the last year, Bob," Gene Smallwood replied, expressing Jiggs' thought exactly.

Having been a second lieutenant in the Marine Corps, a being so low it was said "whale shit looks like fleecy white cloud on the blue horizon," Jiggs knew what it was like to occupy the bottom rung on an organizational ladder. Having been a freshman on a football team ruled by Ronald Bjournquist, Jiggs had weathered more than a few undeserved shots. Then he had known enough to keep his mouth shut. But this was different ... sort of...

He could accept that second lieutenants knew little or nothing of the lessons of war only experience could teach. He understood respect in football could only be earned through demonstration of physical prowess; but the building and maintenance of a strong and vibrant church? If Ladewig had been a Delt, he'd have been making pledges bite the heads off mice.

Still, "there are assholes everywhere," Doc had once told him. "The art is to navigate among them without becoming one yourself." Resolving to kill Bob Ladewig with kindness, however undeserved, not for Bob's sake, but for his own, Jiggs pulled into a parking space opposite his apartment at the end of what had been a sixteen-hour day.

The porch light was on, but no light shown through the drawn curtains on the front window as he unlocked the door. However, when he stepped inside, the room was aglow, not with lamplight, but candle light, dozens of candles scattered around the room.

"What...?"

Before he could complete his question, Carol was in his arms, one of hers wrapped around his neck, the other holding an unopened bottle of wine extended in the air. She stifled his question with a kiss, a big one.

"'What's going on?' asked the happy husband," Jiggs said, wrapping both his arms around Carol's waist.

"We're celebrating my last drink."

"Your last drink?"

"Yes, for at least the next nine months."

"Oh Ho! So the girl's gone and gotten herself knocked up. Hooray." Jiggs started to swing her off her feet, thought better of it and put her down.

"Yup. Pregnancy confirmed. Due date – May 30th. Oh, Jiggs, I'm so happy. Here, open this, please," she handed him the wine bottle, "while I put on some music. The doctor says I can have just one before I go on the wagon."

Jiggs forgot all about Bob Ladewig.

42

January 1973

Jiggs was sitting on the edge of the bed putting on his shoes. Carol was coming out of the bathroom, where she had gone upon getting out of the other side of the bed thirty seconds earlier.

"Jiggs, look at me."

Her face was swollen like an overinflated balloon.

"Look." She held up her hands. Even at a distance of fifteen feet, Jiggs could see they were puffed up well beyond their usual size.

"Jesus. That can't be normal." He glanced at his watch. "Is it too early to call the doctor?"

"Jiggs, it's Saturday."

"I don't care if it's Christmas. You need to see a doctor right away. Apart from the swelling, how do you feel?"

"A little headache maybe."

"Get dressed. We'll go to the Emergency Room."

There were two police cars parked outside when Jiggs drove into the Emergency Room parking lot. No more than thirty minutes had passed since Carol walked out of the bathroom looking as if she'd been stung by a hive full of bees.

Now she was holding her head with one hand and her stomach with the other, unable to decide where the pain was worse. On the way from the car to the door, she threw up.

Just inside the entrance there was a machine that dispensed numbers on a small tab of paper and an electric sign that said number 49 was currently being served. It instructed patients to be seated and wait until their number was called.

I'm not here to order pizza. Jiggs looked at the tab he had taken – 61 – and back at Carol. He went up to the window, practically dragging her. From their chairs in the waiting room, numbers 50 through 60, their friends and family members watched with resentful eyes.

"My wife woke up looking like this." Jiggs gestured in Carol's direction. "She has severe pain in her head and abdomen." An impassive nurse behind the glass looked up at Carol with eyes that said, "If you're not bleeding to death, Honey, go sit down and wait your turn."

"She's pregnant," Jiggs added.

It was as if he'd said "Abracadabra" and the nurse was a genie.

She stood up. "Take her to that door over there." She pointed to her right and began walking in that direction.

Jiggs hustled Carol to the door. Once inside, she was plopped in a wheelchair and wheeled into a curtained examination cubicle. An orderly came in and immediately began to take Carol's blood pressure. "Do you feel faint?"

Carol nodded. "A little."

"Mmmm." The orderly studied his gauge as the blood pressure cuff slowly deflated. "One forty-five over one hundred. A doctor will be in to see you in a couple of minutes."

Instead of a doctor, another technician wearing green scrubs appeared, explained that he was taking Carol to have blood drawn, and wheeled her out. Jiggs hadn't even thought to bring a book, so he paced until he was tired of pacing and sat until he was tired of sitting, then resumed pacing. He was seated again when Carol was wheeled back in forty-five minutes later.

"Someone will be in shortly to perform some more tests." The tech stuck out his hand to Jiggs. "Good luck."

Good luck? Jiggs was about to wonder aloud at that, but one glance at Carol, who appeared not to have heard and to be paying attention to nothing, changed his mind.

Five minutes later another technician, this one in blue scrubs, entered, introduced himself, announced he was taking Carol for a chest x-ray, and Carol was whisked off once more. Another forty-five minutes went by, then another fifteen.

Jiggs was dozing when Carol and her driver reappeared, this time with a real doctor in tow.

"Hello, I'm Dr. Borden. I've taken a look at your blood tests and x-rays, Carol. I'm afraid you're suffering from a fairly advanced case of a condition known as 'pre-eclampsia.' Do you know what that is?"

Jiggs said he did not. Carol shook her head slightly from side to side.

"It's a condition characterized by high blood pressure, swelling, fluid in the lungs, all symptoms that are present here in abundance. Untreated, it can cause damage to the blood and lymph vessels, your kidneys and liver, which, in turn, creates a cascade of additional problems, severe problems.

"This is very serious. It can lead to conditions known as 'eclampsia' and HELLP Syndrome, which are characterized by convulsions and loss of consciousness and, ultimately, death."

Whoa. Jiggs shook his head, wanting to disbelieve what he was hearing, but having no reason. At the word "death" Carol raised her head and spoke in a faint voice.

"What about our baby?"

The doctor sighed. "I'm afraid the only treatment is to deliver the child and terminate the pregnancy. Otherwise, given how far the condition has already progressed, there is a real danger you will die. There is no other treatment at this point."

"But our baby ... I'm only five months ... it can't live ... can it?" Anticipating the answer, Carol started to sob. Jiggs had been holding her hand. His other arm was around her shoulders. He tightened his grip, trying to communicate to her his own effort not to weep.

"Your obstetrician, Dr. Darveau, has been called and is on her way. Once she's had a chance to examine and evaluate the test results, I'm sure she'll talk to you, and a plan of treatment can be formulated."

Thus, on March 22, 1973, Justine Renè Morgan was born, weighing one pound, fifteen ounces. She lived seventy-one hours and nine minutes, and, attached to a ventilator incapable of overcoming the failings inherent in her tiny unformed lungs, died in her mother's arms,.

Three days later she was buried. If she could have, Carol would have crawled into the casket with her.

How do you rescue someone you love from despair, when your own sorrow is so deep that it seems like a sin to smile? "Time," Jiggs told himself, Doc's old saying, "make haste slowly." "Listening," the Camilla Waron recipe. And so he waited, forcing himself to go back to work after a week, while Carol remained at home, sitting on the couch, numb.

Rallied by Susan Karocek, the teens in his Department wrapped their arms around Jiggs in ways that even in the depth of his grief he could not help but appreciate. The initial barrage of casseroles, cakes and pies soon dwindled, but the Monday night meetings, organized and led, not by Jiggs, but by the kids, were so subdued and respectful of his state of mind that even Bob Ladewig could not have complained.

May 30, 1973
Dear Cam,

Congratulations on the Masters degree. Well deserved, I'm sure. Do you plan to stay in New York?

The last few months have been a disaster here. Carol was pregnant and, in March, she developed something called "preeclampsia," a potentially fatal condition, the only treatment for which was termination of her pregnancy just five months along. We had a daughter, Justine Renè, who lived only briefly. You know how sad and unhappy I was when I came back to Okinawa from Viet Nam, well, that wasn't a patch on how Justine's death has made me feel.

As hard as that has been for me to deal with, dealing with Carol's grief has been even tougher. She'd been teaching, but for weeks she didn't go back to work. Then, without saying anything to me, she resigned. When I asked her why, she said she couldn't be around children when her own child was dead. All day long she sits in silence. Whatever she's looking at is something only she can see.

Remembering the kindness you showed me just by listening to my troubles, and how that helped me get them sorted out, I have been determined to do the same for Carol. Problem is, there's nothing to listen to. Carol initiates no conversations. If I make an attempt, I am either met by silence, or, sometimes, by a "yes" or "no," without any elaboration. It does not sound to me like anger, but rather a complete absence of joy. If she eats, as she must, it's while I'm at work. I never see any evidence of it. When I ask her if I can fix her something. "No," is her only reply – ever. Eventually, each night she will get up and go to bed without saying anything. No "I guess I'll turn in," no kiss good-night, no "Pleasant dreams." Nothing.

Her parents have been here, but they have gone home now, as perplexed as I about what to do. All my training in counseling is, of course, Christian-oriented. It's not of much use, because Carol professes not to believe in God, now more than ever, I suspect. I have talked to a clinical psychologist who is a friend of mine from our congregation, but he says if Carol doesn't seek help, there's not much to be done.

I know there will always be a scar on my heart in the place that belongs to Justine, but I have regained my equilibrium. I went back to work a week after the memorial service. The kids in my department have been great, and I found that after a while, I could laugh again. If only the same could be said of Carol.

So, on we go, Carol and I, in this kind of twilight zone. If you have any ideas for me, I will be happy to hear them. In all events, please pray for us. We are in need.

Your friend, Jiggs

Jiggs read over his letter to Camilla at least half a dozen times, and then decided not to send it. Until now, their correspondence had been limited to brief, sunny status reports, new addresses and Christmas wishes. His instinct told him that, while Camilla would want to know if Jiggs was going through a crisis, just as he would want to know the same of her, Carol would not appreciate her struggles being shared, especially with this woman unknown to her. He understood and respected that.

Instead, he wrote congratulating Camilla on her receipt of her Master's, inquiring whether she intended to stay in New York, and described briefly his part in the process of shepherding the teen-agers of Winnetka through their adolescence. He mentioned Justine's birth and death, but omitted the aftermath. He did write of his loss to Larry Nelson, mentioning Carol's anguish only in the context of his own.

> Dear Jiggs,
>
>   I am profoundly sorry to learn of the death of your daughter and of the toll it is taking on Carol. I can think of no greater sadness, no greater test of one's faith, than the loss of one's child.
>
>   In my humble opinion, what's called for is a change of scene for the Morgans, some place like California, specifically, a visit to the Nelsons. It will give Sandy a chance to hear your version of all the stories I have told her about the Hill 410 Follies and Carol a chance to hear mine. Maybe we will even make a wine drinker out of you.
>
>   I'm serious, Jiggs. Come and see us. We would love to have you visit. Meanwhile, you will both be in my prayers.
>
> Regards, Larry

Larry's letter was in Jiggs' pocket as he approached the door to the apartment late in the day. Something seemed different. Jiggs paused. The curtains were open for the first time in almost four months. When he walked in, across the living room in the kitchen, he saw Carol standing at the stove, cooking something.

She looked up and smiled as Jiggs came in. Still wary, Jiggs walked over and put his arms around her, afraid to squeeze, lest it prove unwelcome. Carol responded with a hug of her own, a kiss, and an order that he sit down while she "fetched" him a beer.

Carol sat down across their small kitchen table from him with a beer of her own. Jiggs, consumed in wonder at this unexpected metamorphosis, took a swig. When he set his beer down, Carol reached over and put her hand on top of his.

"Seeing you smile," Jiggs said, "makes my heart sing. What's happened?"

"Nothing 'happened,' Jiggs. It's like my heart's been paralyzed, turned to stone and then fractured into a million tiny pieces whenever I think about Justine. I know I haven't been a very good wife or friend to you while you've been going through the same ordeal, and I'm sorry."

Two weeks later they flew to Los Angeles, rented a car and drove up the coast, their first real vacation in the almost eight years they'd been together. For two nights they stayed at an inn in Big Sur, an old stagecoach station cloaked with flowers. They hiked the rock-strewn beaches and loafed in the sun. A stream ran beneath their window, and they fell asleep listening to its song. As they lay snuggled in bed just before turning out the light on their second night, Carol asked, "Jiggs, do you know what I worry about?"

Of course, he didn't.

"I worry you'll blame me for Justine's death."

Holy shit. "What ... why would you think that?"

"Well, God is such a big part of your life, but no part of mine, not in terms of faith. I worry you'll think her death is God's punishment for my failure to believe."

"Carol, I hope I've never given you cause to think that, because the thought's never entered my mind. I'm not like ol' By The Book Basil, that guy I've told you about. My idea of God isn't one of some guy hurling lighting bolts around the firmament at persons who displease him. Sure, I wish you and I were more together when it comes to our beliefs, but please don't ever think I feel Justine's death was your fault."

"Jiggs, I don't ever want to go back to teaching."

Unsurprised by either the sudden shift of subject matter or Carol's wish to abandon teaching, Jiggs didn't say anything.

"I want to try to become a golf pro, a teaching pro, maybe a coach."

A different kind of teacher. To Jiggs, who for the first three-quarters of his life the idea of making a living playing a sport would have his definition of Nirvana, this seemed a great idea, and he said so. "Do you know how to do that? Do you have a plan?"

Carol did, and she was still explaining it to him long after they turned out the light.

Napa Valley, where Larry lived, was lovely. The two good little Iowans discovered more kinds of wine than either knew existed. But the best part of the three days there was the Nelson family. Larry was able to joke that the prosthetics made him taller; Sandy, was even nicer than all Larry's stories about her back on Hill 410 made her sound; and their two daughters, teenagers now, gave Larry just enough of a hard time to show they thought of him as their friend as well as their father.

Amid his prayers of thanks for Carol's emergence from woe, Jiggs included one of gratitude that here was at least one Viet Nam story with a happy ending.

43

September 1973

Jiggs sat up in his sleeping bag and surveyed the campsite. He was remembering his solemn promise to his body in Viet Nam never to sleep on the ground again if he got home alive. Only embers remained of the recent campfire on this moonless night, not enough light to reveal that twelve of the large boulders strewn about the area were actually sleeping teenagers. At least Jiggs hoped they were asleep. All giggling had stopped, perhaps the last complaint voiced.

Jiggs' small unit leadership instincts told him it would be a good idea to check his lines one last time. He crawled out of his bag, slipped on a pair of shorts and shoes and walked his perimeter. *Oh, oh.* Closer inspection revealed that two of the twelve boulders he'd counted from where he had been lying really were boulders. Two of his flock were missing. Without having to shine a flashlight in anyone's face, Jiggs knew which two.

This is more trouble than a Marine platoon.

Using his best "there are VC in the area" stealth, Jiggs began his search. *Where would I go if I was them?* He walked the path leading from the clearing to the lake. *Bingo.* Off in the shadow of a large tree lay a two teenager sized boulder.

"Ohhh!" Susan Karocek's very healthy heart nearly stopped when she opened her eyes to look at all the stars from where she and Jimmy Blake lay tangled and discovered Jiggs standing above them.

"Hi."

"Oh, Reverend Morgan, ... I ... we ... we didn't hear you." Susan sat up. From what little Jiggs could see in the dark, nothing appeared to be unbuttoned.

"I didn't think you did." Jiggs sat down on the edge of the sleeping bag they were using for a blanket. "I think you were distracted."

Jiggs paused, unsure of what he was going to say next. That this had happened was no surprise. Susan and Jimmy had obviously been an "item" since mid-summer. It was exactly what Jiggs would have done when he was their age if he could have persuaded any girl to go with him. It was going to be tough to be too disapproving.

"Listen, do you like it out here? I mean, camping, hiking, the lake, the woods, the campfire? As long as the three of us are out here, I'd really like to know what you think before I go back."

"I like this a lot," Susan said. "My family never does anything like this."

"What about you, Jimmy? What do you think of it?"

"Yeah, I guess I like it." The boy shrugged. "I mean, you know, ... yeah, I like it.'

Jiggs thought Jimmy only attended Fellowship because Susan did.

"Would you both like to do this again?"

Both agreed they would.

"Would you recommend it to others in the Fellowship who didn't come on this trip?"

Both nodded.

"Do you think there would be any more trips like this if your parents somehow got the idea that I was letting kids go off and make-out? What do you think would happen then?"

"We didn't think about that." Susan looked down at the ground.

Jiggs gave them a long look, stood up and stretched. "Guess I'll turn in. You two come back when you're ready."

Jiggs turned and began to walk back towards the campsite.

"Wait a minute, Reverend Morgan," Susan got to her feet and pulled Jimmy up beside her. "We'll come with you."

Jiggs lay back down and squirmed around in his sleeping bag trying to get comfortable. He was remembering how Reverend Holmgren, whose boar almost ended Doc's career, used to come to the high school dances and prowl the floor, prying apart couples he thought were dancing too closely. Jiggs fell asleep wondering whether the Reverend was still the Central High dance vigilante. The thought the two of them were now in the same business was dismaying.

Morning dawned clear and cold. Suburban children curled deep in their bags, as far from the openings as possible until seduced from their relative comfort by the smell of frying bacon. Still thinking about last night, Jiggs hoped the bacon's seduction was the only one that would take place on this trip.

As they ate breakfast, the sun began to overpower the cold, and the kids' senses of humor reappeared, particularly with respect to Jiggs' cooking. Jiggs told them about how, while camping in Mexico, he had mistaken grapenuts for bulgar in the

340   CHRISTOPHER BRITTON

dark one night, and fried a batch, which he went ahead and ate because he was too tired to start over. His story did not inspire confidence among his disciples.

Suddenly Meagan Cathcart, who was on her way back to the campfire from the bathroom, started yelling. "Snake! Snake! Snake!"

Twelve persons jumped from sitting to standing as one, all looking around their feet, but seeing no snake.

Jiggs hastened to the semi-hysterical girl, who appeared about to hyperventilate. "Where, Meagan? Where's the snake?"

Meagan was breathing too hard to talk, but she pointed at what at first glance looked like a large flat brown stone among other flat brown stones about twenty feet from where she was standing, just over fifty feet from the fire. The snake lay in the sun, its rattles lolling limply back over its coils, warming up, mindless of the proximity of a dozen of its most deadly enemies. Even at rest, its pitted, wedge-shaped head menaced every person in the group, its eyes as colorless and unblinking as the surrounding gravel.

"Kill it," somebody said.

"Yeah, kill it." General agreement all around. Mark Brattin picked up a large stone and raised it over his head as he began to circle behind the motionless animal.

"Wait a minute." Jiggs put his hand on Mark's shoulder. "Mark, put down the rock and let's just go back to the fire."

"What?" Mark looked up at Jiggs, the rock still at chest height. "Are you crazy, man?"

"Yeah, let him kill it," someone piped up. "We don't want any rattlesnakes around."

Jiggs shook his head. "Mark don't kill it. Leave it alone."

"Are you crazy? No good snakes, man."

Jiggs looked Mark in the eye. "Think about where you are. This woods is the snakes's house, not yours. Who's the intruder here, Mark? You or the snake?"

"That snake could bite someone, Rev. Mark's gotta kill it."

"Just leave it alone, and it'll leave us alone. It's not threatening us. It's just trying to get warm. Lots of snakes in the woods, Mark. Can't kill 'em all. It's not bothering you."

"Bothers me, Rev," one of the others said.

"C'mon. Put the rock down, and let's finish breakfast." Jiggs sat back down and picked up his plate.

Slowly the teenager lowered the rock and stepped back, looking around as if to see whether there were any other snakes in the area.

"Shoulda killed it, man," someone persisted.

Mark Brattin walked over to the boy who had spoken and dropped the rock at his feet. "Kill it yourself." He walked away.

Throughout the rest of the meal Jiggs kept one eye on the snake. He could not have said whether his vigilance was for the welfare of his charges or that of the snake. After about ten minutes, it crawled away. None of the kids noticed.

Upon arrival back at the church Sunday evening, Jiggs was carrying Bibles in from the car when Susan Karocek came up to him and offered to help. She picked up the top half of the stack he was holding.

"Reverend Morgan, last night when you were talking to Jimmy and me, you asked what would happen if our folks found out what we were doing."

"Yes," Jiggs said, waiting.

"I mean, do you think they're going to find out?"

"Nothing I could see to find out." Jiggs set down his Bibles on the table just inside the door of the Youth Department. "One thing though. There are lots of things more dangerous than snakes. Going too far too fast's one of 'em. Maybe you and Jimmy and I can talk after Fellowship tomorrow night. I'd like to help you two sort it out."

Susan smiled a big smile. "Thank you Rev. Thank you. I'll be there, and I'll bring Jimmy."

Twenty-four hours later, there was Susan, as promised. But not Jimmy. According to Susan, "Jimmy said he had too much homework."

"Come in, Jimmy. Thanks for coming. Grab a chair." Jiggs had called Jimmy Blake at home on Tuesday when he didn't show up with Susan Monday night. "You get all that homework done?"

Jimmy looked blank. Apparently he had forgotten the homework that kept him from the meeting Monday night. After a moment's hesitation, he sat down.

"Jimmy, I was sorry you couldn't make it to Fellowship Monday night like we planned, but maybe it's better this way, because I want to ask you a question when Susan isn't around. Do you care about Susan?"

A pause. "What do you mean 'care?'"

"Is she someone to whom you would hate to see something bad happen?"

"Yeah. I suppose. Sure."

"Well, if you two keep doing things like sneaking off from a group to go make out on a blanket somewhere, something bad is going to happen to her."

"We weren't doing anything."

"I'm not talking about that, Jimmy. Just by leaving the group and going out there, you put Susan's reputation in danger. Even if the two of you do nothing but 'talk,' people will assume it was a lot more than that."

"Why should I care what other people think?"

"Jimmy, right or wrong, the way it works is, people have dirty minds. They make assumptions. If some of them get the wrong idea about what Susan's doing out there with you, they'll think less of her. Doors of opportunity will begin to close for her, probably without her ever knowing why.

"It doesn't work the same way for guys. Your buddies may even think you're some kind of a 'stud.' But I promise you it won't work that way for Susan."

Jimmy crossed and uncrossed his legs. "Why are you telling me this? Shouldn't you be having this conversation with Susan?"

"I have. But you're a year older and, from what I read on the sports page, kind of a big shot. Susan obviously cares for you. She's probably a little bit flattered by your attention. She wants to please you. That gives you some responsibility. A girl's reputation is a delicate thing, like a tiny china cup – easily broken, almost impossible to completely repair."

Jimmy heaved a "when is this going to be over" sigh and glanced at his watch.

Maybe the little shit doesn't like my analogy.

Jimmy stood up "Is that all?"

Jiggs stood too. "It is if you want it to be. I'll be glad to answer any questions. I can give you some examples, if you're interested. Otherwise, please think about what I said. It's important."

Jiggs stuck out his hand. Jimmy shook it as he was turning towards the door.

Late the next morning, Harry Moorfield walked into the Youth Department for the first time since Jiggs had arrived at First Pres.

"Jiggs, I received a call this morning from the parents of a teen who went on that camping trip with you last weekend. They're outraged and vowing never to let their son go on another outing if you're the one in charge. If what they say is true, I don't blame them."

Oh, oh. "What do they say?"

"They say when a rattlesnake was discovered in the midst of the group, you didn't kill it. Instead, you just let it remain near their children with whose welfare and safety you were entrusted. Is that right?"

Jiggs took a deep breath. "Not exactly. There was a rattlesnake, but it was never closer than twenty feet from any of the kids, and then only briefly. It was a cold morning, and it was trying to warm up in the sun about fifty feet from where we were having breakfast. Once it was discovered, I never took my eyes off it until I saw it crawl off into the brush a short time later. That's what happened."

"So there was a snake and you didn't kill it?"

"Yeah. There was a snake. I didn't kill it."

"Hearing this really makes me question your judgment and fitness to lead such outings."

"What? You think I should have killed it when it wasn't threatening anyone?"

"Absolutely. It might have killed someone."

Should we have drained the lake because someone might drown?

Jiggs held his tongue. "Reverend Moorfield, do you have any interest whatsoever in the reasoning behind what I did?"

"Frankly, no. A snake is a snake. When I see 'em, I kill 'em. I keep an old putter that I've sharpened like a knife in my bag for when I see 'em on the golf course."

Jiggs didn't argue. This conversation wasn't being driven by logic.

"Jiggs, you've done a good job with this department. But you have to be careful. One thing like this can undo all the good work you've done. These people are big financial supporters of our church. We can't afford to have them unhappy. I want you to write them a note apologizing for your lapse in judgment. Here's their address." Moorfield handed a slip of paper to Jiggs.

Pick your battles. Another Doc-ism.

Jiggs took the slip of paper without looking at it and said he would send the note. In response to Jiggs' question, Reverend Moorfield said he didn't need to see what Jiggs wrote before he sent it. Jiggs appreciated that.

Moorfield stood up and turned to go.

"Reverend Moorfield, one more thing." Jiggs held up the still folded slip containing the address. "The parents who complained, was it the Blakes?"

Moorfield looked surprised. "Why, yes it was. How did you know? Did their son say something to you?"

Jiggs shook his head. "Just a lucky guess."

CHRISTOPHER BRITTON

44

October 1973

Two weeks later Hood came to town for the weekend of the Iowa vs. Northwestern game in nearby Evanston, to have a few beers with Reverend Morgan and play some golf with Carol.

"So, how's Doc's doing? Leg okay?"

"Okay, I guess. You've probably seen him since the last time I did. I talked to him on the phone last week. He didn't say anything about it. He's been back practicing for almost a year."

Roger nodded. "Yeah, that's what he told me when he was in the office to discuss the lawsuit in July. But he was still limping. He said Lindy was still taking care of him."

Jiggs laughed. "Lindy's moved in lock, stock and barrel. She sold her house in Iowa City."

"I wondered about that when I heard she was still there," Roger said. "You okay with that? How about your sisters?"

Jiggs shrugged. "Far as I'm concerned, if Doc's happy, Lindy too, for that matter, then I'm happy. I'd guess it raised Marie's eyebrows when she heard about it, but she hasn't said anything. Darcy, hell, she's so easy going, if Doc suddenly said he was going to become a Nazi, she'd knit him an armband."

Roger opened another beer, handed it to Jiggs, and opened one for himself. "Who'd have ever guessed you'd play Cupid for those two?"

"Not sure it's like that. Doc's nothing if not practical. Once he saw they could get along for more than a week at a time, I think he figured there was no reason they couldn't keep helping each other out even after he healed up. Probably tired of eating his own cooking. When Carol and I were there last Christmas, Lindy had made the upstairs her kingdom, while Doc was still bunking down on the first floor.

"But who knows? They go riding together, and Doc's taught her to drive. What a heart-stopping experience that must have been."

Jiggs held up his bottle. Roger did the same "Here's to love in whatever form it chooses to take."

"Speaking of Doc's lawsuit," Jiggs said. "How's that going?"

"Nowhere."

"Nowhere? What do you mean 'nowhere?'"

"Jiggs, the case isn't going anywhere. We got past the State's initial motion to dismiss simply because we stated a claim the law recognizes, that there is no need for this park. But the fact that the legislature passed the law and the Governor signed it creates a presumption the need exists. It's going to be Doc's burden and that of the other opponents to prove it doesn't by what the law describes as 'clear and convincing evidence.'

"We may be able to show that another park isn't needed from the standpoint of recreation, but, in my opinion, we don't have a chance from the standpoint of the need for water conservation. That reservoir will ease a lot of water problems, especially in dry years, help control floods in the wet ones. The

State can get as many water experts lined up to say that as it wants, while I'm still looking for one who will contradict them."

"I presume Doc and the other families know this?"

"I can't tell you what we told 'em, Jiggs. Privileged communication. But can you imagine me telling them anything other than what I really think?"

Jiggs couldn't imagine that. "I suppose you can't tell me what Doc said in response either?"

"You know Doc. He doesn't say much, but he's not backing down."

"Rog, is there anything to be gained by keeping going? Isn't he just throwing good money after bad?"

"Time. He's playing for time. It'll be another year before we get to trial, if the State doesn't get it thrown out first, followed by an appeal, whatever the outcome. Then there will be a battle over valuation of the property. I think Doc's hoping he'll get a new set of politicians in office down in Des Moines, ones who don't have any ownership in this project and want to use the money for something else. In the absence of something like that, once the court sprinkles its holy water ... oops, sorry ... on it and the appeals are exhausted, it'll happen, unless there's a miracle."

Jiggs could imagine an atom being split more readily that Doc being separated from his farm. He looked at Roger and raised his bottle. "Here's to miracles."

45

November 1973 - July 1974

YOUTH YAK
By Susan Karocek

The wheels are spinning in the Youth Department. Reverend Morgan is taking fifteen members of Westminister Fellowship to Iowa at the end of this month to ride in RAGBRAI (Register's Annual Great Bike Ride Across Iowa), a bicycle ride across the state sponsored by the Des Moines newspaper. The ride begins when we dip our wheels in the Missouri River, the State's western border, and ends when we dip our wheels in the Mississippi River, Iowa's border on the East. It will be 437 miles river to river, almost 500 miles of corn on the cob, watermelon, lemonade and fresh tomatoes. YUM!

Reverend Morgan has been leading dawn training rides all summer, a shock to several of us who did not know summer happened or that a bicycle could be ridden before noon. Last Saturday we pedaled fifty miles. Westminister Fellowship is READY!

Let the ride begin.

It had been a year filled with firsts for Jiggs. He performed two baptisms, one wedding and graduated his first confirmation class into full membership in the Church. Scattered among these sacraments were bake sales, car washes, snow shovelings and lawn mowings, as he mobilized his troops to finance the great RAGBRAI safari.

Meanwhile, Jiggs' battles with Bob Ladewig had subsided, not because of any newly discovered love for Jiggs on Bob's part. Rather, with Howard Meeker's words haunting him, Jiggs had gone out of his way not to respond to the self-appointed maestro's frequent provocations. The effort was killing Jiggs. To reinforce his efforts, Jiggs had begun to meditate after reading a book entitled *Positive Addictions*. Borrowing a page from Zen, Jiggs reminded himself, "Be like water. Do not clash with opposing forces, dissolve them." Although his water was often boiling where Rev. Ladewig was concerned, the only person who ever heard Jiggs' tea kettle whistling was Carol.

Carol, too, had been busy. Returning from California, she had won the Church's member golf tournament by four strokes over Jiggs' friend, Gene Smallwood, who had won the preceding three. She was the first woman ever to win. Jiggs caddied.

Her victory propelled her hoped for teaching career, as half a dozen women in the congregation asked her to give them lessons. When the snow flew, she moved her instructional efforts indoors to a large driving range, where her efforts were noticed by management. She accepted a position as an instructor at the range, but, after playing and beating the pro at Harry

Moorfield's club in the Spring, resigned and accepted a teaching job there. She applied for her LPGA membership, and her boat was launched.

The launching was accompanied by her announcement delivered one September morning over coffee that she didn't want to have children. Despite her doctor's assurances that one bout of pre-eclampsia did not create any great likelihood of another, it was a risk Carol declared she could not face. Jiggs was not surprised. He suggested adoption, but Carol's ship was sailing in other directions.

"Has anybody seen Jimmy?" Jiggs was counting noses amid the chaos of six thousand bicyclists. One of his noses was missing. Much to Jiggs' regret, the Blakes had failed to carry out their threat following the affaire d'snake never to allow Jimmy to participate in a trip overseen by Jiggs, and it was Jimmy's nose that was now nowhere to be found.

"I don't know. He just took off when we started this morning," Susan Karocek said. "The rest of us tried to keep up, but we fell back after a few miles. He must have finished a long time ago."

Jiggs had had a flat tire shortly after the day's start. By the time he caught up with his group, Jimmy was out of sight.

Jiggs scanned the crowd assembling in the fairgrounds in Tipton, the evening's host town. Tents of all colors and configurations were sprouting randomly everywhere he looked. By the time the last of the six thousand riders in the rolling carnival that was RAGBRAI arrived, the population of the town would be trebled. Booths sponsored by organizations as varied as the American Legion and the Young Methodist Mothers, were selling tee shirts, bicycle spare parts, lemonade, watermelon slices, corn on the cob and all forms of pork and roast beef sandwich known to man.

"No doubt he's somewhere in that mob. Everyone fan out. Whoever finds him, bring him back here, so he'll know where our tents are. If you don't find him in thirty minutes, come back anyway. He'll have to find us."

Fourteen teenagers fanned out in fourteen different directions. Thirty minutes later, they were back. No Jimmy.

No sense wrecking their last night on account of that knucklehead.

Jiggs turned them loose with instructions not to leave the fairgrounds without his permission and to be back at the tents by ten o'clock. Jimmy would show up sooner or later. Returning to his tent following a shower and change of clothes, Jiggs found Westminister's area deserted except for Susan. She was sitting on top of a picnic table, an open book upside down in her lap. "Susan. Why aren't you out whooping it up with the others?"

The girl who looked up at Jiggs was no longer the scrawny eighth grader he'd met two and a half years earlier. Quite apart from being at least three inches taller, it would have been impossible for Jiggs not to notice that the ugly duckling had become a swan. Lithe and graceful, Susan Karocek radiated youthful loveliness, even when she was crying, as Jiggs could see she now was. She took a quick swipe across her face with her fingertips in an unsuccessful attempt to brush away her tears.

Act like you didn't notice, Morgan. See if she brings it up.

"Oh, I'm just waiting in case Jimmy comes back. He said we could walk around the booths together today. I thought it would be fun since this is our last night, but I guess he forgot."

He didn't forget.

"Well, I was going to wander around a bit. Do you want to walk with me? Maybe we'll run in to him."

Susan slid off the table, closed her book and tossed it in her tent. They strolled in silence among the booths for a few minutes, weaving in and out according to the dictates of the crowd, many of whom were pushing bicycles.

"Susan," Jiggs finally spoke, "I couldn't help noticing you were crying back there by the tents. Are you okay?"

Susan sighed. "Yes and no. I just don't think Jimmy likes me any more, ... and I still like him."

Jiggs shook his head in sympathy. "That's a tough one when you have strong feelings for someone who doesn't feel the same way. But can I tell you something, Susan?"

"What's that, Reverend?"

"It's hard to believe when you're going through it, but the sadness and disappointment will pass. Speaking both as a preacher and a guy, albeit an ancient one, losing Jimmy's no great loss. He's a flashy guy, who spends all his time looking at himself in a mirror, even when there are none around. There's a whole lot more to you as a person than there will ever be to..."

"Junior! Jiggs! Jiggs Morgan!" Jim Hegman emerged from the crowd beyond Susan. He was waving his arms to get Jiggs' attention. "I've been looking for you for five days. Your sister told me you were riding in RAGBRAI this year. Glad I finally found you." They shook hands. "I need to talk to you."

"Jim," Jiggs nodded in Susan's direction, "this is Susan Karocek. Susan, this is an old friend of mine, Jim Hegman."

"Nice to meet you, Susan." Hegman stuck out his hand and Susan shook it.

"Jim, can we meet a little later? I'm kind of bu..."

"No, Reverend Morgan, it's all right," Susan said. "You and Mr. Hegman go on. I'll go find some of the other kids. I appreciate what you said just now. Thanks. I'll think about it."

Susan turned and trotted off.

"Pretty girl." Hegman watched her jog away.

"Sad girl right now," Jiggs said. "She's breaking up with her boyfriend, or, rather, he's breaking up with her."

"Be hard to break up with a girl who looks like that."

"Yeah, and you know the best thing about her? She has no idea how pretty she is."

"Hope she stays that way. Anyway, Junior, it's good to see you again. What's it been? A couple of years at least. Let's go find a place to sit down and have something to drink. You can catch me up on what you've been doing."

Midnight. The last party had waned, the last guest departed. Hardly a light remained with the exception of occasional flashlights – people making their way to and from the restrooms in the dark. Jiggs sat on the same picnic table where he'd encountered Susan that afternoon. He was watching a solitary figure approach, picking his way among the welter of tent ropes, locked bicycles and sleeping bags littering the ground.

Is he a little unsteady, or is it just all the obstacles?

"Hello, Jimmy."

"Ohh ... hello, Reverend. I didn't see you there."

"No. I guess you didn't." Jiggs inhaled. *Beer check.* He couldn't tell, not for sure.

"Been drinking, Jimmy?"

"Ah ... no. Just over there talking to some college guys I met."

"You're almost two hours past group curfew, you know."

"Oh, is it that late. I don't have a watch."

"Too bad. I suppose none of those 'college guys' had one either."

"Dunno. I forgot to ask."

"Jimmy, if you're old enough to come on a trip like this, you need to be old enough to both know and care what time it is, watch or no watch. It makes me want to forget to trust you. Now hit the rack."

Jimmy took a step, then stopped and looked around.

"Hard to recognize which tent's yours, isn't it, when you weren't around to help pitch it? It's the third one over on the right." Jiggs pointed. "Right next to mine. Make sure you don't wake up Brian when you crawl in."

46

August 1974

At the conclusion of Ragbrai, Jiggs handed off his charges to the parents who drove over to pick them up. He caught a ride with Jim Hegman to spend a few days with Doc and Lindy. It was Doc's birthday. As Jim and Jiggs drove through Walnut Grove late Saturday afternoon, they saw Ron Bjournquist coming out of the hardware store and stopped. During their brief conversation, Ron invited Jiggs to come with him to a land auction the following Monday.

It was only a corner, an intersection of two gravel roads somewhere in Colfax Township. Ron parked his pickup with its right side tires a foot or two down the slope of the drainage ditch paralleling the road. Jiggs scrambled out, being careful not to let the heavy door drag him when he opened it on the downhill slope. He joined Ron on the road, and they walked up towards the corner. Something was different.

"Where are all the fences?" Jiggs asked.

"Everyone takes 'em out so as to get another row or two planted."

"What about in a year or two, when they graze it?"

"Nobody grazes cattle anymore."

Except Doc.

"Ground's worth too much for corn and beans. Cattle's all goin' to feed lots."

Jiggs had built too many fences, the kind Doc built, ones designed to outlast the Pyramids, to ever comprehend tearing out perfectly good fence for the sake of squeezing out a few more bushels of corn.

"What about the pheasants?"

Pheasants lived in the grass and weeds that grew along the fences, where it was hard to mow. If wrestling wasn't the national sport of Iowa, pheasant hunting was. "Gone," Ron said. "The pesticides were starting to get 'em anyway. We hunt up in the Dakotas now. They're still around up there."

They joined a group of about thirty men already gathered, a festival of John Deere caps, bib overalls and suntans deeper than any earned on a golf course.

"Morning, Ron. You gonna buy a couple more farms today?" someone in the crowd said. Laughter all around.

Jiggs shook hands with several of the men he knew.

"Good to see you again, Jiggs," said Colonel Clemons, his old employer. "Ain't had any decent help since you left."

"So you're still doing farm sales, Colonel?"

"Not so many. Too much work spreadin' out all the merchandise. Too cold those winter mornings. Make more doin' an occasional land auction though, what with the price of land these days. Only gotta sell one thing and make more than ten equipment sales. Reckon I'll stay in business as long as the Ruskies like eatin'."

The Colonel looked at his watch. "Well, time to get started." He walked into the center of the crowd.

"Gentlemen, ..." he said in a loud voice. Conversation stopped. Everything was still. Through the heat waves rising above the corn, Lawrence Estlund's barn shimmered a quarter of a mile away. The only sound amid that otherwise brief interval of silence was the whirr of insects busy among the weeds in the ditches. Jiggs was sweating just standing there.

"Gentlemen, you all know what we're here for. Bob Ziegler here," the Colonel put his hand on the shoulder of a tall farmer standing next to him, "has decided to put his feet up and start sippin' tall cool drinks with umbrellas in 'em. Now it's up to you guys to finance Bob's plan.

"This here eighty acres is prime farm land. The yield last year was thirty bushels a beans per acre, one hundred bushels a corn the year before that. It's all tiled, drainage is good, never any standing water. Access is easy from either the north or east. Practically farms itself.

"Most a ya already know all that, so who wants a little more ground to plow?"

The Colonel turned his head, surveying the crowd. "Who'll give me seven-fifty?"

"Seven-fifty." Someone in back.

"Seven-fifty. I got seven-fifty. Who'll give me eight?" The Colonel began to sing the auctioneer's song, urging, nudging, cajoling his audience to climb aboard the bidding train, building momentum.

Ron Bjournquist raised his right hand, signaling his bid.

"Eight. I got eight. Ron here's trying to steal this ground. Who'll give me eight-fifty? Good ground, good ground. Got eight, need eight-fifty…"

A hand went up off to the right.

"Eight-fifty. Eight-fifty. Who'll go nine?"

So it went, the price climbing in ever smaller increments as it rose above a thousand dollars per acre, the number of competing bidders soon reduced to two, Bjournquist and a man wearing a short-sleeved sport shirt, slacks and loafers – a dude.

"Who'll give me ten-forty...?"

A hand up.

"... Need ten seventy-five; need…"

Bjournquist nodded his head, still in the game.

"Eleven ..."

The dude hung in at eleven.

"Eleven twenty-five..."

A pause.

"Eleven twenty-five, eleven twenty-five? Pay for itself in a year or two. Gotta have eleven twenty-five." Colonel Clemons chanted on almost too fast for comprehension, but not quite, striving to suck the contestants deeper into the vortex of the bidding.

Bjournquist's hand was in the air, slower this time, but still airborne.

"Eleven fifty. Eleven fifty? Good ground. Good ground..." the Colonel was looking directly at the dude. "Eleven forty?"

The dude looked back and shook his head. "No."

The old auctioneer slowly rotated, his hawk's eyes searching for fresh prey, while he continued his litany, but all the others were keeping to their burrows.

"Eleven twenty-five once, eleven twenty–five twice, sold to Mr. Bjournquist for one thousand one hundred twenty-five dollars per acre.

"Gentlemen, unless something happened around here yesterday I don't know about, I believe we've set a new per acre record for the price of Iowa farm land."

The crowd murmured its approval. A couple of onlookers congratulated Ron, clapping him on the back as they started back to their trucks. The dude shook his hand.

"Who was that guy you were bidding against?" Jiggs asked as they drove away. "He was no farmer."

"Hell no. He's a banker. That's Norm Olds. He's a trust officer at First Iowa. That's the outfit Hegman's working for."

"A banker? Why's a bank want a farm? "

Bjournquist gave Jiggs a look from across the cab.

"First Iowa's the biggest landowner in the County. One of the biggest in the State next to some insurance company from back East. Price of equipment's so high, you gotta have five hundred acres just to make it worth the expense. Banks and insurance companies can afford to farm, but a lot of little guys can't."

I guess that makes you a "big guy," Ron.

Jiggs and Doc were sitting on Doc's porch having a beer. The Cardinal game was on the radio low in the background.

"Went to a land auction with Ron Bjournquist. He bought that eighty Bob Ziegler farmed up in Colfax Township for eleven twenty-five an acre."

"That so. Hmm."

Jiggs could see Doc was doing the math.

"Ninety thousand dollars. Ronald's going to have to raise a lot of corn to pay for that."

"You think it's a bad deal, Pop? All everybody talks about around here is how good grain prices are and all the grain we're selling to the Russians."

"Jiggs," Doc turned in his chair so he was facing his son, "why do you think the price of land is so high?"

"Because the markets are up, I suppose."

"Right, and the price of land isn't the only thing that's up. Equipment, fuel, fertilizer, all those costs climb right alongside the price of beans and corn. I think some guys get hypnotized by the market and lose sight of their margins, what's left after they pay all their bills."

"You think Ron's one of those guys?"

Doc shrugged. "He's probably safe as long as the market stays up, but it sounds like he just crawled a little farther out on the limb today."

As long as the market stays up. "Can't he just sell some land if he's overextended?"

"What if it's no longer worth what he owes on it?"

Agricultural Economics 101. Jiggs had lived on a farm throughout his childhood, but Doc wasn't really a farmer. Cattle and horses were to Doc, the veterinarian, what golf was to Carol's dad, the lawyer. Jiggs had seen corn and beans hauled off and sold by his neighbors, had done some of the hauling himself, but never stopped to think about the overhead.

Doc took a swallow from his beer. "Another thing. If things start to go downhill for Ron, the slope could get steep mighty fast. He's bought all that ground with money he borrowed from First Iowa, and I'll bet he had to mortgage his whole place for security, not just the land he borrowed to buy.

"My guess is Ronald's shoved all his chips into the middle of the table, hasn't held anything back. That's the only way First Iowa will play."

Before they could speculate further about the potential perils of Ron Bjournquist's run at becoming a "big guy," Lindy came out on the porch carrying an envelope.

"Doc, did you see this? It's from Roger's firm. It came in today's mail."

Doc took the letter, opened and read it and handed it to Jiggs., who read Hood's opening paragraph.

Dear Doc,

Today we received the Judge's ruling on the State's motion for summary judgment in *Morgan, et al. v. State of Iowa*. As you will see from the enclosed opinion, Judge Hughes ruled we have failed to raise an issue of fact with respect to whether the reservoir around which the park is planned is needed. In the absence of some facts to support our assertion that the reservoir is NOT needed, judgment has been granted in favor of the State.

The letter went on to explain that Roger had tried to call Doc to give him the bad news and discuss what was involved in mounting an appeal, but had been unable to reach him. Jiggs handed the letter to Lindy. He expected her to start screeching near the end of the first sentence, but she surprised him and began to cry. Jiggs stood up and hugged her. Over the old woman's shoulder, he saw Doc sitting there staring out over the valley. In less than a minute Lindy snuffled that she was "over it," and that "the goddamn bozos down in Des Moines must have better things to do than to throw people out of their homes." Still muttering, she went back inside.

"What are you going to do, Pop? You must have seen it coming. I know Rog hasn't been optimistic."

"Appeal. What else?"

"Doesn't sound from the letter as if Rog thinks an appeal will succeed."

"Jiggs, when you went into the Districts your senior year against Billings, what was your record against him?"

"I don't know. O for 9 or something like that."

"Did that cause you to quit trying or make you try harder?"

"Pop, you're missing my point. I'm not suggesting you quit fighting, if that's what you want to do. But given what you're being told about your chances, you need to think about a Plan B, in the event the case ultimately goes against you, and you have to sell. Start thinking about what you want to do if that happens."

"Jiggs, I'm not leaving. Your mom's buried here, and I will be too."

47

August 1974

Jiggs and Carol were eating out, an Italian restaurant in their neighborhood, to celebrate Jiggs' safe return from the wilds of RAGBRAI.

"I saw Jim Hegman during the ride."

"Jim Hegman, which friend is he? I know you've talked about him."

"Jim was three years ahead of me in high school and then down at the University. It was his wedding I went back for when we were in New Jersey. Nice guy. Smart. He's the President of a bank in Lake City now."

"Was he riding too?"

"Yes. Darcy had told him I was riding. He was looking for me. We had dinner together the last night. He's head of the Session at the Presbyterian Church in Lake City. Jim says the pastor there is retiring at the end of the year ... He wants me to apply. He says he can make it happen."

"The Youth Minister is retiring?"

"No, the head guy."

"Jiggs, that's wonderful."

Wonderful. "Somehow I thought your reaction would be just the opposite."

"No. A church of your own after just three years. No more Bob Ladewig. We didn't think that could happen for at least another three or four years."

Jiggs swirled the sauce into his pasta with his fork. *There will always be Bob Ladewigs.* "What about Arizona? What about golf?"

"Oh, Jiggs. I've been a long time gone from Arizona. Sure, I want to go back there. I still hope that will be our end game, but we've always known you'd need a smaller church before getting a big one. This is a chance to speed up the whole process. Besides, it will be great to be near our families for a change. As for golf, I'll figure something out. What did you tell him, Hegman, I mean?"

"I said I'd talk to you and think it over."

Carol gave him a sideways look. "You don't sound too enthusiastic."

"Well, what if we went there and things didn't go well. I mean, at bottom, I'm a spiritual advisor. That's my business. It's hard doing business with friends. Doesn't take much imagination to foresee having to tell an old friend something he or she doesn't want to hear, maybe supporting causes they oppose. When those things happen in places where you're a pastor first and a friend second, they go down easier."

Carol drummed her fingers on the table, thinking. "I suppose that's true, but how many of our friends are still there? How many are Presbyterians? Besides, everywhere you go, you're going to make friends in your congregation. To the extent giving hard counsel to a friend is a problem, it's one you're in danger of having no matter what. Goes with the territory, doesn't it?"

Carol was right as far as Jiggs' voiced reservations went. But the ones unvoiced, even to himself, weighed on his subconscious. Ministering to guys with whom he'd stolen watermelons, blown up mailboxes, tipped over outhouses, put cows on barn roofs, girls whom he'd dated, felt up or at least tried – somehow it didn't seem right. He hung back. He didn't call Hegman. A month went by and then another month and Jim didn't call.

48

October 1974

The knock on his office door was so soft Jiggs was unsure there was anyone there.

"Come in."

Susan Karocek peeked around the edge of the door. "Reverend Morgan, can I talk to you?"

Jiggs stood up. "Sure, Susan, c'mon in."

Susan came out from behind the door and closed it behind her. She paused and looked around as if she had never been there before, took a step and paused again.

Something's wrong.

"Susan, are you okay?"

Susan looked at Jiggs directly for the first time. Her eyes were full of tears. "Reverend Morgan, I'm pregnant."

Whoa. Jiggs walked out from behind his desk and put his arm around Susan's shoulder and guided her to a chair. He pulled his chair out from behind his desk, sat down opposite the girl and handed her a box of tissues.

Where do I start? "Are you sure, Susan? Sometimes these things..."

"No, no. I'm sure. I went to the clinic..."

"Do your folks know?"

"Oh, no ... just you ... and Jimmy..."

Jimmy, of course. "Jimmy. What does Jimmy have to say?"

More tears. "He ... he said I should get an abortion. Then he said he needed to get to class and walked away. I tried to call him last night, but his mother answered and said he wasn't home. He didn't call back. I don't ... don't think he wants to talk to me."

Jiggs moved the wastebasket over for the spent tissues.

"Susan, you have to tell your parents. You can't face this alone. You need the people who love you around you the whole way. I'll go with you, if that would make it easier."

Susan dabbed at her eyes, then raised her head and met Jiggs' gaze. "Reverend Morgan, do you know my dad?"

Jiggs was surprised to realize that he didn't know either of Susan's parents. He knew they ran a funeral home somewhere in the City, but he had never met or even been introduced to either of them. *How could I have let that happen?*

"No, I'm afraid I don't."

"He'll go crazy. He'll disown me. I'm not kidding. Ever since my sister and I were little girls, he's always said if either of us gets in trouble, brings shame on the family, we're on our own. He'd throw us out."

So much for the deterrence of threats.

Jiggs had a sinking feeling. *By The Book Basil.* "Is your dad named 'Basil?'"

"Yes, Basil Karocek."

"I guess I have met him once, but I don't know him. Don't put too much stock in what he's said in the past. Lots of dads say things like that in hope of scaring their kids into behaving themselves. Once they're confronted with the situation..."

Susan hung her head, shaking it from side to side. "No, no. He will do just as he promised. One night last year my sister came in late from a date. Not very late, like fifteen minutes. She and I share a bedroom, and just as she was getting into bed, he came storming into the room shouting for her to get out, calling her unclean and unfit to sleep in the same room with me. He made her take her mattress down in the basement and sleep and eat there for a month. He didn't say a word to her after that night for the whole month, and he forbid my mom and little brother and me from speaking to her too, whenever he was around. When he came home, he would ask each of us if we had spoken to Tanya against his wishes while he was at work. We had to lie to him and say we hadn't. It was awful."

"What about your mom?"

"She'll cry and beg him not to do whatever he decides to do, but in the end, she'll go along. She can't stand up to him. No one can. Reverend Morgan, what am I going to do? I'm so scared."

"First thing, we're going to tell your folks, you and me, together. Your Dad will probably get mad and make a lot of noise, but as a parent, he has responsibility he has to live up to. There's no reason to postpone this, Susan. He's obviously going to find out eventually..."

"I know, Reverend. Everybody's going to find out."

Jiggs reached over and took Susan's hand. "That's right. And you're going to hold your head up and square your shoulders and walk right past all the petty, small-minded, unforgiving people you're bound to encounter. You're going to remember that this, too, will pass. You are still Susan Karocek, with all the skills, intelligence and charm you've always had, tools that will enable you to deal with things as they arise."

Susan stared back at Jiggs with the same look he had given Coach Bucyk, when the Coach told him he was as good a wrestler as Jim Billings had ever been.

"Second, there's what you're not going to do. You're not going to take Jimmy's suggestion. You're not going to get an abortion. You simply must not do that."

Jiggs listened to himself say the words, discarding the option at the outset, refusing to allow himself to think about it.

Susan sat there, head bowed, staring at her feet, saying nothing.

"Susan, abortion may seem like the easiest answer, but it isn't. The child you're carrying is alive at this very moment, just as much as you and me. Having an abortion is a decision by you to end that life, essentially because it's become inconvenient. Is 'inconvenience,' however great, any reason to kill another person?

"You and Jimmy have done a grown-up thing. You're going to have to grow up fast to deal with the result."

Susan blew her nose. "But what can I do? All I know about being a mother is that I don't' know how to be one, especially if both Jimmy and my family turn their backs on me."

Jiggs let go of Susan's hand and put his fingertips under her chin, raising it as if she was a butterfly that had landed there. "Lots of women have learned to be mothers on the fly. But there are other options. You can give the baby up for adoption. At least you're giving your child a chance to live.

"If you have an abortion, won't you always wonder what that baby would have become? It will be like being haunted."

More tears. "Adoption will haunt me too."

"C'mon, Susan. You don't have to decide right now. You have time to think about what you need to do. Give me both your hands and let's say a prayer. Then we'll go talk to your parents."

Susan laid her palms on Jiggs' outstretched upturned hands. His prayers had been prayed with less conviction and fervor since Justine, but no prayer he ever prayed was more heartfelt than this.

"Father, here is Susan, much in need of your love and guidance. Please help her to see that the circumstances in which she finds herself are by no means as insurmountable as they may seem at this moment. Please help her to know she will live a long and happy life and, with the passage of time, this difficulty may become a blessing. Help her and her child to grow, to find and follow your will as she negotiates the bumps in the road she encounters along life's way.

"Please help me to have the strength and wisdom to help her on her path, to ease its rough spots, so she reaches her destination a healthy, happy person. We ask this in the name of your son, Jesus Christ. Amen."

"Amen." Susan said in a voice no more than a whisper.

Jimmy Blake wasn't in church the following Sunday, nor did he attend Fellowship Monday evening. Late Tuesday afternoon found Jiggs leaning against his car parked next to Jimmy's in the high school lot, waiting for football practice to end.

Eventually the players began to come out. Ten minutes or so after the first emerged, Jiggs recognized Jimmy as he passed under the light above the locker room exit. If Jimmy saw Jiggs in the twilight as he approached his car, he gave no sign.

"Hello, Jimmy."

"Oh, hello, Reverend." Jimmy opened his car door and began to slide in.

"Jimmy, slow down. I need to talk to you ... about Susan Karocek."

Jimmy stopped, half in and half out of his car. "What about her?"

"Jimmy, get out of your car and talk to me. You know what this is about."

Jimmy backed out of his car as if there was a magnet inside holding him in. He straightened up and faced Jiggs in the gathering dusk. Jiggs, just over six feet, Jimmy a couple of inches taller, standing three feet apart.

"Jimmy, Susan tells me the two of you are going to be parents. I was wondering how you're planning to handle that and offer to help any way I can."

Jimmy chewed on his lower lip for a couple of seconds, staring at Jiggs. "I think I've already handled the situation, Rev."

Rev?

"Oh, and how have you 'handled' it?"

"I told her to get an abortion. Said I'd pay for it."

"What if she doesn't want an abortion? What if she wants to have the baby? Keep it?"

"Well, then I guess I'll have to pay for that instead ... if it's mine."

Keep cool, Morgan. Jiggs unclenched his teeth, which had just gone tight.

"Jim, before Susan told you she was pregnant, had she ever given you any indication whatsoever that she had the slightest interest in any guy other than you?"

"You mean someone like you, Rev?"

"Someone like anybody. Be honest with yourself for once."

Jimmy didn't answer.

"That's what I thought. Let me ask you another question. "Did you ever tell Susan you 'loved' her?"

More silence.

"You did, Jimmy. You told her you loved her. What did that mean? 'Susan, I want to get in your pants?'"

"I'll tell you what it didn't mean, Rev. It didn't mean I'm going to wreck my life because she's too stupid to take a pill."

"Susan says you said you were using a condom, but regardless of who was in charge of preventative measures, you have responsibility for this beyond financial. If you think this has potential to 'wreck' your life, how do you think Susan feels right now? One minute you're saying you love her, urging her to give herself to you, and the next minute you won't talk to her. She's facing some tough choices. She could use some comfort and support from the guy who said he 'loves' her."

Jimmy turned and reopened his car door. "I don't know why any of this is your business, Rev. The truth is, I don't give a flying fuck. I told her I'd pay for the abortion."

"You mean your father will pay for it."

"Whatever. If she's too dumb to do that, she's on her own. It may cost some money, but I'm outa that picture."

Good riddance, Shithead.

"Why aren't you eating?" Carol reached across the table and put her hand on Jiggs' forearm. Jiggs stopped his musing and looked up.

"Just preoccupied, I guess."

"Preoccupied with what?"

Ah, the preacher's dilemma. Apart from his friendship with Camilla, Jiggs didn't think he had any secrets from Carol – didn't want any. But there was always the question of how much he could tell her about what he learned by way of confidential conversations without violating that confidentiality. Carol thought of herself as discrete, someone who would never reveal anything he told her. She could see no reason for him to hold anything back, including names.

"What do you think I'm going to do, Jiggs," she once said, when he had answered less than she had asked, "hire a skywriter and publish to the world?"

"That's not the point. The people who come to me must know I'm worthy of their trust. If they can't believe that, my effectiveness as a minister vanishes."

Carol's answer to that was that they would never know.

"But I would," Jiggs had replied.

"A girl in the congregation came into see me the other day." Jiggs picked his words. "Sixteen years old. She's pregnant."

"Someone I know?"

"Yes," Jiggs said, ignoring the implied question, "Who?"

"How far along is she?"

"Seven weeks."

"Has she told her parents?"

"That's a big part of the problem. Daddy's a despot. I went with her when she told them, because she was so scared of him. He started yelling she was a 'Jezebel' and a 'whore.' He grabbed her coat and purse, ran over to the door and threw them out in the yard, told her to go get them and keep going."

Carol shuddered. "How awful. I assume you tried to talk to him."

"Yeah. I went out and retrieved the coat and purse and brought them back inside. Told him that, much as he might want to, he couldn't throw away his child, the law wouldn't allow it. That gave him something to think about. So she's still there, but she's not exactly nestled in the warm bosom of her family. I'm not sure what he's going to do. I'm trying to find somewhere else for her to go."

"It's Susan Karocek, isn't it? Don't bother to answer. I know. Believe it or not, I'm giving his wife some golf lessons. I recognize the father from some things she's said about her husband. This is really heart breaking."

Jiggs didn't say anything.

"What about the baby's father? Where is he in all this?"

"He told her to get an abortion, that he'd pay for it, then walked away from her. I talked to him today. An asshole of the first magnitude."

"Maybe the asshole has the right idea."

"You mean an abortion?" Jiggs narrowed his eyes.

"Yes, I mean an abortion. They're legal now, you know."

"I told her she mustn't have an abortion."

Carol looked at Jiggs, eyebrows raised, mouth open. "'Mustn't have an abortion...' Why not? Why 'mustn't' she have an abortion?"

Here goes. "Well, start with, the fact that having an abortion means taking the life of another."

"Another what, Jiggs? Another something not even half-formed, something that can neither see, nor smell, nor even think, because as yet its brain isn't far enough developed to do any of these things?

"I'll tell you whose life is being taken – that girl's, that's whose. If she decides to carry that baby, she's facing nine months of anguish, mostly alone, it sounds like. You think that won't be communicated to her child? What a great springboard to life! She's going to be forced to interrupt her education, maybe end it, before she even graduates from high school. She'll be left with a distraction and responsibility she's not ready for and from which she may never recover. I can go on and on."

You already are.

"Carol, those distractions and responsibilities are going to be there in one form or another, whatever she chooses to do."

"Maybe so, Jiggs. But they vary greatly in degree depending on how she chooses to balance the equation. What makes me so angry is you telling her from the get go she 'mustn't' have an abortion, you telling her she has to exclude that alternative from her list of choices. Why would you ever do that?"

"Remember who I am ... what I am. She came to see me as a pastor, a representative of the Church. The Church opposes abortion under most circumstances, certainly these."

"Oh, nonsense ... no ... Bullshit, Jiggs. She came to you because you're someone she thinks of as kind and knowing, someone who will be sympathetic to her and whom she can trust. And you, what did you tell her? That she'd go to hell if she gets an abortion? That God, or at least your version of God, says it's a 'sin?'"

"My 'version' of God?"

"Yes, your 'version' of God. The form of superstition you've decided to adopt. The superstition you're now letting get in the way of your really helping someone who trusted you enough to seek your help with as intimate and profound a problem as she's ever likely to have.

"'Mustn't get an abortion.' Bah." Carol put down the fork she'd been waving around for emphasis, stood up and walked across the dining room, through the living room and out the front door. Jiggs did not follow.

"Everybody knows."

Susan Karocek sat again in Jiggs' office.

No tears. Maybe none left.

"When I was at my locker this morning, I heard two girls talking one row over. One of them said, 'Susan Karocek's knocked up.' They laughed.

"The girl who sits next to me second period made a point of sliding her chair further away from me. Bobby Klaus, a boy I dated a couple of times before I met Jimmy, came up to me in the hall and asked why I never 'put out' for him like I did for Jimmy."

Jiggs winced. *The cruelty of children.* He didn't want to say anything until he was sure she was finished talking. *Let her get it out.*

"Everywhere I go in school, I think kids are laughing at me." She stopped talking.

"Your friends aren't laughing, Susan."

"'Friends' ... hmmm." Susan made a sound half way between a sigh and a groan. "I don't know who knows and who doesn't. No one has come up to me and offered to talk, and I can't make myself say anything, because I don't know what the reaction will be. Maybe they'll be like my dad or Bobby Klaus."

"How are things at home?"

"I'm being shunned. He made me take my mattress down by the furnace, and says I have to stay there whenever I'm in the house. He won't let anyone talk to me. I can't eat with the family. My mom leaves a plate of food on the basement steps. I have to sneak up to go to the bathroom. When I get sick, I throw up in a bucket."

"That settles it, Susan. You can't stay there. I've made inquiries. There are homes for girls facing what you're facing, better places. Places that care. There's one in Springfield that sounds nice."

"What then?" A tiny voice.

"'What then?' What do you mean, Susan?"

"What then? I leave school, spend seven months in this home for unwed mothers, have the baby, can't keep it – no money for that – give it up without ever seeing it probably. There I'll be, alone, on the street, seventeen years old with a tenth grade education, a 'whore' to almost everyone who knows me. A 'whore.' Reverend Morgan, this was the first time I ever did it. Anyway, not exactly a recipe for a happy life, is it?"

"We'll work on the 'happy life' part, Susan. The picture you're painting is made up of all the worst assumptions. I don't want to sound like the preacher I am, but this is only an interruption, not an end. There are things to be learned from this that will help you in the future. It's a big world out there."

Susan raised her head and stared back at Jiggs with disbelieving eyes above dark circles. She stood up as if it was an effort, as if she was already eight months pregnant.

Jiggs gave her a gentle hug and a smile. "I will find out more about this home in Springfield for you. Things are going to turn out all right. We will make it happen, you and me. Let's say a little prayer before you leave."

"Reverend, can we pray for a miscarriage?"

49

November 1974

Two days after his discussion with Carol about his advice to Susan Karocek, Jiggs arrived at work still dragging anchor. He and Carol seldom actually fought. Their disagreements, sometimes deep and wide, usually resulted in both saying to themselves, "Suit yourself," tamping down their discontent and going on with their life together. Not this time. Carol had walked back into their apartment that night just as angry as when she walked out. The only sound before bedtime was that of doors slamming. If Carol was awake at all during the night, she gave no sign. If she had, Jiggs would have known, because he was wide awake. Things had not improved during the ensuing thirty-six hours.

On his way to the Youth Department Jiggs stopped at his mailbox next to the Church office. There among the advertisements for church conferences, religious supplies and pitches for various charities was a letter from Camilla, the first he had received in almost two years. Jiggs' capstan began to turn. By the time he reached his desk, he had weighed anchor. Before he even sat down, he grabbed his letter opener and was beginning to slit the envelope, when his phone rang.

"Is this Reverend Morgan?" A woman's voice that sounded far away.

"Yes."

"Reverend Morgan, this is Bella Karocek, Susan Karocek's mother. I am calling to tell you Susan died this morning."

Camilla's letter still impaled on the opener hit the floor, but Jiggs didn't hear it. He didn't hear anything, including an anguished mother's description of how she had found her daughter unconscious on a blood soaked mattress in the shadow of the furnace, a bloody coat hanger nearby and of how all efforts to revive her had failed. All Jiggs could hear were the words, "You and me," his promise to Susan, his promise to Saucers. Same words. Same result.

Jiggs hated to even get in the car after Susan's memorial service. He knew the still angry Carol assigned him a large measure of fault for Susan's death, although perhaps no more than he assigned himself.

The turnout had been amazing. It seemed as if half of New Trier High School was in attendance, lots of teen-age tears. Jimmy Blake did not attend; neither did By-The-Book Basil. The rest of Susan's family was in the front row, from where Bella Karocek's very un-Presbyterianlike wailing lament echoed throughout the sanctuary.

Jiggs and Carol were waiting at a stoplight, neither having uttered a word since leaving the Church, when Carol said, "Well, Jiggs, you've always said you wanted to 'make a difference.' I think you've finally made one."

For the first time since the day he spent with Carol in Arizona on his way back from Mexico, Jiggs felt something other than love for her. Not even his own sorrow at Susan's death could preempt the flash of disdain he felt at that moment. Upon reflection later, he thought his sadness probably heightened it.

Somewhere he had read, "silence is the most eloquent expression of scorn." The light changed, but Jiggs stayed put, . turning his head and looking at Carol without saying a word. He continued to stare until the car behind him started honking.

"What was that look supposed to mean?"

Jiggs said nothing.

"You think I'm wrong, Jiggs? You think your telling that poor girl not even to consider an abortion played no role in what she did? Let me ask you a question. Fifteen years from now, if Justine had come to you with the same sad news, would you have given her the same advice?"

Low blow.

"Because if you can't answer that question with an unequivocal "yes," then your hypocrisy and superstition have just proved fatal."

Arriving at the apartment, Jiggs pulled to the curb instead of into their carport. "I'm dropping you off. I need to go for a walk, and I think it needs to be by myself. Your recriminations aren't doing either one of us any good. You have a key?"

Jiggs' walk was the saddest he'd taken since Tony Capini's death almost five years earlier. He was beginning to think Carol might be right about his unwise career choice, maybe even her view of the belief system at its foundation. Saddened as he was over Susan's death, it was these dawning uncertainties that grieved him most, these, and the fact he had begun not to care what Carol thought. *Come on, Morgan. Don't shoot the messenger.*

It was almost dark when the cold wind off the Lake drove him back to his car. Unwilling to go home and listen to more railing, he went to his office instead. As he sat down, he stepped on something lying underneath his desk where nothing ordinarily was. He glanced down, and there was Camilla's letter, paper knife still protruding from the envelope.

Cam. Just when I need you most.

He picked it up. It was heavier than correspondence he'd received from her in the past. This envelope contained at least a couple of pages. He leaned back, propped his feet on his desk and proceeded to read.

> Dear Jiggs,
>
> I blush to admit I cannot remember the last time I wrote a line to you, but I know it was right after you finished seminary. You have been a better correspondent than I. Your note mentioning the loss of your daughter caught up with me about six months after you wrote it. It made me so blue, I couldn't even pick up a pen. By the time I re-inflated, it seemed like so much time had passed, my sympathies might just pry the lid off healing hurts. But I have felt guilty about not having written ever since. I am so sorry that happened to you and Carol, Jiggs. My heart continues to ache for you.
>
> That was January of '73. I still have your note. I was in Bolivia, working in the Peace Corps at the time, but came home shortly thereafter and married a guy I'd been dating since my last year at Columbia. Our plan was to move to California, where I intended to enroll in a doctoral program in English at UCLA. Mark (the spouse) had a job as a pilot for Hughes Aircraft.
>
> Alas, the best laid plans, etc. We got married in New York, and our honeymoon was to be our trip to

California. We were going the long way, which included a visit with Mark's family in South Carolina. At the end of our week there, when I was literally opening my suitcase to pack and begin heading west, Mark announced that HE had decided we should live there, in South Carolina. His family has a peanut and tobacco farm, a pretty big operation, and they wanted him to stay and work in the family business.

You might think the unilateral nature of that decision was not a very promising way to start a marriage, and you'd be right. After voicing my objections and being met with an utter unwillingness on Mark's part to reconsider, I gave it a try for a few unhappy months, but it didn't work out. I told him we needed to pursue our original intent or some other plan in which we both had input, and he refused.

So I left. Rather than go to California by myself, I have come to Washington and enrolled in the doctoral program at Georgetown. The language skills are keeping me afloat financially, and, thanks to the Peace Corps, I have added Spanish to the mix. Mark and I are divorced now, and with luck (and lots of long hours), I will be Dr. Waron in about eighteen months. Wish me luck.

Enough about me. What about Rev. Morgan? How is your ministry progressing? Are you finding the satisfaction and sense of purpose you were seeking? What is Carol doing? How are your dad and sisters? Tell me all, Jiggs. No more post cards, no more brief notes, at least not until we are once again abreast of each other's lives.

While I was in Bolivia, I thought of you and your determination to make a contribution. See, you inspired me. That sounds like a joke, but it isn't. I continue to think of you often and hope you are well and happy. Write to me, Jiggs.

Your friend, Camilla

P.S. Written any poetry lately?

Two weeks later, Jim Hegman called. Hegman's invitation to apply for the position in Lake City forced the orbits of Planet Carol and the Planet Jiggs, so completely concentric for almost a month and nearly so for much longer, to intersect.

"Carol, I know you're still pissed about my advice to Susan, but I need to ask you something, and I ... no, we, need more of an answer than you just getting up and walking into the other room."

Carol put down the newspaper she was reading and looked at Jiggs without saying anything.

"Even assuming I was wrong in giving Susan that advice, it seems to me your anger goes way beyond the bounds of that mistake. We obviously disagree on a lot of things, big things, but I always thought you respected my right to believe as I do, just as I respect yours."

Carol folded her newspaper and tossed it on the coffee table, a sign that Jiggs had her full attention.

"Despite our differences," Jiggs continued, "I thought we always loved being with each other more than with anyone else. Now I'm not so sure we still feel that way. It seemed like after Susan died, you were really trying to hurt me.

"You must have thought about these things too. What do you think is happening to us?"

Carol looked down at her hand, where she was twirling her wedding ring around her finger with her thumb, as she tried to compose her thoughts into words.

"Jiggs, it's true I've been disappointed ever since the day you came home from overseas and told me you wanted to be a minister. There are still times when you will say or do something so reminiscent of the old Jiggs, the one I fell in love with, still love whenever he shows up, that I can almost forget the reality of what you've become."

But not quite.

"Don't get me wrong, Jiggs. You are not sanctimonious. As pastors go, you are probably among the most humorous and irreverent, and I appreciate that. I do. But, at bottom, you are still a clergyman. You are motivated in so much of what you say and do by ideas and beliefs that I think are profoundly wrong." Carol met Jiggs' gaze and shook her head, sadness written all over her face. "These beliefs thrust you into the midst of other people's problems for which I usually have not an ounce of empathy. And in those rare instances when I do empathize, situations like Susan's, I see those beliefs leading you in catastrophic directions."

Nothing new in any of this. It was still hard to hear. "Okay. What's left? Where do you see us going from here?"

Carol shook her head. "You're the counselor, Jiggs, not me. I want to try, but at this point I don't know how."

"Well, Roger once told me a lawyer who represents himself has a fool for a client. That probably goes for counselors too. What would you say if we try going to some third party, a marriage counselor?"

"Not another minister?"

Jiggs laughed. "No, not another preacher. A neutral."

IV

LAKE CITY

50

December 1974 – March 1975

It was cold the week Jiggs and Carol came back for Jiggs' interviews with Session at Lake City Presbyterian. They were staying in town with Carol's parents, in order to be closer to the week's activities. The afternoon before everything was to begin, Jiggs went out to see Doc.

The house was dark when Jiggs drove up the lane, and no one answered the bell. Jiggs still had a key, but thought he'd check the farm buildings first. There he found Doc getting ready to go for a ride. There were five horses in different stalls outside the tack room, nickering, twitching and shifting their weight as they scoured their feed boxes for the last oat in their measures.

As Jiggs approached, Doc looked up from saddling a big black horse named "Bill," whom Jiggs had met on an earlier visit.

"Hello. Jiggs. I heard you were coming. What brings you here from the big city?"

"I have a surprise for you, Pop."

Doc paused, holding Bill's bridle. "What's that?"

"I'm here for a job interview at Lake City Presbyterian. They're looking for a new pastor. Jim Hegman's Chairman of the

Search Committee. There's a good chance Carol and I will be moving back here."

"Did I just hear what I think I heard?" Lindy came out of the tack room. "Jiggs, that's wonderful."

"Jim Hegman, eh?" said Doc.

Jiggs knew Hegman and his bank were spearheading efforts to get the dam and park built.

"We're about to go for a ride, Jiggs." Lindy gave her horse a gentle push to turn it around and head it out of the stall. "Come on, Marilyn, move your ass."

"Want to come along, Jiggs?" Doc asked. "I reckon you still remember how to ride. I'll get a saddle down for you."

"Sure." Jiggs looked around. "Where's Freckles?"

Freckles had been Jiggs' horse ever since Jiggs used money he earned pulling weeds from soybean fields to buy him for eighty dollars. Jiggs had been eleven, Freckles six. Jiggs could not remember ever riding any other horse after that.

"Got a surprise of my own, but it's not a good one." Doc paused at the tack room door and turned to face Jiggs. "I had to put Freckles down. Legs were shot. He lay down one day about a month ago and couldn't get himself up. I finally got him on his feet, but he lay right back down."

Doc was looking at his boots as he talked. He took off his old Stetson, ran his fingers through his hair and looked up at Jiggs. "Couldn't find anything wrong with him – just old. I let that go on for the better part of a week, hoping he'd snap out of it and feel like standing again, but he was going downhill, stopped eating.

"It was rough. He'd been here a long time. I should have called you, but I didn't have the words. Still don't."

Jiggs didn't have any words either, no good ones. After a few seconds, "He had a good life," found their way around the lump in his throat.

"Yeah," said Doc. "At least he got to stay to the end on the place he lived most of his life." He disappeared through the door.

The park. Jiggs turned in Lindy's direction. She returned his look and shook her head. The winter wind seemed more raw than ever.

They rode across the east meadow and over the hill behind the house. As they rode, Lindy talked about the recent election. Beezer, Jiggs' best friend in high school and Darcy's husband, had just been elected County Sheriff after the incumbent Sheriff retired. Beezer had become another apple of Lindy's eye. She had worked on his election campaign, stuffing envelopes, putting up signs, using her new found driving skills to ferry elderly and disabled voters to the polls. "When Beezer won, damned if it didn't feel like I'd got elected too. Finally going to get some decent law enforcement in this goddamn County."

As they came over the crest of the hill and rode out on to a knoll overlooking a large pasture just this side of the river, Doc reined in. "Hold up a second. Jiggs look over there." He pointed towards a field on the far side of the line of trees bordering the river, land belonging to Arnie Johanssen, Doc's neighbor.

There were two men walking away from them in the distance. One of them was carrying something over his shoulder. As Jiggs watched, they disappeared into a distant copse of trees. *Hunters?* It wasn't the right time of year for hunters. Jiggs turned towards Doc, his eyes asking the question.

"Surveyors. Arnie's already agreed to sell out. We lost the appeal, Jiggs. The Court's allowing preliminary surveys for the dam to go forward."

Expectation fulfilled. The news made Jiggs wince. "What's left, Pop?"

"Roger says we can appeal to the State Supreme Court, but unless we post a bond that costs about a year's income, the State can go ahead and start condemnation proceedings against those who won't agree to sell."

"I suppose that includes you."

"What do you think?"

"Gonna appeal?"

"Already filed. But I'm not putting up the bond. Appeal will be decided before the condemnation trial wraps up."

They rode down the hill, across the pasture and into the trees along the river, following a cattle trail along its bank. They were in the shadow of the bluff on which Jiggs' mom was buried.

Without warning, Doc stopped and dismounted. He handed the Black's reins to Lindy and walked ahead a few yards to where Jiggs saw a piece of wood driven into the ground with a red flag nailed to it, a surveyor's stake. Doc jerked it out of the ground, returned and stuck it in his saddle bag.

He glanced up at Jiggs as he remounted. "Sons a bitches don't own this place yet."

51

March – May 1975

Who counsels the counselor? Who consoles the consoler? The answers, Jiggs found, were elusive. It was easier to determine who couldn't than who could. Certainly not Dr. Adrian Rothstein, the marriage counselor he and Carol first turned to in the wake of Susan's death. His approach seemed to be to let the two of them sit and vent for fifty minutes a week without any input from him, on the apparent assumption that, if they talked about it long enough, they would eventually figure things out for themselves. Jiggs thought he and Carol had already been talking about their problems for six years without progress. *Why not continue to fail for free rather than pay for the privilege?*

Next in the line-up of love doctors was Colleen Kerrigan, Ph.D. Dr. Kerrigan had lots of suggestions, each of which seemed founded, at least insofar as Jiggs could see, on the belief that all men are idiots, religion is the province of the Middle Ages, and Carol's acceptance of Jiggs' wish to become a clergyman, however reluctant, was a compromise far outweighing Jiggs' surrender of his hopes to become a missionary and a father. Even Carol recognized the imbalance, and it had been she who suggested they leave Dr. Kerrigan in the dust.

Although he thought it unlikely, Jiggs recognized it was at least possible that one, if not both, marriage counselors might have proved more helpful, but for the fact that the person he really wanted to talk to about his troubles was Camilla Waron. Jiggs suspected her undisclosed existence could not help but be a barrier to anyone seeking to understand and assist them.

There were times when he longed to just sit in Camilla's room at the Quonset on Kadena late into the night reading poetry back and forth, pausing now and then to discuss the world, or to scramble to the top of the sea wall at sunset and sit in shared silence as the Earth continued to turn. So it was to Camilla he revealed himself, but never all the way. He would write her long letters. Then, both because he believed he owed it to Carol not to share their problems with someone who might be part of them, and because he didn't want to be a complainer or a "my wife doesn't understand me" guy to Camilla, he would not send them. The writing was itself therapy, a journal sporadically kept. To Camilla, Jiggs wrote of his life only insofar as it did not creep into realms of discontent. He wrote of his take on world events and of his interest in the life she was living.

Ultimately, Jiggs and Carol decided a move to Lake City might be something more helpful than anything the science of psychology could provide - a fresh start. Both remembered what they once had been and wished for its resurrection. They moved to Lake City, relying mostly on hope.

Over the years, the inevitable jitters that preceded Jiggs' public speaking efforts had diminished and finally all but disappeared. He had come to think of standing up in front of a group as just another time at bat. But not today. Pastor Morgan's first time in the pulpit as Pastor of Lake City Presbyterian Church was accompanied by jitters akin to those he experienced during the run up to his last match with Jim Billings.

As he stood in the narthex waiting behind the choir for the processional, Jiggs studied notes he held in hands not entirely free from sweat. He closed his eyes, visualizing. The organ boomed out the opening notes of *Faith of Our Fathers*, the choir line began to move. He reopened his eyes and stepped into a blur, shaking hands with people he knew on both sides of the aisle. The invocation, call to worship, hymn of praise, recitation of the Apostle's Creed, the congregation's exchange of greetings, the offering, scripture reading, anthem, sermon, closing hymn and benediction - a torrent of adrenalin-drenched sights and sounds washing in and out of his brain as the service progressed - all but one that would never go away.

When Jiggs stood and faced the congregation to give the Invocation, there were his sisters, Lindy, even Roger, who had driven up from Des Moines. Jim Hegman and his family were in the first row, Carol and her parents, all people he expected to see. No Doc, of course. But farther back, sitting like a mountain among foothills, sat Ron Bjournquist.

Jiggs knew Bjournquist was a lifelong member of Walnut Grove Lutheran Church. Generations of Bjournquists had been baptized, married and buried at Walnut Grove Lutheran. It would have been no exaggeration to say that Bjournquist men had built that church, and for more than one hundred years generations of Bjournquist women had sustained it. There he sat, Charlene immediately to Ron's right, four bristle-haired little clones sitting like stair-steps to his left. So moved was Jiggs by Ron's presence that throughout his sermon, he had to remind himself to turn his head, to speak to the entire congregation, instead of preaching to this one surprise worshiper, like some kind of torch singer trying to seduce a single member of her audience.

Afterwards, standing beside Carol in the receiving line, he waited for his giant friend as others in the congregation filed past. At last Ron loomed in the church entrance and came down the steps, family in tow.

"Nice sermon, Junior." Jiggs' hand was engulfed in the mighty paw, so calloused that Jiggs had seen it pick French fries out of a deep fat fryer filled with bubbling grease without so much as a wince.

"Ron, what a great surprise to see you here. How are the Lutherans going to get along without you for a Sunday?"

52

October 1975

Sitting on the wooden bench, hard as any pew, Jiggs pondered whether Roger felt about courtrooms the way Jiggs once felt about churches. Were they more than just a workplace? Were they a place where something sacred, something the world needed doing, could be done? Awaiting the judges' appearance, the air heavy with the feel of what was at stake, Jiggs hoped his friend was finding more to like in the law than he was finding in religion. Then, putting his professional misgivings aside, and with Carol, Doc and Lindy on his left, Marie, Darcy and Beezer on his right, Jiggs silently prayed that the thing the Morgan family most needed doing would be done in this place today.

"All rise."

A door behind the high bench at the front of the room opened. Seven judges in black robes trooped in and took their seats.

"The Supreme Court for the State of Iowa is now in session, Chief Justice Donald Gormanson presiding. Be seated."

Chief Justice Gormanson looked like Rip Van Winkle to Jiggs, and to either side of him sat Methuselah and Hammurabi. The remaining four justices sitting outboard of those three

---

looked equally like refugees from the Old Testament. Jiggs glanced out of the corner of his eye at Doc. What was his father thinking? Doc sat, expressionless as the judges themselves. It occurred to Jiggs how foreign this place must seem to the man whose entire life had been spent outdoors in all weathers doing rough work, usually alone. It would almost be better to have the issue decided in a face off on a dusty street in some forlorn western town. High noon. Even if he lost, the result would be easier for Doc to understand. He would have less sense of having been robbed.

This was the third time Jiggs had accompanied Doc to court. He had read the briefs Roger sent him, listened to the arguments, all wrung dry of any emotion by the dispassionate language of the law. Their path to the Supreme Court was littered with losses, much as Roger had predicted. Jiggs had no faith this time would be any different.

The Chief Justice looked down at a clerk seated at a lower desk just in front of the judge's bench. "Call the first case."

That was another thing. Theirs was the third case of six on the Court's docket that day, a single hour assigned for the hearing. The threat gnawing at the hearts of the seven people seated there just behind the bar was being thrown into a bushel with five other matters, as if fungible, like a bucket of corn. The disproportion between the importance of this outcome on Doc's life and through him on all of theirs and the amount of time and individual consideration the Court allotted to it further darkened Jiggs' mood as he sat unlistening through the arguments in the two preceding cases.

"Morgan v. The State of Iowa," the clerk droned.

As Roger stood and walked to the podium, Jiggs glanced at his watch. Eleven–thirty. Something told Jiggs it was not to their advantage to be the last case before lunch. Probably the half of the judges not still thinking about the previous case, which had involved pornography and sex traffic, were already thinking about the approach of their BLT's.

"Counsel," the Chief Justice began as soon as Hood finished formally stating his appearance, "do you agree Iowa law entitles the State to condemn and acquire the property of a citizen when it serves a public purpose?"

"Yes, Your Honor, as far as that goes."

"Do you further agree that the construction of a reservoir and state park are public purposes?"

Jiggs figured Roger could see the corner into which the Judge was trying to paint him.

"No, Your Honor, not in this case. In this case, the so-called public purposes, are a mirage, an illusion, a barrel of political pork. The question that needs to be asked is, when the public does not need the facility for which condemnation is sought, is it still a public purpose? The third largest state park in Iowa is less than ten miles from the property here in question. Within twenty-five miles there is a lake larger than the one contemplated by this project. Population in the area to be served is actually declining. Under these circumstances, seizure of a citizen's property is an abuse of governmental discretion."

"But Counsel," this from Methuselah sitting on the Chief's right, "aren't two parks better than one, two lakes better than one?"

"With all due respect, Sir, that is an oversimplification. One ice cream cone may taste wonderful, but a second make you sick. – the proverbial 'too much of a good thing.' Justice in Iowa has always involved a weighing of competing interests. When a second park, a second lake, neither of which are needed, compel the taking of a citizen's home, then every other citizen is entitled to ask, might this also happen to me? That is a question, the mere asking of which corrodes the public confidence. In this case, two are not better than one."

"But, Counsel, assuming for the sake of argument that there is no need for more recreational facilities in the vicinity, doesn't the un-contradicted evidence show the reservoir will supplement flood control in the Des Moines River Valley, to say nothing of providing water reserves during periods of drought?"

This, Jiggs knew, was their Achilles heel. As Roger had once explained, the hydrologists were all against them.

"What 'flood,' Your Honor?" Roger shot back. "What 'drought?' The so-called 'evidence' is nothing more than hypotheticals, models concocted by hired experts unsupported by history. There hasn't been a significant flood in the area that would be served by the proposed reservoir in fifty years, interestingly, ever since that lake I mentioned earlier twenty-five miles to the north was built. As for drought, we're not talking about the middle of the Sahara here. The longest period without measurable rain in Central Iowa in the last fifty years has been nine weeks. Throughout that period, yields have consistently risen. Once again, just as a park would give people unneeded additional places to play, this reservoir would create an equally unneeded resource."

So it went, back and forth. Roger's time expired and the lawyer for the State was tossed some fat pitches, questions she could knock out of the park. Finally, the red light signaling the end of all argument flashed.

"Very well, this case will be taken under submission. Court will stand..."

"Just a minute!"

Two of the judges were half out of their chairs when Doc's voice brought them to a halt.

"When you decide this case..."

"You, Sir, are out of order..."

The Bailiff, startled out of some daydream, rose from behind his desk and hastened toward where Doc was standing.

Doc raised his hand as if he held a thunderbolt. "Never mind that." The grimness of his tone returned Jiggs' mind to the dirt street showdown he had earlier imagined. "When you gentlemen decide this case, try to think of the property being seized as your own homes, homes you built with your own two hands on land where your wives are buried. Toss that into your scales of justice." Doc turned and walked out of the courtroom.

53

November - December 1979

Dear Cam,

When was the last time you stopped at a soda fountain? Not many of those antiques left, but here in Lake City one such dinosaur survives. Horton's may be the only sporting goods store in the world with a full service soda fountain. It was the place I hung out when I was growing up. If I wanted to find out how poorly I wrestled on Friday night, all I had to do was stop by Horton's on Saturday. Some local would surely be there to enlighten me. It's the place where I bought my first baseball glove, Carol, her first set of golf clubs. The place is still thriving, just as it has for the last fifty years. I still get coffee there on my way to work most mornings. Small town America. Just thought you'd be interested.

You asked me once whether I have found the satisfaction and sense of purpose I sought. I still have your letter. At the time I received it, I was at a very low place. A wonderful young person in my Youth

Department had just died tragically despite my misguided efforts to help her. Carol and I were having some big differences. If I had answered your question at that moment, you might have thought I was about to step off a bridge.

Not long after that, Carol and I came back to Lake City. I won't tell you that life suddenly became bathed in golden light, as if some switch had been thrown, but I have gained some perspectives. One of which is that the ministry often gives me the opportunity of doing some good, of helping people in need of material assistance, some direction in their lives, or maybe just a hug. However, in my experience, religion itself rarely brings genuine comfort or relief to persons in the midst of real desperation, including, in a couple of instances, my own. Sometimes it gets in the way.

So, to your long ago question, I guess my answer is "yes" and "no." Yes, I have found a sense of purpose, that of trying to use my abilities to help others, but no, the avenue I have chosen has not been particularly satisfying. What was it you once told me, it's the trying that's important? Well, I'm still in there pitching.

Meanwhile, life goes on. I hope the first paragraph of this letter gives you some of the flavor of Lake City. Most Lake Citians are prosperous and content. We have been here more than four years now, and I have many friends. Carol is happy in the summers, when she works in the golf shop she owns in partnership with the Country Club. She spends a couple of months each winter in Arizona now, where she can keep an edge on her game, make some money coaching and stay in touch with the golf merchandise market much more readily than she can in Lake City, Iowa.

I'm afraid my dad is among the not so content. I have mentioned in earlier letters that he is threatened with loss of his farm to the State for creation of a new park. The hearing on his final appeal to the Iowa Supreme Court took place, and, as expected, he lost. Condemnation proceedings have been dragging on for a couple of years - competing appraisals, depositions, endless negotiations. Ugh.

When it became apparent Pop will eventually lose, I suggested he offer to sell all but the couple of acres the house is built on. To my surprise, he went along with that, albeit grudgingly. Unfortunately, his offer was rejected, even though the house isn't located near the area that will be flooded for the new lake. Apparently the State wants his house as a home for the Park Ranger. As you might imagine, the idea that they're going to take his home just to let someone else, who could live almost anywhere in the vicinity, live in it, is impossible for him to swallow, and he's more determined than ever to resist the project any way he can.

Having just re-read what I have written, I realize it sounds awfully somber. Upon reflection, that is probably as it should be. I have this sense that my life is yet to be lived, and that there is some defining event somewhere over the horizon that will propel me in whatever direction I need to go from here. I thought it was Viet Nam, but I'm no longer so sure. So, although perhaps somber, I am hopeful.

I hope, too, that this finds you well and happy. You make Washington, D.C. sound like an exciting place. Please write whenever you get the chance.

Your friend, Jiggs

Another letter written, but unmailed.

"The only constant is change," according to some philosopher Jiggs once read. Less than a month after Jiggs wrote the letter, Lake City, that mostly "prosperous and contented" place, discovered that philosopher was also a prophet.

On December 24, the Russians invaded Afghanistan. The Kremlin had chosen Christmas Eve to make its move, surely just a coincidence. It meant that few Lake City residents knew of the invasion that day. Even fewer thought about it enough to care. Ron Bjournquist both knew and cared.

Jiggs was in his office getting ready for big doings at church later in the day, when his phone rang.

"Junior, this is Ron Bjournquist."

Ron had remained a Lutheran after one dip of his toe in Presbyterian waters. Jiggs had not seen him for several weeks. "Merry Christmas, Ron."

"Merry Christmas, Junior. Hey, I'm in town doing a little last minute Christmas shopping. Want to have a cup of coffee?"

Jiggs eyed the pile of notes he'd was trying to get into some kind of order before he had to preach the first of two Christmas Eve services. To Jiggs' ear, Ron's casual inquiry had a studied quality about it, maybe not so casual as it seemed.

"Sure. Want to meet down at Horton's in half an hour?"

"See ya there." Ron hung up.

The big man was already pouring his coffee back and forth between his cup and saucer to cool it when Jiggs arrived, took off his coat and stepped behind the counter to pour himself a cup. They had the place to themselves. Norm Haverkamp, one of the owners was back in the merchandise area helping a last minute customer.

"There, coffee's all saucered and blowed." Ron took a sip as Jiggs sat down. "You hear what the Russians did today?"

"Outlaw Christmas?"

"Worse. They invaded Afghanistan."

"You think that's worse that outlawing Christmas? I suppose it is for the Afghans."

"It is for me too, and a lot of other guys in this County, Junior."

Ron's not here to crack jokes. Jiggs tried to think why a Russian invasion of Afghanistan was bad for Ron Bjournquist in Walnut Grove, Iowa.

"Radio says Carter's already meeting with his advisors to consider an appropriate response. You know what that response is going to be, don't you, at least part of it?

"Carter's going to cancel the Russian grain deal." Ron answered his own question. "What else can he do short of declaring war, and you know he's not going to do that."

Clearly, Ron had already worked this out in his head. Jiggs didn't interrupt.

"Carter does that, and grain prices go in the tank. A few months after that, so do I, and about half the other farmers in Iowa along with me, I think."

Ron spent the next thirty minutes and two refills explaining to Jiggs the impact a sudden twenty-million-bushel reduction in demand for U.S. corn, wheat and soybeans would have on the farm economy. Jiggs wasn't sure he agreed things were as dire as Ron foresaw, but he was filled with amazement at his friend's grasp of economic complexities. Here was the tobacco-chewing brute who had all but obliterated him in ninth grade, explaining supply and demand, net profit margin, excess capacity, the rule of unintended consequences, blow-back. Jiggs was tempted to take notes.

"Well, Junior, I've griped enough. I reckon I better get home. We got a house full a company, and Charlene says I gotta be Santa Claus. I sure don't feel very jolly. Thanks for listening to me. I heard about this Afghanistan thing on the radio while I was driving into town this morning, and the consequences just kinda washed over me. I needed to talk to somebody, an' I couldn't call Hegman. He's my banker."

They both stood up.

"I'm glad you called, Ron. I hope you're wrong." Jiggs stuck out his hand, and they shook.

"Me too, Junior. Me too."

Seven hours later, the "Family Service," included a live donkey in the Bethlehem tableau, something that would never have happened in Winnetka. The donkey was a tough act to follow, but Reverend Morgan soldiered on. He had changed his message following his conversation with Ron Bjournquist to a homily focusing on the stable owner who gave Mary and Joseph shelter and the importance of charity in a community's time of need.

The donkey didn't come back for the grown-up service at eleven, but Jiggs preached the same lesson. He was followed by the choir, each member holding a lighted candle in the otherwise darkened church, filing out of the choir loft and surrounding the congregation while it sang *Oh Holy Night*. Gathered thus, in the bosom of the music on this "night divine," Jiggs pronounced his Christmas benediction.

Father,
As in the shadow of Christmas
We gather this day,
Help us to remember
As we humbly pray.

In the midst of our plenty,
Help us to recall
Your Son's humble birth
In that Bethlehem stall.

In the songs of our choir
Bring to our ears
The voices of angels
Across two thousand years.

In the warmth of our hearth
Help us be filled
With the wonder of shepherds
In the cold of the hills.

By the words of your disciples
Help us be imbued
With the wisdom of kings
Who became pilgrims for You.

Let the lessons of Christmas
Be rekindled more bright
Than the star that You sent
To guide them by night.

The Herods of the Earth
Give us strength to oppose
And compassion for the victims
Of tyranny's woes.

Help us both to find and to give
The comfort Joseph gave Mary
And to emerge from this hour
Determined to carry

Christmas –
To all who might hear,
Not just this season,
But throughout the year.

Amen

54

January 1980 – October 1982

DATELINE 5 JANUARY 1980: CARTER ANNOUNCES RUSSIAN GRAIN EMBARGO

President Carter announced yesterday he is suspending all future shipments of grain to the Soviet Union in response to Russia's invasion of Afghanistan on Christmas Eve last year. Since the Russian Grain Deal negotiated in 1972 by the Nixon administration, Russia has purchased more than twenty million tons of U.S. corn, wheat and soybeans per year. The current commitment entered last year calls for the purchase of twenty-five million tons of grain by November of this year estimated to be worth 2.6 billion dollars.

Suspension of these sales could ultimately cost American farmers more than 3.5 billion dollars in lost export revenues, according to the Department of Agriculture. ...

The story trailed off into a discussion of available grain storage capacity and possible alternative markets, including a push for a major commitment to production of ethanol. Jiggs put down the paper. Having momentarily forgotten Carol had left for Arizona the day before, his first thought was to discuss what this meant with her. He needed to get used to batching again for a while. He decided to call Ron Bjournquist.

"What's Carter? President of Brazil? Argentina? That's who's going to be selling corn and beans to the Russians instead of us. Carter should move to Rio. That's in Brazil, or one of those places, isn't it?"

Jiggs and Ron were sitting at the fountain at Horton's. Ron had been doing all the talking, Jiggs the listening.

"Maybe the Ruskies will get out of Afghanistan rather than go hungry."

Jiggs didn't think the decision makers in Russia were the ones who would go hungry.

"Oh, well, it won't last forever. Carter won't be president much longer. I figure two years tops. Once we get a sane man in there… "

Have you got two years, Ron?

In December 1979, corn had been $8.00 per bushel. By the end of 1980, it was $6.50. In April, 1981, three months after his inauguration, Ronald Regan, lifted the embargo, but, like Humpty-Dumpty, the market bubble had burst. Despite the efforts of all the king's men, it could not be put together again. By the end of 1985, corn was well below $3.00 per bushel.

It was a busy time for Midwest preachers. Bankruptcies, alcoholism and divorce spiked as one after another farms and the businesses that relied on them closed up shop. Central Avenue in Lake City looked like a ghost town. Every third space was vacant. Those stores remaining open carried little inventory. "We can order it for you," became the retailers' mantra.

For two years Ron Bjournquist cut every corner he could to stay afloat, stretched every dollar, exhausted his credit. "You know what I tell the bill collectors, Junior?" Ron and Jiggs were back at Horton's. "I tell 'em that at the end of each month I put all my bills in a hat, then draw 'em out and pay 'em until the money runs out, and the guys who give me a hard time, I won't put their bills in the hat."

Jiggs couldn't help laughing.

"You know, it's ironic," Ron continued. "For years your dad and I have been fighting that park project, paying lawyers, signing petitions, meeting with legislators..."

Legislators? Jiggs could not imagine Doc meeting with "legislators."

"... trying to prevent our land from being taken, and now I'm praying they'll take it, before First Iowa gets it."

Only a small part of Ron's land was inside the proposed park. The State had been concentrating on bigger fish.

"Why wait for the State, Ron? Why not sell it to someone else?"

"Nobody will buy it. Banks won't loan 'em any money or they're waiting for the price of land to fall even further. It's already worth less than half what I paid for it."

"Jiggs, I have some good news and some bad news." Roger had just arrived at Jiggs' house, having come north for a meeting with Doc the next day about negotiations for Doc's land. He had been there just long enough for Jiggs to hand him a beer.

"Give me the good news, Rog. I've spent my whole day listening to impoverished farmers and distraught wives."

"The State's withdrawn its offer to buy Doc's place."

Three months earlier, in an effort to avoid the expense of going to trial to determine a sale price, the State had offered Doc just over $200,000 for his one hundred eighty acres, including the house, a little north of a thousand dollars an acre, a phenomenal amount in light of the local economy. Doc had not responded.

"That's supposed to be good news?"

"Sure. It's going to delay everything."

"Then what's the bad?"

"It's finally dawned on the sovereign State of Iowa that it's overpaying. The next offer will be much lower. State's withdrawn all pending offers to those who are yet to sell. Doc should have taken it when it was on the table."

"Hell, Rog. He was never going to accept it anyway. If this buys him a little time, it's all good news as far as he's concerned, but I worry about some of the other owners. They're all out of alternatives. "How long is this going to delay the trial?"

"It's scheduled now for June. State asked for a six-month continuance in order to get a new appraisal. The new date will probably be sometime next January or February. But, I have an idea for an offer of our own that might appeal to Doc, under the circumstances."

Right. "What could that be?"

"Well, figure that of the $200,000 the State was offering, about $50,000 was for the house. Doc was willing to sell all but the house three years ago. So why not offer to sell the whole place for $150,000, in other words, the offer that was just pulled, minus the value of the house, but with this condition, Doc and Lindy get to stay in the house for the rest of their lives. Then it goes to the State. What do you think?"

"Who knows? Doc may go for it, but won't the State see that all you're doing is subtracting $50,000 of value that probably no longer exists anyway, while at the same time requiring it to give up the right to immediate possession of the house?"

"Maybe, but it's kind of like sex, can't hurt to ask."

Grinning, Jiggs folded his hands and bowed his head. "Please, young man. Have a little respect for my collar."

By July, 1982, Bjournquist had run out of corners to cut.

"I'm going to lose it all, Junior."

"Your whole place, Ron? It's that bad?"

"Worse. The land isn't worth the amount of my loans, not even with all the buildings and equipment. If I'm forgiven the difference between what it's worth and what I owe, the IRS will treat that amount as income to me. It's called 'phantom income,' which means I never saw any of it, but have to pay taxes on it anyway. I figure it'll come to around $190,000 that I'll owe."

That's worse. "No chance of an extension? This thing has to turn around sooner or later."

I met with Hegman about that. He said the bank doesn't extend loans that are already in default."

"What about restructuring the loan, so you could pay it?"

"Talked to him about that too. Said he couldn't recommend it to the Loan Committee. He's the head of the Loan Committee, so..."

"Couldn't recommend it?"

"That's what he said. Said if he did it for me, he'd have to do it for a hundred other guys who are in the same boat."

"Maybe he should ... do it for the other hundred guys, I mean."

Ron's gaze met Jiggs, and he shrugged. "I suppose Jim's got shareholders to keep happy, directors. Bank's gotta perform, or sooner or later they'll get somebody new to run it – just like a farm."

"What about other banks?"

Ron shook his head. "Tried 'em all."

The two men exchanged another glance, this one of helplessness, both shaking their heads.

"You know what makes me saddest, Junior?"

"What it means for your family, I suppose."

"Yeah, not just Charlene and the kids, but all those who came before." Jiggs heard a catch in Ron's voice. "My grandparents who ate nothing but bread and beans, sometimes for more than a week at a time, during the depression, but managed to hold on to the land. My folks, my mom, who farmed the place with my older brother, who was only twelve, me and my sister crawlin' around at her feet the whole time, while Dad was away in the war. Somehow they all managed to hang on to the land in worse times than these. What must they be thinking? It's like I've dishonored them." Ron pulled a blue bandana out of his hip pocket and blew his nose. Jiggs thought he also wiped his eyes.

"I don't think you should be so hard on yourself, Ron. You were trying to take care of your family the best way you knew how. There's no dishonor in that."

Bjournquist stood up from the table. "Maybe not." He looked down at his feet and then back up at Jiggs. "But I've come to recognize there's a fine line between honest ambition and greed, and I still kick myself for sometimes having stepped over that line ... live and learn." He shook hands with Jiggs and went out the door.

At the end of September, Horton's closed after more than fifty years. Ball gloves and milk shakes were no longer in most people's budgets.

In October, the Cardinals won the World Series. A catcher, Darrell Porter, was the MVP. That was the only ray of sunshine in the Morgan family that month.

Jiggs and Carol had dinner at Doc and Lindy's on the night of Game Seven. As they sat in the living room watching, Doc said, "I need to tell you, Jiggs. I'm going to retire. I've sold my practice or what's left of it, to Phil Klinger over in Harcourt."

"More like he gave the goddamn thing away," Lindy said.

Doc gave Lindy an annoyed look. "Hard to sell something that's losing money."

"How old are you, Pop? Sixty-eight? Seems like it's time, although I always thought you might just die with your boots on." Jiggs laughed.

"So did I." Doc didn't laugh. "But it wears on you working for people who you know can't afford to pay you, especially if they're lifelong friends. They either let their livestock languish until whatever's wrong becomes impossible to treat, because they're embarrassed they can't pay, or they try to barter something I don't need and probably can't sell. It's impossible to say 'no,' when you know some animal's likely to die if you refuse to help. Vicious circle."

On the last day of October Jiggs was in his office wrestling with an objection he'd received from one of his flock regarding Halloween decorations in the church, "celebrating a pagan holiday." The sound of a knock was followed immediately by, "Happy Halloween, Junior."

Ron Bjournquist came in and sat down in a chair that all but disappeared beneath his bulk. "I come to say 'Good-bye.' Hope I'm not interruptin' anything important."

Nothing more important that this. "So today's departure day, eh? Still can't talk you into staying?"

"Nah. Tomorrow's the sale, and I don't want to be anywhere around when that happens. Charlene and the kids are over at her sister's. That's where we stayed last night. I just wanted to stop by and say thanks for all your listening. You been a good friend."

It would have taken more muscles than Hercules possessed to keep Jiggs' face from falling into a near weep. He gritted his teeth with the unsuccessful effort.

"You know, Ron, there's still a lot you could do around here. You're losing your farm, not your friends."

"I know that, Junior. It's just that, well, I was an important citizen hereabout for a few years, on the schoolboard an' all. Now what am I gonna do if I stay around Walnut Grove, be a hired man? Nothing wrong with that, except I'd always think folks were rememberin' where I'd been and be feeling sorry for me. I would hate that. I think it's time for a fresh start somewhere else. Charlene and I talked it over, and she agrees."

"Where have you finally decided to go?" Jiggs felt like he was choking.

"Kansas City. My cousins live down there already, so there'll be family in the area."

"Any idea what you're going to do?"

"Got a line on a job as a high school custodian. Won't be the boss, but it's a start. Charlene's a nurse. She's gonna try to get back in the game now that Riley, our youngest, is in school. She's got a lot of catchin' up to do though."

"You seeing anyone else before you leave?"

"Wasn't going to. But Hegman and his wife came over to my sister-in-law's last night."

"No shi ... really? How'd that go?"

"Good. I come away from it understandin' much better just how little choice he had in the whole deal. Charlene's still real bitter though. She went in the bedroom when they showed up and didn't come out 'til they left. Too bad, 'cause her and Karien Hegman were good friends once upon a time, and no part of this is Karien's fault. Natural though, I guess. Charlene loved that house we built. Can't stand the thought of someone else livin' in it."

Sounds familiar.

Ron stood up. "Anyway, Junior. I gotta get on the road. You keep spreadin' the word around here." He stuck out his hand, and Jiggs shook it with as much warmth as he had ever felt for that simple ceremony.

"So long, Ron. Hang in there. I have to tell you. I don't think I could have handled the kind of reversals you've had with even half your grace and dignity."

Bjournquist held onto Jiggs' hand with his inescapable grip and grinned. "Aw, you preachers say that to all the girls, Junior."

He let go of Jiggs' hand and was gone.

The sale of Bjournquist Farms took place on the steps of the Adolphus County Courthouse on November 1, 1982. Jiggs attended the sale. He wasn't sure why. He knew Ron wasn't going to be there.

The way it worked was that the Sheriff or one of his deputies would read the description of what was being sold and any required terms and conditions. Anyone in attendance could submit a written bid, and the highest bidder would be declared the buyer. No Colonel Clemons goading his listeners, beguiling them into paying a little more than they originally intended.

When Jiggs arrived, his brother-in-law was already out on the steps setting up. "Morning, Beezer. I didn't know the Sheriff himself was going to preside at this affair."

"Just this one." Beezer looked at Jiggs and grimaced. "Rough as he sometimes was, I always looked up to Ron. He put a lot into this County, always helped out whenever he could. If he can't make it, who can? If he doesn't deserve to make it, who does?

"Anyway, I reckon this is as much of a funeral as anything I'll ever go to. Just thought I ought to do it myself out of respect for the man."

"Well said." A familiar voice came from just behind where Jiggs and Beezer were standing. Jim Hegman.

Mr. First Iowa.

"Didn't expect to see you here, Jim." Beezer echoed exactly what Jiggs was thinking.

"Came for the same reason it sounds like you came for, Beezer. You, too, Jiggs, I suppose."

Both men nodded. Beezer looked at his watch. "It's time. Looks like no one else is coming. Let's get this over with."

Beezer read his script. When he finished, Hegman handed him First Iowa's bid. There were no others. Thus did fifteen hundred acres of prime Iowa farmland, three hundred twenty of which had been in the Bjournquist family since being homesteaded by Rueben and Burt Bjornquist in 1866, leave the family for almost three quarters of a million dollars less than the amount Ron owed on it.

Later that day, Jim Hegman's head appeared around the edge of Jiggs' door.

"Junior, can I come in?"

"Sure." Jiggs gestured Jim towards the same chair from which Bjournquist had said his good-bye the day before.

"Ohhh." Hegman groaned as he sat down. "Feels good to sit down."

"Rough day, huh, Jim?"

"Can't remember the last smooth one, Junior."

"Well, I think by going over to see Ron night before last, you made his departure a lot less painful than it otherwise would have been. I know Ron appreciated that."

"Oh, so Ron told you about that. Did he tell you my news then?"

"News? No. What news?"

"I resigned from the Bank this morning after the sale. I told Ron I was going to do it."

Holy shit. A dozen things Hegman's resignation might mean tried to force their way into Jiggs' brain through the barrier of his surprise.

"Is the Bank okay, Jim? Or is that something I'm not supposed to ask?"

"Bank's fine, Junior. Not exactly flourishing, but in no real danger. I just couldn't be part of the disintegration of this community any longer. Holding the purse strings on my friends' lives was killing me. I would rather have cut off my arm than call Ron's loans, but they were past saving. No choice. It was like each desperate conversation I would have with customers was taking a bite of flesh out of me that would never grow back."

Wow. "I can see how you'd feel that way, Jim. But I'm still stunned. That's all. What's next? You staying in town?

"Like to, but who'd hire a broken down banker whose conscience finally got the best of him?"

"I suppose not as many as might prefer to hang you."

Hegman laughed a "things sure didn't turn out the way we thought."

"No. I'm going to Chicago. Going to be Chief Financial Officer for a company that makes steel drums, barrels, all sizes. Friend of mine from business school owns it. Let me know if you need any barrels. I might be able to get you a deal."

"When's this all happening? I mean, you're not leaving tomorrow or the next day, are you? Is this good-bye?"

"No, Junior. I'll be around for a few weeks yet. I gave thirty days' notice, and I don't start in Chicago for sixty. I just wanted you to hear it from me before word got around. I know I was the one who talked you into coming back here, and I'm sorry. You've done a good job."

That night at dinner, Jiggs told Carol of Hegman's resignation.

Carol nodded. "I heard it out at the shop this afternoon. So, another rat leaves the sinking ship."

What kind of a crack is that? "You think Hegman's a rat?"

"A lot of people around here do, but I don't necessarily agree with their reasons for thinking so, just their conclusion. He didn't force those people to borrow his bank's money. I think he's a rat for leaving. I thought captains were supposed to go down with their ships. He's certainly been one of the captains in this town. So was Ron Bjournquist. What chance do Lake City or Walnut Grove have if people like them leave?"

As unwilling as Jiggs was to think of Ron Bjournquist as a rat, or even Jim Hegman after their conversation this afternoon, he could see Carol's point.

"Maybe so. But the more I think about it, the forces that got us all into this mess and will eventually get us out aren't anything the Jim Hegmans and Ron Bjournquists can control."

Carol put down her fork. "Are you talking about God?"

That was what Jiggs had long believed or believed he believed or wanted to believe or thought he was supposed to believe.

"No," Jiggs replied, "I'm not."

55

January 1983

"Jiggs, Honey, can I come in?"

Lindy stood in the doorway framed by the dark, a small suitcase in her hand.

"Lindy, what are you doing here in the middle of the night?"

"Oh, Jiggs, things are kind of a mess right now. Doc told me he wanted me to leave, and that I can come back and get my stuff tomorrow." Jiggs could see that the old woman's eyes were brimming with tears through the lenses of her glasses. Her wrinkled face looked more forlorn than he believed possible.

"Wha ... what? Jesus, Lindy, what happened? C'mon into the living room. I have a fire going. Get warm."

Jiggs pulled two chairs near the hearth. "Want some tea or something?"

"Put some bourbon in it. I think my goddamn heart is frozen."

Jiggs came back into the living room with two cups of tea and handed one to Lindy. "All right, what's going on?"

"Same thing that's been going on for years now with that goddamn park. Roger called today and told Doc the State rejected his offer to sell the farm if we could live in the house until we died, and that the case is going to trial next month.

"I could tell by listening to Doc's end of the conversation that Roger was telling him he ought to just sell and move and put an end to it. The State's new offer's still more than the place's worth on the open market. Doc cut him off and told him to get ready for trial.

"After he hung up, Doc and I got in an argument, because I took Roger's side of things an' told him we oughta just move. I mean, he's gonna lose the place. If he goes to trial, the only issue is how much the State has to pay, and it's not gonna be any more than what's being offered, maybe less. Hell, what's the point?

"Doc, he listened. He didn't yell or anything. You know how he is. He just looked at me real hard and said he wanted me to leave, go live somewhere else."

Jesus. It's come to this. Jiggs stared into the fire. He stood up, walked over to Lindy's chair and put his arm around her. "You can stay here forever, Lindy."

They sat drinking their tea. Lindy described how Doc, never chatty, now talked of nothing except fighting the State. "It's getting to be an obsession with him, Jiggs. Hell, I don't want to argue with him. He's the best friend this old woman ever had, but I gotta tell him what I think. Once upon a time I believe he valued that."

"I know he did, Lindy."

Next morning, having slept little, Jiggs was up early. He thought of calling Carol in Arizona to tell her what happened, but was unable to make the effort necessary to overcome the oil slick of apathy widening between them. Besides, he was too busy wondering what he was going to say to Doc.

Jiggs found his dad in his workshop sharpening a chain saw.

"Hi, Pop. Going to cut down a little shade?"

Doc looked up from what he was doing. "If you're here to talk about Lindy, save your breath."

"Seems to me Lindy's not the issue, Pop."

"Then what is?"

"The issue's where you're going to be living a year from now, cause it's sure not going to be here. I talked to Roger this morning, and he says the outcome at trial's about as close to a slam dunk as there is in law. Once that's final, the State can evict you. Rog says even with appeals you've got less than a year at best."

Doc set the chain saw on his workbench and turned to face Jiggs. "Seems to me, where I live is my business."

"Pop, do you remember when you got me fired from Willets to keep me from dropping out of college before I even started?"

Doc's only reply was a look that said, of course he remembered.

"You told me then that there were a lot of ways to drown. Well, you're drowning now. Drowning in your own hate. You began this fight out of love for this place, but that's not what's driving you now. If it was, you wouldn't have thrown Lindy out last night for doing no more than telling you the truth."

Doc looked at Jiggs through narrowed eyes. "It was time for her to go."

Jiggs shrugged. "Maybe so. Under the circumstances, she probably would agree with you. But, like I say, that's not the point. Pop, you've always been the wisest man I know. For sure it's a bad fact that pretty soon, it's going to be time for you to go as well. What I can't believe is that the wisest man I know is letting one bad fact ruin his life."

Doc walked over to the open door and looked out at the farmyard. Little eddies of snow curled in its midst in the January wind. Across the way, Bill and Marilyn and the other horses stood nose to tail in the lee of the tack room. Beyond them the leafless trees along the river stood stark against the gray sky. It seemed to Jiggs Doc was inhaling the scene, breathing it in, the very sight of the place the incense of his life.

Finally, Doc turned back towards his son. "It's my life, Jiggs. I know what I'm doing."

Jiggs glanced at the clock beside his bed as he groped for the phone. Three twenty-two a.m. *Now what?* He was a preacher. Midnight calls were almost routine, especially the last couple of years.

"Jiggs, this is Beezer. You better get out to Doc's right away. The place is on fire. I just got the call. Darcy and I are leaving right now. Will you call Marie and then come on?"

"What, you mean the house?"

"Yeah. The house and maybe some other stuff as well. Don't know much."

"What about Pop? Is he okay?" *He's not.*

"Don't know."

"Yeah, okay. I'm on my way."

The night sky was overcast. Jiggs could see the underside of the low clouds illuminated in smoky red light off to the east while still two miles away from the valley. As he came over the crest of the hill from the west, it was as if dawn had arrived three hours early.

At the bottom of the hill by the entrance to Doc's lane two fire trucks were parked, red emergency lights blinking. It looked like the lane itself was on fire. At the upper end, the house was engulfed in flame. One hundred fifty yards down the road, the barn, machine shed and tack room were all burning brightly. Flashing lights told Jiggs there were more emergency vehicles down there.

This is no accident.

As Jiggs got out of his pickup he saw Beezer walking towards him in the headlights.

"Holy shit, Beezer..."

"Doc's burning the place down, Jiggs. Look at the lane."

The ten walnut saplings he and Doc had planted when they started construction on the new house almost thirty years ago, five on each side of the lane, had grown to more than forty feet in height, but they were no more. They lay instead, ten horizontal walls of fire, crisscrossing the lane at ten yard intervals, too evenly spaced to leave any doubt about how they happened to be there or why.

"There's a ten-foot-wide ditch all the way across near the top," Beezer said. "No way these rigs can get up there, even if we could clear those trees. They're trying to drag a hose up from the pumper now, but the fire guys say they don't begin to have enough water to make any difference."

"Any sign of Pop?"

Beezer shook his head.

"What about down below?" Jiggs gestured in the direction of the farm buildings.

"Same story. Another ditch across the drive."

Jiggs started for the meadow to the right of the lane. "I'm going up there."

"I'll go with you, but you can't get within seventy-five feet of the house." Beezer fell in beside Jiggs. "I been up there once already."

They post-holed through the deep snow in the meadow to the base of the hill. As they crossed, Jiggs notied the horses huddled together in a corner as far from the conflagration as they could get. *What must they be thinking?*

Sparks from the flames had ignited the dry weeds still standing on the nearly vertical hillside where no snow had been able to cling. Jiggs and Beezer were forced to weave their way around fiery clumps, scrambling, sometimes using their hands as well as feet as they climbed. Twice Jiggs had to slap at his jacket to put out places that had begun to smolder from the embers. The air became ever hotter as they ascended. It hurt to breathe. Jiggs' eyes felt as if they might liquefy from the heat.

One look once they were at the top told Jiggs the place was beyond salvation. The house was an inferno from end to end. Tongues of flame leapt up, licking the upper branches of the maple they'd planted to commemorate Jiggs' mom, the bottom branches already seared.

"Doc must have painted the house, those trees, with gasoline," Beezer muttered as they stood watching the conflagration.

Jiggs scanned the hillside behind the house in the firelight for some sign of Doc up there surveying his handiwork. Nothing. "He didn't half-step when he built it. No reason to think he'd do so when he destroyed it."

Deep inside Jiggs knew exactly where Doc was. Deep inside. Maybe Carol'd be pleased. At least one captain had chosen to go down with his ship.

"C'mon, Jiggs. Let's get out of here. There's nothing to be done."

"You go, Beez. I think I'll just stay up here a while and say good-bye."

As Beezer's head disappeared below the rim of the hillside, Jiggs sank to his knees, arms to his side, head bowed touching the melting snow.

56

February 1983 – September 1984

There was no memorial service for Doc. Where would it have been held? Not in any church. The absence of a service didn't bother Jiggs. Doc had staged his own. It would be a long time before anybody in Adolphus County forgot what he had done.

Jiggs would never forget what Doc had done or how he had done it or how Doc's own son, the last person to speak to Doc insofar as anyone knew, had failed to deflect his father from his path to self-destruction.

Carol called around noon the day of the fire. She'd heard the news

"Jiggs, why didn't you call me? Were you ever going to call me? Are you okay?"

"No."

"No what? No, you're not okay?"

"No. I'm not okay. Would you be okay, if something like that happened to you?"

"It did happen to me, Jiggs. Do you think Doc didn't mean anything to me? Do you think you have a monopoly on grief?"

Jiggs was tired of all the questions, and so he stopped answering.

"Jiggs, are you still there? Do you want me to come home?"

Not if you have to ask.

"I don't care."

Two days later Carol arrived. It had snowed heavily the previous afternoon and evening. When she drove up to their house, the sidewalks and driveway were unshoveled. The morning paper was still on the steps. The curtains were drawn, the front door unlocked. Inside, Jiggs was sitting on the couch in the dimness.

"You were right," Jiggs said when Carol entered the room.

"Right about what?"

"I should have never become a minister. What does 'minister' mean, after all? To minister to the needs of others? First Susan Karocek, now Pop. I'm a real source of comfort."

"Jiggs, I may have thought you shouldn't be a minister, but not because you weren't good at it. What's happened is tragic. No doubt about it. But it sounds to me as if you're not grieving for Doc. You're grieving for yourself."

Jiggs didn't say anything. Isn't that what happens when someone dies? The survivors grieve for what the death means to them, not what it means to the deceased. The deceased is beyond suffering. He stood up and walked into another room.

Instead of returning to the pulpit after a reasonable period of mourning, whatever that might be, Jiggs took three months leave of absence. How could he continue to praise a god who allowed such things to happen? Jim Billings, Saucers, Tony Capini, Ellen Kelso, Justine, Susan Karocek, Doc, inquisitions, crusades, wars, famines, plagues, millions and millions of unjust, undeserved deaths. What did free will have to do with Justine's death? Jim Billings? Bah. Free will was no explanation. The sheer caprice of life impeached the faith he had struggled so hard to embrace for the last fifteen years.

How could I be so fucking dumb? The question returned again and again during his months of mostly silent reflection. At the end of his leave, he resigned. To have resumed would have been fraud.

A door slammed.

"Jiggs! Jiggs, where are you?"

If Jiggs heard Carol, he did not respond.

Carol stomped into the study where Jiggs had been busy looking out the window.

"What's this I hear about you resigning?"

"I don't know. What did you hear?"

Carol's lips compressed against her teeth in a look of exasperation. "Don't be coy. Half a dozen people came up to me today at the shop and said how much they regretted your resignation."

"I resigned."

"From what? The church? The ministry? What?"

"All of it."

"Just like that? Without even discussing it with me?"

"No, not 'just like that.' I gave it a lot of thought. I thought you'd be pleased."

Carol stood in the middle of the room with her hands on her hips. "You know, Jiggs, it's one thing not to begin a career many thought ill-advised, and quite another to abandon one after a successful investment of fifteen years…"

Successful?

"…without even discussing it with me. You didn't think I'd be pleased. You knew it would embarrass me not to know."

It occurred to Jiggs to reply that Carol had taken as little a part as possible in the career in question ever since he launched it, so why should he discuss its termination with her? "Do you find it ironic that you're angry at me for ending something you hated?"

"That's not my point, Jiggs, and you know it."

Jiggs was tired of arguing and didn't respond.

The next day Carol returned to Jiggs' study, not stomping this time. She sat down at one end of the couch, her back resting against the arm, one leg cocked up on the cushions, facing him.

"Jiggs, where do you see our marriage going?"

Jiggs sat down at the other end, shook his head and shrugged. It was only ten o'clock in the morning, and he was already tired.

"Do you care?"

Another shake and shrug.

Carol gave a little gasp."That's what I thought." She had closed her eyes as she spoke. "In that case, I think one of us should leave. I'm thinking of staying with my parents until we get this sorted out."

"It's a cinch I can't stay with mine."

In July, after doing everything she could think of to cheer Jiggs up, Lindy left to move in with Darcy and Beezer. On the day of her departure, the two of them stood at the door.

"Jiggs, Honey, you understand I have to leave, don't you? I'm almost eighty years old. I spent a lot of years watching Doc tear himself apart. I don't have the heart to watch you do the same. If I thought I could prevent it, I'd stay. You know I would. But you're going to have to do this for yourself."

"I know, Lindy. I understand." Jiggs gave her a hug, picked up her suitcases and walked with her out to her car.

"We'll still see each other, Jiggs. Won't we?"

"I'm sure we will, Lindy. I'm sure we will." But they didn't. Darcy invited him to dinner lots of times. Usually he declined. A couple times he accepted, but didn't show. He thought he wanted to, but couldn't when the time came. Eventually the invitations stopped.

Carol filed for divorce in August. She called to warn him. Jiggs did not contest. They sold the house, the only one Jiggs had ever owned. He sold most of his stuff and moved into a one-bedroom apartment over what used to be Horton's. His money wouldn't last forever.

On January 28th, the anniversary of Doc's Armageddon, the final divorce hearing was held. It was the only one Jiggs was required to attend. Apparently the Judge wanted to look Jiggs in the eye when he pronounced him no longer married. Of course, Carol was there with her lawyer. She was lean and fit from miles of golf and wearing her Arizona tan. She cried throughout the fifteen-minute proceeding.

As soon as the Judge finished reciting the terms and conditions of the termination of the marriage and said, "It is so ordered," Jiggs stood up and headed through the swinging gate and down the aisle leading out of the courtroom. Just as he cleared the gate, he felt a hand on his shoulder, Carol's hand.

"I guess this is 'good-bye,' Jiggs. I've sold the shop. I'm going to stay in Arizona."

Jiggs nodded. *Another rat.*

"You know, Jiggs, I knew I'd be sad on this day, but it's worse than I expected. It's just that, despite all the mistakes we made, I never thought there would be a time when you didn't love me." She gave him a hug and walked out the courtroom door ahead of him.

Jiggs went back to mentally throwing cards at a hat, going for walks with no destination in mind, starting books he never finished, keeping a journal with mostly blank days. It had been a year since Doc's death. Throughout that time, he had not written to Camilla, because there was no realm of his life where disappointment and discontent did not dwell. *How could I be so fucking dumb?* Now more than ever, while needy and angry at life, he was determined not to seek her out. He feared that might mean forever, but his self-imposed ground-rule remained in place.

He didn't pray either.

Doc was dead, Lindy had left, Darcy and Beezer had given up, now Carol was gone. Winter became Spring became Summer became Fall. Roger remained. Week after week, month after month he drove up to Lake City, one hundred and two miles door to door each way, uninvited, just to sit. They would watch meaningless games on television and drink beer, Roger was prepared to listen, if only Jiggs had been prepared to talk.

More than eighteen months passed without discernable change. Roger Hood was no psychologist, but he thought the situation called for dramatic action.

V

THE WORLD

CHRISTOPHER BRITTON

57

October 1984

Central Avenue was dingy. Tired old brick buildings coated with the translucent gray film, the legacy of decades of exhaust. It was a disappointment after one hundred miles, one hundred two to be exact, of vast fields of dry corn and soybeans being gobbled up by giant green machines beneath world-class blue sky. Monotonous, perhaps, unless it was the home of someone you once had loved, may still love, might always love, if only he will give you the chance. That possibility infused the terrain with vivid imaginings of a tall, dark-haired boy with a scar on his nose busily becoming the man she knew, or once had known and hoped to know again, among fields such as these.

"Go slow," she reminded herself for the thousandth time, as she climbed the wooden stairs leading up from the alley and knocked on the door. There was no bell.

The door opened, and the forty-year-old version of Jiggs Morgan appeared. He didn't look that different, a little more filled out and in need of a shave. Not the disheveled wreck that had populated the worst of her fears. If she still resembled her twenty-five-year-old self that closely, she would have been delighted.

Jiggs' initial look of inquiry became a gape. He looked down and then back up and shook his head, as if to clear it. "Cam, is it you?"

"In the flesh. How are you, Jiggs? Not so good, I hear." Camilla opened the screen door between them that Jiggs appeared too stunned to operate. She stepped inside and gave Jiggs a hug. "You don't mind if I invite myself in?"

It was not a one-way hug. "If I had known you were coming, I'd have baked a cake."

Camilla felt a wince as Jiggs spoke the words. She leaned back to look at him, his arms still around her waist. "Jiggs, what is it? Is something wrong?"

"No. Nothing's wrong. I just realized that, pitiful as it was, I made a joke. Haven't done that in a while."

Jiggs let go of her with one arm, the other still encircling her, and pivoted around to face the interior. Gesturing with the free one, he invited her to enter.

"Have a seat. Let me take your jacket and get you something to drink before you tell me what brings you here."

"I'll have a Coke, if you have one." Camilla sat down on the couch as Jiggs retreated.

"I'm afraid all I have is beer and tap water," he called from around the corner. "I can make some coffee."

"I'll have a beer. That seems to be our get acquainted beverage." No response from Jiggs.

"Okay," Jiggs said once they were settled, "tell me what's going on."

Camilla reached into her purse. "This is probably the best place to start." She handed him a letter. "Go on. Read it."

September 30, 1984

Dear Ms. Waron (Camilla),

My name is Roger Hood. You and I don't know each other, but we share a mutual friend, Jiggs Morgan. I know this because once, back in 1968, after he returned from overseas with the Marines, Jiggs asked me to contact you in the event of his death (NO, Jiggs is not dead) and let you know what happened. Over the years he has given me some changes of address for you, but no other information. So I have no real idea of the nature and extent of your friendship, but it must be pretty special.

I am writing now, because, although not dead, in my opinion Jiggs is dying, not of any disease, but of sadness and disillusionment. He has had a succession of sorrows and disappointments in his life the last few years. I won't go into specifics. Perhaps you already know the details. If not, and if you're interested, it would be better to hear them directly from Jiggs, and I hope you will.

I don't know what it will take to snap him out of his malaise, so I am hoping you have some magical incantation. Seriously, even if you don't possess any supernatural powers, but your friendship is such that you wish to see him again while he still is at least a shadow of his former self, I urge you to get in touch with him. He is being eroded by his unhappiness.

Jiggs address is: 765½ Central Avenue, Lake City, Iowa 50501. His telephone number is 555-623-1918. If you need to reach me, my number is 555-343-2275.

I hope it is not presumptuous of me to have written. I can think of nothing else to do.

Best regards, Roger Hood

P.S. I have always assumed the fact Jiggs requested me to contact you in the event something happened to him meant that his wife, Carol, did not know of you. She is no longer in Jiggs' life, so there is no need for that to be a concern.

Jiggs put down the letter and looked at Camilla. "Rog only wrote this a week ago. You must have had to scramble to get here so quickly. I hope it wasn't too tough to make those kinds of arrangements."

"Well, he sounded so dire, I didn't know how long you'd last. You don't look like you're ready to expire."

"No, but sometimes I wish I would."

The sun had set, the sound of traffic on the street had disappeared, and the clock atop the courthouse half a block away had announced the most recent hour with a single chime, before Jiggs completed his chronicle of heartache and regret.

For hours they had been sitting in the cone of light cast by a single lamp situated on a table just behind the couch. Camilla, who had been holding both Jiggs' hands in hers since his account of Justine's death, heard a hardness creep into his voice as he finished describing Susan Karocek's ordeal.

"And do you know what?"

Camilla couldn't imagine what he was about to say.

"It was right then that I should have quit. It was right then that I wanted to kill Susan's father, Jimmy Blake, myself. It was like Howard Meeker said. I couldn't forgive any of us our frailties, our mistakes. Still can't. Any one of us might have saved her."

The smell of coffee awakened Camilla the next morning. She had left the window open an inch or two, and it was cold in the room. A breeze was stirring the hems of the curtains just above the sill. She snuggled deep beneath the comforter covering Jiggs' bed. He had insisted she sleep there. He would take the couch. "I wake up and pace a lot at night," was his excuse. It was hard for her to believe where she was.

"Aren't you going to eat breakfast?" Jiggs had just refilled their cups for the second time. Camilla was hungry. Supper last night had been preempted by history.

Jiggs shrugged. "Seldom do."

"Breakfast is the most important meal of the day."

"You sound like my mom." He set the coffee pot back on the stove and began to rummage around in the cupboard. "There might be some cereal in here somewhere." Camilla had already had a look in the refrigerator. Beer, hot dogs, some eggs, not much else. She was not hopeful.

"How about I fix us some eggs?"

"Cam, you don't have to cook for me."

"Jiggs, sit down." Camilla gestured towards the other chair sitting at right angles to hers beside the tiny kitchen table. "I know I don't 'have' to do anything. I'm not here out of duty or compulsion, you know. I'm here to be with my best old friend, and whatever happens, whether it's breakfast or..." she caught herself, "... a banquet, it's all purely voluntary on my part. Can we agree on that?"

Jiggs nodded, and Camilla fixed the eggs. As she cooked and they talked, she noticed Jiggs had shaved.

After breakfast, Camilla re-inspected the apartment. The morning sun through the east facing windows brightened what had seemed like a dungeon when she had arrived late the preceding afternoon. The coating of dust she had noticed on most of the furniture yesterday had not disappeared overnight. Camilla had to resist the urge to write "Dust me," on several surfaces as she checked things out. Otherwise the place was reasonably neat, if only because it contained so little. Leaning against the wall behind the door to the outside was a black bicycle that looked like it had enough gears to climb Mount Everest. Both tires were flat.

"How long's it been since you rode Man O' War over there, Jiggs?" Camilla nodded towards the bike.

"Long time. Autumn before Pop died, I think. I was going to sell it when I moved here, but I just couldn't make myself part with it. You ride?"

"All the time. Most days I commute on my bike. How about we go for a ride today? It looks like it's going to be nice. Is there someplace I can rent a bike?"

"There isn't even a bike shop in Lake City anymore. There was for years, but it closed over a year ago."

Jiggs wasn't sure whether he was happy or sad there were no rentals to be had. His bike had stood where Camilla found it for all the months he had lived there. It taunted him daily, an ever present reminder of all he no longer was, but might be again if he could just make himself get back on.

Without knowing exactly what he was thinking, Camilla could see Jiggs was reaching for something inside himself. He took a deep breath. "I think my sister has a bike. Maybe we could borrow hers."

"Great. Why don't you call her, while I try to pump up these tires?" Camilla removed the tire pump from its bracket on the bike's frame. As she pumped, she listened.

"Hello, Darcy, this is Jiggs."

...

"Yes, it has been a long time. Listen, do you still have your bike? If so, do you mind if I borrow it? I have a friend in town, and we'd like to go for a ride."

...

"Yeah, I know yours is a girl's bike. That's okay. My friend is a girl."

Darcy and Beezer lived in a new neighborhood out on the east edge of town. Darcy was out the door and half way down the sidewalk by the time Jiggs and Camilla got out of his truck. She was followed by her youngest, Molly, who hadn't been walking the last time Jiggs had seen her, and Lindy, who was walking with a cane.

Once Lindy finished hugging him, Jiggs introduced Camilla to Darcy and Lindy, and he knelt to say "Hi," to Molly. Then they loaded Darcy's bike and said their thanks and good-byes.

Carmichael Lake was an artificial lake five miles north of town. Jiggs parked in the parking lot of Trevelyn's restaurant, Lake City's "Finest," now closed and boarded up, and they pedaled north along a County blacktop. The only other vehicles on the road were occasional tractors pulling big wagons filled with grain.

They turned into the park and, coming to a Y in the road, went right, following the shoreline for about two miles to the west edge of the lake, where they stopped to use the bathroom and have a drink. It was a beautiful day, leaves were drifting from the trees in the breeze, and apart from the two of them, the park was empty.

When Camilla came out of the bathroom, she saw Jiggs sitting atop a picnic table in the sun looking out at the water, his back to the road. He didn't say anything as she came over and sat beside him. Their silence continued for a couple minutes. Overhead a V of geese flew south, specs in the sky, punctuating their passage with an occasional honk. "Jiggs, I have to ask. Is this the lake the State took your dad's farm to build?"

Jiggs shook his head. "No. That one's not finished. They're still building the dam. Nothing's been flooded yet."

"Can we go out there before I have to go home, or would that be too tough? I'd love to see where you grew up."

Jiggs took so long to reply that Camilla didn't think he was going to answer, but then he said, "Maybe."

Jiggs did not seem motivated to climb back on the bikes, and, apart from a nudge now and then, Camilla was determined to follow his lead on this voyage of re-discovery. "Go slow," she reminded herself once more.

After a few more minutes of quiet, Jiggs turned his eyes from the water towards Camilla. "You know how I was telling you last night about how I think I wasted all those years in the ministry?"

Camilla nodded.

"My biggest regret isn't my failure as a minister. My biggest regret is the consequence my decision had on my marriage. I destroyed the most worthwhile thing in my life and Carol's in pursuit of a foolish and, for me, unachievable goal."

"Why 'unachievable,' Jiggs? No, first tell me why you decided to become a minister in the first place. When I left Okinawa, I had no clue."

"'Why did I decide to become a minister?'" Jiggs half laughed, half sighed. "Boy, how many times have people who know me asked that question? How many times have I asked myself?

"I think I went into Viet Nam kind of taking the existence of God for granted. I hadn't thought about it much. Then I saw terrible things, and I tried to explain them to myself in terms of God and couldn't. I think that's where I was when you and I were talking about it. Remember how we about wore out that seawall discussing God?"

Camilla nodded, remembering.

"Of course, the thing that troubled me most was my having persuaded that kid, Saucers, to stay in combat by using the story about the 23rd Psalm, when I knew he was pretty devout. I also knew that even more than the rest of us, he didn't belong there. Knowing all those things, I kept him in a war I didn't believe was even worth fighting. How could I have been so fucking dumb?"

"But Jiggs," Camilla put her hand on his knee, "what you told him about that Psalm and how it played in your head was true, wasn't it? That wasn't just a story?"

"That's just it, Cam. It wasn't just a story. After you left the Island and baseball was over, I spent most of my time trying to reconcile the illogic of what I had seen with the existence of God. With the fact I seemed always to want to believe, so somewhere deep down I must. Otherwise, where was that Psalm coming from? I decided maybe Saucers' death was just my punishment for having used God to persuade that poor kid to remain in that ungodly war, part of God's plan for me."

Jiggs looked up at the sky, shaking his head, blinking his eyes.

"I had always thought I was 'blessed,' for want of a better word, with a lot of gifts. For a long time, ever since that trip to Mexico I told you about, I had wanted to do something to help people who weren't as lucky as I was. Becoming a minister seemed like a way. I would grow that seed of faith I could see was inside me, really explore it. I would give something back to God, for whatever I had taken away by keeping Saucers in the war. Does that make any sense?"

Over the years, Camilla had figured atonement must have been among Jiggs' reasons. His account of his trip through the minefield remained vivid in her memory. "Well, then why do you say the ministry was an unachievable goal for you, Jiggs?"

"Ah, Cam, the seed never grew. I thought the seminary would feed and water it, but faith there was presumed. Seminary just taught you how to make a living with it. At least that's how it seemed to me. I continued to want to believe for a long time. There would be moments when the beauty of a service, some piece of sacred music, Christmas, would move me, give me a shot of adrenalin, encourage me. But, little by little, all those things we talked about last night gnawed away until not even the seed was left. Eventually, I think Doc was the only force or whatever you want to call it, I still believed in. And then he was gone."

Camilla sat, arms folded over her chest resting on her knees, head down, listening. When Jiggs paused, she raised her head and looked across her shoulder at him. "Jiggs," she said in that voice he would have recognized as hers whenever and wherever he heard it in the universe, low and cool, "Doc's not gone. He will live on as long as you remember him, as long as all those things he taught you, as long as the example he always gave you, continue to guide you.

"Even at the end, that last conversation you had with him, when he was clearly committed to a path perhaps only he could understand, what you told him about the futility of allowing himself to be consumed with hatred, was born of the wisdom he bestowed on you. It was the kind of thing he would have said to you, Jiggs, once upon a time. The wheel of life had turned. It was your turn to be wise. The fact that it didn't save him doesn't diminish his gift in any way. Doc's not gone."

Watching, trying to communicate the sincerity of what she was saying with her entire bearing, and not just her voice, Camilla saw a single tear trickle down Jiggs' cheek. She reached up and brushed it away and smiled. Jiggs smiled back.

When they returned the bike to Darcy, she and her retinue were again at the curb almost as soon as Jiggs and Camilla emerged from the pick up. This time they came up to Camilla, not Jiggs.

"Camilla, how much longer are you going to be in town?" Darcy asked.

"What's this? Monday? I have to leave Thursday morning. Two more days."

Darcy glanced at Lindy out of the corner of her eye. "Will you and Jiggs come over for dinner tomorrow night? We'd love to have you. If that doesn't work, then the night after. Either one."

Camilla looked down at Jiggs, who was back down at Molly's level pretending to steal her nose. "What do you say, Morgan? Your social calendar's not all booked up, is it?"

Jiggs looked up at his sister. "You sure you want to have me, Darcy? I haven't been a very reliable guest."

"If you don't come, Camilla can come by herself. Either that or I'm sending Beezer over with his cuffs."

Lindy took Camilla's hand. "Camilla, Honey, make him come, will you? He needs to see his family. Besides, look at him. He needs the goddamn nourishment." She had whispered the last part so Molly wouldn't hear.

"Are you ready for the third degree?" Jiggs asked as he and Camilla were driving back to Darcy's for dinner the next evening.

"Third degree?"

"Yeah. My guess is you're about to experience an interrogation more intense than any murder suspect has ever undergone. Darcy's probably even called up Marie out in Seattle and invited her to submit questions regarding who you are and why you're here."

Camilla hadn't thought about it, but as soon as Jiggs said it, she knew he was probably right. Who is this mystery lady who suddenly flushed Jiggs out of hiding?

"Do you think we need to get our stories straight?"

"Nothing to straighten out as far as I can see. Stick with the truth. It's easier to remember."

Camilla wasn't entirely convinced. "Was Darcy or Lindy close to Carol? Do you think our friendship on Okinawa might generate some hostility on account of that?"

"Cam, as I recall, you and I worked pretty hard on Okinawa not to give anyone anything to be hostile about."

"You and I both know that, Jiggs. But all Darcy and Lindy know is that I'm a woman you met during the year you were away, but never mentioned to anyone, including your wife, for the next fourteen years. What kind of inference do you think they're likely to draw from that?"

Jiggs shrugged. "I think Darcy and Lindy are both willing to think the best of me. Even if they think I was misbehaving, they won't hold it against either one of us. Marie might be a little more prickly at first, but she won't be there tonight."

As foreseen, Camilla was afforded full opportunity to tell most, if not all her life story. She didn't go into her adoption, but described growing up on an apple farm in Northern Virginia, going to school at Duke, her decision to teach overseas, where she met Jiggs, on Okinawa, then in Germany for a year. She told about living in New York and working at the United Nations, what it was like when she was in Bolivia in the Peace Corps, life in Washington, D.C., first as a student and translator at the State Department, and later as a college professor at Georgetown, where she currently worked. She even mentioned her brief fling at marriage.

No matter what they thought might have happened on Okinawa, Darcy and Lindy were both too polite to ask. Besides, apart from Darcy's one trip to Seattle to see Marie and the years Lindy had worked in a cafeteria in a defense plant in Chicago during World War II, neither of them had ever been out of Iowa. It was as if Camilla was from another world.

"Camilla, Honey, when I listen to you talk about the Andes Mountains and the United Nations and all those things, I feel like I'm listening to a goddamn female Indiana Jones." Lindy cackled at her own joke.

Camilla laughed. "No. No uncharted territory or international intrigue for me, I'm afraid, Lindy. Wherever I flew, it was at much lower elevations."

As they were departing, Jiggs opened the pickup door and held it for Camilla. She was getting in and simultaneously waving good-bye to Beezer, Darcy, Lindy, Molly and Allan, Molly's older brother, who were all standing on the porch waving back. "You've dazzled my family, Cam."

"Nice people, Jiggs. I like finally finding out where you come from."

"Want to go for a drive?" It was Wednesday morning, Camilla's last day.

Camilla looked up from the newspaper. "Sure, where to?"

"Around."

They headed out of town to the west and after a mile or so turned south. As they drove, Jiggs pointed out places where stories he'd told Camilla in the past had happened. Camilla leaned back, meditating with her eyes open, hearing without listening, seeing the highways and fields and farmhouses, the grain elevators and rural churches, their silos and steeples outlined against an infinity of blue. A collage. After twenty minutes and a couple of turns, they passed a sign that said, "WALNUT GROVE 2 MI." Two miles later the road began a long sweeping S curve, left and then right, at the end of which a business district a short two blocks long ended at the bank of a river spanned by an old-fashioned bridge that looked like it had been built with an erector set. Most of the buildings appeared to be vacant. There was no one on the sidewalks.

"This is it, Cam, my hometown on its way to becoming a ghost town."

It was true. Camilla could think of no reply. They crossed the bridge and turned up the hill that loomed above the opposite bank. At the top, more flat, treeless farmland spread before them, but after only another four miles the road dove down a steep hill. At the bottom there was a driveway on the left with a locked gate across bearing a "NO TRESPASSING" sign. Jiggs pulled in, turned off the engine and got out. Camilla followed. She met him in front of the truck and they leaned side by side against the hood facing the lane. It led up the hillside about one hundred yards and then turned to the right onto a level space carved into the side of the hill.

"That's where the house stood, Cam."

"Have you come out here much since it happened, Jiggs?"

Jiggs nodded. "A bit. I don't stop here though. I usually go on down around the corner and park and walk. If you feel like walking, I'll show you."

Camilla felt like walking.

They climbed back in the truck and Jiggs drove down to an intersection, turned left and after a tenth of a mile, pulled into the entrance to a field barred by another gate, another lock, another sign.

"C'mon," Jiggs climbed over the gate, Camilla right behind him. They walked across a pasture that obviously had not been mowed or grazed in more than a year through grass and weeds as high as their waists. On the far side, they came to a small stream and followed its bank until they reached a log that had fallen across. They tight-roped over, traced the opposite bank for a few minutes and then began to climb a steep slope through a grove of walnut trees, their green fruit the size of golf balls, ungathered, littering the ground.

They crested the hill onto a small plateau where several graves stood in the middle of a weed free circle of mown grass. Whatever had been inscribed on all but two had worn off long ago. On the two still legible, Camilla read:

Mary Agnes Morgan
September 9, 1915 –
February 4, 1962

James McAlister Morgan, DVM
August 2, 1914 –
January 28, 1983

Camilla stood beside Jiggs, who looked down at the graves and then away across the large valley. The timbered hillsides were draped in a tie-died autumn cloak.

"Are you the person who has been tending these graves, Jiggs?"

"Mostly, I think. I've become quite a gardener."

"It's beautiful, Jiggs. The whole setting is breath-taking."

"The employment's temporary. It will all be under water in another couple of years." Jiggs voice was low, but it was not soft. After a few seconds he said, "Let's walk some more."

As they were going along, Camilla, although no equestrian, was thinking how great it must have been to ride over these hills on horseback, when Jiggs asked, "How are your folks doing, Cam? Still growing apples?"

"They're still on the place, but my dad's slowing down. My sister, Mara, and her husband pretty much run the business now, with Dad helping and, of course, telling my sister what she's doing wrong. My mom's still going strong, though. She bakes more things in a week than I've baked in my whole life."

"How long have they been married?"

Camilla stopped to think. "Thirty-seven years. We had a big celebration for number thirty-five a couple of years ago." She resumed walking.

Jiggs sighed. "I was just thinking, this would have been my parents' forty-first. They got married in January '43, just before Pop went overseas. That was an act of faith, getting married in the middle of a war."

"You did the same thing, didn't you, Jiggs?"

"Yeah, I guess I did. Somehow when I did it, it didn't seem so risky. Don't know why. Maybe in some ways, it was the war that wrecked us. Who knows what direction our lives would have taken if we'd waited or there'd been no war?

"Strange, isn't it. Our folks grew up and got married in times at least as turbulent as ours and managed to stay married, and here we are, both divorced. Even though divorce was going on all around me, I never thought of it happening to me until it did. I guess your situation was a little different, but do you ever think about it?"

"Oh, yes..."

The emphatic tone of Camilla's response turned Jiggs' head as they walked.

"... What I think about is how I've missed the boat on being a mom. I might have even stayed with Mark in South Carolina in order to make that happen, but before too long, I decided if I had kids, I didn't want him to be the father. He was dishonest. We'd go to a restaurant, a buffet, and he'd insist only one of us pay and go through the line, piling enough food on one plate for both of us to eat.

"A few months after we were down there, we had a workman doing something, installing cable television, I think. He left a drill at our house. When he discovered what he'd done, he came back for it no more than an hour later. Mark told him he hadn't seen the drill. Mark kept it. After that, I was pretty sure he'd lied to me in the first place about being willing to go to California. He hadn't just changed his mind.

"Either way, that was it for me. But now I'm almost forty and my biological clock is in the red zone. I guess you can't outplan fate."

Jiggs put his arm around Camilla's shoulders; she slipped an arm around his waist. They walked on.

"You remember that joke Lindy made last night about you and Indiana Jones?"

Jiggs and Camilla sat facing each other in a booth at a coffee shop on the outskirts of Lake City – their last supper.

"She got it wrong."

Camilla looked up from her menu. "Wrong how?"

"You're not Indiana Jones. You're Mary Poppins, flying in for a few days to make everything right."

"You think I'm your nanny?"

"Well, I wouldn't take the comparison that far. Maybe you're Indiana Poppins."

Camilla put down her menu. "What do you think's going to happen next, after Indiana Poppins flies away?"

"Next?"

"Yes, next. Judging by your friend Roger's letter and from what Darcy and Lindy told me when I was out in the kitchen with them last night before dinner, you've talked to me about your troubles more in the last three and a half days than you've talked to the entire world in almost two years. I think that's a good thing, don't you?

"Cam, I love that you came to see me. But you have a life. What do I have? A room over an empty store. I think of the years I squandered and the lives I wasted, and I feel like such a fool. I just want to go off by myself and hide. All I can think about is all the things I regret. It's hard to see that changing. Knowing you wish to help me, is the nicest thing I know. But I would rather not try, than try with you and fail and wind up with you frustrated and disappointed when you think of me."

"Jiggs, if that's how you really feel, then you shouldn't have let me come in last Sunday afternoon. Because now it's too late. Do you really think I can go home tomorrow and just forget all about you? It sure didn't work very well the last time we tried it."

Before Jiggs could answer, the waitress came to take their order. When she left, Camilla resumed.

"Shall I tell you what I think should happen?"

Without giving Jiggs a chance to say "no," she continued. "You need to come see me. The bleakness of these towns, Jiggs, the things that happened here – there are too many ghosts. What's to prevent you from coming anyway? Your room over the store? Make whatever arrangements you have to make and cast off. You've shown me your town. Let me show you mine."

The next day, Jiggs walked Camilla down to her car in the early morning twilight.

"Promise me again that you're coming, Jiggs."

"I'll try."

"No, not good enough. Promise. 'I, Jiggs Morgan, will come visit Camilla Waron in the very near future...'" She almost said "... so help me God," but caught herself and shut up.

"Okay."

"Okay, you'll come?"

"Okay, I'll come."

"You understand you can come any time, no notice required. Just show up. That's what I did."

"Yup."

Camilla gave Jiggs an enormous hug. As she stepped back and before turning to open the car door, she reached up and touched his cheek. Once in the car, she rolled down the window. "And Jiggs, if you drive, bring your bike."

Jiggs nodded, and Camilla drove away.

58

November 1984

Lindy leaned her head back against the top of her chair and sighed a deep sigh. "Thanks for coming tonight, Jiggs."

"Eightieth birthday, Lindy. Too big to miss."

"Yeah, but your record hasn't been too good when it comes to showing up. I was worried."

Darcy, Beezer and the kids had all gone to bed. Jiggs and Lindy were sitting in the living room. Jiggs was picking the semi-popped kernels from among the tooth-crackers in the bottom of the popcorn bowl. Just like the old days. The old, old days.

"Lot of candles on that cake, Lindy. Did you make a wish before you blew'em out?"

"Sort of."

"Sort of?"

"Jiggs, Honey, most of my wishes have already come true. These last twenty years have been the happiest of my life. How many eighty year olds can say that?"

"Even with everything that happened?"

"You mean what Doc did?"

Jiggs nodded.

Lindy didn't say anything for several seconds. She was sitting with her hands folded in her lap. She was staring at them when she finally spoke.

"When Doc told me it was time for me to leave, those words seared my heart. Worst hurt ever. The next night, the fire. I understood. Making me go. Doc's final act of kindness."

Lindy leaned over and reached in the popcorn bowl, but found only Jiggs hand foraging ahead of her. She held it.

"Course, I didn't understand right away. Doc dying, the way he did it, knocked me down for a long time. I kept asking myself if there was something more I coulda done. But in the end, I come to see what he did as a triumph, not a tragedy. I mean, losing him was like I was swallowed alive. Saddest thing ever. To think of him finally cornered like that is hard, even now. But his response, his defiance at the injustice of it all, that was like some goddamn Viking."

Jiggs sat in silence watching his ancient friend as she shook her head, adrift in the thought of her dead hero.

"Think about it Jiggs. Can you imagine Doc in some goddamn apartment in town? Might as well a tossed him in prison, and he was smart enough to know it."

"That's a good way to think about it, Lindy."

Neither spoke for several minutes until Lindy retrieved them from their reverie. "You hear anything from your friend, Camilla?"

"No."

"Have you called her?"

"No."

"Did you write to her?"

"No."

"Damn, Jiggs," Lindy leaned forward in her chair. "Why not? How did you two leave off when she went home?"

"She wants me to come there ... to Washington."

"When are you going?"

"I don't know."

"Jiggs! What's holding you back?" Lindy let go of Jiggs' hand and held hers out, palms up as if handing Jiggs the answer. "That woman loves you, Jiggs. She didn't come all the way out here on a moment's notice just because you used to be her pal. Do you care about her? What's the matter?"

"What difference does it make, Lindy? What have I got to offer her at this point?"

"Jesus Christ! Jiggs Morgan, do you really want to know what I wished for my birthday? I wished that you would finally get your shit together and stop feeling sorry for yourself. That's what I wished." Even by Lindy's lofty standards of imprecation, this tirade, although brief, lacked nothing in the way of vehemence.

"That's the question, isn't it, Lindy? What shit do I have to get together? A career built on a cracked foundation? A preacher who can't make himself believe?"

Even behind bi-focals as thick as coasters, Jiggs could see Lindy's eyes narrow.

"Your big failure isn't the ministry, Jiggs. It's your failure to overcome failure, if that's what you want to call it. Moping around wallowing in self-pity." Lindy stood up and began to hobble toward the door. "I'm tired. Going to bed." She disappeared into the back of the house still muttering.

Two weeks later when Lindy answered the bell, Jiggs was standing on the porch, wearing galoshes and holding a bouquet of flowers. Over his shoulder, she could see his pick-up parked at the curb, his bike in the back.

"Jiggs, what in the name of..."

"Good-bye, Lindy. These are for you. A peace offering."
He handed her the flowers, sat down on Darcy's porch swing
and began to take off the boots. "These are for you too. I won't
need 'em any more. I've stopped wallowing."

Lindy began to cackle.

"Going to Washington ... and Lindy, I don't know when
I'll be back."

"Jiggs, Honey, knowing that gives me all I need.
Whatever you do, give it all ya got. Doc'll be proud of you ... and
so will I."

Jiggs bent down and Lindy stood on her tiptoes and they
gave each other a hug and kiss. Then he was gone.

59

December 1984

A month went by. Each day Camilla would crane her neck as she rode down her street towards home after work, straining to see if there was a green pick up parked in front of her house. She had been sure Jiggs would come, would keep his promise. She debated calling him, but decided not to. She had made her wishes clear. This was a step Jiggs needed to take on his own without further urging. Thanksgiving came and went.

Saturday morning, December 1st. No Saturday classes this semester, Camilla could sleep in. Much to her annoyance, the phone rang just before seven a.m.

"Hello, Camilla, this is Sharon from across the street. There's a man sitting on your front steps. He looks like some transient or homeless person. Should I call the police?"

"No, but thanks, Sharon. I think this transient is pretty harmless."

Camilla pulled on her robe. As she hurried to the door, the buoyance she had lost without even knowing it while waiting to see whether Jiggs would keep his promise, washed over her. Relief mixed with joy. "Jiggs, what are you doing sitting out here in the cold? Get in here. The neighbors are thinking of calling the cops."

Jiggs closed the book he'd been reading, stood up and stretched. "Can only sleep in the cab of a truck for so long. I arrived too late to knock. Could use a cup of coffee though."

After a brief period of instruction, Jiggs made the coffee while Camilla dressed. They spent half the morning talking about Jiggs' trip. Somewhere in its midst, breakfast happened, it being the most important meal of the day.

"I decided to take back roads, no freeways, and camp my way out here," Jiggs explained. "The first night I only got as far as Springfield, Illinois. I saw a billboard advertising the Lincoln Museum there and decided to stop. I was always interested in Lincoln and the Civil War. Wound up spending a whole day. I was going to camp another night along the way, but the farther east I went, the colder it became. So I drove on through. Got here about three-thirty."

"You should have knocked anyway."

"If I knocked on a girl's door at three-thirty in the morning, somewhere in the universe my mom would know it and disapprove."

"Your mom has telepathic powers, does she?"

"Doesn't yours?"

By ten o'clock, Jiggs was nodding off. Camilla put him in the guest bedroom and didn't see him again until dinnertime.

The next morning, having slept sixteen of the last twenty hours, Jiggs was up before Camilla. Utilizing his recently acquired mastery of Camilla's coffee maker, he chased away the fuzzy residue of too much sleep, and read until Camilla showed up an hour later.

Camilla had arranged her living room so that two of her chairs faced a bay window that looked out on her side yard and across a low fence towards a park on the far side of her neighbors' back lawn. Jiggs and Camilla sat there, side by side, watching squirrels busy making their eleventh hour preparations for winter. It was starting to snow.

"Still up for going to the museum today?" During dinner the night before, they had discussed going to an exhibit of Christmas ornaments that had once belonged to the Tsars, "Christmas With The Romanovs."

Jiggs last visit to Washington had been to protest the war in '70. Not much sightseeing that time. Any place or no place was fine with him. He was just glad to be here. "Sure. Do you think the snow will be a problem?"

"We can take the Metro. Parking's terrible down there anyway, even on weekends."

As they came out of the station and started walking, the wind almost spun them around. Leaning into it, and with Camilla, who knew where she was going, leading the way, they found the gallery they were looking for among the Smithsonian labyrinth.

Most Washingtonians were too busy getting ready for their own Christmases to bother with that of a vanished era. Coupled with the weather, that meant Jiggs and Camilla had the room to themselves except for a security guard who never budged from her post by the door.

They bought a pamphlet describing the history of each of the items on display and took turns reading aloud about the careers of the exquisite ornaments. So abundant were the precious stones, gold, pearls and ivory, so delicate and fine the workmanship, that appreciation of the individual pieces was made difficult by their excess. Jiggs wondered whether the Czars had had the same problem.

When they'd toured the room completely, Jiggs informed Camilla he had just purchased an angel made of more than a thousand pearls outlined in gold and he was giving it to her for Christmas.

"Oh, merci, Monsieur." Camilla's jaw dropped in mock astonishment at his lavish gift. She had just read that French was the language of the Russian imperial court.

"And for you, I have this." She led Jiggs to a carved wooden drummer boy attached to a stick in such a manner that when twisted back and forth, the child soldier beat his drum. It was easily the most humble member of the magnificent collection, and the only one that might ever have been handled by a child.

The tenderness of Camilla's choice was not lost on Jiggs. "Oo la la," he said, exhausting his supply of ersatz French.

Leaving the wonderland of Fabrege's version of Christmas, they went back outdoors. It was still snowing, but only lightly. The wind had died.

Before starting to walk, Camilla put her hand on Jiggs' arm. Jiggs was making jokes. He was reading. He seemed cheerful. She thought what she was about to propose would be okay. "Jiggs, I'm going to make a suggestion, but if you don't want to do it, please just say so. Do you want to go see the Viet Nam Memorial?"

He had thought about the Memorial as he was driving out. He'd followed its construction a few years earlier. It had not surprised him that even the monument dedicated to those who fought and fell in that unpopular war had been accompanied by discord and recrimination. Jiggs took a deep breath. "Yeah. I think I do."

A twenty-minute walk brought them to the end of a long plaza that sloped gently down away from them towards the

bottom of a wide V formed by huge polished black stone walls
bearing the names of the war's dead. Jiggs had read somewhere
that the Memorial was visited by a thousand people a day. The
place was going to have to have some big days to make up for
this one if it was going to maintain its average. Like the museum,
it was deserted.

The only sign they were not alone was a single pair of
footprints marching towards the wall across the otherwise
unmarked coverlet of snow from near where they were
standing. The prints weren't fresh. They were partially filled
with snow. Neither Jiggs nor Camilla could see anyone
anywhere around, but there were no tracks retreating from the
wall in any direction.

"Been here before?" Jiggs asked.

Camilla shook her head. "Hard place to come alone, and
you were the only one I could of think of with whom I wanted
to be here."

Without speaking, Jiggs took her hand, and together they
walked, taking care not to step in the track of their mysterious
predecessor. Jiggs was moving slowly, not with hesitation but,
it seemed to Camilla, with reverence. Their traverse reminded
her of some wedding or, more likely, funeral march. She wasn't
going to interrupt Jiggs' reverie with a lot of questions about
how the place made him feel. She knew he would eventually tell
her if he could.

Besides, she was having enough trouble sorting out her
own emotions at being in this bleak spot on this snowy, gray
afternoon. What was it she was feeling? Did her feelings arise
from being there with Jiggs and seeing him so strongly affected,
or was there more to it than that? The war, the tumult, the
anguish of the times didn't just belong to those who fought

there. Camilla, too, had come of age during the war in more ways than one. She had her own ghosts.

As for Jiggs, the black stone, no more than ankle high at the top of the V, now loomed above him like a storm. There were the names, more than fifty thousand of them, inscribed one after another, name, dot, name, dot, name, dot, like some word processor gone mad. Jiggs knew they'd be there. He'd seen the pictures, but the foreknowledge made their immediacy no less gripping. It was as if the names, the tens of thousands of dead names, were sucking him right into the wall, making him disappear with their owners into the vacuum of their fate.

At the nadir of the V, the single pair of footprints that preceded them turned to face the wall. There against its base lay a small brown and tan teddy bear, very old, its fur worn off in patches, a crack in one of its wooden button eyes, a single snowflake on its tiny red felt tongue. Jiggs made a soft choking sound at the sight and stopped, saying nothing. Without being aware of it, all tension left his grip, and his hand slipped from Camilla's and fell limp at his side. His eyes scanned the panel in front of him, neither reading nor even seeing the individual names, only the unending stream.

After several minutes standing in place beside Jiggs, Camilla moved away. She, too, knew several names on the wall. She had made up her mind not to try to find them. They were there. She didn't have to see them to be reminded. The boy her sister, Olga, dated in high school, the blond boy from Richmond with whom she'd studied for her geology final her sophomore year at Duke, her second cousin, Bret.

Camilla walked the length of the wall. Random names caught her eye. Montoya, Brubaker, Peters ... and she wondered who they were, where they were from, who they left behind, how their families coped with their sorrow. Without thinking, she reached out and touched the wall with her hand. The stone was cold to her touch, her fingers traced some of the letters as she thought of the war as she had seen it on television, soldiers in baggy uniforms walking slowly through tall grass, in staggered columns on either side of a road, in a chow line somewhere on Christmas. It hadn't looked very deadly on TV. The demonstrators always looked more ferocious on television than the soldiers. Maybe that was because the demonstrators knew what they were fighting for.

Camilla remembered the boys on Okinawa, just a three-hour plane ride from the war. They would be there tomorrow; they had been there yesterday, but on Okinawa, they were mostly irrepressible, happy American boys. Camilla wondered if the names of any of the men she met there were on the wall. They would fly away from the Island, some to the war, some back home to America, and she would never see them again, never know what became of them ... except for Jiggs.

As her mind's eye gazed back across the years towards that last stepping stone to the war, Camilla wandered over to where the statue of the three bronze soldiers stood, eternal sentinels to the grim obituary. Unblinking eyes staring out of youthful faces, looking back at the wall, silently asking all who passed how such a thing could have happened. Their somber look of wonder made Camilla's throat ache, awakening her from her musings. She glanced around to see where Jiggs was.

Jiggs hadn't moved. He was standing in the exact spot where he'd been when she walked away, only now his head was resting against the wall. He stood there, a statue himself, the snow gathering on his shoulders and the top of his bowed head. His arms were up, and the palms of his hands were pressed against the stone. As if he sensed her watching, Jiggs turned and began walking with that same reverent tread toward where

Camilla was standing. As he drew near, he pursed his lips in the unconscious way he had of beginning to smile, a gentle smile, more eyes than mouth. He shook his head. "Ready to go?"

They walked on, climbing the steps of the Lincoln Memorial, just across the way. There they stood in awe of the man who one of Jiggs' professors at Iowa once described as the closest thing to an American saint.

"That book I'm reading is a biography of Lincoln. I picked it up in the museum in Springfield."

Camilla had read once that, with the exception of Napoleon, there had been more biographies written of Lincoln, than of anyone in history. "What's the title?"

"'With Malice Towards None.' A phrase from his second inaugural address. Pretty decent sentiment, don't you think?"

Once back home, they had a drink and watched it get dark. Neither talked much as they digested their day. "What do you want to do about dinner?" Camilla finally asked, overcoming the temptation to sit there all night. "I can fix something or we can go out. There's a nice quiet place just about five blocks from here, an easy walk. Sometimes they have live music, just jazz, nothing loud. It's not fancy, but the food's good."

The snow had stopped a couple of hours earlier. It had never snowed hard, but now a raw wind had resumed blowing. It whipped at the hem of Camilla's skirt and the collar of Jiggs' jacket as they walked. It was cold and there were no stars. The lights of the city were reflected off the bottom of the low clouds churning above them. Last leaves fell from already barren trees, tumbling across lawns frosted white. Jiggs took Camilla's hand for the second time that day as they walked along.

It was as cozy inside the restaurant as it was frigid outside. Off to the right of where they stood waiting to be seated was a lounge area. A fire burned in a fireplace across the room, and a three-man combo was playing. Two couples were dancing.

"Hi, Camilla." One of the couples, both the woman and the man, waved when they saw her. Camilla waved back.

"Friends of mine."

Camilla's life. For the first time in a while, Jiggs felt once again like the man who lived in a room over a store.

"What's your theory about those footprints at the Wall?" Camilla asked, as the waiter was pouring the wine. "It was as if some guy just walked down to the bottom of the V and then disappeared."

Jiggs gnawed his lower lip, thinking. "The drifts were a little higher over on the other wing of the V, probably from the way the wind swirled inside there. I think they must have covered up all traces of the guy's departure. But, maybe whoever it was did fly away. All I know is, that teddy bear ate me up."

Camilla reached over and put her hand on Jiggs' hand. "Me too."

"All those names gave me a serious case of the 'Why me's?' Seems unimaginable that so many guys died over there, and here I am all these years later, alive and unscathed. Made me think of men I know whose names are up there. Saucers."

Camilla didn't necessarily agree with the unscathed part, but she knew what Jiggs meant. "I don't know how to say this, Jiggs, but it made me think of Saucers too, and all the things you've told me about what happened. Seeing all those names ... don't you think that for virtually every one of those men, there was some lieutenant, some sergeant, who, in hindsight, wished he had done something different?"

Jiggs stared down at his hands folded on the table in front of him. "I don't know. Probably a lot of 'em. I never thought of it that way before."

Camilla took a sip of her wine. "Even Lincoln. No commander in our history ever sent more men into battle. He must have had some monumental regrets, but he kept going, doing what he thought was right."

"That's the difference. I already knew the war wasn't right."

"Maybe the war, Jiggs. But on an individual level, didn't you ask Saucers to reflect on how he wanted to think of himself in that time and place later in his life? You didn't do that to keep him in the war, did you? You did that out of regard for him as a man. That was not a wrong thing.

"Jiggs, I listen to what you did, both on that day and on the day Saucers died, and to a certainty the Jiggs Morgan I know was doing the best he could, would never have done less. Think about that Wall, Jiggs. Viet Nam was a frightfully dangerous place. There was no way you could do what you were charged with doing without some losses. You weren't alone in that. Your best, Jiggs. That's all you can ask of yourself. You're bound to have regrets, but I don't think there's any room for self-recrimination."

They ate in silence for a while. Jiggs ruminated on all that Camilla had said. He'd just been reading about Lincoln.

"You know, Cam, what you said about Lincoln. You're right. All those casualties almost crushed his spirit. That, and losing his son, dying in a White House bedroom while Lincoln carried a nation on his back ... and yet he kept on. "

Camilla didn't know how far she could extend this line of thought, but Jiggs was responding to it. She was determined to take it as far as it would go. "Jiggs, do you see any parallels between being an infantry lieutenant and being a pastor?"

Jiggs had become a minister in the hope of getting as far away from infantry and war as he could. "No. Do you?"

"Well, for one thing, both jobs put the people who do them right in the cross hairs of tragedy. Like the infantry, when your job is to minister to people's spiritual needs, Jiggs, there are going to be some losses.

"You may make mistakes. I know you think you made a big one. But who's to say what was a mistake in that situation? You were trapped in the midst of what might be the most divisive issue in the history of this country since slavery. I grew up a good Catholic girl, Jiggs, and right along with most other good Catholic girls of my generation, I took birth control pills and said a prayer of thanks to my Catholic god for making them available."

That made Jiggs smile.

"Is abortion wrong? I think the Supreme Court got it right. Each of us has to decide for herself. But the advice you gave that girl was no different than what literally millions of others would have given her, including, I think, her own father based on what you've told me about him. Point is, you were doing your best. You were, Jiggs. You were."

All during dinner music from the bar had wafted into the dining room. Mostly, it was clarinet music, haunting and indistinct, a silken thread running through a lovely evening. As they walked past the lounge on their way out, the musicians began to play "Stranger On The Shore."

"Oh, Jiggs, let's dance to just this one song, please."

Jiggs did not have to be asked twice. Although neither ever acknowledged aloud that "Stranger" was "their song," it was on the jukebox at the pizza restaurant across from Futema

Air Base on Okinawa. Whenever they went there, they always played it. Its beguiling suggestion of discovery seemed so like their discovery of each other. Throughout the years, Jiggs had always stopped whatever he was doing to listen when it played on the radio. He always paid his quarter whenever he saw it on a jukebox, a small price for the memories it evoked.

They walked onto the dance floor, and Jiggs took Camilla in his arms. She laid her head against his chest, and for three minutes they floated into the past, their first slow dance.

The wind that had been blowing as they walked to the restaurant was still up, fresh and sharp out of the West. They paused on a bridge across a small creek, leaning against the rail looking down at the frozen stream threading its way between some trees. Camilla stood in the lee of Jiggs, out of the wind, his arm around her shoulders.

"Do you ever wonder if we'll return to Okinawa some day?" Camilla asked.

"I return all the time in my mind, Cam. But I'm not sure I actually want to go back. That was a special place and time, the kind that's hard to recreate. There are other places and times out there just waiting for us to make them special too."

Jiggs' words, Camilla's thoughts, all one. As he spoke, she turned, raising her hand to his cheek, and he kissed her. First kiss.

They smiled at each other, their faces the combined length of their noses apart. "Whew," Jiggs said, "First dance, first kiss, big night for the two little farm kids."

"Yes. And you know the best part?" Camilla half turned and leaned back against him, his arms encircling her. "It's not over."

Camilla doubted it was the music that awakened her, but there in the dark on her bedside radio Karen Carpenter was singing, "Make Believe It's Your First Time." The sound was so low the slightest rustle of the covers obscured the music, but when Camilla lay absolutely still, it was very clear.

Without otherwise moving, she reached for Jiggs and her hand touched his chest. He was sitting up. "Jiggs," Camilla was half-whispering as she scooted around so that she lay across him, facing him, propped up on one elbow. "Are you all right?"

"Yes, I'm fine, just a little sad."

"Sad. Why?"

"Because as lovely as this is, I have to go away, if it's going to stay lovely."

"Go away?"

"Cam, right now I'm still the guy who lives over a store. I have to do something, rebuild my life so that there's at least some rough parity between us. I don't want to be an emotional parasite, and I'm sure that's not your goal either. It would get old fast."

"But why does that mean you have to go away?"

"I've been thinking about it ever since you left Iowa, about what I need to do. I haven't done anything but think so far. I wanted to talk to you about it, see where you think we're going. We've kind of answered that question in the last twenty-four hours. So the remaining issue is, whither Jiggs Morgan?"

"Jiggs, I agree with all of that, but what else have you been thinking, ... about the 'going away' part, I mean?"

"Well, in my heart of hearts, my goal hasn't changed, Cam. I still want to make a difference. I know that's kind of a cliché, but deep down, I want to be a giver, not a taker. I just don't want to do it as a churchman. For a long time I wanted to be a missionary. That idea got squelched, but there are lots of international charities whose missions don't involve religion, just helping others. I think I need to do something like that, not just for me, but for both of us."

Camilla saw the riddle. What has to be apart so it can be together? Answer: Jiggs and Camilla. She knew Jiggs' dream had been stifled by his first love. It must not be stifled by his second. "Ohhh." She could not entirely suppress the sorrow accompanying this realization. "Jiggs, so long as I know you're always coming back to me, go and seek your fortune. I'll even pack your lunch." She leaned forward and kissed him.

Breakfast was early the next morning. Monday was a workday for Camilla. Jiggs cooked. As they were sitting down, the English Professor in Camilla asserted itself.

"So, Jiggs did you ever write any more poetry after you left Okinawa? You were off to a pretty good start."

"A few, but none for a long time until about a month ago. Then I wrote one about you. Want to hear it? I brought it with me, hoping you'd ask."

"Of course."

Jiggs retrieved the poem from his suitcase and began to read.

I hear the music
In my ear,
A song so gentle,
Soft and clear;
Like a stream
In the air,
Meandering here,
Rushing there.

I heard it first
Years ago.

Where it would lead
I did not know.
Seasons passed,
It came and went.
For years it seemed
Its strength was spent.
Then came a time
I was more low
Than I ever dreamed
That I could go,
When the song reappeared,
Began to grow.

Now I hear it
Everywhere.
Its haunting beauty
Fills the air.
I hear it as we
Walk hand in hand,
Laughing about
Things we planned.

I hear it on
The mountaintops,
In parks, cafes,
It never stops.
On quiet mornings
In the rain,
Like drops trickling
Down the pane,
The music trickles
In my brain.

On sunny days
And starlit nights
The music dances,
Darts, delights.
Late at night
The music hovers,
Serenading us as lovers.

The music's magic
Is growing still.
I have perfect faith
It always will.
And of that magic,
This I know,
You are the musician
Who makes it so.
Camilla.

Camilla's eyes were still damp when she left for work.

EPILOGUE

December 1986

As Camilla came down the jetway at the Athens airport, she wondered whether Jiggs would once again be as malnourished as he had appeared when he came home on leave from the Sudan the previous June. Then he had been even more gaunt than when Camilla first saw him on Okinawa after being medevaced out of Viet Nam.

"My God, you look like one of those refugees you've been writing about for the last year," she said. "We have to fatten you up."

Camilla had bundled Jiggs into her Volkswagen camper the day after his return. For five weeks, as they camped their way around the country, Jiggs grazed on cold beer and ice cream, wallowing in the luxury of abundant refrigeration, one of the many things in short supply at the Dumlah refugee camp in northern Sudan.

In Des Moines, Hood finally met his mysterious pen pal.

"Camilla, Jiggs told me you saved his life on Okinawa," Roger said, as the three of them lounged on his deck the afternoon of their arrival. "Said he was mad at the whole world, and you helped him scale back and just be mad at selected parts. What's your version?"

"Oh, I think Morgan was probably already on the road to recovery when we bumped into each other. Besides, he had a lot to be mad about. It just took him some time to calm down."

"Well, from what I can see, you're batting two for two when it comes to salvaging Morgan. He's lucky to have a guardian angel like you. I salute you." Hood raised his bottle. Jiggs did the same.

"That's what I keep telling him," Camilla replied.

Rivers, the Ohio, Mississippi, Missouri, Red, Pecos, Colorado, American, Columbia, Snake, Jiggs and Camilla crossed them all. Three days before Jiggs was to return to Africa and Camilla to teaching shortly thereafter, they re-crossed the Potomac and came home. The weeks had flown past, but they were slow in comparison to those last three days, when looming separation made both wish time would stop.

At the departure gate at Dulles, they reprised earlier partings except that this time more than ever before both knew they would be together again.

"Here's to Christmas in Greece, Cam," Jiggs had said between kisses. Camilla nodded, fighting back tears. Christmas would only be ten days, which was all Jiggs could coax out of his relief agency. Everyone wanted time off at Christmas. It was semester break at the University; Camilla would have three weeks, so she was the one traveling the farthest. Camilla had suggested somewhere warm, but Jiggs kept raving about a place in central Greece called "Meteora," where he had gone the preceding Christmas with two co-workers from Dumlah. He wanted to show it to her. They could leave and go elsewhere if it turned out to be a disappointment. The place didn't make much difference to Camilla. So Greece it would be.

"Last call for Flight 441 to Cairo now boarding at Gate B36." Jiggs' flight.

"Cam, before I go, may I have this scarf?" Between his fingers Jiggs held the end of the blue silk scarf Camilla was wearing. "Something to remember you by."

"My scarf? Sure." Camilla unwrapped it from around her shoulders and handed it to him. It was the first memento he had ever asked her for.

"Thanks." Jiggs fingertips on Camilla's lingered as she handed it to him. After a couple of seconds, he took his hand away with what might have been a smile, might have been a wince of pain. He folded the scarf and stuffed it in his jacket pocket. "I'll take good care of it. Now I have to run."

They had kissed once more and he was off.

Now, after six months of letters filled with more stories of latrine building, treatment for camel bites, hunger and disease, the holidays had finally arrived. The civil war ravaging Eritrea continued to flood Dumlah, just across the border in Sudan, with people fleeing pestilence and starvation. According to Jiggs, Dumlah might ease their suffering, but for all but a rare few, only death would end it. Camilla marveled at Jiggs and others he wrote about who found fulfillment in such a place.

Jiggs shepherded the jetlagged Camilla through customs, out of the airport and to the train station, where they embarked for Meteora, Jiggs' Shangri-La. Camilla slept the entire three jolting hours, awakening only long enough to wobble off the train into a taxi. When they finally arrived at their hotel, a tiny inn, they both climbed into bed in a room once occupied by the innkeeper's grandfather. They slept until morning.

After breakfast, they walked out on the hotel veranda. It was cool, but the sun was shining. The rounded peaks and sharp spires of ancient mountains covered with pine and oak forests surrounded them, some crowned by what looked like palaces out of a Tolkien novel.

"Jiggs, this is beautiful."

"Now do you see what I mean? 'Meteora' means 'suspended in air.' Those buildings are monasteries, some of them as old as the Eleventh Century."

"I've been a lot of places, Jiggs. I've never seen anything like this. Thank you. Thank you for bringing me here."

Jiggs took Camilla's hand and walked with her to the far end of the veranda. He pointed east across a narrow valley. "Cam, look over there. Do you see that cliff?" Jiggs was pointing at a mountain face so steep no trees had bothered trying to grow there. He handed her a pair of binoculars. "Tell me what you see."

Camilla fiddled with the focus until she got it right. "It looks like a bunch of prayer flags in the entrance to a cave just below the top. What are those, Jiggs?"

"You're right, sort of. The people of Meteora hang scarves there in honor of a saint. Each year the young men of the town replace them. Part of the tradition is that a man must get a scarf from his lover and hang it there before she will marry him. Look way over to the right side of the cave entrance. What do you see?"

Camilla scanned the place Jiggs indicated. Separated by a boulder from the rest, a bright blue scarf fluttered in the breeze. Camilla almost dropped the binoculars. She remembered. "Jiggs Morgan, is that what I think it is?" She turned to look at the beaming Jiggs. "Did you really put my scarf up there?"

"How else was I going to get you to marry me?" Jiggs fished a ring out of his pocket, knelt and offered it to her. "I love you, Cam."

Camilla slipped the ring on her finger and threw her arms around Jiggs' neck. "Of course I'll marry you. I'm just glad you survived that climb."

"Well, I have a little confession to make. I had our host's son put it up there. I couldn't get here to do it before you arrived. Plus, I probably couldn't have hauled myself up there anyway. I hope it's the thought that counts."

It was.

For three days they wandered the forests and caves of Meteora, places, Jiggs assured Camilla, populated by nymphs and satyrs, to say nothing of the ghosts of Agamemnon and Ulysses. Then they entrained for Mykonos, a whitewashed Aegean island, where, Jiggs announced, "If I lived here, I would never die. I would just eventually melt into the sea." Near the end of their ten days, when it was almost time for Jiggs to melt back into the Sudan, Camilla asked to go with him.

"Why not, Jiggs? I have almost two weeks left. I want to see the place that keeps taking you away from me."

"I don't think you have the shots for Dumlah, Cam. It took me three months to get all the necessary vaccinations before I could go there."

"Yes, I do, Jiggs. I've been a busy girl."

From Athens to Cairo to Khartoum, was the easy part of the journey. The bus ride from Khartoum to Kassala and beyond took longer. It was accomplished over a track that made the roads of Bolivia from Camilla's Peace Corps days seem like a four lane. The last two hundred yards were traversed in a vessel old enough to have been one of Noah's lifeboats, in which they crossed the Atbarah River that ran just east of Dumlah. The crewmen had dragged their boat almost half a mile north of the camp before putting in. By the time they pulled across, the current swept them back down to where they collided with the muddy bank not far from the camp's entrance. Jiggs told Camilla that when he'd first arrived during dry season, he walked across the riverbed without getting his feet wet.

The guards at the gate waved and shouted something, the only part of which Camilla understood was "Mr. Jiggs." Jiggs waved back. They slogged through the mud for five more minutes. Camilla followed Jiggs as they threaded their way among dozens of tents, some with signs identifying the activity within, some anonymous. Camilla was contemplating calling a rest stop when there was a yell, "Mr. Jiggs!" A coffee-skinned wraith no more than four feet high with long braided hair came streaking out of one of the tents and leaped at Jiggs, clinging to him. After a few whispered words and a nod from Jiggs, Camilla saw two eyes that shone more blue than sapphire peer at her over Jiggs' shoulder, the most extraordinary eyes she had ever seen. Jiggs put the child down. "Cam, this is Komina, my assistant. 'Komina' means 'hope' in Arabic. Komina, this is my fiancé, Camilla."

"Hello, Komina." Camilla knelt in the mud and extended her hand. Komina put her chin on her chest and drew back.

"Go on Komina. Camilla is a friend. I promise."

After another moment's hesitation, Komina reached out and took hold of Camilla's fingertips with her own. Camilla smiled. Komina smiled back. Together the three of them walked into Jiggs' tent. The inside was partitioned into two halves. There was a cot in each.

Putting their suitcases down, Jiggs turned to Komina. "Komina, will you please go down to the supply tent and see if you can get another cot for Camilla and bring it back here? Tell

Mr. George it's for my friend who's staying with us for a few days."

The girl flew out the door.

"She never walks anywhere," Jiggs said.

"Komina lives here with you?"

"Yup. For almost a year now. She's an orphan. We think she's about eight. I found her wandering on the outskirts of the camp. No one knew who she belonged to. Mother probably died. The father, too, although around here fathers don't pay too much attention to children until they're about six. Before that, the odds are pretty good they'll die, so why bother."

Camilla sighed and shook her head at Jiggs' confirmation of everything she'd seen since their arrival.

"I checked around. When nobody claimed her, I took her to the orphanage, but she was suffering from malaria. They were afraid she would infect the other children. Then I took her to the hospital, but as usual it was full. A doctor I know there said her chances were better if I took care of her than if she was in hospital anyway. Too much chance of her catching something worse there. He gave me some medicine. So I took care of her, and she's been here ever since."

"Why haven't you ever mentioned her in your letters?"

"Oh I wanted you to meet her first. I figured you'd come nosing around here sooner or later."

Camilla spent six days at Dumlah. The morning after her arrival she had been put to work at the school, Professor Waron, the teacher's aide, helping students with their lessons, readying whatever meager school supplies were on hand for use that day, discussing ways to teach reading with the teachers, most of whom had learned to read in the same room where they were now teaching only a couple of years earlier.

"You know what I've noticed, Jiggs?" With the help of Komina, who was bursting with pride because she was the new teacher's friend, Camilla was re-packing on the eve of her departure. Jiggs was just sitting, brooding over the prospect.

"What?"

"You're about the oldest westerner here, with the possible exception of that English doctor you introduced me to."

"Well, I got a late start, but you're right. It's a young person's job. People get old fast at Dumlah."

"How old are you going to let yourself become here, Jiggs?"

"Not much older. I've applied for a post at head-quarters in Washington. I hope to have a young wife there about the time it comes through. One problem though."

Camilla didn't know about the "young wife" part, but she knew the problem. "Bring Komina with you, Jiggs. Maybe I'll get to be a mother after all."

JIGGS' POEMS

JUSTINE

Your arrival
Anxiously awaited.
Your visit
Expected
To last
A lifetime.
Mine,
Not yours.

Susan Karocek

Your vibrance
Lighted lives.
You made us laugh.
Then you
Made us cry.

CHRISTOPHER BRITTON

Doc

Wise as the hills
And meadows,
Deeper than the river,
Quiet as dawn.
Long-seeing,
Kind.

Lindy

Tough as
Old leather.
Tender as
Ripe fruit.
Smart.
Loyal.

Cam,

Do you ever stop and wonder
Though we're thousands of miles apart
Whether I'm seeing what you're seeing
Not with my eyes, but with my heart?
Do you ever stop and watch a cloud
Like a ship sailing in the blue
And wonder if by some magic chance
I can see it too?
Do you pause to listen to the leaves
Stirring in some gentle breeze
And imagine walking with me
Among those whispering trees?
Do your fingers brush your cheek
Where mine did so long ago,
As you recall the words we spoke
When I said "I love you so."
Are you by the spider's web reminded
As it dances in the morning sun
Of bonds even finer
Reaching out to make us one?

Jiggs

The Magic Room

We are stepping
Across the threshold
Of a magic room –
A place to dance,
To toast romance,
To howl at the moon.

Within this room
The walls all stretch
And boundless
Pulse with life,
Sensitizing feelings
More keen than any knife.

Beneath the window
Of this magic room
Stretches all the world –
A flower in bloom,
A weaver's loom,
A wondrous flag unfurled.

Within this room
Laughter and tears,
Pain and joy and sorrow
Are all absorbed, embraced,
Caressed and soothed
Before today
Becomes tomorrow.

Within this room

We weightless float,
Seamless,
Sometimes breathless.
Our shadows frolic
On the walls
Celebrating feelings
That are deathless.

Within this room
The only light
Shines from within
Our souls,
Entranced, enriched,
Embraced, entwined,
An undivided whole.

Our hands are clasped,
Our hearts are clasped,
Within this room
We're one,
Each independent,
Yet allied by bonds
That will not be undone.

This room, this room,
This magic room,
Where we are hand in glove,
This vibrant, vital,
Breathing place,
This magic room.
Is Love.

Cam,

If you will be with me,
I will give you pine needles
Glistening in the sun
And Chopin in a darkened room.
I will give you silent places
Where you can hear
The sound of your own heart
And easy, dancing laughter.
I will give you skies so blue
Their depth exceeds all
But that of my caring
And an old age
Where youth survives.
I will give you my ideas
In an understanding way
And seek your thoughts
That you would have me share.
I will give you whatever strength
I have to give,
Nor will I hide from you
Whatever tears I cry.
If by my side is where you wish to be,
I will give you me.

Jiggs

Made in the USA
San Bernardino, CA
03 November 2016